SOUND THE TRUMPET

THE LIBERTY BELL

🔔 🔔 🔔

1. *Sound the Trumpet*

THE HOUSE OF WINSLOW SERIES

★ ★ ★ ★

1. *The Honorable Imposter*
2. *The Captive Bride*
3. *The Indentured Heart*
4. *The Gentle Rebel*
5. *The Saintly Buccaneer*
6. *The Holy Warrior*
7. *The Reluctant Bridegroom*
8. *The Last Confederate*
9. *The Dixie Widow*
10. *The Wounded Yankee*
11. *The Union Belle*
12. *The Final Adversary*
13. *The Crossed Sabres*
14. *The Valiant Gunman*
15. *The Gallant Outlaw*
16. *The Jeweled Spur*
17. *The Yukon Queen*

SOUND THE TRUMPET

GILBERT MORRIS

BETHANY HOUSE PUBLISHERS
MINNEAPOLIS, MINNESOTA 55438

Cover illustration by Chris Ellison.

Copyright © 1995
Gilbert Morris

Published by Bethany House Publishers
A Ministry of Bethany Fellowship, Inc.
11300 Hampshire Avenue South
Minneapolis, Minnesota 55438

Printed in the United States of America.

Library of Congress Cataloging-in-Publication Data

CIP applied for

ISBN 1–55661–565–5   CIP

To Johnnie—From her husband

A bag of golden coins is mine.
Each one is made of precious days, my dear,
A glowing token of each lovely year
We've spent together. Ah, what a lovely time
Those tender days when first we knew such bliss—
When we were young and tasted love's desire!
Why, every second seemed a jewel of fire—
Each minute precious as a crown of amethyst!
Those youthful days—they are not gone from me.
When my spirit fails, from my treasure chest
I count my golden coins! Like flowers pressed
They breathe a fragrant memory of thee!
A miser soul, my six-and-forty coins I hold—
Each one, my love, with you a year of gold!

GILBERT MORRIS spent ten years as a pastor before becoming Professor of English at Ouachita Baptist University in Arkansas and earning a Ph.D. at the University of Arkansas. During the summers of 1984 and 1985 he did postgraduate work at the University of London. A prolific writer, he has had over 25 scholarly articles and 200 poems published in various periodicals, and over the past years has had more than 60 novels published. His family includes three grown children, and he and his wife live in Orange Beach, Alabama.

CONTENTS

PART FOUR
The Shot Heard Round the World
1770–1775

PART ONE

ENGLAND

1743–1749

1

A Bleak Christmas

BY THREE O'CLOCK IN THE AFTERNOON, myriads of snowflakes had gathered in the dull skies over the royal palace and soon were drifting to earth, some of them as big as shillings. Within an hour the dark and dirty street leading up to the palace was covered with a light blanket of clean white snow. The palace itself no longer looked dark and foreboding with its turrets now robed in white. In the fading light of the late afternoon, it seemed transformed into something out of a fairy tale.

As the snow continued to fall, the crowd that had gathered in front of the palace gates began to shiver. The cold air whipped across the grounds and the open courtyards, turning noses red and ears blue. Most of the people who stood milling around the palace grounds on this twenty-fourth day of December in 1743 were poorly dressed. It had been a difficult year for England. The War of Austrian Succession had drained England of many of her resources and had stripped even the poorest commoner of any hope of securing warm, new clothing. In fact, it was a common sight to see people dressed only in thin woolens, or even less, as a guard against the cold, bitter wind that numbed their faces and hands and feet like frozen blocks of ice.

Yet today the crowd hoped to find a few moments of respite from the hard times surrounding them. The memory of how the royal court's generosity was sometimes displayed on Christmas Eve brought these poorly clad onlookers here in hopes of receiving some free morsel to celebrate Christmas. From time to time the royal family would have more food than was necessary—prepared for the royal banquet during these festive days. As a demonstration of His Majesty's benevolence, the leftovers would be dispersed to the poor who had gathered outside.

This particular year the crowd was larger than usual. A great many children stood shivering against the cold—children who should have been at home in front of their warm fireplaces on this freezing Christmas Eve had been drawn by the hope of food.

As the crowd shifted, a woman up near the front gate stumbled and fell into a tall, burly man who was standing in front of her.

"Wot's this?" The man turned his face, pinched with the cold, and shoved her back. "Watch wot you're doing, woman!" he growled, giving her arm a rough shake. "Bad enough to freeze my toes off waiting for them blighters in there to give us a crumb without having you fall all over me!" He gave her another shove, which caused her to stumble back and fall. Just as he was about to turn his back on her, he heard the challenge.

"You leave her alone!" A tall and gaunt boy about thirteen years of age shoved himself between the fallen woman and the large man. The lad was dressed in tatters, his worn shoes wrapped with rags to keep the soles from flopping. His bony arms protruded from an ancient black coat that had obviously belonged to a much larger person, and his fingers were blue from the biting cold. "You leave her alone!" he said again, louder this time, with anger in his voice.

The burly man did not complete his turn but whirled to face the boy. "What'll you do if I don't?" he growled. When he reached down to touch the woman again as she struggled to her feet, the young boy threw himself forward, fists flying, and pummeled the large man in the ribs. He caught the man off guard and drew a *woof* of shocked surprise from the lips of the bully.

"Daniel! Don't do that!" the woman cried, reaching out to stop the boy.

But she was too late. The huge man's face flushed with rage, and with a bearlike motion of his hand he caught the boy a blow on the side of the head, sending him sprawling in the snow. "Keep your 'ands to yourself!" he grated. Then he reached down, grabbed the boy by the frail coat lapels, and jerked him to his feet. Raising his fist to strike the boy again, he snarled, "I'll teach you to 'it a man, you young rogue!"

Suddenly a powerful hand reached out and clasped the man's wrist in a steely grip. Surprised at the strength he felt restraining him, the bully cried out, "Wot's this—?" He dropped the boy and turned to face the man who was holding him with one hand. "I'll bust your face!" the bully scowled. He tried to wrench his hand loose but to his surprise found it as fixed as if it had been bound in cold steel.

The man who held it stared at the attacker with a pair of menacing pale blue eyes and lips drawn thin with anger. He was not as large as the bully, but there was a solidness in his upper body and something in his face that gave warning to the large man to pause.

" 'Ere now, I wasn't going to 'urt the boy."

"Take yourself out of here, then," said the newcomer as he released the man's wrist. "Get off with you. If I see you again, you'll be the worst for it."

The bully weighed him carefully, then decided to leave, muttering, "Too cold to fight, otherwise, I'd show you something."

"Henry!" The woman came and stood beside her rescuer, a small smile on her face. "I'm so glad you came."

The boy got to his feet and glared after the departing form of their assailant. "If you hadn't come, I'd have given him something!"

"I suppose it's well that you didn't get into too serious a brawl with the likes of him," the man called Henry said. Then he turned to the woman and said, "Leah, you shouldn't be out in this weather."

"I know," Leah said quickly, "but I wondered perhaps if we couldn't be here when the food was given away."

Henry Partain had known Leah Bradford in better days. It grieved him now to see the thinness of her face and the paleness of her cheeks. He remembered suddenly how rounded and beautiful and rosy she had been when he had first seen her. Things had been much better back then, when she had a home and a husband. Now all that was gone, and Partain felt a flash of anger to think that such a fine young woman had suffered such loss and hardship. "Come along, now," he said. "It's too cold. They won't be giving any food away here, I can tell you that."

"But, Henry, sometimes they do."

"Sometimes they do and sometimes they don't—but you can't

stay out in this cold." Even as he spoke, Partain saw the woman sag and begin to cough. "Come along, now." He put his arm around Leah and began to edge through the crowd. "I'll see you home. Come along, children."

The boy, whose name was Daniel Bradford, set his teeth, and his jaw formed a firm line. He had wheat-colored hair that crept out from beneath the wool cap, and eyebrows of the same color. He looked at the man with a pair of penetrating hazel eyes, which were oddly colored with just a touch of green. "I'll come along after a while, Mr. Partain," he said. "You take Mum and Lyna home."

At once the girl who had not said a word began to protest, "I want to stay with you, Daniel."

"No, you go on with Mum," Daniel insisted. "I'll be home soon."

"You be careful!" Partain said. "Don't you get into any mischief." Then he turned and led the woman and the girl away.

As they left, Daniel called out, "And I'll bring you home something for Christmas dinner, too—see if I don't!"

He looked around angrily as a laugh went up from those around him. One ancient crone cackled, "You won't get nothing 'ere except some stale bread, maybe, and you'd 'ave to fight the rest of us to get that."

Casting an angry look at the woman, the boy shook his head, then pressed his way through the crowd. For some time he had been carefully studying the grounds and the garden. Trying not to draw attention, Daniel slowly moved along the street until he came to an iron gate that barred the entrance between two buildings. He glanced quickly around. *Nobody looking*, he thought. *I can get over that gate.* He reached up and caught the gate, the cold metal burning his bare hands. As agile as a squirrel, he scampered over the top, dropping to the other side. At once he got up, brushed the snow from his ragged knees, and darted into the gathering darkness between the two buildings.

Alert and wary, Daniel made his way out from the buildings and followed the curve of a long hedge that led to a lighted section of the palace. His nose told him that he was getting near the kitchen, and his mouth seemed almost to water as he smelled the rich aroma of food cooking. His stomach was knotted up and he muttered, "I'll get something for Mum to eat. See if I don't!"

Daniel Bradford was a bright lad. And thirteen years on the streets of London had sharpened his wits considerably. However, the last three years since his father had died had been a hard struggle for him, for he felt the heavy burden of caring for his sister and ailing mother. He darted silently as a cat into an open space in front of one of the buildings, determined somehow to find something for them to eat. When one of the servants came out, Daniel slipped in unnoticed through the door. He found himself in a large, open room flanked on one end by four large fireplaces burning brightly. He kept his head up and walked along as if he were one of the helpers in the kitchen. Past experience had taught him that people will trust someone who seems to know where they are going and what they are doing. So, with an air of determination, he moved along toward the outer door.

As Daniel looked around, he couldn't believe what his eyes saw. In all his days, the young lad had never seen so much food. The kitchen of the palace was filled with the smell of cooked meat, baked bread, and all sorts of delicious-looking food. Daniel took in the turkeys that were roasting on spits over open beds of hot coals, the steaks that were sizzling over hot fires, the huge loaves of bread that the cooks were removing from mammoth brick ovens. He moved directly onward, having no plan but knowing there was food enough here to feed an army—and he only needed a few handfuls of it.

" 'Ere now—where you going, boy?"

Alarmed, Daniel turned, ready to dash out the door, but saw one of the cooks staring at him impatiently. "Make yourself handy. Take this 'ere to the end of the banquet room and be quick about it."

"Right you are," Daniel said with alacrity. He picked up a pewter dish weighed down with a huge turkey just removed from the spit over the hot coals. The cook stared at him and said, "Can you 'andle that?" he asked suspiciously. "You don't look strong enough if you ask me."

"I can handle it," Daniel assured him, then marched away toward the large doors from which issued the sound of music. His shoulders and wrists ached from the weight of the heavy platter. The huge bird was right under his nose, and he longed more than anything else to lean down and take a bite out of the crusty breast that lay so close. Just then an attendant swung open the large door and Daniel quickly passed through it, finding himself in a room the likes of which he had never even dreamed of, much less seen.

The royal banqueting room was *enormous*. The vaulted ceilings rose high, with windows to allow light in from the outside during the day. On this dark wintry evening, the huge hall was brightly lit with countless candles and warmed by blazing fires from the large hearths on each side of the room. As Daniel looked around, he saw that every square inch was packed, it seemed, with long tables. Having no idea which way to go, Daniel moved along between two lines of tables, noting that they were loaded with every sort of food imaginable. When he reached the end of the line, a tall man said, "There, boy, put that turkey down for His Lordship."

Quickly Daniel obeyed, putting the large platter down, half reluctantly. One of the richly dressed men at the table grinned at him and said, "You look like you'd like to bite that bird in half, boy."

Daniel blinked, not knowing what to say, and finally muttered, "It looks very good, sir."

"Why, here. Try a bit of it yourself." The man reached out, lifted a knife in his left hand and, grabbing one of the huge legs, severed it from the body. "There!" he said. "How does that suit you, lad?"

Daniel looked at him suspiciously, but seeing that he had a friendly look on his face said, "Thank you, sir." He took a bite of it, trying not to snatch at it like a hungry wolf, and nodded. "It's very good, thank you."

"Here, you can eat that on your own time." Daniel turned and saw a tall man sitting across the table frowning at him. "Clear these dishes off the table," he ordered. "Get busy, boy! Bring in some more food."

Holding the huge drumstick in one hand, Daniel moved quickly. Whirling around he headed back through the door and for the next half hour moved from the banqueting room to the kitchen, carrying empty trays and returning with new ones laden with succulent dishes. All the time he kept his eyes moving, making his plans for his own Christmas dinner. He had carefully stashed the turkey leg the nobleman had given him behind a pile of dishes, hoping it would be there when he returned.

King George II of England had caught sight of the young boy

as he left with the dishes in one hand and the turkey leg in the other. He had smiled and said in his thick German accent, "That boy got himself a turkey leg!" He laughed so uproariously that the queen, who was seated across from him, took notice and looked toward where Daniel had just disappeared through the door.

She smiled at her husband. "He deserves a drumstick, I suppose, dear."

The king was a small man, frail and rather ugly. His face was characteristic of the Hanoverian features: he had a long receding forehead, with bulging eyes and baggy eyelids. His nose was thick and long, drawn down to a pouting mouth above a flabby, swinging double chin. Unlike his father, George I, who had spoken no English at all when he had come to the throne as the first Hanover, George II had made the effort to learn to speak English—although his speech was amply carried along with a rather thick German accent. Like his father, George had never learned to like England. At one time he was heard to say emphatically, "No English cook can dress a dinner. No English player can act. No English coachman can drive, nor are any English horses fit to be ridden. And no English woman can dress herself." Left to his own desires, he might have gone back to his native land, but one does not easily give up the power and prestige of the throne of England.

"Your Majesty, you have outdone yourself," a thick-bodied man sitting next to the king remarked casually.

"Aye, Walpole." King George nodded with satisfaction. "We have a good feast, *ja*?" He looked over at his prime minister, Horace Walpole, and his eyes gleamed as he said, "You remember what we were doing earlier this year?"

Walpole, who was the first prime minister of England and the primary reason King George II had not destroyed himself politically by his own foolish actions, leaned back and said what he knew the king wanted to hear. "Why certainly I remember, Your Majesty. You were courageously leading your troops into battle at Dettingen." He smiled, adding, "England has never seen a king lead a charge with more ferocity than yourself."

The fulsome flattery pleased the king and served to bolster his confidence. He nodded with satisfaction. "*Ja*, and I will do the same to the filthy Scots. See if I don't!"

Queen Caroline, who had been endowed with a better sense

of judgment than her husband in these matters, said quickly, "Perhaps they will draw back. We do not need another war, my dear."

"I fear they will not draw back, Your Majesty," Walpole addressed the queen. He shook his head desperately and added, "Those Scots! You can kill them to the last man before they'll change their stubborn heads. It was a sad day for England when our two countries were united."

But George was not disturbed. "I will lead the charge that will trample them to the earth!" he cried out. He grasped a tankard of ale, lifted it high, and shouted, "Blast the Scots!"

All around the room a laugh went up and the cry echoed, "Blast the Scots!"

As the king and queen and Walpole carried on a lengthy conversation about how best to crush the Scottish rebellion sure to occur, Daniel had returned from the kitchen with another huge platter of food. As he distributed it among the nobility, he was amazed at the dress of the people attending the royal banquet.

Never in his life had he seen such a display of color and craftsmanship. The brilliance of the aristocratic male reminded him of the colorful plumage of a royal peacock. The men's coats sported every imaginable color and shade—blue and green, scarlet and yellow, violet and pink. Most were lined with ermine or white satin, laced with gold and silver thread, and had brocade sleeves.

Every piece of their outfits was an elaborate declaration of wealth and artistry, carefully designed and sewn with expertise by gifted tailors from throughout the city. Even their waistcoats were elegant, blooming with embroidered flowers or birds. And upon every button was a family crest in gold or silver or a miniature of the weaver's latest love. Their breeches, of contrasting silk or satin, were worn with silk hose of every color. Their shoes shone with buckles crafted from precious metal, and on their heads rested the powdered wigs of nobility.

The ladies were no less varied in the brilliance of their attire. Their billowing gowns and sacques, spread over lace petticoats, upheld by vast hooks of whalebone, conferred upon them a daintiness and feminine allure. Upon these flashing, rippling gowns were embroidered baskets of colorful flowers, fruit and grain, golden seashells, or silver branches. The light cast by the candles on the tables along with the blazing fires from the hearths made the jewelry donned by the ladies of the court a living sunburst. It seemed every head was crowned by a tiara, and all the bare white arms gleamed and glittered with bracelets studded with precious stones, while at the waist was laced "the stomacher," woven almost solid with diamonds and other precious gems in intricate patterns.

As fascinated as Daniel was with the sights and sounds and myriads of lords and royalty, he knew that he was in a dangerous position. Passing by the very platter that he had left on his first journey into the room, he saw that the turkey had lost its remaining leg but otherwise had not been touched. A thought came to him and his eyes narrowed. Quickly, he picked up the platter and started out of the room. His heart was beating faster, but he kept his head high and tried to appear as busy as the other servers. As he passed through the door, he spied a white apron hanging by a nail on the wall. Casting a furtive look around, and seeing that no one was watching, he placed the platter on the floor. He ripped the white apron from the nail and in one quick motion wrapped it around the turkey. To avoid drawing attention, he straightened up and looked around the room. Everyone was busy scurrying about, trying to keep the food served up, so he dodged quickly around the side of the room and passed out the same side door he had used to enter not more than an hour ago.

Instantly he was enveloped by the welcome darkness. For a moment Daniel stood there, his heart pounding in his chest for fear someone had seen him leave. Knowing that he could not go through the hungry crowds that waited outside, he made his way back to the iron gate. It took some agility to climb the gate, holding the heavy turkey, but he dropped on the other side, snatched up his precious burden, and began to run. The raucous noise of the banquet slowly faded behind him as he made his way down the dark streets, illuminated only by the yellow gleam of street lanterns that cast eerie shadows as he ran by.

♜　　♜　　♜

The snowfall that had started that Christmas Eve lasted only for a day or so. As fires were continually stoked in thousands of fireplaces, clouds of black smoke rose from the chimneys, creating an ebony cloud that hung over the white city. Instead of perfectly formed flakes of dainty creations, dirty particles of ash began to flutter to the ground. Soon the city was covered with a mantle of

21

blackened snow. The day after Christmas the weather turned warm, and as passersby made their way through the streets, the snow was transformed into a leprous-colored mass that stained the boots and clothing of all who ventured out. The warming did not last long, as a cold, bitter wind moved in, causing the city to suffer under an intense cold snap. The streets remained dismal and the air itself seemed almost palpable with a choking flood of half-burned coal fumes that seemed so heavy it could not rise from the earth.

Late on a Thursday afternoon, a few days after Christmas, Daniel approached the door to a small building, carrying an armload of wood. He shivered as a fierce wind came sweeping down the street. It bit at his face and bare hands and seemed to suck his breath. When he loosened one hand to open the door, several pieces of wood fell, but the door swung open and he quickly entered.

"Daniel! You're back." Lyna came quickly to pick up the pieces of wood that had fallen and then shut the door.

Daniel moved across the dark room, dumped the wood beside the fireplace, and turned quickly to ask, "How is she?"

Lyna Lee Bradford, though only eleven, already gave promise of a grave beauty about to blossom. She had gray-green eyes set in an oval face. Her skin was smooth and fair, and her mouth was graced with clean, wide-edged lips and a firm chin. The bony structure of her face made definite, strong contours, making her seem older than her actual years.

She glanced at the door that broke the side of the single room and shook her head. "Not well. She's very sick." Feeling the fear rise again, she said, "Daniel, we've got to fetch a doctor!"

The thin lips of the boy tightened. They were blue from the cold, and he hugged himself, trying to soak up the faint heat that came from the fireplace. "How would we pay him?" he demanded as he angrily pulled his cap off and threw it across the room. "I don't know what to do, Lyna."

From behind the door a faint voice came, and the two young people looked at each other. "Has she eaten anything?" Daniel asked.

"No. She won't eat a bite."

"She's *got* to eat! Come on, I'll go talk to her."

When they entered the adjoining room of the small apartment,

Daniel moved at once to the wooden bed and bent over the frail form that lay under several worn blankets. He was chilled by the gauntness of his mother's face but tried not to let it show. "Well now, I've got some firewood, Mum, and I'm going to cook up some of that turkey. Turkey stew is what we'll have tonight!" he said.

Leah Bradford's body had shrunk to almost a skeleton. The sickness that had ravaged her had left her eyes sunken, and her lips were thin as she put them together, obviously in pain. Her breathing was shallow and she whispered, "Daniel—"

"It'll be all right, Mum. Mrs. Green is coming over. She said she's got some medicine that will do you some good."

"Daniel, you and Lyna come closer." She held out one hand to each of the children, and they came and sat beside her on the bed. "Listen to me," she said. "I've been praying, asking God what to do."

"He's going to make you well, Mum," Lyna said eagerly. "I know He will."

"But if He doesn't," the sick woman said, "I want you to go to my uncle who lives in Bedfordshire. His name is George Porter. Can you remember that? George Porter. If anything happens to me, you're to go to him."

"Nothing's going to happen to you, Mum," Lyna whispered in a frightened tone, but the pale gray of her Mum's face and the fragile feel of her hand brought fear to her eyes. "You're going to be all right."

"Write it down, Daniel," their mother insisted. "George Porter. He was good to me when I was a child. He's getting on in years now, but I've written him a letter. He was always a kind man. He'll be glad to take you in. I should have taken you there and made a place for you after your father died."

"We'll get you well first, Mum, and then we'll go," Daniel said. "Now then, I'm going to make up some of that stew and we'll have a nice supper."

The two young people went back into the other room, and Daniel asked, "How much of that turkey's left, Lyna?"

"Not very much. We've been living on it ever since Christmas. I'll get what there is." She stepped outside, went to a crevice in the house, and pulled up a loose board. The meat she had kept there was frozen, and when she brought it back inside she shook her head as she took it out of the paper it was wrapped in. "Not very much."

"I've got two potatoes," Daniel said. "We'll bake those. Then we can slice everything up and make a stew."

While Daniel threw more wood on the small fire, Lyna did the best she could to help with the meal. Shortly they had concocted a bland stew from the remains of the turkey.

"That's all there is," Daniel said, looking at the bones that were left. "We'll have to do something else tomorrow."

"Let's see if we can get Mum to eat some of this," Lyna said. She filled three bowls and carried them into the other room.

"Let me help you up, Mum," she said, putting one of the bowls down and helping her mother into a sitting position. "Now then, this is going to be real good. It'll make you feel better. It's hot and will help take some of the chill out."

The sick woman managed to get down two or three swallows, then gently pushed Lyna's hand away. "No, that's all I want right now. You eat the rest of it."

No amount of persuasion would change her mind, and finally, when the children had eaten, she said, "Daniel, read me some more from the Bible."

"All right, Mum." Daniel went to get the worn Bible, the only book in the house. When he returned he sat down with it on his lap and asked, "Where do you want me to read?"

"Read from the last chapter of the Book of Revelation. . . . It's the last book in the Bible." She waited until Daniel had found the place, then whispered with a thin, reedy voice, "Start with the third verse."

Leaning forward so that the light from the single candle illuminated the pages, Daniel put his finger on the lines and began to read: "And there shall be no more curse: but the throne of God and of the Lamb shall be in it; and his servants shall serve him: and they shall see his face; and his name shall be in their foreheads. And there shall be no night there; and they need no candle, neither light of the sun; for the Lord God giveth them light: and they shall reign for ever and ever. . . ."

Daniel read on throughout that old book, and the longer he read, the quieter and more peaceful the woman became. She lay back, her eyes closed, her frail body scarcely seeming to breathe. Finally, Daniel looked over at her and for a moment felt fear. He leaned forward and asked in alarm, "Mum, are you all right?"

The pale eyelids fluttered open and the lips moved in a whisper, "Yes, I'm all right. Read some more."

As the candle slowly burned down, Daniel read on far into the night. When they were sure their mother was resting, Daniel and Lyna quietly slipped out and lay down in the next room on pallets.

With the first rays of dawn, both children were awakened by their mother's faint call. They jumped up, a look of fear in their eyes, and ran into her room. When they entered they saw their mother half fallen out of the bed.

"Mum!" Daniel cried. Gently he lifted her and put her back in bed, her arms draping to the sides. He put her arms under the cover and slid the pillow under her head. Tears rose in his eyes, for he did not know what to do. "Mum! I'll go get a doctor—"

"No." The woman's lips barely moved. Her eyelids opened and she said more strongly, "No! There's no time."

"Mum! Mum!" Lyna cried and threw herself across her mother's thin body.

Leah Bradford's hand slowly caressed the honey-colored hair. With her other hand she reached out to Daniel, who caught it with both hands and put his face on it. She felt his hot tears and whispered, "Don't cry! You must not cry."

"Mum!" Daniel whispered. "You can't die! You can't!"

"It's hard, but the Lord's told me that you will be all right. You will be in His kingdom. Promise me you will serve Jesus all your life. Promise me!"

Daniel lifted his head. He looked at his mother and saw that her eyes were not cloudy, but clear. He whispered, "I'll do the best I can, Mum."

Lyna lifted her tear-stained face. "Mum, what will we do?"

Their mother's voice grew weaker, and she whispered, "You'll have no father or mother—but God has promised to be the Father of the fatherless. He will take care of you. It may be hard at times, but never forget that Jesus is Lord of all. Will you promise to remember that?" she asked again, her voice falling away.

They both promised, nodding, unable to speak. Their voices were choked by the tears that rose. The dying woman looked at them and began to talk. She spoke of how God had come into her life and how she had always served Him. How their father, Matthew, who had died four years earlier, had been a fervent Christian. Finally, she said, "You see me now, sick and dying. I can't even walk. But, do you know what I'll be doing in just a little while?"

"What, Mum?" Daniel whispered.

A smile touched the thin lips of Leah Bradford. She squeezed his hand and raised her other hand to gently stroke Lyna's cheek. "I'll be dancing on streets of gold. . . !" she whispered.

The two children stared at her and Lyna said, "What? What did you say, Mum?"

"I always wanted to dance and I never could. Life has been hard, but as soon as I leave this place, I'll be with the King and I'll be dancing on streets of gold. I'll be with my Lord!"

She closed her eyes and grew still. At first the two young people looked at each other, overcome with grief. They thought they had just heard her last words, but then she stirred. For the next hour Leah Bradford whispered many encouragements to her children. Finally she lifted herself up in the bed.

"It's time for me to go. Be faithful," she whispered. "I love you more than anything on earth, but I must go to be with the Lord. Don't forget your promise." And then she settled back and took a deep breath. When she released it, her body lay completely still.

Daniel held the limp hand as he put his other hand on Lyna's shoulder, who was weeping. Tears were running down his own face. The children had seen death before, but now the one thing on this earth that they loved more than anything else had been taken from them, and the sorrow and grief bit bitterly in Daniel's throat. He looked over at the small form of his sister and put his arm around her. "Don't worry. We'll be all right, Lyna," he whispered.

For a while they stayed there, holding on to that limp form and staring at the peaceful expression on their mother's face. Then Daniel rose up and said, "I'll go get the neighbors."

🔔   🔔   🔔

Death, for the rich, meant heavy oak caskets, carriages filled with mourning relatives and friends lining the streets, elaborate sermons by bishops in ornate cathedrals, and then interment in the magnificent inner-city cemeteries.

But for Leah Bradford, it meant a small gathering of a few poor neighbors, dressed in thin coats standing around an open grave, a curate who had come after much persuasion to say a final prayer, and then the throwing of the red clots of raw earth on the top of the simple pine box.

Daniel and Lyna Lee stood beside the casket as the overweight curate read from the Scriptures in a hurried fashion, drawing his scarf around him to keep the cold wind out. He finished by reading a few lines from the Book of Prayer, reached down, picked up a clot of dirt, and threw it in on the coffin. "Dust thou art to dust thou returnest," he said, then put his eyes on the two young people. "God be with you in His mercy."

Then it was over. But when Lyna and Daniel turned to go, they found themselves confronted by two gentlemen they had never seen, dressed in long, thick black coats, well protected against the biting cold by fur gloves and heavy boots. One of them, the taller of the two, said, "I am Mr. Peevy and this is my assistant, Mr. Havelock. We are the agents for the county."

The two young people looked at each other, and it was Daniel who spoke up. "Yes, sir? What is it?"

"I'm afraid," the taller of the two said, "we have distressing news for you young people. We have contacted your mother's uncle in Bedfordshire, and I'm afraid there is no possibility of your going to live with him. He is, as a matter of fact, very ill and requires others to take care of him."

Daniel swallowed hard, not knowing what to do, for he and Lyna had no other plans. "Well," he mumbled, "we'll have to do something else."

"I'm afraid," the shorter of the two men said, "you cannot go back to your house. The rent is due and the owner insists on your vacating it immediately."

Daniel shot back angrily, "We paid our rent every month! We never missed."

"Ah," Mr. Peevy said, "but that is over now and your mother, rest her soul, is gone. Now, you must make other plans."

"We'll get by." At the age of thirteen Daniel Bradford had learned to struggle for life. He lifted his chin and said, "We don't need that old room anyway!"

"But I'm afraid you must do something," Mr. Havelock said, "and all that remains is the workhouse."

"The workhouse?" Lyna Lee asked, her voice trembling. Somehow the word had an ominous character, and she clutched Daniel's hand. "What is that—the workhouse?"

"It's the place where people are cared for who can't care for themselves," Mr. Peevy explained. "Arrangements have been made for you to go. You, my boy, are almost old enough to make your own way, but your sister is not. I assume you will choose to go with her for a time?"

Daniel wanted to tell both of them to go to the devil. He felt overwhelmed by the black grief within him, but he would not allow these callous men to see the tears he had shed. "Yes," he replied, "we'll go there. Let us go get our things first."

"No need for that. We've already gathered them," Mr. Havelock said. "Come along, we'll take you to the workhouse."

🜚 🜚 🜚

The workhouse was a bleak building located in one of the poorer sections of London. It was a dank, wooden structure that seemed shrouded with an aura of misery. As the carriage pulled up to the front of the building, Lyna Lee looked at it and whispered, "I'm afraid of this place, Daniel."

"It'll be all right," the boy said quickly with more assurance than he felt. "If we don't like it, we'll run away."

The two got down out of the carriage and were directed to the front door, which opened when Mr. Peevy knocked firmly. A tall man in a dark suit stared down at them. "Ah, Mr. Peevy, Mr. Havelock. I assume these are the two orphans? Please come in."

"Yes, sir, we leave them in your charge," Mr. Peevy said promptly. He looked at the two young people. "I trust you will be duly grateful for the mercies of God. This is Mr. Simon Bardolph. He and his good wife, Emma, run this respected establishment and will see that you are fed and clothed. We bid you good day. Thank you, Mr. Bardolph."

As soon as the two men left, Bardolph closed the door, then turned to look at the two newcomers. He was a tall, thin man with pale eyes and brown hair. His hands had long, skinny fingers that he clutched and rubbed together as he examined the pair standing before him. "Well," he said rather sharply, "I'll expect no trouble from you two. I do not permit trouble here at the workhouse. You understand me, young man?"

"Yes, sir," Daniel muttered.

"Speak up! No sullenness here, boy, no sullenness."

He turned and called, "Mrs. Bardolph!"

A short, fat woman soon appeared in the hallway. She had a red face, and when she spoke, her voice was louder than it should have been. "Are these the pair?"

"Yes, my dear. Now, we must give them instructions. I have already warned them that no trouble will be tolerated in the work-house."

"I hope you made it plain," Emma Bardolph said loudly. "If they don't keep the rules, they know what to expect. You've told them that?"

"A touch of the stick! A touch of the stick!" Bardolph had the habit of repeating everything twice, and his own words seemed to amuse him. He stared at the two grimly and nodded. "Come along. I will show you your places."

Daniel and Lyna Lee Bradford never forgot that first day at the workhouse. Etched in their memories were the long, narrow rooms where they shared hard cots with the other unfortunate clients. The evening meal was composed of one bowl of rather watery soup, one hard roll of bread, and a quarter of one potato. They would never forget the same hopeless expression of desperation and defeat on the faces of every denizen of the workhouse. Whatever hope had once been there of youth and goodness and joy had been washed out. And now, both the old and young moved about as if they were slaves condemned to a galley, an empty hull of a ship that would take them nowhere.

The next morning after a breakfast consisting of another bowl of the same watery soup and another hard roll of bread, Lyna Lee looked at her brother. Her eyes were red from weeping long into the night. "We can't stay here," she whispered. "I'll die. I can't stand it, Daniel! Let's run away."

Daniel felt much the same way, but he knew what lay outside the walls—the dead of winter with hard times across all of England. There was no hope. "We can't," he said grimly. "We'll stay here until we're able to go." Then he reached over and took her hand in his and tried to smile. "I'll get us out of here, Lyna. I promise."

"Will you, Daniel, will you?" she whispered, holding on to his hand with both of hers.

Daniel looked around the sooty, grim surroundings and noted

the hopelessness in the face of an old man shuffling along, ready to die, ready for the grave. Then he looked back at Lyna. "Yes, I'll get us out of here, Lyna. We'll stay here as long as we have to. If it gets too bad, we'll run away, but we'll wait until spring."

At that moment, Simon Bardolph came by and saw the pair talking together. "None of that! None of that!" he barked. "Get to work."

Daniel squeezed his sister's hand and breathed his promise again. "I'll get us out of here, Lyna. You just wait and see!"

2

DANIEL MAKES AN ENEMY

WHATEVER HOPES DANIEL AND LYNA HAD of finding the workhouse to be more pleasant than its reputation were shattered during those first few days. They were not physically beaten, but the grim existence they endured proved at least that they were hardy. Day after day the food was mostly the same, with little variation. For breakfast they were usually served a thin gruel, a bowl of some sort of greasy soup for lunch, and a sparse serving of vegetables with a single slice of bread for dinner. The monotony of the diet did not, however, cause their appetites to diminish, for every night they went to bed hungry. They both lost weight, and by the time they had endured fifteen months of such scant rations, the coarse garments issued to cover them that first day they arrived now hung on them loosely.

The barracks where they slept were crowded with hard cots, and often they were kept awake by the coughing and wheezing of their fellow inmates. In winter they shivered from the numbing cold, and in summer they gasped for breath in the sweltering heat. Not infrequently a still form would be discovered in the morning, having given up the feeble struggle for survival during the night. The body would be carried out and wrapped in a blanket, then placed in a raw hole in the ground, whereupon Simon Bardolph would read the funeral services to the collected inhabitants of the workhouse.

It was on a raw morning in 1745 that an old woman was found

dead in the barracks. A shabby group had already gathered for the funeral outside, and they stood there shivering in the cold March wind. Lyna had been late for breakfast and her stomach ached as she moved closer to Daniel. He slipped her two pieces of hard bread, whispering, "I filched it for you. Eat it later. . . ." She squeezed his hand, but then before she could thank him, Mr. Bardolph came to stand at the head of the gaping grave.

A blanket-wrapped form lay beside the hole in the red earth, and the head of the institution frowned and shook his head with displeasure. *A shame to waste a blanket—she won't need it now,* he thought. He had once resorted to dispensing with the covering, but the dirt falling on the naked, helpless face of the dead man was more than even *he* could take. *Well, it's an old blanket—cheaper than a coffin, and will serve just as well.* Stepping forward Mr. Bardolph glanced sternly over the thin, pale faces—rather blue with cold—and began to read the now-familiar service they had heard several times during the winter. He was wearing a fine heavy wool topcoat bought with the funds reserved for clothing for the paupers. He had spared no expense in his selection, for a man in his position could hardly be seen in an inferior garment for such a solemn occasion!

He read the service quickly, skipping over the more lengthy sections, then slapped the book shut. "We will now pray for the departed soul of this sinner. . . ." Simon Bardolph had a nasal voice that always raked on Daniel's nerves, and when he was finished, he nodded at the two men who stood back with shovels in their hands. "Very well, do your duty," Bardolph said impatiently. Then he turned to the band of spectators who stood silently. "Be off with you now—get to your work! Get to your work!"

Daniel and Lyna turned with the others and made their way back to the shed where they both had been picking oakum for use in the Royal Navy. It was a dreary, monotonous work, and their fingers were soon rubbed raw from the tedious task. After a few more hours, the bell used to announce meals was rung. At once they moved along with the others to the dining hall where they ate their watery soup as slowly as possible to make it last longer. When they arose and started back to the oakum shed, Emma Bardolph appeared, snapping, "Go to the office, both of you."

"The office, ma'am?" Daniel asked, startled. He felt Lyna

clutch his sleeve. He could sense her fear, for a visit to the office of Mr. Simon Bardolph usually meant a caning for some minor offense. As they walked slowly toward the red brick house that served both as home and office for Mr. and Mrs. Bardolph, Daniel whispered, "Don't be afraid, Lyna—we haven't done anything wrong."

He knocked on the front door, swallowing hard, for in the last six months he himself had taken more than one beating from the hand of the cruel master. But as he waited for the door to open, a stubborn anger rose in him. *He can beat me—but he isn't going to touch Lyna!*

When the door opened, Mrs. Mason, the housekeeper, was standing there looking at them. "Come into the kitchen," she said abruptly, then motioned them over in front of the large fireplace. She poured a basin of hot water and commanded the two, "Wash your faces—and get into them clean clothes."

Astonished at her command, Daniel and Lyna obeyed when the tall, angular housekeeper spoke sharply to them. She grew impatient and finally took a cloth and began to scrub their faces until Daniel and Lyna both feared their skin would be removed. Next she brushed their hair with a harsh brush, then stripped off their dirty clothes from working in the oakum shed and had them put on the clean clothing laid across the chair. She tossed them shoes, which were not new but had soles and tops, and nodded. "Now into the study, both 'o you—and mind your feet!" Both the young people obeyed and followed Mrs. Mason down the long hall toward the study.

Lyna cast a questioning look at Daniel just as they reached the door, but he said nothing and shrugged his shoulders.

"Here they are, sir," Mrs. Mason announced, leading the pair inside.

Daniel glanced quickly at Mr. Bardolph, who was standing by the fireplace beside a very large, portly man with brown hair and brown eyes. Beside the well-dressed man sat a very short and overweight woman in a large chair. When the children entered, the woman turned to look at them. She had light hair, rather faded blue eyes, and was wearing expensive clothes. "Are these the children, Mr. Bardolph?" she asked, peering at them in a shortsighted fashion.

"Yes, indeed, Lady Edna," Mr. Bardolph answered. He gave a warning glance toward the pair, nodding shortly. But he smiled cheerfully, saying, "I thought of them the moment I received your request, Sir Edmund. I believe they are just the right young people to meet the needs you mentioned." He walked over and, standing between them, put his hand affectionately on the respective shoulders of Daniel and Lyna, giving them a fond look. "They're rather favorites of Mrs. Bardolph and myself. Since the tragic passing of their mother, we've been like a father and mother to 'em!"

"I trust they're not spoiled," the large man said, his eyes fixed on the pair. "We'll expect them to know how to work and to keep their station."

"Why, I should hope we've instilled those good qualities into them, Sir Edmund!" His hand closed cruelly on Daniel's thin shoulder, and he demanded, "I think you'll be able to give Sir Edmund and his good wife, Lady Edna, assurance that you're not afraid of hard, honest work, eh, Daniel?"

"No, sir," Daniel spoke up. He was mystified by the sudden change of behavior in Mr. Bardolph but quickly decided that the couple here in the study in search of some sort of workers was the best opportunity they had of escaping the dismal workhouse.

"What we are in need of," Sir Edmund went on, "are two young people to be servants. Particularly, we need a young man who can learn the skills of working with the horses and later drive the carriage. And we need a young woman who can do housework and later become a lady's maid." Staring at the two youths, he asked pointedly, "Do you think you might be able to do that?"

The offer was the open door Daniel had been praying for, and without a moment's hesitation he said with alacrity, "Yes, sir. My sister and I would very much like to do such work, wouldn't we, Lyna?"

"Yes, please," Lyna whispered. "We'd try very hard to please you both."

Lady Edna smiled at the girl but turned to her husband and said, "They're both very young, aren't they, Edmund?"

"Daniel is fifteen and the girl is thirteen," interjected Mr. Bardolph politely. Then he turned to address the two young people. "You will be taken into service as indentured servants. That means that for five years you will serve Sir Edmund Rochester and his good wife, Lady Edna. At the end of that time, you will be given the choice to serve longer if you wish. If you choose to go elsewhere, you will be provided with clothing and a small sum of money." Mr. Bardolph then turned back toward the woman and added smoothly, "I'm sure Your Ladyship is aware that in such matters as these, it's important to get the children at a youthful age. In that way they won't have picked up any vicious habits and can be trained to please you."

"I rather think that's true," Sir Edmund nodded. He was a bluff individual with a red face, and he had a tendency to bluster. He prided himself on his ability to make quick decisions, which were as often wrong as they were right. Pleased with their selection he now said, "Well, sir, I believe they will do fine. When shall they come to us?"

"Why, at once, I think," Mr. Bardolph said, smiling benevolently at Daniel and Lyna. "We'll miss them greatly, of course, but I couldn't think of depriving them of an opportunity to serve such as yourself, Sir Edmund—and you, Lady Edna!"

"Very well, send them by carriage—I'll pay their fare, of course." He turned to his wife, saying with satisfaction, "Now, my dear, I think we may consider the matter settled. Come, we'll be on our way."

As soon as the pair was gone, Mr. Bardolph dropped his feigned smile. "Now, I trust you will be properly grateful—but I doubt it." His cold eyes examined them critically, and he added, "If I ever hear of your speaking a disparaging word of your experience here, I'll convince Sir Edmund that you don't deserve positions with him. You'll be brought back—and I'll have you for it! You understand?"

Daniel nodded at once. "Yes, sir. We—we thank you for your kindness—don't we, Lyna?"

Lyna held tightly to Daniel's arm, and when the pair had satisfied their benefactor that they would never entertain any thought other than warm gratitude, he promptly dismissed them. His wife came in at once, demanding, "It went well?"

"Yes, my dear, very well." He picked up a bag of gold coins from his desk and smiled briefly. "I wish that we could get rid of the rest of the beggars on such profitable terms." He opened the bag and let the coins fall into his palm, making a most satisfactory musical tinkling, more enjoyed by the happy pair than any other form of music. "I'll make arrangements for a carriage to take them tomorrow. No sense paying for food when we'll not get any more work out of 'em!"

T   T   T

"Daniel—it's so *big!*" gasped Lyna.

Daniel stepped out of the coach and reached up to help his sister make the long step. Only then did he look at the imposing brick house that dominated the green lawn outlined by hedges and flower beds. The house consisted of three stories, with large mullioned windows on three sides. Enormous chimneys crested the structure, emitting curling tendrils of smoke, and to the rear was a carriage house larger than any dwelling either of them had ever seen.

A tall, thin man with salt-and-pepper hair came forward to meet the carriage and said, "Daniel and Lyna Bradford, I take it? I'm Silas Longstreet, manager of Milford Manor." He had a kindly look and nodded at their luggage—which consisted of two small bags. "Didn't come overloaded with this world's goods, eh? Well, come along and I'll show you around." He turned on his heels, adding, "You'll sleep in the carriage house, Daniel, and you'll have a place with the house servants in the attic, Lyna. Did you have a good trip. . . ?"

Daniel could feel Lyna holding his hand tightly and gave it a squeeze. "Yes, sir, a good trip." The two of them followed the manager to the carriage house, then to the second floor where a small room had been framed up at one end.

"This will be yours, my boy," Longstreet said. "Not fancy, but I daresay it will do."

Daniel glanced over the small room. It had one window which allowed the warm sunshine to fall over the simple furnishings: a cot, a table, two chairs, and one chest topped by a white basin and a pitcher.

"Well, you wait here," Longstreet ordered, "while I take your sister to the house."

"Yes, sir," Daniel said. He smiled at Lyna, saying, "We're in a good place, sister. Go along and be a good girl."

Lyna seemed a bit frightened by the newness of it all, but she returned the smile. "I will—and you be a good boy!" she said, winking at her brother.

Longstreet chuckled, shaking his head. "I see she knows you, Daniel! Well, both of you do your work, and you'll have no trouble. Come along, lass."

Daniel opened his bag and put his few clothes on nails, arranged his other belongings in the small chest, then sat down on the bed. *This will be good!* he thought. *I like Mr. Longstreet—he seems like a kind man.* He lay down on the cot, found it comfortable, then rose and went downstairs to look at the horses he heard in the stalls below. He was stroking the nose of a black horse when an elderly man came in and gave him a searching glance. He was small and bent with either age or illness, and when he spoke it was in a querulous tone.

"Ye'll be the new boy. Wot's yer name?"

"Daniel Bradford."

"Humph. I'm Bates." He was carrying a small saddle in one arm and gave the boy a sour look. "Do ye know horses, boy?"

Daniel was tempted to say he did but knew he'd be found out soon enough if he lied. "No, Mr. Bates—but I'm a quick learner. Just show me what to do, and I'll try my best to do it!"

The boy's eagerness and good manners seemed to pacify Bates, and his tight lips relaxed. "We'll soon see about that," he grumbled. "Might as weel start now. I'll saddle Midnight there, and then we'll see if ye'll do."

Daniel had never saddled a horse in his life, so he watched carefully as the gnomelike little man went into the stall and saddled the horse. "All right," Bates said, stripping the saddle from the horse and stepping outside. "Let's see what ye can do."

At once Daniel stepped into the stall, and for one moment he felt a jolt of fear. The horse towered over him, a mass of nervous muscle and hard hooves and large teeth. But he pushed the fear away and spoke quietly to the animal. Giving a snort, Midnight turned to look at him curiously. Daniel picked up the small mat and placed it on the broad back, then put the saddle over it. He had some difficulty getting the straps buckled but did the best he could. Finally he stepped back and turned to face the old man. "Is that right, Mr. Bates?"

"Not bad," Bates admitted grudgingly. Stepping into the stall, he examined the saddle. "A bit tighter, mind you." Then he turned to look at the boy. "Ye've never saddled a horse, ye say?"

"No, sir," answered Daniel.

"Weel, maybe I'll make a good helper out of you." This was high praise, as Daniel was to learn later, and the Scotsman nodded, saying, "Now, the bridle—that is a harder thing. Watch how I do it, boy. . . ."

By the time Silas Longstreet returned, Daniel had managed to put the bridle in the horse's mouth. "Well, what about it, Bates?" Longstreet asked. "Can you make a horseman out of him?"

"I'll nae say so—but we'll see." A dour smile came to the thin lips of the old man, and he nodded slightly. "We'll know better after he gets nipped and his toes trod on a few times. He's nae afraid of a horse—but he don't know how dangerous the beasts can be."

Daniel asked hesitantly, "Do . . . do you think I might learn to ride, sir?"

"Ride!" Longstreet exclaimed. "Why, Daniel, that'll be a big part of your work. Midnight here needs a workout every day— and you'll see to it that he gets it—after you learn how. Bates will teach you. Oh, your sister, she'll be rooming with one of the maids, Martha Ives. She's a kindly sort of girl—so you don't need to worry about her."

"We're very glad to be here, Mr. Longstreet."

"Be easier than the workhouse, I'll vow!" Longstreet shook his head. "You had a pretty hard time there, I suppose?"

A temptation to speak of the hardships leaped into Daniel's mind, but remembering Mr. Bardolph's threats, he shook his head, saying, "It . . . wasn't too bad. But I'm very glad to be here, sir. I'm not too smart, and I don't know much about horses—but I'll work as hard as I can."

The two men exchanged glances, and Longstreet gave the boy a friendly slap on the shoulder. "I expect you're smart enough for the work here, Daniel—eh, Bates?"

Bates took out a clay pipe and slowly stuffed it with coarse black tobacco. He searched for a match, found one, then struck it on the post of the stall. When he had the pipe going, he took a long look at the eager, thin face of Daniel Bradford. Bates was growing old, coming to the end of his active life, and knew he was facing his replacement. For a long time he had dreaded the meeting, afraid that the new boy who'd come along would be cheeky and intolerable in the manner of some he'd met. Fortunately, Sir Edmund had heeded Bates' insight on some of the young hired help and had to dismiss a few of them along the way. The old man knew his horses and was not one to give his approval quickly.

"Weel, we'll have tae see," he said, the burr of the Highlands rough on his tongue. He sent a curl of purple smoke into the air, then nodded. "I think we can do something with the lad, Silas—if he don't get his neck broke first." Then as if he'd been too kind, he plucked the pipe out of his mouth and jabbed it at Daniel, saying harshly, "Don't be gettin' yerself killed, ye hear! It's too hard to break in a new boy!"

"I'll do my best, Mr. Bates," Daniel said. He was feeling a gust of relief, for he knew that these men might be hard, but they would be fair. "I'll do my best to please you both," he murmured.

♜   ♜   ♜

Lyna found her work easy—a pleasure really—after the endless harsh toil in the workhouse. She enjoyed polishing the heavy silver knives and forks, and helping to take care of Lady Edna's fine silk and linen dresses pleased her. She liked to let the smooth material run through her fingers—so different from the coarse linsey-woolsy most garments were made of.

She found Mrs. Hannah Standridge, the housekeeper, difficult—though not as harsh as Mrs. Bardolph or Mrs. Mason had been. Mrs. Standridge was a tall, angular woman with an imposing bust and manner to match. She demanded perfection from the staff, and the house servants despised her for it. Lyna quickly learned, however, that the housekeeper was not cruel, and the girl managed to do her work so well that she seldom incurred the sharp tongue of the woman. In fact, the older woman gave a rare nod of approval at Lyna's work from time to time.

The first two weeks of their service went well. Daniel and Lyna usually ate together and after supper often had a few moments to walk together around the grounds of Milford Manor. After the workhouse, they both were happy in their new situations, and when Daniel complained, it was Lyna who was able to end his bad mood by saying, "Think how it was at the workhouse." Her reminder always worked, and Daniel would smile and take her hand. "Right! God's been good to us, Lyna. I'm an ungrateful whelp!"

Daniel seemed to have a natural ability with horses, and so his work progressed very well. He exceeded Bates' expectations—which came as a shock to most of the other workers.

"Ain't nobody ever been able to please the old goat!" Rob Mickleson complained sourly. He was a heavyset man of twenty who worked on the farm under Longstreet. "I started out doin' yer job," he told Daniel once. "But there warnt no satisfying 'im! Don't see 'ow you done it, Dan'l."

Daniel had laughed, saying only, "I guess I like horses so much, it don't seem too hard."

This was, indeed, the "secret" of young Bradford's success with the animals. He loved the horses and even tackled the job of mucking out the stables with as much enthusiasm as any boy could. Bates watched him carefully as the days went by, noting the lad's gift with the horses. Pleased by what he saw, Bates poured his vast knowledge into Daniel, flattered at the devout attention the boy paid to his every word. When Sir Edmund asked him about the boy, he'd said, "Weel, sir—except for meself—I've never seen anybody who took to horses as the boy does. He'll make a fine jockey—except he'll be too big if he keeps growing. He's skinny now, but if he grows into his frame, he'll be a big 'un!"

Sir Edmund and Lady Edna were well pleased with their latest acquisitions. Although it had been his wife's idea, Sir Edmund took full credit for the addition to their house. He boasted of the pair to his neighbor, Mr. Henry Davon, saying firmly, "I told Edna it would be well to look to the workhouse for servants. They aren't guilty of spoiling them there!"

One fine afternoon, Lyna was helping to clean the master bedroom, when Mrs. Standridge entered. "Lyna, take these bedcovers out to the washhouse. Be sure and tell Maud not to use the strong soap on them."

"Yes, Mrs. Standridge," Lyna answered. She gathered the bedcovers into her arms and left by the back door. The washhouse was located close to the carriage house, and Lyna saw a plume of smoke rising from fires under the huge black pots where the clothes were being washed.

She passed through an opening in the hedge that led to the area, but the bedcovers were piled so high in her arms she failed to see the young man standing with his arms crossed in the middle of the path. She bumped into him, drawing a surprised grunt, and she staggered, dropping the load of bedcovers.

"Well, what have we here?" A tall boy with very light blue eyes and a carefully combed head of brown hair stood grinning at her.

He was not over sixteen, Lyna judged, but was very tall and strong. He was wearing a pair of tight doeskin trousers and a white linen shirt with full sleeves that was open at the throat. His bold eyes fastened on Lyna in a way that made her feel uncomfortable.

"Haven't seen you before—you must be the new maid."

Lyna scrambled to pick up the bedcovers, but he reached out and took her arm and held it with a strength that made her gasp. "You're a pretty little thing—what's your name?"

"Lyna—please let go, you're hurting my arm."

The young man slackened his grip but still held her fast. "Lyna? Why, that's a pretty name—to go with a pretty girl."

"I—have to get my work done," Lyna said. She had no idea who the young man was. She didn't think he could be one of the servants; his clothing was too fine for that. *Maybe he's one of the young men from the neighborhood,* she thought. "Please, let me go—"

"Yes, let her go!"

Lyna turned and saw Daniel standing in front of them. His face was pale, his lips drawn into a thin line. He reached out and struck the arm of Lyna's captor, then pulled her to his side. "Go back to the house, Lyna," he said. "I'll take—"

But he never finished what he intended to say, for a hard fist caught him on the cheek. He was driven to one side but caught his balance. Without a word he threw himself at the tense form of the young man, and in a moment the two of them were swapping blows. Daniel got the worst of it, for his opponent was taller and heavier than he. Three times Daniel went to the ground, and three times rose again. His mouth was bleeding and his left eye was closed, but he refused to give up.

"Here, now—!" Strong hands caught Daniel, and he recognized the voice of Silas Longstreet. "Daniel, stop this!"

"Who is this lout?" demanded the young man.

Longstreet held Daniel firmly. "His name is Daniel Bradford—and this is his sister." Silas kept his hold on Daniel's arm and his voice was firm. "I don't think I should mention this to Sir Edmund. He's still upset over your—attention—to Mary."

Anger washed over the bold features of the young man. "Oh, very well," he muttered. He glared at Daniel, adding, "You put your hands on me again, and I'll have you horsewhipped and driven out of Milford!"

As the young man strode away, Daniel wiped the blood from his mouth. "Who is he?"

"Someone you shouldn't have touched," said Longstreet, shaking his head. "That's Leo Rochester. He's the only son of Sir Edmund and Lady Edna."

"I don't care—he shouldn't have bullied Lyna!"

"He's done it to other young women," Longstreet said grimly. "But his father and mother won't hear any bad word about him. Just stay away from him, you hear?"

Longstreet turned away, and as soon as he had gone back to the carriage house, Lyna whispered, "Daniel—let's run away from here!"

But Daniel knew that leaving was not the answer. He shook his head slowly. "No, Lyna. We've got to stay. We've got no place to go—except back to the workhouse. We can't do that."

"I hate him! He's awful!"

"Just stay away from him."

"He'll try to get back at you, Daniel," Lyna warned. "Did you see how he looked at you?"

"I can't help that." Daniel knew he'd made an enemy, but he managed a smile. "Come on, now, don't be afraid. It'll be all right." Daniel bent down to pick up the bedcovers, saying, "You go on back to the house, now. I'll take these things to the wash-house for you."

Lyna gave Daniel a grateful smile and helped pile the bedcovers into his arms.

"Let's go down to the river tonight after supper," Daniel offered. "Maybe we'll see the kingfisher again. . . ."

His words had helped distract Lyna from what had just happened, but as she turned and walked back to the house, Daniel was thinking of the blazing anger he had seen in the eyes of Leo Rochester. *Lyna was right—he hates me. I'll have to watch my step all the time, or he'll find a way to get even with me.*

3

The End of a Season

"HAPPY BIRTHDAY, LYNA."

Startled, Lyna took the small package that Daniel extended toward her. Her face flushed with pleasure, and she exclaimed, "Oh, Daniel, you didn't have to get me anything!"

"Why, sure I did," Daniel exclaimed. "A girl's fourteenth birthday is important." He leaned against the wall of the milking shed, smiling at his sister. The year of good food, plenty of rest, and outdoor exercise had transformed him from a skinny, pale-faced stripling into a sturdy young man. He had shot up during this year to only an inch under six feet. He was lean, but his upper body, after long hours at the forge and in the saddle, was padded firmly with strong muscles. At the age of sixteen, he was stronger than many fully grown men. He brushed a shock of wheat-colored hair from his forehead and grinned. "And, besides, if I didn't get you something, you wouldn't get me a present on *my* next birthday."

Lyna laughed, then carefully untied the string. When it slipped off, she unfolded the paper and stared at the gift. She stared at it so long without speaking that Daniel shifted uncomfortably, asking finally, "Well, what's the matter? Don't you like it?"

"Oh, Daniel—it's *beautiful!*"

She picked up the locket, letting the paper flutter away, caught by the soft May breeze. When she lifted her eyes to face Daniel, she was blinking back tears and her lips were trembling. Holding the small gold chain with the heart-shaped gold locket up to him, she whispered, "It must have cost all the money you had!"

Daniel had been saving money for a year—working in his free time for a neighboring farmer—in order to buy a fowling gun. He had used one belonging to Silas Longstreet's brother when they invited him to go hunting once. Since then he'd borrowed it often and longed for his own gun. But when a traveling peddler had passed through the village two weeks earlier, Daniel hadn't been able to resist using the money he'd saved to buy the locket for Lyna.

He was rewarded by the look of delight on Lyna's face and said quickly, "Oh, don't worry about that. Put it on."

"It's too fine for work—but I'll just try it on now."

As she reached back and fastened the catch, Daniel thought, *She's grown so much in this past year—won't be long until she's a woman.* He admired the long honey-colored hair that caught the sun and the graceful form which was not hidden by the plain brown cotton dress. *Some man's going to get a fine wife in a few years.* Aloud he said, "Now that looks fine, sister!"

Lyna reached up and kissed him on the cheek. "Thank you, Daniel. It's—it's the best present I've ever had." She hugged him, then stepped back and removed the locket. The paper had blown down the path, and she went to retrieve it. Carefully replacing the locket, she tied it up, then put it in her pocket.

"Maybe you can wear it when we go to London," Daniel suggested.

"Yes! I can do that. With my new green dress." The "new" green dress was one that had been given to Lyna by Eleanor Rochester, Sir Edmund's daughter. It was out of style and had scarcely been worn, since Eleanor never really liked it. "I'm so excited, Daniel," Lyna went on. "Do you think we can have some time to ourselves?"

"Hope so." Daniel straightened his back, adding, "Be plenty to eat from what Josh tells me. Well, I've got to get busy. There's work to get done."

Lyna watched him go, then turned and entered the milk shed. One of the farmhands saw her and said, "Come to get the milk, 'ave you?" He gave her a bucket of frothy milk and pinched her arm. "Wot about givin' me a kiss, lovely?"

Instantly Lyna pushed him away. She had grown defensive,

for her youthful beauty had the unpleasant side effect of drawing many of the men and boys to her like flies to honey. "Keep your hands for the cows, Simon!" she said stiffly. She ignored his rude reply and hoarse laugh and turned and made her way back to the house. She poured a glass of the frothy milk, then left the kitchen and went upstairs. She knocked on the door of the large bedroom and waited.

When Lyna heard Eleanor say, "Come in," she opened the door and entered.

"Here's your milk, Miss Eleanor—fresh as can be," she said brightly.

Eleanor Rochester took the milk and sipped it languidly. She was a tall girl with rather small brown eyes but a beautiful complexion. At sixteen, she was already being sought after by suitors—which had the effect of making her proud. She was both kind and cruel to Lyna, according to her mood. "Bring me my white dress—the one with the red lace," she commanded. She rose and Lyna started to help her dress, but Eleanor cried out and cuffed the girl. "You're so clumsy! Watch what you're doing."

"Sorry, Miss Eleanor. I'll be more careful."

"See to it, then. If you don't do better, I'll leave you here and take Mary to London instead."

"Oh, please, Miss Eleanor—don't do that!" Lyna's face grew distressed and she begged, "I'll be very careful, indeed I will!"

"See that you do, then!" Satisfied that her maid was properly cowed, Eleanor allowed the girl to brush her hair. She had no intention of taking the other maid, for Lyna was very quick and had learned what pleased her mistress very well. She closed her eyes and said, "I suppose your brother is going to London?"

"Yes, miss. He'll be driving the big carriage."

"Better keep him out of my brother's way." Eleanor had heard of Leo's encounter with Daniel and knew he had taken a dislike to the young man ever since. And time had only intensified the rancor the younger boy seemed to stir in Leo. "He dislikes Daniel—I suppose he still resents him from that fight they had when you two first came."

"I wish he still didn't hold that against Daniel, miss. But Mr. Leo—"

Eleanor caught the hesitation in the girl's voice and demanded, "What about Mr. Leo?" She drew her head back and stared at the girl, noticing her attractive figure and full lips. "Has he been after you?" When Lyna stared back at her, speechless and flushing, Eleanor laughed. "Well, he's been after everything in skirts ever since he was out of nappies! It's a compliment, in a way."

"I—wish he wouldn't, Miss Eleanor. Couldn't you—ask him not to bother me?"

"No. It's really none of my business. You'll have to take care of yourself." Actually Eleanor well knew that her brother was beyond any sort of rebuke she might give. Her mother had long since given up trying to exert any authority, and her father could only control Leo by threatening to cut off the money the young man spent so recklessly. Curiosity, however, got the better of Eleanor and she demanded, "What did he do to you, Lyna?"

"Oh, miss—I don't like to say!" But when Eleanor insisted, Lyna dropped her head and said in a low voice, "He . . . he's always touching me. And he grabs me and kisses me when none of the family is around. He says . . . that I have to give in to him because I'm only a servant." Lyna lifted her troubled eyes and begged, "Please, Miss Eleanor, don't you think you might talk to your father—ask him to speak to Mr. Leo?"

"Oh, don't be such a *puritan*, Lyna!" Eleanor exclaimed. "He's not going to force you. And a few stolen kisses won't kill you." She rose and put the matter from her mind. "Now, we'll take the rose dress and this one!"

The London that Lyna and Daniel found on their journey in June of 1746 bore little resemblance to the one they remembered. The Rochesters and the attendants who had accompanied them were guests at the palatial home of the wealthy family of Colonel White. The home contained numerous rooms and a ballroom ornately decorated for the special festivities to be held that very week. The room was so large that two hundred people could easily be accommodated.

Lyna was kept busy, for Eleanor was constantly changing clothes—or else out on a shopping spree buying new dresses to keep up with the latest fashions. Lyna accompanied her most of the time, and the effort of keeping the spoiled young woman washed, made up, dressed, and in good humor for the numerous social events was enough to exhaust the young maid. But Lyna was grateful for the privilege of accompanying Eleanor, and thoroughly enjoyed the music and color of the balls that were held almost every night, so she made no complaints.

Daniel was kept busy, too, driving the family through the streets and into the country. He had become an expert driver and soon learned the major routes of the great city. Bates was getting on in years and had been left at home, too stiff with aching bones to make the trip, so Sir Edmund charged Daniel with the task of transporting the family on their many trips around the city.

Colonel Adam White, the youngest son of the Earl of Wilton, took notice of the young man's efforts and was appreciative for all of Daniel's help with his own horses. Daniel had gone out of his way to shoe some of the colonel's favorite mounts. It did not go unnoticed, for Colonel White was a professional soldier, holding a commission in the Cavalry of King George, and had extensive knowledge of both men and horses.

"That young fellow is very able," the colonel remarked one afternoon to Sir Edmund. "See how firmly he handles that horse? We could use some like him in my troop." He watched with interest as Daniel hitched a pair of spirited matched bays, then added, "He's been with you for quite a while, I expect, Sir Edmund?"

"As a matter of fact, no." Sir Edmund glanced at Daniel, who sprang into the seat. "My wife and I took him and his sister from the workhouse a little over a year ago—more or less as an experiment. I thought it might be easier to train young people accustomed to discipline." He smiled with satisfaction. "It's turned out very well, sir—the young fellow has a positive gift with horses. Can do anything with them, it seems. And he's become quite a good blacksmith. Does a great deal of the shoeing for my stable."

"Very interesting," Colonel White commented. The two of them climbed into the carriage that Daniel pulled up in exactly the right spot. The colonel leaned forward and said, "Your master gives a good account of you, young fellow. What's your name?"

"Daniel Bradford, sir." He spoke to the team, which moved away smartly, then added, "I'd be a poor servant indeed if I couldn't serve Sir Edmund."

Sir Edmund's face flushed with pride and he said, "Tell Colonel White your new idea about forming and fastening the shoes, Daniel. I'm sure he'd find it most interesting."

As they rode on, Daniel explained how he had been experimenting with a new method of forming the shoes of the horses, one that seemed to be superior to the established method. When he ended, Colonel White nodded with appreciation. "Why, that sounds very practical, my boy. I'd be interested in learning how the experiment comes out." Leaning forward with a sly gleam in his gray eyes, he whispered, "Now I'm not a man to recruit from a good friend, but if you ever *did* decide to leave your present position, I think I could make you an interesting proposition."

"Here now, none of that, Colonel!" Sir Edmund protested.

Colonel White acquiesced, lifting his hand and laughing. "I surrender, sir! But I congratulate you on finding and training such an excellent young man for your service."

Daniel dropped the two men off at their destination, and as he waited for them to return, he smiled to himself. Colonel White's compliments had made his day, and he felt proud to be of such valuable service to Sir Edmund. When Sir Edmund and Colonel White returned, Sir Edmund slipped a crown into Daniel's hand and said, "Take your sister and see a little of London, my boy."

When Daniel completed his duties and finally found Lyna that afternoon, she told him Eleanor was exhausted from all the activities and had decided to spend a few hours in her room resting. Lyna had been ordered not to bother her mistress until it was time to dress for dinner.

With the crown in his pocket and a few hours of free time, the two set out walking along one of the busy streets of London. Daniel told Lyna of Colonel White's words, and she beamed at him. "How nice of him to say so—but it's only what you deserve."

They wandered around taking in the sights. After a few hours they headed back to the home of the Whites. As they walked through one of the poorer streets, Lyna shivered and said, "This reminds me of where we used to live—I don't like to think about it."

"Nor I. It was a bad time, Lyna." He saw that she had lost her gaiety and said gently, "We're better off now, aren't we? Mum would be happy for us."

At the mention of her mother, Lyna grew silent and pensive. Finally she said, "I still miss her, Daniel."

The woeful look on Lyna's face troubled Daniel. Putting his

arm around her, he said quickly, "Why, Lyna, don't you remember the last thing she said to us?"

Lyna looked up and asked, "What was it?"

"She said, 'I'll be out of this dark place—and I'll be dancing on the streets of gold!' Remember that?"

"Yes!" Lyna brightened and gazed up into the skies. "Think of that—Mum dancing and singing in heaven!" They walked on for a time, thinking of those early days. "We made her a promise, didn't we, Daniel? To serve God all our lives."

"Yes, we did."

The two walked on, and when they reached the front of the imposing mansion, they stopped for a moment. Daniel reached out and touched the gold locket, smiling at her. "It looks nice on you, Lyna. And so does the dress. You're very pretty."

With chores to be done, Daniel hurried to the carriage house to check on the horses. And Lyna rushed inside to finish some last-minute tasks before waking Eleanor. An hour later Lyna was walking down one of the broad hallways that opened up into a number of bedrooms, thinking of which dress Eleanor was to wear for that evening. Suddenly she heard a door open, and without warning, a pair of strong arms went around her, causing her to cry out with alarm.

"My, don't you look pretty!" Leo Rochester spun her around and grinned as she tried to pull away. "Where'd you get that gold locket? One of your lovers?"

"Please—let me go!" Lyna pleaded.

"All right—just one little kiss, and I will."

Lyna was helpless, for Leo Rochester was an extremely powerful young man. He pulled her closer, and when she tried to turn her head, he simply grabbed her hair and held her face toward his. His lips fell on hers and he kissed her despite her pleas. Then he released her hair and said, "Why don't you be nice to me, Lyna?" he demanded in a hoarse whisper, his penetrating eyes full of lust and craving. "A girl needs to be loved. Come on—" He pulled at her, dragging her toward his bedroom and laughing as she tried to wrench free of his grasp.

Lyna felt a choking kind of fear and did the only thing she could do. She was on the threshold of the bedroom when she turned and sank her teeth into his forearm, biting as hard as she could! At once Leo cried out and yanked his arm away. Instantly,

Lyna whirled and dashed down the hall with Leo's curses ringing in her ears. "I'll have you—you hear me?" he screamed after her.

Running into her small room she quickly closed and locked the door, then fell on her bed, trembling and crying at the same time. She was afraid of what could happen if she tried to mention anything. The one time she had brought something like this up to Eleanor, her mistress had simply laughed. So Lyna said nothing to anyone about Leo's actions. She understood that the family would not listen, and she was afraid of what Daniel might do.

She kept away from Leo that night, but when she met him while attending to Eleanor, she couldn't help but notice his pale blue eyes were as cold as ice when he looked at her.

He'll be after me all the time—I'll have to be very careful, she thought. The pleasure of the trip to London was over for her.

𝕿   𝕿   𝕿

Leo Rochester was born with a capacity for doing tremendous good—or enormous evil. Like most firstborn in titled English families, the cultural and economic system of that nation had endowed him with power and means denied others. Leo was gifted with more than an average share of intelligence, not to mention a strong body and fine appearance. This combination could have made him a champion of virtue, a potent enemy of vice.

However, like most who enter this world with such power conferred upon them at birth, the young lord quickly learned that his social position could be used to indulge his own avarice and self-serving motives. After a few less-than-chivalrous indiscretions, he soon discovered that the system rarely called those in his social standing to account for their actions.

By the time Leo had reached early manhood, those who watched him most carefully knew that nobility was not the major element in his character. Over the years his parents had turned a blind eye to his faults, so often excusing his behavior as youthful exuberance that they became powerless to deal with it. But the people beneath him quickly learned that the young lord had a personality bent on cruelty. His "idle pranks," as his mother called them, went well beyond the limits of childish play. If he had been a commoner, he would have been beaten—or worse—for his behavior. However, who could stand against the future lord of the manor, especially when his parents were so indulgent?

A few unfortunate ones painfully learned about Leo's vengeful nature. He never forgot a fancied wrong, and even his equals in society learned to their sorrow that to cross Leo Rochester was to court a bitter harvest. Timothy Defoe, one of Leo's best friends, learned this early in life. He beat Leo at a horse race three times in a meet and thought little of it. He remembered it six months later, however, when his favorite hound was found with its throat cut. No evidence was discovered to link Leo to the cruel act—but one look into Leo's cold, triumphant eyes and Timothy knew the truth.

Leo might appear to forget offenses, but deep down he nurtured hatred against those who crossed him—and he never forgot his first meeting with Daniel Bradford. True, he had not been injured by the few blows that the young man had been able to land. Leo had been the stronger of the two back then and had bloodied young Bradford considerably. The thing that Leo could not stand was being challenged, and Daniel had done that before his friends. Ever since that day, Leo had made life unpleasant for the young servant.

And Lyna's resistance of his advances burned in the heart of the young man. He was used to having his way with the servant girls, even if it meant coercion. His father had warned him sternly about this, and he had repented—on the face of the thing. But the people who served Sir Edmund well knew exactly how much Leo could be trusted. They kept their daughters carefully away from him—and those young women who had no such protection either left or suffered humiliation.

Leo sat in his room late one morning, his head aching from too much ale the night before. He was in a foul humor, and when he glanced into the mirror on his wall and saw the marks of Lyna's teeth on his upper arm, rage surged through him. "I'll teach her better than that!" he muttered. As he dressed, he thought of the pleasure he would derive from breaking the girl's spirit, but he thought of his father's warning: *"Stay away from the servant girls, Leo. Some of them have brothers and fathers who are capable of killing a man for such things. And I'll not stand for such crass behavior in my son. One more incident—and you'll discover what a world without money is like—I warn you!"*

Leo wasn't sure if his father would really carry out that threat, but the thought of losing his inheritance gave him sufficient reason to plan his moves carefully. "All right—so the brother is in the way. Get rid of him, and who's to stop me from having her? Without Daniel around, Father will most certainly never find out." Leo spoke this aloud, and a thin smile touched his lips. He had a quick mind, and by the time he'd gone down to breakfast, he'd already thought out the details of his plan.

The working out of his scheme was going to take some time, but the doing of it was pleasing to him. Horses played a large part in Leo's life; he was an expert rider and owned several fine racers. The one thing in young Bradford's favor, in Leo's mind, was that he was good with the horses. Daniel groomed them properly and had learned from old Bates how to keep them in top form. Leo had always been rough with his orders to the young groom, but from that day forward, he became vicious. Every day he found some reason to get at Daniel, cursing him for the least fault and inventing offenses where none existed.

Bates observed this, of course, and tried to intervene—but he was roundly cursed for his efforts. "He's got his knife out for you, boy," Bates warned Daniel. "Don't aggravate him."

As much as Daniel tried, he found no way to please young Rochester. Time after time Leo would strike and curse him, and somehow Daniel managed to control his growing anger. But finally the time came when Daniel couldn't stand it anymore.

Leo had invited a group of young people to Milford for a week-long visit. It was common enough, but it threw a great deal of extra work on Daniel. Bates was physically almost helpless by now, kept on at the manor only for his expert knowledge and experience with the horses. Consequently, Daniel was responsible for seeing that all of the guests had animals to ride. Inevitably there were delays, and Leo never failed to give him the rough side of his tongue when they occurred.

One day the group came for their day's riding, and Daniel worked feverishly. He had all the group mounted, except for a young woman named Emmy Price. "The mare for Miss Price is lame, sir," Daniel explained to Leo.

"What? Then saddle King for her."

Daniel shook his head. "Mr. Leo, King's too much horse—"

"Shut up and do as I say!"

Daniel nodded slowly, but as he saddled the big rangy bay he knew it was a dangerous thing to do. Reluctantly, he brought the horse forward, gave the young woman a hand up, then handed her the lines. But even as he stepped back he saw the whites of King's eyes roll—and knew he was going to buck. "Miss—look out!" he called out, but it was too late. The horse gave one tremendous thrust with its hind legs, throwing the surprised young lady out of the saddle. Daniel managed to catch her before she hit the ground, then quickly helped her away from the bucking animal. She was unhurt but visibly frightened by the ordeal. "It's all right, now—" Daniel soothed.

Suddenly a blow struck his neck like a streak of fire. "You imbecile!" Leo raged, his face red. "You frightened that horse—Miss Price might have been killed! You need a whipping—and I'll see you get it!"

Daniel covered his head with his arms, but the riding crop struck him with cruel force. It cut through his thin shirt and left red welts on his shoulders and back. He gritted his teeth and backed away, but Leo followed him, his powerful arm delivering whistling blows of the crop.

All of the young men knew better than to interfere, but Miss Price ran forward. She grasped Leo's arm, crying, "Do stop, Leo! It wasn't his fault!"

Leo was breathing hard but allowed her to hold his arm. "He might have killed you, Emmy!" he said angrily. Then he put his arm around her and said, "Go back to the house. Ted—see to her." He waited until the girl was escorted away, then turned and delivered a blistering speech to Daniel, shaking the crop in his face. He ended by saying, "This is just a taste of what you'll get from now on! Now get out of my sight!"

Daniel turned away, shaken and angry. His upper body burned like fire, and he gingerly touched the painful welts on his neck and left cheek. He went at once to the carriage house and packed his belongings in a sack, then walked to the house. He asked to see Lord Rochester and waited until Sir Edmund came down.

The color drained from Sir Edmund's face as he caught sight of Daniel standing at the foot of the stairway. "What's happened, Bradford? Who did this to you?"

"I'm asking to leave your service, Sir Edmund," Daniel said in a dead voice. "I thank you for your kindness—but I must go. I'll have to owe you the amount of my indenture."

"Why, we can talk about this, Daniel—"

"No, sir." Daniel was certain that Sir Edmund knew very well who had done this to him. He had an affection for the older man and knew that to speak of his son would have been both painful and useless. "I have to go, sir."

"I'm so sorry, Daniel. I'm sure this wasn't your fault. Perhaps we can work something out—we certainly don't want to lose you."

"No, sir. I've made up my mind. I believe it's in everyone's best interests for me to leave." He hesitated then said, "I will ask one favor of you, sir. Not money. Would you—look out for my sister? She'll be all alone when I'm gone. And the world's a hard place for a young girl with no family."

Sir Edmund looked into the eyes of this young man who showed so much maturity and promise—and felt deep shame over what his own son had become. He knew, of course, what lay behind Daniel's request. He had heard of Leo's attentions to Lyna and had spoken at length to him about it. But now he knew he was being asked to do more than that. A thread of anger ran through him that Leo's indiscretions had created this situation. His son was a constant embarrassment, and now his behavior would cost Milford Manor a good worker. He said forcefully, "My boy, I give you my word as a gentleman—no harm will come to your sister while she is under my roof." He added with determination, "I will make it plain to the staff—and to *anyone else*—that she is under my protection."

Daniel swallowed hard, a look of relief and gratitude on his face. "That's very good of you, sir—but you were always good to me and Lyna. Goodbye, sir—please tell your good wife how much I thank her for all her kindness to me."

Later that afternoon Leo found himself enduring the most painful half hour of his life. He had been called into his father's study, and as soon as he saw the wrath on his father's face, the young lord knew he had to be very careful. He stood at attention as his father thundered out loudly his many faults—knowing that his friends could hear most of it. Finally Sir Edmund said in a quieter tone, "I will be speaking with the boy's sister from time to time. And I will ask her if you have shown any insolence or offered her any affront. If she merely *nods*—I promise you, Leo, you will not be the next master of Milford. You will be thrown out of this place and on your own! I have tried to show kindness to you, but apparently force is all you understand. Do I make myself clear?"

"Yes, Father."

When Leo left his father's study, his hands were trembling and black fury raged in his heart. He was shrewd enough, however, to realize that he had gone too far. *The wench isn't worth it*, he thought, and from that day decided to leave Lyna strictly alone.

Lyna had no idea of what had transpired in the study, for she was busy helping Eleanor with a new dress that had just arrived from the seamstress. There was a light tap on the bedroom door, and a maid entered, saying, "Your brother wants to see you. I think he's in trouble."

Lyna excused herself with her mistress's permission and went down at once. When she saw the welt on Daniel's cheek and his bag at his feet, she began to cry.

Throwing her arms around him, Daniel held her, telling the story. Finally he said, "Sir Edmund won't let Leo bother you. I have his word on it, and he won't break it."

"But what will you do? I want to go with you, Daniel!"

"I'm going to join the army," Daniel said. "I've been thinking about this for some time now. Colonel White offered me a position—and it will be a place where I can learn a profession. . . ."

He spoke quickly, then finally drew back. "When I'm able, I'll send for you, Lyna. We'll be together again."

Lyna watched him as he walked away, watched until he disappeared down the road. Then she turned blindly and ran away into the garden, where she cried until her body ached. Finally she rose and walked dully toward the house, feeling more alone than she had ever felt in her entire life.

4

"Give Them Cold Steel?"

IN THE MID–1700s ENGLAND FOUND HERSELF surrounded by enemies—so much so that His Majesty's army made a thin red line protecting her borders. France had declared war on England and Austria, with Prussia forming an alliance with France. The repercussions were even felt across the sea in America, where part of this conflict became known as King George's War. This was only one in a series of bloody struggles for control over Canada, which eventually drew the Colonies into the fray.

As if foreign battles were not enough, England now faced a challenge on her own shores. Charles Edward Stuart, known as Bonnie Prince Charlie, landed in Scotland, gathered supporters, and started a Jacobite rebellion. He was victorious at Prestonpans but, for lack of support, dallied for weeks in Edinburgh. His failure to press forward after that initial victory gave the beleaguered English sufficient time to assemble an army to meet the challenge from the north.

Daniel Bradford was among the thousands of British troops who were sent to crush Bonnie Prince Charlie's insurrection. The entire force consisted of ten thousand men under the command of William, Duke of Cumberland.

Daniel knew little of politics and was rudely awakened one morning by his lieutenant, a blustering old soldier misnamed Jolly. "Get out of that sack, soldier!" shouted Lieutenant Jolly as he ripped off the bedcovers without apology. Daniel awoke instantly as the freezing air hit him. The officer grinned at the shivering young man, jeering, "Come on now, the troop's pullin' out."

Jerking his uniform on hurriedly, Daniel stared at the big man in confusion. "Pulling out for where?" he asked, yanking his boots on.

"For Scotland—now, no more questions. Get over to the mess tent and get a bit of breakfast, then see to the gear." Jolly turned to leave, then wheeled around, his red face serious. "You'll hear the cannon this time, Bradford. We're going to put a cap on the Young Pretender! About time we stomped on the cursed Jacobites!"

Daniel stared at the lieutenant blankly, but he had become enough of a soldier since he had enlisted to know that it was his job to obey, not to understand. That's why there were experienced officers in command. Throwing his coat on, he hurried to the mess tent, ate his portion of corn mush and salt meat, washed down with a large draught of ale, then went at once to tend to his work.

The time he'd spent serving in the 6th Royal Cavalry had been hard—but exciting. As soon as he had left Milford Manor, Daniel had gone to see Colonel White. The man had asked no questions but said instantly, "Here's your shilling, Daniel Bradford." He handed the boy a shilling, which sealed the enlistment, then added, "Obey orders and you'll make a fine soldier. After your training, I'll see what can be done about using you in my personal service."

The training had been rigorous those first months, but Daniel was accustomed to long hours and hard work. His keen ability with horses was recognized from the start, and he was assigned to work with the army's mounts. He was with the horses constantly, and Lieutenant Jolly was very pleased with what he observed. "He'll make a good 'un, sir," the big lieutenant nodded one day as he gave his report to Colonel White. "For a young man, he knows more about horses than most—and he's a good blacksmith."

"Will he make a good trooper?"

"Sir, he will! Rides like a centaur, he does!"

A few days later Daniel had been called to the tent of the commanding officer. "I need someone to take care of my own mounts, Private," Colonel White said. "Would you be interested?"

"Why yes, sir," said Daniel, shocked to hear of his new duties.

"I remember your theories about a new method of fastening the shoes on a horse. Did it work out?"

"Oh yes, Colonel White," Daniel nodded. "And I've figured out a way to put the weights on the shoes to make the gait easier, too."

"Very well, you'll serve me personally. I need a messenger fairly often, and when none of my officers are available, you can see to that." He smiled as he added, "I can't have a private serving me personally. I promote you to sergeant as of this moment."

"Thank you, Colonel. I'll try my hardest to do my best," said Daniel, pleased with the promotion.

"I have no doubts about that from what I've seen and the good reports Lieutenant Jolly's been giving me." With a smile, the colonel said, "You're dismissed, Sergeant. Go see to your new duties."

Daniel had proved a valuable asset to the colonel, who took great pride in seeing that his horses were well cared for. At first, Daniel had to endure severe taunts from some of the troops because of his rapid promotion, but he shrugged them off, determined to make the best of his time in the army so that he could make a place for Lyna. In fact, a day never went by that Daniel didn't think of his sister back at Milford.

That cold morning the camp was in a state of confusion as Daniel went about getting the gear ready. Finally, however, the 6th moved out in advance of the foot soldiers. They expected no contact with the enemy for several days, and soon the order of the march became clear. Daniel kept busy seeing to the mounts each day, picking up what information he could along the way about the battle to come.

Fires dotted the countryside on the third evening of the march, and Daniel worked late with the horses and gear. Several of the officers' mounts needed attention, and Daniel toiled with Simms, the blacksmith, at a portable forge. Daniel was cinching the last shoe on Colonel White's favorite horse, a mottled gray stallion named Ranger, when he heard steps behind him.

"Well, now, how does he seem, Sergeant?" Daniel looked around to see Colonel White, who had come to watch. The officer approached and bent over to peer at the shoe. "Looks fine to me."

"Yes, sir, it'll hold." Daniel dropped the hoof, patted the side of the horse, then took off his apron. "That's the last of them, sir. All in good shape."

"Fine—you and Simms come along. One of my officers found a suckling pig. There's a good bit of it left, and you two have earned it."

Ten minutes later Daniel was eating the roast pork with relish, listening as Simms spoke to the colonel about the condition of the troop. Since the troopers were only as good as their mounts, both Simms and Daniel played an important part in the scheme of things as the army advanced.

The brawny blacksmith gnawed thoughtfully on a bone, then said, "Colonel, I don't rightly understand this war we're going to fight." Simms was a Cornishman and spoke with such a thick accent that it had taken Daniel some time to understand him. "Who will we be a-fightin'? The frogs or the Spaniards?"

Colonel White was sitting in his camp chair, holding a pewter cup filled with ale. Shaking his head, he answered, "Neither of those, Simms."

"Who, then, sir?"

"Scotsmen, mostly, with some English."

"Another civil war, Colonel?" Daniel asked.

"Not really." White leaned forward, his hair giving off reddish tints from the leaping tongues of fire. "When James II was driven from the throne, many people thought he was the rightful king of England. Since then we've had several rulers, now a German prince named George, one of the Hanoverian line. But the supporters of James II have never given up their hope of seeing him and his descendants returned to power. They're called 'Jacobites,' which means 'James' in another language." He sipped his ale, nodded thoughtfully, then added, "The son of James is called the Old Pretender. And *he* now has a son whom many call the Young Pretender."

Simms shook his head, took a large bite of meat from the bone in his hand, and chewed thoroughly. "And it's him who's coming to take over."

"His friends call him Bonnie Prince Charlie," White explained. "I think he must have a powerful way to stir people. He's managed to draw considerable support—much of it from our own people. . . ." The colonel spoke on for some time, relating the course of Charles's victories. "It's not a civil war—not yet," he said grimly. "Call it a rebellion, for that's what it is. In any case, our standing army is very small here in England. We're stretched to the limit, what with the war against Spain and the one in North America."

"Will we win, sir?" Daniel asked.

Colonel White gave the boy a direct glance, then stood to his feet. "We have to," he nodded sharply. "If we don't, England will become Catholic again. And if that happens, we'll see days such as we saw under Bloody Mary. Get to bed when you finish—it'll be a hard day's march tomorrow." He drained the last of his ale, then said almost to himself, "When we meet Bonnie Prince Charlie—the fate of England will be on our lances. . . !"

☩   ☩   ☩

When Charles Stuart led his army across the English border, he proved to be a wily foe for the soldiers of His Majesty's army. For weeks there were pitched battles in the Scottish Highlands. Daniel did indeed hear the cannons and endured the rigors of war. During much of the fighting he was not on the front line where the action was. He spent his days tending to his duties, making sure there were always fresh mounts, or carrying messages for Colonel White. At times he rode with the cavalry when it was sent on wide sweeping movements to seek out enemy positions. He rode for hours in the van of the troop, his eyes constantly on the mounts.

On two occasions, he was caught up in actual battle, when the troop made wild charges against the enemy. Once Colonel White's horse was shot from under him, and immediately Daniel was there to provide a fresh mount. "Good man!" White shouted, then turned and rode right into the mouths of the cannon. Daniel, having no orders, kept just to the colonel's rear, and he saw men go down, their breasts stained crimson. One of the lieutenants riding directly in front of Daniel uttered a shrill cry. Throwing his hands up, he went down, falling in a heap. Daniel pulled up his mount to protect the still body, and when the troop roared by, he slipped to the ground and bent over the wounded officer. "Are you hurt bad, sir?" he asked.

"Bad enough—but I'd be worse if you hadn't kept me from being trampled under the horses." Lieutenant Mullens struggled to his feet, and Daniel helped him onto his own horse, then swung up behind him. "We'll get you to the field surgeon, sir," Daniel said. Holding on to the sagging form of the lieutenant, he rode until he found the medical staff. When he pulled up in front of the tent, two attendants helped him carry the wounded man into the tent.

Later, after the battle was over, Daniel was working with a black mare with a gaping wound in her flank when Colonel White stopped by. "You probably saved Lieutenant Mullens' life, Sergeant," he said. "He told me how you pulled him off the field." He smiled and nodded. "It was a fortunate day for me—and for Lieutenant Mullens—when you took the king's shilling."

"I was glad to be of help to the lieutenant," Daniel flushed. He was weary and saw that the colonel was dirty and very tired as well. "Will we be moving on tomorrow, Colonel?"

"I think not—but very soon." White removed his hat and mopped his brow with a soiled handkerchief. "How many horses did we lose?"

"Too many, sir. We'll need replacements—and some like Lady here will need to rest up until they're healed."

For over a week, the troop remained in camp licking its wounds. One night after his duties were completed, Daniel wrote to Lyna. A few days later he was delighted to receive a long letter from her.

She assured him that there had been no more trouble from Leo—but she also informed him that Sir Edmund was very ill. "He had pneumonia earlier and can't seem to get over it," she wrote. "I pray that he recovers, for he has been very kind to me ever since you left."

Daniel had been saving every penny of his wages and had worked for some of the officers to make a little extra. As he read the letter, he thought, *If something happens to Sir Edmund, Lyna will have to leave. I've got to have enough money so I can find her a place. . . .*

The rebellion was slowly crushed by the English forces, though not without some cost. Daniel learned firsthand about the horrors of war. And what few romantic illusions he'd had about military exploits were gone by the time winter set in. Death on the battlefield was a terrible thing, and by the time the 6th Royal Cavalry came to grips with the last remnants of the rebels, Daniel heartily hoped he'd never again see a bloody corpse or endure the lingering stench of dead bodies strewn across a battlefield.

The end came at Culloden Moor. Daniel had risen early and taken extra care to prepare the horses for the colonel and several of his staff. At nine o'clock the Duke of Cumberland, the son of George II, came thundering up on a white horse, followed by his staff officers.

"Colonel White," he called out, his bulging blue eyes glittering with excitement, "we have them now—send your troop across that field! Swing around behind the enemy and we will crush them to chaff!"

"Yes, General, at once!"

"And there will be no quarter given, do you understand?" The duke's face was firmly set, his mouth drawn up into a grim line. "I want them finished! There are to be no more Jacobite rebels to disturb our kingdom!"

Colonel White shouted, "All right, my brave fellows—charge!"

The charge across the broken field was like nothing Daniel had ever experienced. The troop kept together fairly well at first, but soon gaps began to appear in the ranks as the desperate enemy found the range for their cannons. Nonetheless, they were cornered and knew that they could expect no mercy from the army of George II, so they fought like demented wolves.

The cannon's breath touched the face of Daniel Bradford, but it merely blew his hat off. He charged his horse into the midst of the enemy gunners, sending two of them sprawling. The third wheeled, pulled a sword from his belt, and hacked at Daniel with a vicious backhand blow. Daniel had drawn his own saber, with which he had never drawn blood, and managed to parry the blade. The force of it nearly tore the saber from his hand, but he wheeled his mount around and slashed at the tall soldier with desperate strength. The tip of the saber seemed to barely graze the man's throat, but Daniel had sharpened it to a razor's keenness.

The man nodded and blinked his eyes, then stared at Daniel with a look that haunted the young soldier for months. Blood cascaded from the soldier's throat, drenching his shirt with a rich crimson. Dropping his sword, the man grabbed his throat in a futile effort to staunch the flow, and his cries were pitiful—a series of gurgles that continued as he fell to the ground. He looked up at Daniel, his brown eyes pleading, held up one bloody hand as if for help, and then his heels dug into the earth as he kicked in protest against the end he could not flee.

Daniel, trembling uncontrollably, whirled and saw Colonel

White far ahead urging the riders forward. Ahead of the colonel loomed a wide ditch, too wide for a horse to jump, it seemed to Daniel. Nevertheless, White's red stallion lunged forward, sailed through the air, and hit the ground, staggering from the force of the impact. Daniel saw a group of the enemy move forward with gleaming bayonets, determined to capture the officer.

Right then Lieutenant Jolly came flashing by, shouting, "Come, boys! We've got to save the colonel!"

Daniel yelled something, a rage coming over him, and he spurred his mount forward. When he came to the edge of the gully, he saw several of the troop who had tried and failed to make the jump and were wallowing with their floundering steeds. He had a good horse, a fine jumper, and screamed as he reached the edge and threw his weight forward. "Up—Jupiter—up!" He felt the powerful legs of the animal as it lunged and left the earth and, for a frozen moment of time, felt gravity lose its power.

At first he thought the horse would fall short—but the powerful animal landed on the brink. Daniel kept his seat by some sort of miracle. With a wild look he turned around and saw that he and Lieutenant Jolly had succeeded in making the jump. Even as he mastered Jupiter, Jolly yelled, "Come, Bradford—give them cold steel!"

The two riders drove their horses into the midst of the enemy, driving four of them to the ground. But they could not get them all, and Daniel saw one of them riding furiously to where Colonel White struggled to get to his feet. The soldier had his blade lifted as he bore down on the colonel. Daniel wheeled his horse and drove into the fifth soldier, but saw that he was too late to help the colonel.

Just before the soldier reached Colonel White, Lieutenant Jolly, screaming and cursing, rode up from the side and struck the man in the head with his saber, killing him instantly. Daniel cried out, "Good, Jolly! Good—!"

But then an explosion rocked the earth, and Daniel suddenly found himself flying out of his saddle. The world seemed to whirl and finally came up and struck him a blow in the back that drove the breath from his body and his mind into a black, whirling pit.

🔔　　　🔔　　　🔔

"Come, my boy, wake up!"

Daniel woke to find himself looking up into a smoke-blackened face. He coughed and then realized that it was Colonel White who was holding him.

"There, now, that's better!" Colonel White's face showed relief, and as Daniel sat up and looked around, he saw that the battle was over—or almost so. The enemy was fleeing, but the remaining Jacobites were being cut down without mercy. The colonel pulled him to his feet, saying, "I was afraid they'd done you in, my boy. Are you all right?"

"Y-yes, sir," Daniel stammered. He looked to his left and gave a start—Lieutenant Jolly lay with his eyes open staring blindly at the sky. "Lieutenant—!" he cried out but knew at once that the man was dead.

"Poor fellow—he caught the blast of the cannon," Colonel White said, shaking his head. Then he took a deep breath and said quietly, "If it hadn't been for you two, I'd have been cut to pieces." He placed his hand on Daniel's shoulder and his eyes were sad. "I wish I could bring the lieutenant back. He was a fine soldier. I can't do that—but I'll never forget him. And I'll never forget you, Sergeant Bradford. A man would be a poor wretch indeed to forget the sight of you and Lieutenant Jolly sailing over that ditch!"

"I'm glad we were able to help, sir." Daniel looked over the field and was sickened by the senseless slaughter that was taking place. "Do they have to do that, Colonel? They're beaten badly enough."

But Colonel White knew there would be no mercy. "The king has ordered the Jacobites eradicated. There will be no future rebellions from that source!"

In the end the clan chiefs were stripped of their authority, and the wearing of tartans and kilts, and the playing of bagpipes and the owning of weapons were forbidden on point of death.

Daniel had survived the battle, but the aftermath left haunting memories he would never forget. He looked away as often as he could from the execution of the prisoners. Some of the captured were cruelly allowed to starve, while others were sold as slaves to American plantations. The prisoners were kept in the open, chained to trees and exposed to the inclement weather. Daniel noted one of them was a dark-skinned individual and stopped to ask, "You're not a Scot, are you?"

A pair of obsidian eyes met his, and for a moment the prisoner kept his silence. "I am Mohawk," he muttered.

"What's that?"

"Indian—from across the great sea."

Daniel was fascinated. He had read of the red savages of America but had never seen one. He noted that the man's lips were cracked with thirst. "I'll get you a drink and something to eat." He ran to get some provisions, but when he returned, the guard protested. Daniel boldly used Colonel White's name and had no more trouble from the guard. He squatted down and watched as the Mohawk eagerly drank the water, then devoured the food.

"Why do you help your enemy?"

Daniel could sense the man's suspicion and shrugged. "Why, I guess we've had our fight. I'd let you go if I had my way." He studied the coppery face, then asked, "What's your name? How'd you get all the way to this place?"

The Mohawk proved to be talkative. "My name is Orcas. I am the son of a great warrior chieftain." He related how he'd become friendly with some of the officers fighting against the British, and they'd offered to make him a great chief if he came to the Continent with them. "They lied—white men always lie," Orcas said bitterly.

"I'm sorry you got captured," Daniel said. "I'll do my best to bring you food until—"

"Until they kill me?" A grim smile touched the face of the Indian, and he seemed totally unafraid.

For the next three days, Daniel saw to it that Orcas had food and a blanket to stave off the cold. He talked often with the Mohawk, and Colonel White asked him once, "What do you find so fascinating about that savage?"

"Why, he's a long way from home, sir, and about to die." Daniel struggled to find the words to describe what he was feeling. "I guess I can't hate him much. If I was in his shape, I'd sure appreciate it if someone was kind to me."

"Very commendable," White said absently. "But he'll be shot tomorrow morning, I understand. Perhaps you'd like to take him a good meal tonight."

"Yes, sir. I'll do that."

Daniel never knew what possessed him, but after the camp had quieted down and the soldiers were asleep, he crept out of his blankets and quietly made his way to the tree where Orcas was tied. "Be very quiet—" he whispered as he cut the ropes that bound the Mohawk and handed him a small leather purse and a knife. "There's a little money there—if you can get to a port in Scotland, maybe you can make it home. It's all I can do, Orcas."

The dark eyes of the Indian never left Bradford's face. "Why do you do this?" he demanded.

Daniel shrugged. "I don't know. Now—get going."

Orcas suddenly reached out and grasped Daniel by the shoulder. "Give me your hand," he whispered. When Daniel only stared at him, Orcas lifted his own left arm and made a cut in his forearm. Then reaching out, he took the arm of the young man, made a similar cut, and held the two wounds together. "We are one blood now—blood brothers."

Daniel felt the pain of the cut and, staring into the Indian's eyes, could only say, "Go now, before they catch you—God be with you!"

Orcas nodded, his eyes gleaming. "Maybe not *all* white men are bad." Then he faded into the darkness without making a sound.

The next day the sentry who had been in charge of the prisoners was given ten lashes for permitting one of them to escape.

Colonel White said nothing for two days, then he murmured casually, "That Indian you liked so much—you did give him a good last meal, didn't you?"

Daniel looked into the eyes of the officer and said evenly, "Yes, sir. He was glad to get it." He waited for the colonel to speak, but the officer merely smiled strangely and turned to move away. For days Daniel was tense, waiting to hear that Orcas was recaptured. Finally he decided that the Mohawk had managed to get safely away or perhaps had even made it to a port and secured passage back to America.

T　　T　　T

Finally the battle at Culloden Moor was over, and when the troop returned to England, Colonel White didn't forget Daniel's faithful service, nor the fact that he had saved his life in battle. He kept Daniel close, praising him to one and all. A few days later, the colonel called Daniel to his headquarters. With a smile on his face, he said, "Draw a horse and go see your sister, Sergeant.

You've earned leave, so have a good time."

Daniel obeyed instantly, and two days later, he drew up in front of Milford. Wanting to surprise Lyna, he tied his horse in the rear of the main house, then made his way toward the cottage occupied by Silas Longstreet. Longstreet was very pleased to see Daniel and, after getting a report on the young man's travels, agreed to bring Lyna to his house. "Be quite a surprise for her," he smiled. "She's kept the whole household informed of your heroic deeds."

Daniel waited impatiently, then when he saw Lyna walking toward the cottage, he stood behind the door. When Lyna entered, he grabbed her and lifted her clear from the floor.

Lyna cried out in alarm, but when she twisted her head and saw who it was who held her, she squirmed free and threw her arms around him. "Daniel! You beast! Why didn't you tell me you were coming!"

"Because I didn't know," Daniel grinned. He held her at arm's length and shook his head at what he saw. "I leave a little girl, come back later—and find a woman!"

Lyna flushed, but her eyes were bright. "*Me* grown up! You've grown a foot!"

"Only an inch or so," Daniel protested. But he stood at attention for her while Lyna walked around him, admiring his soldiery stance. "If you don't look fine in that uniform!" she exclaimed. "How many girls have you had chasing you?"

"Not so many—and none as pretty as you." He caught her hand, saying, "Come on, let's go down to the river. I'll tell you how I won the battle at Culloden Moor singlehanded. . . ."

For the next three days, the pair had a wonderful time. Sir Edmund was still very ill, but Daniel was permitted to make a brief visit. He was shocked at how frail his former master was but did not allow it to show in his expression. "I'm very grateful for the kindness you've shown to my sister, sir," he said warmly.

"Nothing at all—nothing!" Sir Edmund was sitting up in bed, and his eyes were bright with fever. "I received a letter from Colonel White, Daniel. He told me what a heroic thing you did at the battle. Lady Edna and I are very proud of you, my boy!"

Daniel tried to make little of his deed, but he could see that the sick man took pride in his accomplishment. His visit was brief, for he didn't want to tire Sir Edmund. As he closed the door and turned to leave, he met Lady Edna in the hallway. "I'm very sorry to see Sir Edmund so weak."

Lady Edna's face was thin, and she shook her head. "I fear for him, Daniel. He's not making progress."

The days sped by, and Daniel said to Lyna one evening, "I have to rejoin my regiment day after tomorrow." He saw her face grow apprehensive, and he added quickly, "I've got some money saved. In another three months I'll have enough to send for you. Then we'll be together. Just be patient a while longer."

On the day before Daniel's departure, Leo Rochester returned. He had not heard of Daniel's visit and was more than a little drunk that day. As he rode in, he saw Lyna walking across the back pathway. He rode his horse across the yard and quickly dismounted. Coming to the ground, he blocked her way, saying, "Well, now, aren't you glad to see me?"

Lyna had not been troubled by Leo since Daniel left, but she saw at once that he was drunk. "Your father will be glad to see you, Mr. Leo," she nodded briefly.

She would have turned, but he caught her and, despite her struggles, kissed her roughly. He would have kissed her again, but he was suddenly seized and thrown back so forcibly that he staggered. Catching his balance, he glared at Daniel, who had stepped between him and Lyna. "You again!" he gasped. "You dare to put your hands on me!"

"Keep your hands off my sister and we'll have no trouble." Daniel turned and took Lyna's arm. The two walked away, not looking back. With a maniacal look in his eyes, Leo moved to his horse and opened the saddlebag. He pulled out a brace of pistols, checked the loads, then cried out, "Bradford—!"

Daniel turned to see the muzzle of the pistol in Rochester's hand level on his chest. Instantly he shoved Lyna to his left, falling with her. The explosion rang out, and he heard the hissing of the ball as it went by his ear. He leaped up and ran toward Rochester, who had dropped the one pistol and was coming up with the other loaded one. Daniel caught Leo's wrist, and the two struggled for possession. Daniel's months working with the forge had given him great strength, and he twisted the pistol away from himself.

Leo cursed and tried to resist—and then the air was shattered by a loud report. Daniel was shocked as Leo released his grip and fell to the ground, his side drenched with a sudden flow of blood. "You've killed me—!" he gasped.

The two shots drew an instant audience, one of them Silas Longstreet. His eyes widened as he saw Leo on the ground and the smoking pistol in Daniel's hand. "What have you done, boy?" he gasped.

"He tried to murder me!" Leo shouted. He propped himself up on one elbow, glared at Daniel, and cried out to the men who were running to the scene. "Take that pistol away—and hold him. He's a murderer!"

Lyna started to protest, but Longstreet knew there was no use. "There'll be a fair hearing for you, Daniel," Longstreet said sadly.

But Daniel was staring at the face of Leo Rochester. He had risen to his feet and apparently had suffered only a superficial wound. His eyes were burning as he glared at Daniel. "You'll hang for this, Bradford—I swear it!"

Daniel was taken at once to the local jail, and when Lyna was allowed to see him, he sat silently with her. "It was *his* fault!" she protested. "They can't hang you for that."

But Daniel had seen enough to know that his chances for gaining his freedom were slight. He held her hand and tried to pray, but when she left, he lay down on the filthy straw and wondered if there even was a God in heaven.

5

THE TRIAL

IF SIR EDMUND ROCHESTER HAD BEEN ABLE to attend the hearing, the trial of Daniel Bradford might have been more charitable. Judge Brookfield was an old friend of Sir Edmund's, and it is possible that he might have been prone to listen to the background surrounding the case.

However, Sir Edmund's health was in critical condition, so that even his wife was not able to be present at the hearing. At her husband's request, however, she did send the family barrister to defend the young man, but Emmett Sissons was more of a solicitor than a trial lawyer. He had plenty of experience in handling wills and torts, but he was out of his element when it came to a criminal case.

On his first visit with his client, he said, "Well, Mr. Bradford, what have you to say for yourself?"

"I'm not guilty, Mr. Sissons."

"Oh my! Dear me!" Mr. Sissons clucked his disapproval and insisted, "But, sir, you were found with the weapon in your hand and Mr. Leo Rochester on the ground with your bullet in him! Not guilty? Oh, dear me, no!"

When Daniel offered his sister as a witness to what had really happened, Sissons sighed and looked pained. "I will call her as a witness, but the prosecution will make short work of her, I warn you!"

On the day of the trial, Mr. Ronald Child, arguing for the prosecution, brought forth a series of witnesses who testified they had come on the scene to find Leo Rochester lying on the ground wounded and Daniel Bradford standing over him with a smoking pistol. After skillfully questioning each of the witnesses, the shrewd lawyer capped his case by calling Leo Rochester to the witness stand—who proved to be a most effective witness.

"And do you insist, Mr. Rochester, that the defendant removed your pistols and shot you without provocation?"

"Well, I must admit, sir," Leo said calmly, "Daniel Bradford has never liked me ever since he came to Milford Manor. We have had trouble more than once, I daresay."

"What sort of trouble, may I inquire?" said Mr. Child, leading the witness on.

"Oh, he was careless with his work, and I had to rebuke him many times."

"Were these serious rebukes?"

"One of them was. . . ." Leo then proceeded to give a twisted account of how Daniel had nearly caused serious injury to one of Leo's guests. "I was so provoked that I struck him with my riding crop. I shouldn't have done that, of course."

"What did Bradford do at that time?"

"He left my father's service—and the last thing he said to me was, 'I'll kill you for this—see if I don't!' "

"I never said that!" Daniel burst out as he came to his feet. "He's lying!"

"Mr. Sissons! Keep your client silent, do you hear me?" ordered Judge Brookfield.

"I apologize, m'lord!" Sissons pulled at Daniel, whispering, "Sit down, you young fool! Keep your mouth shut!"

Mr. Child was very adept at making the most of Leo Rochester, who presented a very good appearance to the judge. He showed no sign of anger, and at one point during the questioning Leo even said, "I feel very sorry for Bradford. He has good stuff in him, but he's got a temper like fury, and I had the misfortune to anger him."

When the prosecution was done, Sissons was given time to cross-examine Leo, but his manner and style were so gentle that there was no danger that Leo's testimony would be damaged in the slightest.

"Why didn't you make him tell the court how he's persecuted my sister?" asked Daniel when Sissons sat down.

"He'd deny it—and nobody would believe her."

Finally Judge Brookfield asked Mr. Sissons to give the defense.

When Lyna was called to testify, she related the story of what had happened. But when Ronald Child began to cross-examine her, she was soon reduced to tears. "The defendant is your brother. Is that correct, Miss Bradford?"

"Yes, sir."

"Your *only* brother—in fact, your sole living relative?"

"Y-yes, sir, but—"

"You love your brother very much, don't you?"

Lyna twisted her fingers nervously and nodded. "Yes, I do."

Mr. Child put his eyes on the girl and asked in a kindly fashion, "You would do a great deal to help him, would you not?" When the girl nodded, he insisted, "You would, in fact, do *anything* to keep your brother from being hanged or from going to prison?"

By this time Lyna was in anguish. She stared at Mr. Child and again nodded.

"I put the question to you, Miss Bradford," the tall man said, his eyes fixed on hers. "Would you lie to save your brother's life if necessary?"

Lyna cried out, "Yes, but I'm not lying!"

Child lifted his eyebrow. He had expected the girl to be more difficult. "M'lord, you have heard the witness. She has declared that she would lie to protect her brother. I move that she be declared no proper witness and that her testimony be stricken."

"So moved and so declared," said Judge Brookfield. He turned to Sissons then and said harshly, "Do you wish to call any other witnesses, Mr. Sissons?"

"Yes, m'lord. I call Colonel Adam White as a witness for the defense."

A stir of surprise ran over the courtroom as the well-known officer moved to the front of the courtroom to stand at the bar. He took the oath, and then Sissons said, "Colonel White, please state your profession, and tell the court your opinion of the defendant, Daniel Bradford."

"I am in command of the 6th Royal Cavalry," White said, his voice clear and even. "I first met the defendant when he was an indentured servant of Sir Edmund Rochester. . . ."

Daniel kept his eyes on the colonel as he set forth his account—a very fine one. But Daniel was also watching the judge and could tell he was not impressed.

" . . . and I can say that Sergeant Bradford is a fine soldier, one who has defended his country with honor and courage. I find it impossible to believe that he is guilty of attempted murder."

Sissons, feeling quite pleased with his witness, said, "Thank you, Colonel White." Then turning to the prosecution with a satisfied look, Sissons said, "Your witness, Mr. Child."

Child approached the officer carefully. He was a crafty man and had no intention of trying to intimidate such a formidable man as the one who stood watching him. "Colonel, the prosecution is second to none in its admiration of our fine officers and men. We are all aware of the noble service you and the 6th performed at Culloden Moor. We would be degenerate indeed were we to do anything to degrade any man in His Majesty's service." He waited until a murmur of approval had died down, then said smoothly, "Colonel, I will put to you a single question. I know you have confidence in the defendant—but were you present when the shooting took place?"

Colonel White had no choice. "No, sir, I was not."

"Thank you, Colonel," Child nodded, then turned to the bench. "It was thoughtful of the colonel to come and give a testimonial concerning the defendant. However, his testimony has no bearing on the case, for as he himself admits, he did not witness the incident."

Child waited until Colonel White had been dismissed from the stand and then proceeded to summarize the case with great skill. "The case is quite simple, m'lord," he shrugged. "We have called *many* witnesses who all agree that they came upon the scene immediately after the shots were fired. They all agree that Mr. Rochester was on the ground, and that standing over him with a smoking pistol was the defendant. You have heard Mr. Rochester testify of the bad humor of Bradford, and there is no other possibility but willful attempted murder. The prosecution rests."

Sissons realized his client had no hope of being acquitted and made a feeble plea for mercy on the grounds of Daniel's youth and his good service for the king.

Daniel sat quietly, observing the final proceedings, knowing that he was lost.

Judge Brookfield said finally, "Let the defendant rise. Daniel Bradford, I find you guilty as charged of attempted murder." Ignoring the cry that came from Lyna, he proceeded, "I sentence you to ten years in prison, term to be served in Dartmoor prison. This court is adjourned."

Lyna fought her way past the guard and fell against Daniel, sobbing. She wept until she was led from the court by Silas Longstreet. When she looked back, she saw Daniel being shackled hand and foot. When he looked at her, his eyes were bleak and hopeless. He didn't move or return her cries but turned and shuffled away, his arm grasped by a heavy guard.

☫   ☫   ☫

For two weeks after Daniel's trial, Lyna listlessly moved about doing her work, her face pale and her lips tightly drawn together. It was a difficult time in any case, for Sir Edmund was dying. The servants were kind, and Lady Edna said only, "I'm sorry about your brother, my dear."

Leo stayed at Milford, saying nothing at all to Lyna. He showed concern for his father and gave himself to comforting his mother and his sister. Only once did he speak to Lyna. They met by accident in the hall, and he halted, his eyes on her. She stared at him silently, and in an odd tone of voice he said, "After my father is gone, we'll make better arrangements for you."

The words echoed in Lyna's mind for a week. She knew very well what Leo's *arrangements* would be! She began to think of leaving, but she had no place to go. Sir Edmund had been her sole protection from Leo, and when he was gone, she would be helpless.

When the doctors showed up early one afternoon, whispers spread the word that the master was dying. Just before dinner the family was called, and Mrs. Standridge announced, "Sir Edmund, Lord of Milford Manor, is dead—God rest his soul!"

For the next few days the house was very busy making preparations for the funeral. It was an impressive occasion. The church was packed, and the bishop came from London to give the funeral sermon. Lyna attended, as did all the servants, but she heard very little of what the bishop said. She was thinking about how she could get away from there.

However, the apprehension that she entertained faded as the days passed. Leo was forced to spend a great deal of his time in London on legal business, and when he did come home, he did no more than give her a penetrating glance.

Maybe it's going to be all right, she thought. She was miserable and lonely, weeping over Daniel's fate and longing to see him. Dartmoor was far away, and she was not even certain that visitors were permitted—but she determined to go and see him somehow. Night after night she lay awake, and during the day she spoke little to anyone. She had never felt more alone. When her mother had died, she'd had Daniel, but now she had no one.

"I'll find a way!" she murmured one morning after a sleepless night. "I'll go to see him, no matter what it takes!"

6

THE RUNAWAY

THE DEATH OF SIR EDMUND ROCHESTER brought great changes to the estate of Milford. The family, of course, made the adjustments to the loss of the head of the family with some difficulty. Lady Edna Rochester took the loss the hardest. She had been totally dependent on her husband, and it was perhaps natural that she should now look to her son for every need. If she had been a more robust woman, she might have remarried, but she was overweight and given to nervousness, which did nothing to attract any suitors. Sir Edmund had left the estate to Leo, with provisions that he would care for his wife and daughter, and Leo saw to it that his mother's needs were met. Soon she settled into the dull routine of a wealthy widow.

Eleanor Rochester was an astute young woman, and though she missed her father greatly, she quickly adapted to a new way of life. She and Leo were much alike and came to an understanding almost at once. "Look around and find yourself a rich husband, sister," Leo advised her. "You're good-looking and have some property to offer as a dowry. Shouldn't be too hard to snare the son of an earl."

"And what about you, Leo?" Eleanor had countered.

"Oh, I'll marry, of course," he had shrugged. "But I intend to enjoy my liberty for a time. Father was all right, but he kept me on a pretty short chain. Now I'm my own man and can do as I please."

The servants of the house and the farm were all somewhat doubtful of their new master. Leo had never made any attempt through the years to befriend any of them, and some of them had been abused by him. He was totally selfish, they well knew, and the young maids were careful to avoid him whenever possible. Now that Sir Edmund had died, there was no one to restrain him.

Lyna had been warned by Silas Longstreet shortly after the death of Sir Edmund. He drew her aside one afternoon, saying, "Lyna, I'm leaving Milford."

"Oh, Mr. Longstreet—!" Lyna exclaimed. "You've been here so long!"

"Aye, but it's time to go. We'll be moving next week." Longstreet had grown fond of the girl and now said, "It'll be hard on you here with Sir Edmund gone."

Lyna knew exactly what he meant. "I wish I could leave here— but my time of indenture won't be up for two more years," she sighed.

"That's what I want to talk to you about," Longstreet nodded. "I've spoken with my new employer about you. He says he can use a maid and is willing to buy the time remaining in your service from Sir Leo—if you want to come."

"Oh yes!" Lyna said instantly. "There's nothing for me here— now that Daniel's not here. Please, will you speak to Sir Leo?"

Later that day Longstreet was going over the books with Leo, and when they were finished, he said, "I think all's in order, sir. The new man should have no trouble."

"It seems very well, Longstreet."

"One more thing, sir. My new employer needs a lady's maid. I thought of Lyna and mentioned her. He's willing to buy the remainder of her indenture if you'd care to sell."

Leo shot an angry glance at Longstreet. "The girl will remain here!" he snapped.

Longstreet gave Leo a steady glance. "Sir, I have an affection for both Lyna and her brother. Not to be offensive, but the girl has no friends here. I feel responsible for her. As a matter of fact, I promised Daniel—"

"You heard me! The girl stays—now you're free to leave!"

Longstreet had seen Leo Rochester before in such angry moods. He said no more, for he knew to push it further was useless, and it would only make things worse. Sadly he went to his house and told his wife, "I spoke to Sir Leo about Lyna." His brow clouded, and he shook his head. "He won't let her go." He ran his hand through his gray hair, adding, "He'll have the girl now. I hate to think of it!"

When Longstreet told Lyna of Leo's refusal to release her, the poor girl began to cry. She had dared hope that she would be able to go with the Longstreets, but at the thought of having to stay, a heaviness settled over the young girl.

For two weeks after the funeral, Lyna went about her work, seeing little of Leo. He was spending most of his time with the new manager, so he was seldom seen in the house. Lady Edna became more demanding, and Eleanor increasingly more so. The house servants seemed to settle into the new way of life, but Lyna feared that sooner or later Leo would notice her.

Two days after the Longstreets left Milford, Lyna was approached by Betty, one of the housemaids. "Sir Leo, he wants to see you, Lyna—in his study."

Lyna at once grew wary. "What does he want, Betty?"

"You'll have to ask him that," Betty shrugged. "He don't tell me his business." She gave Lyna a sly grin and said, "Better watch out for him, though. He's a one with the girls, he is!"

Lyna moved down the hall and knocked on the door of the study reluctantly, her heart beating faster. When a voice said, "Come in," she opened the massive oak door and entered. Leo was sitting at the walnut desk, which was littered with papers and ledgers. Looking up, he smiled, "Well, come in, Lyna."

"Yes, sir." Lyna moved closer. "You sent for me, sir?"

"Yes, I did." Leo replaced the goose quill into a gold holder. Then he rose and moved to stand beside the high window that admitted bars of yellow sunbeams. He was a handsome man— and well aware of it. He had a tall body, kept strong through an active life of riding and hunting, and always wore the finest of clothing. He was wearing a pair of ash gray breeches cut to fit very tightly.

Leo's shirt was pure white, his cuffs cut back in the newest fashion, his collar high in the latest style, and a pure silk ruffle blossomed at his throat. He wore a maroon waistcoat and a pair of shining black boots that covered his calves. On his right hand he wore a large red ruby set in a massive ring, which glowed as he lifted his hand and ran it through his thick brown hair.

"Well, now," he said, his blue eyes fixed on her, "I haven't seen much of you lately, have I, Lyna?"

"No, sir," said Lyna nervously.

"You're looking well. Let's see, how old are you now?"

"S-seventeen, sir."

"Ah, yes, seventeen." Leo moved across the room, coming to stand beside her. His eyes roamed over her, and the corners of his lips turned up in a smile. "I remember when you first came to Milford," he said. "You were skinny as a stick and pale as paste." He reached out and let his hand fall on her shoulder. "You've blossomed since then—my word, you have!"

Lyna felt uncomfortable and desperately wanted to pull away from his hand. She looked up quickly, saying, "You wanted to see me, Sir Leo?"

Leo gave her shoulder a squeeze. "I can make things a lot easier for you, Lyna. No need for you to work so hard."

Quickly Lyna said, "I don't mind work, sir." She moved away from his touch and lifted her chin in a defiant manner. "If that's all, sir. . . ?"

The girl's quick movement away from his touch amused Leo. He was accustomed to easy successes with women, especially with young servant girls. Somehow Lyna Bradford's resistance pleased him. He saw it as a challenge, and now that his father's heavy hand was not present, Leo knew it would be only a matter of time before he bent the girl to his will. "That's all—for now," he said and watched as she left the room. "You've got pride—but so did your brother," he murmured, then smiled at the thought of Daniel Bradford buried alive in a dark and foul prison cell at Dartmoor.

🕊   🕊   🕊

A sound broke through her fitful sleep, coming to Lyna only faintly. She rolled over, moving restlessly under the heavy weight of blankets, vaguely aware of the absence of Betty, her customary bed partner. A faint clicking sound caused her to start. She struggled out of sleep, lifted her head, and asked, "Betty—is that you?"

When no answer came, alarm flooded her at once. Betty, she remembered, had gone to spend the weekend with her parents. It had been a luxury, having the tiny garret room to herself. The room was located in the extreme east corner, over the ballroom. It had become a citadel for Lyna, a haven where she retired as soon as her duties were over. She had a few books and a candle, and reading had been her only entertainment.

One window broke the west wall of the small room, and as Lyna sat up with alarm, the full moon sent silver beams through it—outlining a large form that loomed beside her bed!

Lyna cried out, but at once Leo Rochester's voice broke the silence, "Now, don't take on, Lyna—" When he pulled the covers back, Lyna made a frantic lunge to escape. A powerful hand caught her, closing on her arm with a viselike grip. Lyna caught the smell of liquor and knew that he was drunk. His voice was hoarse, and he pulled her back, holding her fast.

"Let me go!" she panted, pushing at him with all the strength of her arms. Fear ran along her nerves, and she knew if she didn't think of something soon, all would be lost!

Leo captured her wrists and held them tightly in his big hand. "That's all right, sweetheart," Leo gloated, his voice slurred with too much wine. "Fight! I like it—but you'll give in soon enough!"

Lyna screamed, "Help me—someone!"

"Nobody to hear you. You can't hear anything in this room in the main house. Scream all you want—"

Lyna could see his face in the cold moonlight, and her mind reeled with terror. No one would come to her aid. Unexpectedly, an idea broke through her panic. To Leo's surprise, she suddenly went limp. When she stopped struggling, Leo lifted his head and laughed.

"You give up pretty easy, girl." He released her hands and started to pull her close—but the moment she felt her hands free, Lyna lunged away from him. His hand slapped at her, but she managed to come off the bed as he cried angrily, "Come here— you can't get away!"

Lyna knew he would put himself between her and the door. Her mind was racing now. She had only one hope. A heavy pewter candlestick sat on the table beside the bed—the only thing that could be used for a weapon. Desperately she seized it, then turned to face him.

The moonlight fell on Leo's face, which was twisted with drunken anger. "Come here, Lyna! You can't get away!"

Lyna held the heavy base of the candlestick tightly in both hands. When he came toward her with his hands reaching for her, she thrust it at his face with all her strength! It caught Leo in the mouth with a sickening sound of breaking teeth, and a wild cry burst from his lips. He lifted both hands to his mouth, and when he did, Lyna took the candlestick by the top of the stem and with all her force swung it again. It caught Leo in the left temple, and he crumbled to the floor instantly. He lay there so loosely that Lyna thought she had killed him. But when she leaned over, she saw that he was still breathing.

"Got to get away!" she gasped. Instantly she wheeled and went to the small closet. Frantically she threw on a dress and her one heavy wool coat, then stuffed her meager possessions into a rough cloth bag. Leo was beginning to groan as she stepped past him. She took one look at his face, which was covered with blood, shuddered, then ran from the room.

Lyna quickly went to the kitchen. Opening a cloth sack, she put a few potatoes, two loaves of bread, and some dried meat inside. Quietly she stepped outside into the numbing cold wind and went at once to the barn. Daniel's old room was vacant except for his old trunk containing his personal belongings he'd had to leave behind when he was arrested. Digging through the trunk, she took some of his things, including two books and one of his old outfits—not knowing why, but wanting something of his. As she left the barn, she heard the sound of the horses stirring but nothing else.

The moon cast a silver glaze on the fields as she made her way south. She had no destination, but Lyna knew instinctively that Leo would search for her. *He'll never forget what I did*, she thought grimly. *I'll have to hide during the day and walk nights. Maybe I can reach the coast and get on a ship. . . .*

She made a pathetic figure as she fled from Milford. Several times she passed cottages where warm fires burned. And each time she thought of how nice it would be to have a little house— to be safe inside. But she knew no house in the country would be safe for her, and as the moon gazed down on her, she walked doggedly along the road, not looking back a single time.

𝕀   𝕀   𝕀

Drifting snow streaked across the fields in a ghostly haze and swirled in little eddies at her feet as Lyna made her way down the frozen road. Dawn was beginning to redden the low-lying hills to her left as she stumbled over the rutted way. She was cold and tired, and her shoes, never made for heavy outside wear, had not stood the journey. Both soles had come loose sometime during the night, and her attempts to bind them up with strips of an old blouse had not been very successful.

She stopped, dropping the heavy bag, then pulled off her thin gloves and blew on her fingers. *Got to find a place to stay!* she thought numbly. It was her third night on the road, and twice she had been forced to sleep in haystacks. She had burrowed into the musty hay to shiver through the cold, lying there all day until night came. The other time she had been fortunate to find an abandoned barn and had managed to make a small fire. She had roasted two of the potatoes she had brought and ravenously ate them along with some of the bread.

The wind was picking up now, and the blowing snow was forcing its way into every opening in her scant clothing. She knew she would freeze if she didn't find shelter. Slowly she turned and saw, against the glowing red of the early morning sky, the outline of a large house. Picking up her sack she moved toward it. A dog's bark broke the frigid silence and stopped her dead still. A small mongrel appeared from around the corner of the house, its head down and a menacing growl in its throat.

"Good dog!" Lyna whispered and held her hand down. The dog halted, seemed to consider her—then began to wag his stubby tail. He came closer, and Lyna pulled a piece of bread from her sack and offered it to the animal, who took it eagerly. "Good dog," she said, patting his ragged fur. "Come on, now."

She skirted the house, having seen the outline of a barn in the meadow behind it. She was frightened, knowing that if seen she could be shot for a prowler. But in the icy wind the swirling snow soon screened the house. When she reached the back she saw two barns—one new and the other ancient. The older one was leaning at an impossible angle, ready to fall, it seemed. The sound of animals in the new barn gave her an idea. She slipped inside and, by the dim light of the rising sun, saw three cows in stalls, chewing slowly.

At once Lyna found a bucket, then speaking soothingly to one of the cows, sat down on a three-legged stool. Soon the rhythmic sound of streams of milk hitting the bottom of the pail came, and when she had drawn about a pint, she lifted the pail and drank thirstily. The rich taste of the frothy, warm liquid was the best thing she'd ever tasted! She quickly milked the other two cows, not taking much from either, and drank until she could hold no more. Then she made her way to the older, deserted barn—a better hiding place, she surmised.

Climbing into the rickety loft, she found enough old straw to cover herself. Outside, the wind moaned, muting all other noises. Exhausted from walking all night, and comfortably full from the warm milk, Lyna fell asleep as if drugged. Once she woke up to the sound of a voice from the next barn. But soon that ended, and she knew that the farmer had milked the cows and fed them, so she dropped off to sleep again.

When she awoke, the sun was declining in the west. She rose stiffly, blew on her hands, and wished for a fire. The dog met her as she came down the ladder, and she spoke softly to him. "Nice dog," she murmured, noting that her lips were stiff with the cold. She peered out the door and could see a man chopping wood in the backyard. Smoke was rolling out of the chimney of the big house, and she longed for the warmth of a fire.

A fresh snow had fallen while she slept, for the land was covered with a pristine white blanket that reflected the golden rays of the dying sun. She drew her coat around her, and then slipped unseen into the new barn. After making her supper of all the fresh milk she could hold, Lyna began a careful search of the barn. Toward the back wall, she found a small barrel of apples, which she sampled at once and found good. She took half a dozen of them and also a small sack of the corn used for horse feed. It could be soaked and cooked, she knew.

As the last rays of the sun slowly faded, Lyna got ready to start another night's walk. Though the food and rest had helped, she knew that she was in great danger. She had come some twenty miles from Milford, but a long journey still lay ahead of her. *If I could just travel during the day,* she thought, *I'd be all right—but I'll freeze trying to walk at night.* She looked outside and saw that it was finally dark—but also that fine grains of snow were being swirled by a rising wind. It would be harder going now in the deeper layer of snow. Discouraged, she went back inside the barn and sat down. The small dog whined and came and put his head in her lap.

"I wish I had fur like you," she whispered. She rubbed his head, trying to think. "If I were a boy, it would be easy," she added, pulling at his ragged ears.

If I were a boy—

The thought echoed in her mind, and she stood up so suddenly that the dog gave a startled yelp and backed away. Lyna had a quick mind, and once the idea had come, she rapidly worked it out.

"I've got some of Daniel's old clothes," she muttered, "and nobody would be looking for a *boy* runaway." She thought for no more than two minutes, then nodded, her eyes gleaming with determination. "I can't make it to safety as a girl—so I'll become a boy!"

At once she pulled Daniel's old clothes from the bag, stripped off her dress and petticoat, and put on the trousers and shirt. They were too large for her, but the very shapelessness of the garments helped hide her figure. She picked up the soft cap—then paused. Her hand went to her long hair and she whispered, "Got to get rid of this—but I don't have scissors—or even a sharp knife."

She made another search of the barn and was delighted to discover a pair of sheep shears. She tested their edge, then with her left hand took a heavy lock of her blond hair. Placing the shears in position, she took a deep breath, then snipped the hair. It fell to the floor, and soon was followed by other locks. Cutting her own hair was awkward, but Lyna worked carefully, leaving it long enough to fall over the edge of her collar.

"There—now you're a boy," she said to herself. She ran her hand over her head, whispering, "It feels so *odd!*" Then she carefully scooped up the loose hair, wrapping it in her cast-off petticoat. She stuffed everything into the bag and determined to rest until nearly dawn the next day.

"I've got plenty of food here, and I'll leave before dawn. Maybe I can get a ride on a wagon," she murmured. She started to walk across the floor of the barn and laughed. "It feels so— *funny!*" Lyna had been wearing skirts all her life, and now the feel of the rough trousers on her legs was shocking. She walked around and thought, *Boys walk different than girls—they take bigger steps—and they swagger sometimes.* She practiced a few times, and after several strides was finally satisfied. Finding a blanket in one of the horse stalls, Lyna decided to risk staying in the snug new barn. She milked one of the cows, drank all she could hold, then patted the side of the animal, saying wistfully, "Wish I could take you with me, cow."

She wrapped up in the blanket and slept well. An hour before dawn she woke, had her last liquid breakfast, then picked up her bag and left the barn.

The dog came to nose her, and she bent over to pat his shaggy head. "Goodbye," she whispered. Then she shouldered her bag and made her way around the house to the road. By the time the sun cast its first rays across the land, Lyna was already two miles away, walking down the snow-packed road.

She heard the sound of horses' hooves and looked back to see a wagon with runners replacing the wheels. The man who drove it was wrapped up in a huge coat and his cap nearly covered his eyes. However, as he pulled alongside her, he called out cheerfully, "Hello, young fellow. Goin' to town?"

"Yes, I am."

"Hop in. It's too cold to be a-walkin'." When Lyna climbed into the seat beside him, the farmer asked, "Whereabouts you headed, lad?"

"Going to Dover."

"Well, I ain't goin' so far as that—but I can put you down in Faxton. What's your name, boy?"

Lyna had not yet thought of that, but the answer came naturally. "Name is Lee." Daniel had called her by her middle name when she was small, and now she smiled at the thought. "Just call me Lee," she said. She sat there beside the driver, suddenly filled with hope for the first time since leaving Milford. For some reason, she thought of her mother and the last prayer she'd prayed for her and Daniel.

As the sled moved smoothly along the glistening ribbon of snow, Lyna Lee Bradford prayed a childlike prayer: *Lord, help me find my way!*

7

An Unexpected Visitor

DARTMOOR PRISON WAS DESIGNED for the confinement of prisoners—not for their comfort.

The guards were callous men who often vented their anger and frustrations on the inmates. Warden Pennington G. Sipes was dedicated to wringing the last pence from his budget. The last thing either he or anyone else cared about was the misery and dismal suffering of criminals. He was fond of stating his philosophy of penology to the inspectors who made rare visits to see that funds were not wasted on excessive food or fine clothing for the prisoners.

"It is my task to demonstrate to the prisoners that those who break the law must suffer for their crimes. We are not running a resort here at Dartmoor, but a prison. Those who have pride will be broken—and if some perish, what complaint can they have? Had they been respectable citizens, they would not be here."

After almost a year of fighting to survive the rotten food, the sweltering heat in the summer, and the numbing cold in winter, Daniel Bradford had lost almost every normal reaction that he'd brought into the prison. The days were endless drudgery, and the nights a horror. The thought of spending ten years in a hell such as Dartmoor brought a mindless terror so consuming to Daniel that he wanted to scream and beat his fists against the stone walls.

From the very beginning, however, he learned to obey orders instantly—*any* orders—for any minor infraction in the eyes of the

89

cruel guards was ruthlessly punished. His spirit was crushed almost at once, and he soon found out what the inmates meant when they spoke of "going to the shower." Something in their voices and the fear in their eyes frightened Daniel. If these hardened men were filled with terror over whatever the punishment was, how could he bear up to it?

The grim reality came one day when he failed to put away his tin plate used for all meals. A hulking guard named Jesperson caught him by the arm, his small eyes gleaming. "All right, Bradford, you didn't last long, did you now? Come along—you can use a shower."

Fear threaded Daniel's nerves, but he kept his face stolid as the guard dragged him away. He saw the grins on the faces of the other guards—and some of the inmates joined them.

Jesperson led him to a section of the prison walled off from the rest. When they entered a room set off to the back, Daniel looked around apprehensively.

"Got a new man, Pinkman, name of Bradford." Jesperson grinned. "Needs a taste of a shower."

"Well, I reckon we can accommodate him." The guard was small and had a sharp face like a ferret. He measured Daniel with his slate-colored eyes in a way that frightened the young man. His smile was a mere twitch of thin lips, and he nodded toward a device against the wall. "Just 'ave a seat, and we'll take care of you right enough."

Jesperson shoved Daniel into a heavy wooden chair fastened to the back wall. Over the chair was a pipe with a circular head pierced with many small holes. Daniel had time only to glance at it, when Jesperson fastened his wrists with leather straps to the arms of the chair. Then the other guard swung something that was attached to the wall in front of his face. It was a large cuplike device that pressed against his throat and came up to the level of his eyes, clamping his forehead tightly with a steel band.

"Not too tight, is it?" Pinkman asked anxiously. "Let me know if it binds. We aim to please. Are you ready now?"

"He's ready," Jesperson grinned. "Let 'im have it, Pinkman."

The small guard reached out and turned a handle, and at once cold water sprayed over Daniel's head. The shock of it made him gasp, and he struggled to move, but his head was clamped fast by the steel band. He opened his eyes and saw the two men grinning as they watched. When he looked down he saw the water collecting in the cup, and suddenly terror ran through him.

They're going to drown me!

He felt the water touch his chin, then slowly rise until it lapped against his mouth. He shut his lips, but as the water crept up over his upper lip and touched the base of his nose, he fought against his bonds with all his strength.

The water soon rose over his nose, and he held his breath as long as he could. Finally the pain in his chest forced the air out—and when he inhaled, water choked him instantly. It was agony, and he coughed and gagged as the water hit his lungs. His arms and legs strained mightily, but the horrid torment went on until finally he passed out.

He came to, coughing and gagging and heaving as he recovered. He shivered and opened his eyes to see Pinkman and Jesperson watching him with interest. "All right now?" Pinkman asked, his voice strangely gentle but his eyes filled with an unholy joy.

Daniel nodded weakly, and Pinkman winked at his companion. "A tough one, ain't he, now? Well, let's have another shower, eh?"

Daniel almost screamed as the guard turned on the water again. A mindless terror clawed at him, and as the torment was repeated, he fought until he went under again.

How many times the ordeal went on, Daniel could never remember afterward. The world became a fiendish nightmare as the two guards again and again waited for him to regain consciousness, then watched as he strangled and gagged helplessly.

Finally Pinkman looked down at the pale face of the young man and nodded regretfully, "Guess that'll have to do—for this time. He's a tough one, eh?"

"He ain't no crier, that's for sure," Jesperson said, a reluctant admiration in his pale eyes. "Not a word out of 'im!"

"Well, well, next time we'll do better," the small guard nodded as he unfastened the straps and allowed the limp head of the prisoner to fall to one side. Pinkman's ferret eyes gleamed and he urged, "Be sure you bring this one back, Jesperson—he's an interesting case. Kind of a challenge, you might say. . . ."

Three times during the past ten months Daniel had been taken to the "shower," despite every attempt to avoid it. He had nightmares now of those times, and a deep-seated hatred for Jesperson and Pinkman burned in his belly. He would have killed them instantly if the chance had ever come, but it never did, of course.

Dartmoor had few individual cells, only large tomblike rooms in which fifty prisoners were crowded together. These oversized "cells" were little kingdoms, where Daniel had discovered those first days after arriving that the strong ruled and the weak served. He had been challenged almost at once by a hulking inmate named Perry, who demanded that Daniel give him his blanket. When Daniel refused, the big prisoner struck out at him. Though the man was muscular, he was slow and ponderous. Daniel slipped under the impact and instinctively drove a tremendous right-hand blow into the convict's mouth, knocking him down. Daniel was strong and healthy and had had his share of fights in the army. When the convict got up, cursing and raving, Daniel proceeded to coolly knock him down again and again.

Finally Perry crawled to his feet, his face a bloody mask. He stared at the young man, who was not even breathing hard, spat out a tooth and muttered, "Who needs yer blasted blanket?"

"Good on you, lad," one of the prisoners murmured. "He'll leave you alone now."

"That's what I want—to be left alone," Daniel muttered. He turned to face the prisoner who had spoken to him, an undersized man of some thirty years. He was emaciated and bore the marks of suffering on his gaunt face, but he seemed to be of a better sort than most of the others. "My name's Bradford," Daniel offered, sitting down next to the thin man and leaning back against the dank, foul-smelling wall. "You can call me Daniel."

"James Boswell—call me Jamie." He extended a bony hand, then asked, "How long is your sentence?"

"Ten years."

"And the charge?"

"Attempted murder."

"Ah? Well, Daniel, ten years is better than goin' to the gallows."

Daniel looked around the abysmal surroundings and shook his head. "I don't know about that," he said bitterly. Then he stared at Boswell closely, asking, "What about you?"

A slight smile appeared on Jamie Boswell's thin lips. "Well, the charge was treason. I was arrested for being a supporter of Bonnie Prince Charlie—for being a Jacobite."

"And were you?"

"Oh no, not really. But the hunt was up and I'd made political enemies. The Crown needed a scapegoat and my enemies needed to get rid of me, so—there it was."

Daniel had been filled with bitterness since his arrest and was puzzled at how calmly the small man seemed to take his fate. "I guess you'd like to pay those back that put you here?"

"Oh no, that's not for me, Daniel. The Scripture says, 'Vengeance is mine, I will repay.' "

Incredulous, Daniel stared at the man, and Boswell quickly added, "But I can't take any credit for not harboring hatred. In the natural I suppose I'd be filled with hatred by now, what with the way I've been treated. But since the Lord Jesus came into my heart, why, I find it's possible even to pray for those who locked me up here."

"I'll never pray for the man who put me in this place!" spat Daniel.

Boswell didn't answer for a time but gently laid his hand on the young man's shoulder. "Well, I'm sorry you're in this place, my young friend, but we'll make the best of it. Perhaps I can be of help from time to time. I've learned how to get by, and you shall too."

Daniel relaxed in the presence of this calm and gentle man. "It's a terrible place. How long are you in for, Jamie?"

"Six more years to go. Now, first of all, come and make your bed next to mine—if you'd care to, that is."

Daniel liked the open honesty of the small man and agreed at once. Those next few days Boswell had guided him through the worst of it all. And when Daniel saw how badly some of the newcomers had fared, he was very thankful for the advice.

He was able to repay Boswell almost at once. On the second day of Daniel's imprisonment, Perry came to stand over the pair. He ignored Daniel, but putting his eyes on Boswell, he demanded, "You got yer money today—hand over me share."

At once Daniel realized that the hulking bully had been forcing Boswell to pay extortion. Standing to his feet, he said, "Perry, get away from here or I'll smash your face to jelly."

The words were not loud, but Perry immediately took a step back. He glared at Daniel, but his lips were still crushed from the young man's hard fist, and he whirled and walked away, cursing under his breath. Daniel took his seat, saying nothing. But Boswell clapped his thin hand on Daniel's shoulder. "Thanks, Daniel. He's been robbing me for months."

From that time on the two kept together, and Daniel profited from the relationship. He discovered that his new friend was a scholar of sorts and had been a writer and a printer before he'd been imprisoned. "Had to learn how to print to get my things published," Jamie informed him. "My pen gets out of hand at times."

Visitors were rare at Dartmoor. The prison had been built in a location very difficult to reach, so that it involved considerable expense and trouble to make a visit. Getting letters out was hard, for the guards demanded a bribe, and Daniel had almost no money. He did send one letter to Lyna but received a reply from an unexpected source—Sir Leo Rochester.

When the letter came, Daniel stared at it in disbelief. The envelope was sealed in wax with the family crest of the Rochesters. The letter itself was written on fine paper with the same crest at the top of the page.

"Your sister is no longer at Milford," the letter read. "She left shortly after my father's funeral. However, I have gone to great lengths to find her. I know you will be pleased to know that when I do, I shall see to it that she is properly cared for. My father having passed away, I am now master of Milford. I trust you are enjoying your présent environment."

Daniel felt a wave of hatred rush through him, and he tore the letter to shreds. He was so troubled about Lyna's plight that he shared his history with Jamie, who showed quick sympathy.

"Well, from what you tell me, she's better off away from Leo Rochester. Thank the Lord she's out of his power."

"But—where *is* she?" Daniel groaned. "She could be hungry or sick—"

"Let's think better things," Jamie answered at once. "She's an orphan, and God has a special love for those people. He calls himself the Father of the fatherless." Boswell had a pair of mild light blue eyes, and he spoke quietly as a rule. "When I came here I raged at God—cursed Him and dared Him to strike me dead."

Somehow this side of the man didn't fit the image that Daniel had formed of Boswell. "Can't see you doing that," he said finally, "but it's what I'd *like* to do. What changed you?"

"God did—but not until I'd almost destroyed myself." Jamie hesitated, then said, "Mind if I tell you about it, Daniel?"

"Go ahead—but it won't do me any good."

Boswell ignored Daniel's skepticism. He settled down with his back against the stone wall and began to speak. He went far back, relating how his own family had been devout Christians. Then he spoke of how he'd gotten away from their faith when he went to the university.

"Which one was that?" Daniel asked.

"Christ's College, Oxford," said Boswell.

A bit surprised, Daniel paid more careful attention to the quiet voice, for he'd formed a high opinion of educated men.

"I became an atheist," Jamie acknowledged. "I made fun of my parents' simple religion and used to laugh at ministers." He paused and asked, "I don't suppose you're an atheist, are you, Daniel?"

"No. Only a fool would deny there's a God!"

"Well," Jamie shrugged, "I was a fool for several years. Made myself a reputation in the printing world, plenty of money—everything I needed." He paused and ran his hand over his sandy hair. "You know, there are times now as a Christian when heaven and all that seems terribly improbable—but there were many times when I was an atheist when hell and judgment seemed terribly probable. . . ."

The two sat there, and for almost an hour Boswell described how he nearly lost his mind buried alive in Dartmoor. Then he told how a minister had come once and held a funeral service—and had preached the love of Jesus for all sinners. "It hit me like a physical blow, Daniel," he confessed. "I began to tremble, and when the minister finished, he came to me. He said, 'Man, call on the Lord for forgiveness! Jesus died for you—don't miss out on heaven!'"

"What happened?" Daniel asked. He could not doubt the sincerity of the small inmate, for there was a quiet light of joy in those blue eyes.

"I did what the man said. I called on God, and the moment I asked for forgiveness in the name of Jesus Christ—everything changed!" He shook his head, saying, "Oh, I still grew weary and sick—the food was still awful, and I still endured some misery from Perry and the guards—but there was a peace inside me that I can't explain, Daniel! Before I was converted, Jesus was just a man who lived two thousand years ago, but by some tremendous miracle I can't explain—why, He's inside me now!"

Daniel listened but made no comment. Later, as the weeks passed, from time to time Jamie would share something from the Bible with him. He quoted scripture liberally, and once after quoting the entire eleventh chapter of Hebrews, Daniel asked, "How much of the Bible do you know by heart, Jamie?"

"Why, all the New Testament—but not that much of the Old."

Daniel stared at his friend in disbelief. "*All* the New Testament? You must be a genius!"

"Oh no, not really," Jamie denied. "I've always had a good memory, and since I've been in here, I've had little else to do. I memorized most of Plato when I was an atheist. But it's nice to have the Bible with you all the time."

The months passed slowly, and Daniel grew more and more sullen and withdrawn. He never heard from Lyna and dully assumed that she had left the country—or perhaps had died. He moved through the days like an animal, sitting for hours staring at the walls, his mind a blank. He deteriorated physically, of course—as did all those in Dartmoor. The deplorable conditions, the rotten food, the lack of exercise, and the horrors of "the shower" reduced even the strongest of men to empty shells of hopelessness. Some had even committed suicide to escape the baneful existence.

If it had not been for Jamie, Daniel would have found a way to kill himself. Weapons could be obtained—for a price. He could have hanged himself by making a rope of his clothing, which one poor soul had done a few days earlier. But though he came close to killing himself, just when things grew worse, Jamie Boswell would be there, encouraging him. Jamie was a ray of light in that dark place, and Daniel vowed if the time ever came, he would find a way to repay the man for his kindness.

Finally winter came again, and the bitter cold gripped every man in an iron fist. Each inmate put on every thread of clothing he owned and spent the days and nights wrapped in the thin ragged blankets that served as bed and cover alike.

One bleak December morning, Daniel was sitting beside Boswell, half asleep. He shivered involuntarily from time to time, but this had become so habitual that he paid no mind. He was dreaming of the time when he and Lyna had walked beside the small stream that flowed through the woods close to Milford. A vivid image of her dear face, fresh and eager, came to mind. It almost seemed as though he could hear her clear laughter.

And then he felt a boot nudge him, dispelling the pleasant reverie. He looked up and saw Adams, one of the better guards, standing over him. "You've got a visitor, Bradford. Come along, now."

Daniel blinked with astonishment, then came to his feet at once. "It's got to be Lyna," he whispered to Jamie. Then he turned and followed Adams, stumbling on numbed feet. He walked behind the guard out of the cell, then down a long hall that led to the main section of the prison. Door after door opened, then closed behind him with a clanging that echoed down the cold corridors. Adams came to a door, opened it, then nodded. "Wait here, Bradford."

The room was not heated, but it was warmer than his cell. A table and three chairs sat alone in the otherwise bare room. Daniel stood staring at the door, trembling with excitement. He had given up hope long ago, but now it came back with a strength that flooded him.

He waited for five minutes, then the door opened. Daniel stepped forward, expecting to see Lyna—but a shock of bitter disappointment ran through him when Leo Rochester stepped inside!

Rochester stopped and stared at Daniel, a look of smug satisfaction creeping over his face. "Well, I suppose you were expecting your sister, Bradford." He removed his heavy black wool coat and hung it on the back of a chair. Daniel's ragged condition stood in marked contrast to Leo's elegant attire—finely woven gray woolen trousers, a green brocade waistcoat, and a white silk shirt. Leo carefully set his beaver hat on the table, dusted off the chair with his kid leather gloves, and sat down. "Well, now, let's have a talk," he said brusquely. "How've you been? Not too badly, I hope?"

Daniel would have allowed himself to be pulled to pieces with hot pincers before giving Rochester the satisfaction of hearing him beg or complain. "As well as can be expected," he said. "What do you want?"

Rochester slapped his thigh and laughed. "Well, sink me! If you aren't as incorrigible as ever. I thought Dartmoor would take the starch out of you—but I'm glad to see it hasn't."

"Glad to see you're still interested in my welfare," Daniel said bitterly. He was struggling with the rage and hatred that rose in him at the sight of the man—but kept his face immobile. "You have nothing better to do than come torment me?"

"Torment you?" Rochester lifted his eyes in mock horror. "Now *there* you do me an injustice."

"Just pure Christian charity, is that what brought you here?"

Rochester seemed pleased with his caustic responses. "Daniel, you're as tough as a boot! I always said you were, you know. We've had our differences—but I confess, you've got the one quality I admire in a man—and that's toughness."

"I'd like to go back to my cell, Mr. Rochester. The company's better there."

Leo shook his head, saying, "Why, you haven't heard what I've come for." He sat forward and leaned on the table, studying Daniel carefully. "You'll be pleased to hear that I've managed to lose a great deal of money since I came into my property."

Daniel smiled for the first time. "I'm pleased to hear it."

Rochester blinked, then laughed. "I knew you would be. Well, let's talk business. I have an offer to make you." He waited for Daniel to ask what it was, but silence filled the room. "Oh, you're not going to ask? Well, I shall tell you anyway. I want something from you, and I'm willing to make it worth your while if you give it to me."

"What could you possibly want from me?" Daniel spoke abruptly. "Your lies put me in this place! Isn't that enough revenge even for you?"

"All right, I did lie. You infuriated me—always have. But that's over, past history as it were." He leaned back and studied Daniel carefully. "I actually *do* have a proposition for you. I'll make it, and if you choose to say no, I'll walk out of here and you'll never hear from me again. Here it is—I've sold everything I own in England and bought a large tract of land in Virginia—a plantation, you'd call it." Rochester uttered a nervous laugh. He bit his lips, then shrugged his shoulders. "I haven't the least idea of how to manage such a place, but it's a chance for me to recover my fortune. Land's very cheap there, and with luck and time, it can be done."

"And what do you want from me?"

"I need all the workers I can get—and I want your life for the next seven years."

Daniel was stunned, unable even to utter a response. Rochester smiled at the young man's obvious shock. "That surprises you, I see. Well, there it is, Daniel. You go with me to America as my indentured servant. Serve me for seven years, during which time you'll be well provided for. At the end of the time, you'll be a free man. I realize you have good cause to hate me—but anything would be better than this place, I'd think."

Daniel stood stock still, wild thoughts racing through his mind. He thought of spending the next nine years like a blind worm in the hole of Dartmoor. He knew if he remained here he would come out a broken man. On the other hand, he had heard many speak of land that could be had for pennies in America. A man at least had a fair chance there!

Rochester watched Bradford's face but said nothing for a time. Finally he said, "I'm leaving next week. I'll have to have somebody—if not you, I'll hire another man. Make up your mind."

Daniel asked, "How do I get out of here?"

"I've already taken care of that. It's done all the time—prisoners released to go serve as indentured servants." He rose and picked up his coat and hat. "Well, what shall it be?"

Daniel knew that he was putting himself into the hands of a man who hated him, who would humiliate and grind him down as much as possible. But he would be out of the dank dungeon of Dartmoor. And he'd never have to suffer "the shower" again.

"I'll go," he said abruptly. "But only on one condition."

"And that is?"

"There's a prisoner here, his name is Jamie Boswell. You see to it he gets out, and I'll do what you want. . . ."

Leo listened carefully, then nodded. "Very well. I'll get him a place here with one of my friends. Agreed?"

"Yes."

Rochester said instantly, "Done! I'll see to it that you go as my servant." Reaching into his coat, he drew a legal-looking paper from his inner pocket, saying, "I had the papers drawn up for you. Sign it, and I'll have someone come for you." He gave Daniel a long, searching look, then said in an odd voice, "Seven years—you'll do as I say. You know I'm not an easy man. There'll be no turning back, you understand."

"Have you found Lyna?"

The question took Rochester off guard. He put his hat on, pulled it down over his brow, then looked directly at Daniel.

"I thought you knew," he said finally.

"Knew what?"

"I wrote you about her—you never got the letter?"

A chill gripped Daniel. "What—did the letter say?"

Rochester dropped his eyes as he pulled on his gloves. "This will be hard for you," he said. Looking up he said, "I traced her to Liverpool, but by the time I got there—" He shook his head and his voice fell. "By the time I got there, she had died. There was an outbreak of cholera, and she was one of the first to go."

Daniel felt as if his heart had been ripped from his body. He stood staring at Rochester, a burning hate raging through him. *If you hadn't driven her away from Milford, she wouldn't have died*, he thought.

Rochester said only, "Sorry—I thought you knew." He turned and banged on the door, and when the guard opened it, he left without a backward glance.

Daniel stood in the room, not moving. When the door slammed shut, he said out loud, "I'll be serving the devil in human form—no mistake about that. Leo Rochester will make life miserable for me!"

Finally Adams returned and led him back to the cell. Jamie took one look at his face and asked, "What's wrong, Dan?"

"My sister—she's dead."

"Ah, lad, I'm sorry to hear that—!"

The two sat for a long time, and finally Daniel said, "Jamie, we're leaving this place . . ." He explained what he had done, then said, "Leo will see you get out—if you don't, write to me and I'll see it's done."

That night Daniel couldn't sleep. All he could think of was Lyna's dear face and how they'd loved each other. He finally whispered, "Lyna, I'll never forget you—and I'll try to live a life for both of us!"

PART TWO

THE
MASQUERADE

1750–1752

8

At the Red Horse Tavern

VERY FEW THINGS DISTURBED SIR LIONEL GORDON so much as the behavior of his younger son. Gordon had served with distinction under the Duke of Marlboro, who had commended him to his staff, commenting, "Gordon is a *steady* man. He never allows the enemy to rattle him. A man like that is invaluable!"

But if the great duke could have seen the object of his admiration on the morning of June 4, 1750, he might have been forced to revise his high opinion of the man.

Mild summer weather had ushered out the last traces of the terrible winter. A warm, gentle breeze stirred outside, carrying the sound of birds through the window of the smaller dining room where Sir Lionel sat with his wife and older son. The grass spread out from Longbriar Manor like an emerald green carpet, but the owner of the great estate was taking no pleasure in the fair weather or the beauty of his estate.

"Well, so he's managed to get himself thrown out of Oxford!" he exploded.

Sir Lionel's fist struck the heavy mahogany table, causing the china dishes and crystal goblets to tremble as if in alarm at the loud voice. He was a large, well-built man of fifty, with steady blue eyes and a thatch of reddish hair. "I'd have thought that was impossible—even for Leslie. Some of the greatest chuckleheads who ever drew breath have managed to stay in that place!"

"I told you it would come to this, Father." Oliver Gordon was a small man of twenty-eight years, made in the mold of his mother rather than his father. His eyes were brown like hers, and there was a cold, almost impersonal air in his sharp features. Oliver held his hands out and studied them thoughtfully. His fingers were long and tapered, and he was an expert musician—almost his only passion. Picking up the knife from the snowy-white tablecloth, he pared a slice of beef from the portion on his plate, then took it into his mouth. Chewing slowly, he nodded toward the woman who sat across from him. "Mother and I warned you that he would never settle down there. He's not the type to become a man of letters."

Lady Alice Gordon was not yet fifty years of age. She was plain, though all that could be done to improve a woman's looks was evident. Her brown hair was carefully arranged in the latest fashion, and cosmetics made her smallish eyes appear larger. She wore a maroon silk dress trimmed with Dutch lace at the collar and sleeves. When she lifted her wineglass to sip the clear wine, the light from the chandelier reflected from the large diamond ring on her finger. "You really *must* do something with him, dear," she insisted.

"Do *what*?" Sir Lionel demanded. "He's twenty-four years old, Alice—a little late to take a stick to. And too strong, I might add." He allowed some of his pride in his younger son's physical strength to creep into his voice, but at once shook his head. "I wish he'd marry some rich woman and waste *her* money instead of mine!"

"I think you should send him to one of the Colonies, Father," said Oliver, looking up suddenly to meet the older man's stern eyes. "We need a man to oversee the property in Virginia that Uncle Robert left. Send Leslie."

"Why, he can't even take care of his *clothes*! He could never manage a property in a place like that—" But the idea caught at Sir Lionel. He stroked his neat beard thoughtfully, then said, "On the other hand, it just might do, Oliver. It's a rough sort of place, filled up mostly with criminals and Indians. The experience might do him some good."

"Leslie needs some sort of challenge like that, Father," Oliver said. He had little use for his younger brother, and the idea of sending him to America had come to him sometime earlier. He was aware that despite his father's anger at Leslie's wild ways, he concealed a streak of fondness for his younger son. Oliver would one day be master of Longbriar, and at the age of twenty-eight he was already as competent in the running of the vast estate as his father. He was his mother's favorite and now turned to her for support. "Don't you think it might do Leslie good to be on his own, Mother?"

"You've often said that it was the making of you, Lionel—leaving home and serving with the regiment." Lady Alice knew how to handle this husband of hers. She had brought him a large sum of money as her dowry and knew quite as much about managing their affairs as he. "Think about it, at least, my dear. You're so good at things like this."

Sir Lionel Gordon was better at managing his horses than at managing his family. He stared at the table, thinking hard, then sighed. "I'll have it out with him, then. He can't go on like a schoolboy for the rest of his life. . . !"

Oliver and his mother exchanged satisfied glances, and later in the afternoon, Sir Lionel faced his younger son in the library. The two men were much alike, having the same tall, robust frames and the same half-handsome features. They had been close when Leslie was at home, as they shared a love of hunting and fishing. But the later years had not been happy, for Leslie Gordon had not found his way. He had no desire to enter a profession—especially law or medicine, which he hated equally. He knew the estate well but had become a profligate as he passed through his later teens, spending his time with a small group of rather wild young men.

Now Leslie braced himself for the lecture he was certain lay before him. Oliver had smiled when Leslie had arrived, saying, "Father wants to see you, Leslie." Something about the smile of his older brother gave Leslie caution.

Standing before his father in the study, he said tentatively, "It's good to be home, Father. I've missed our times of hunting."

Sir Lionel did not smile but said sternly, "You may get a different kind of hunting, Leslie. I'm sending you to America to manage the plantation there."

The statement struck Leslie like a bucket of cold water thrown into his face. For a moment he stood stock still. "But—sir," he finally managed to say, "I don't know anything about that kind of thing."

"You don't know about anything, Leslie—except fast horses and tavern wenches. But you're going to learn. There's no point arguing. My mind's made up!"

But Leslie *did* argue, giving his father several very good reasons why he should not go to America. Finally he said, "Father, I'd be a waste over there. But there's one thing I could do well, I think."

"I'd be pleased to hear it," Sir Lionel said bitterly, more disappointed in the young man than he showed. *He's so much like I was at his age,* he thought, studying the broad shoulders and electric blue eyes. *Full of life—and of the devil! What a waste!*

Leslie loved his father and was heartily ashamed of his own life. At Oxford he had tried to throw himself into the life of a scholar. But almost from his arrival Leslie had discovered that the dusty world of books was not meant for him. He loved activity and physical action, but as much as he tried, he could never apply his mind to his studies as Oliver had done.

He had, however, come home with a plan, which he now presented. "Father, I know I've been a great disappointment to you—but no more than to myself." He began to pace the floor, speaking for some time about how he had learned that the life of a scholar was not for him. "I have no talent for it—nor inclination," he said, pausing to stand before his father, who was slumped in a chair behind a massive rosewood desk. "But there is one profession I think I might be suited for. It's what I hurried home to speak with you about."

"What profession might that be?"

"One you love very much, sir," Leslie said instantly. "You've always spoken of your time in the army. I've often thought it was the part of your life you liked best."

Sir Lionel stared at Leslie somewhat surprised, and his features relaxed. "You know, I think that's true—but don't say so to your mother. She hates the army." He stroked his beard thoughtfully, his eyes half-lidded. "I remember those days. It was a fine time for me. Hard, mind you, but a man needs hardness, Leslie. I still think of those times with old comrades. Many of them are dead now, but I think of them as they were—bronzed, strong, and filled with life. By Harry, we had *life* in those days!" He blinked, then demanded, "Are you saying you want to go into the army?"

"Yes, sir, I am."

"I offered to buy you a commission when you were twenty. You laughed at the idea."

"Yes, but that was before I knew what other professions were like."

"It's a hard life, Leslie. Oh, I loved it—but there's danger, boredom, and injustice in that world. And quite frankly, you haven't shown any inclination to accept discipline. I'm not so sure you would succeed. A soldier has to accept rebuke—something you've never been able to do."

To Sir Lionel's surprise, Leslie admitted, "You are right, sir, I never have. But I've thought of this for almost six months. And I've been talking with General Drake, your old friend."

"Morton Drake?" Sir Lionel's eyes opened wide. "Why, he must be as old as the hills!"

"No, sir, he's hale and healthy. I've gone to see him, and he talked a great deal about your military service together. He still thinks the world of you, sir."

"Morton Drake—I haven't seen him in years!"

"He's retired, of course. But he introduced me to Colonel Adam White, who's in command of the Royal Fusiliers, stationed at Sandhurst. . . ." Leslie saw that this information interested his father, so he spoke rapidly of his visits to the general. Finally he said, "I asked him for his advice—about going into the army, and he said the same as you, sir. But he took me with him to meet Colonel White."

"Did he now? I'd like to see him again."

"Why don't you, sir? He's very fond of you. He'd be glad to see you again after all these years."

"Well—perhaps I will."

"I'd like to make the army my career, sir. I believe I'd make a good soldier." Leslie said no more but stood before his father, waiting, his face serious.

"I'll think on it," was Sir Lionel's only response. But for the next two days he thought of little else. He was aware that his wife and older son were waiting for him to announce that Leslie was to be sent to America, but somehow he could not bring himself to do it.

Finally at dinner on Tuesday, he said abruptly, "Alice—and Oliver—" He put his fork down and looked toward Leslie. "Leslie has made an interesting proposal. He wants to make the army his career." Sir Lionel sat there listening quietly as the two protested, but finally he shook his head. "I feel he would not do well in America, but he has the qualities to become a good solider—if he can learn discipline."

"He never has," Oliver said shortly. But it was obvious that his father had made up his mind, so he shrugged and added, "It's as good as any for him, I suppose."

Lady Alice hated the army and said so, but Sir Lionel stuck to his guns. "It's a chance for him to make something of himself. I'd like to see him learn how to be a man—and the army is the place for that," he said with finality.

For the next two weeks Leslie and his father spent most of their time hunting and riding while they waited for the legal processes of purchasing his commission to settle. It was the finest time they had enjoyed for years, and when it was time for Leslie to leave, he took his father's hand, saying, "I'll do my best, sir." He'd made his farewells to his mother and brother, but parting with his father was different.

Sir Lionel felt the strength of his son's grasp and said huskily, "I'd like nothing better in this world than to see you become a good soldier! I . . . I sometimes wish I'd stayed with my regiment, but that's past praying for." He suddenly stepped forward and embraced Leslie—something he'd not done for many years. Then he stepped back, saying brusquely, "Well, be off with you—and take care of those horses, you hear me?"

Leslie was moved by his father's embrace, so much so that he could not speak for a moment. He covered his confusion by turning and stroking the nose of Caesar, one of the two fine horses his father had given him to take along. Grabbing the reins, he mounted and took the lines of the other horse, a mare named Cleo, then smiled, "I'll write you often, sir—but come and visit when you can."

Sir Lionel watched the departure of his son with a feeling of hope. He stood there until the distance swallowed up the young man, then turned and slowly walked back into the house.

"He's got the makings of a fine soldier—if he can just put his mind to it!" he said to himself.

T   T   T

Lyna paused wearily and looked up at the sign that swung

gently in the slight breeze. A bright red horse with flaring nostrils and long legs was outlined against an ebony background.

Red Horse Tavern, she thought wearily. The hot sun had sapped her of strength. Weak and thirsty, she moved to the wooden trough where two horses peered down at her. Grasping the pump handle, she had to struggle to get a trickle of water flowing, then drank thirstily. She caught some of the cool water in her cupped hands and splashed it on her hot face, then dried it with a ragged cloth she used for a handkerchief.

Got to have something to eat, Lyna thought as she turned to face the door of the tavern. It was late afternoon, and she had plodded along the road all day since early morning. She had left the farm two days ago where she'd spent most of the winter and spring. When she'd been allowed to stay and work for her keep at the place, she'd been grateful. The winter had been unusually bitter that year. Henry Tate, the owner of the small farm, had said roughly, "Can't pay you nothin', but you can sleep in the shed and you won't starve. Expect you to work hard, though."

She hadn't starved, but she had worked long hours, and the food had been sparse and ill-cooked. Tate's wife, Harriet, was a sour-faced woman who measured out each morsel of food as if it were fine gold, and she demanded hard labor from everyone.

Though it had been difficult, she'd had a place to sleep and something to eat. But Tate's nephew had arrived the previous day, and the farmer had said, "Can't keep you no more, Smith. You'll have to find yourself another place."

Lyna had left at dawn without a word of farewell. Hoping to find work on another farm, she stopped at several. Soon, however, she discovered that no one needed help. *"Get to London—you'll find something there, boy,"* had been the last advice she'd gotten.

But after two days of hard walking in the heat of summer, she was exhausted. A kind lady from a small farm had given her a bowl of fish soup for breakfast, but that had been hours ago. Now with her stomach knotted from hunger, she approached the Red Horse and entered without much hope.

The interior was dim, lit by two small windows and several candles. A big man was standing beside a table, pouring some sort of liquid into the cup of a customer. The smell of hot food caused another contraction of Lyna's stomach. It was a small place, with only three customers, and Lyna knew it was unlikely that they'd need more help.

She waited until the innkeeper went back to the bar along one wall, then moved toward him. He turned and took in her ragged clothes and pale face with a practiced glance. "No begging here, now—on your way!"

"Please, could I work for something to eat?"

"Don't need nothin' done."

Lyna was desperate. "Please, I'm starving. Let me work for scraps—anything."

"I told you, there ain't nothin' here for you!"

Lyna would have been intimidated by the man's roughness, but she stood before him, saying, "I'll do anything!"

The innkeeper came from behind the bar. He was a short, burly man with a bald head and a fish-hook mouth. Grabbing her arm, he began to drag her toward the door, saying, "You deaf? I said for you to get out!"

"Just a minute, Tapley. . . ."

The innkeeper swiveled his bullet head to glance at the man he'd just served. "I don't mean to be hard, sir, but these beggars come around like stray cats! Why, you feed them once, and they ain't no way to get rid of them!"

"I think I can spare half my meal. Let the boy sit down."

Tapley hesitated, but then shrugged and released his grip. "None of my business," he muttered. "You 'eard the gentleman—now mind yer manners!"

Lyna was feeling very faint, when the man at the table said, "Here, lad, have a seat." He kicked one of the heavy chairs out from the table. "Bring another plate and cup, Tapley." When the innkeeper left, he added, "Well, sit down. You look like you could stand a good meal."

Lyna walked unsteadily to the chair and sat down. "I . . . can eat in the kitchen, sir," she whispered.

"No need for that. What's your name?"

"Lee Smith."

"My name is Leslie Gordon." When Tapley came with the extra utensils, Gordon cut a generous slice from the large slab of roast pork and put it on the pewter plate. "Bring us a pitcher of ale," he ordered. Then he cut a large slice from the bread that was on his left and transferred it to the plate of his guest. "Get yourself on the outside of that, Lee," said Gordon, then he began to eat his own meal.

Gordon didn't stare at the youth, but he noted that despite being at least half-starved, the young fellow ate in a mannerly fashion. *If I were that hungry, I'd stuff my mouth like a dog,* he thought. Without appearing to pay attention to Smith, he made some quick observations—*Pretty frail—and not much good for heavy work. Looks like he's had a hard time of it—ragged as a scarecrow. Not a bad-looking chap, though—if he were cleaned up, he'd look fine.*

"Been on the road, have you, Lee?"

"I've been working at a farm—but I got put out for another fellow."

"Oh? Well, that's too bad, but you'll find something. Here, wash that down with some of this ale. It'll put some color in your cheeks." He watched as Smith drank the ale, then asked, "Do you have any family?"

"No, sir."

The brief answer took Leslie Gordon by surprise. The idea of having no family and no place to go was something he'd never had to think of. He stole another glance at the small form, taking in the fineness of the face and the hollow cheeks. Now as he studied the young man, pity rose in him. *I'll have to give him a little money,* he thought, *and maybe buy him something to wear. Those rags are past help!*

Lyna ate until she was full and then said, "Sir, can I groom your horse for the meal?"

"Do you know horses?"

"My brother taught me a little."

"All right, come along." Leslie rose and led her to the rail. "I think I'll stay the night. Come along to the stable. Here, you can lead Cleo."

Lyna was glad for the times she'd spent helping Daniel with the horses at Milford. Some of the good advice Daniel had learned from Bates and passed on to her helped her now. She spoke gently to the mare, who eyed her, then followed docilely.

Gordon made the arrangements with the hostler, then said, "Lee, I'll be leaving soon. Give them both a good grooming and I'll pay you well."

"Yes, sir." Lyna didn't waste any time in setting about her task.

She liked horses, and by the time Leslie Gordon returned, both the animals were gleaming.

"Why, they look fine!" Leslie said with pleasure. "Never saw a better job of grooming!"

"Thank you, sir," Lyna said. Then she swallowed hard and asked the question she'd been planning. "Would there be a place for me at your home? I'll work for food."

The question caught Leslie. He looked into the gray-green eyes that were fixed on his and stammered, "Why, I . . . I'm sorry . . ." Seeing the sudden disappointment sweep over the boy, he said quickly, "You see, I'm leaving my home. I'm going into the army— as a lieutenant."

Lyna pleaded, "But won't you need a young man to take care of your horses? Don't officers have servants?"

"Why, yes, I believe they do."

"Then take me, sir!" Lyna began to speak quickly. "I can cook for you, Mr. Gordon—and I worked for a tailor for a time, so I can keep your clothes and boots for you—and I'll see that your horses are in good shape—please, sir!"

Leslie knew that it was customary for officers to have servants, but he had not thought of hiring one. Still, the idea of having someone to take care of his uniforms was appealing—and the boy *could* groom a horse.

Lyna stood before him anxiously waiting. She felt as if her fate were hanging in the balance. Her eyes were enormous as she kept them on the young man's face. And she prayed as hard as she ever had in her life.

"Well, I don't know—" Leslie said slowly, then he slapped his side and grinned. "Why not, though? It'll have to be all right with my commanding officer, you understand?"

Lyna blinked in surprise at his answer and quickly said, "Why, thank you, Mr. Gordon. I'll be a good worker, you'll see."

"I'm sure you will, Lee. But—you can't be my servant in those clothes."

"I . . . don't have any more, Mr. Gordon!"

The notion took a swift hold on Leslie. He fished into his pocket, pulled out some coins and said, "There's a shop beside the Red Horse. Go buy yourself something to wear. Better get two outfits, I think."

Lyna was stunned with the suddenness of it. She took the

coins, then looked up into the face of the man. "How do you know I won't steal this?"

"Never thought of it," Leslie said. "You won't, will you?"

"No, sir!" She turned and left the stable at a run.

Leslie laughed and slapped Caesar's side. "Well, you'll get all the attention you want now, I think." He turned to the hostler saying, "Saddle them both."

"Yes, sir, that I will!"

Lyna found the shop, and when a tall man came to give her a disparaging look, she opened her hand to show the coins Gordon had given her. "Mr. Gordon wants me to dress well enough to be his servant," she said.

At the sight of the coins, the shopkeeper beamed. "Well, I think we can take care of that!" He soon discovered that his advice was little needed, for the young man knew *exactly* what he wanted. Lyna went through the stock, made her selection, then went into a back room to change. Quickly she took off her brother's old clothes. She tore the shirt into strips and bound them around her bosom, then put on the loose-fitting tan shirt and brown breeches. Over the shirt she donned a dark green vest that helped disguise her figure. She sat down and slipped on a pair of white stockings and the new shoes. Stepping outside, she stopped to look at her image in the mirror and was startled. For a final touch, she chose a tricorn felt hat. After paying the shopkeeper, she left the shop and went at once to the Red Horse.

Leslie looked up from his seat at a table in the back of the room when she entered and exclaimed, "Well, now—clothes do make the man, after all! Let me have a look."

Lyna felt her cheeks burn as he studied her and she held her breath.

"You look very well, Lee. Now, let's see if we can make a few miles before dark."

"Yes, sir."

When they left the tavern, and Lyna realized Gordon intended her to ride his other large horse, she had a moment of panic. She'd ridden a few times, but never such a spirited horse. She put her foot into the stirrup and awkwardly got into the saddle.

Cleo began to buck, and Lyna would have fallen if Leslie had not come to grab the lines. "Calm down, Cleo!" he ordered. When the animal had quieted down, he looked at her. "You've not ridden much, I take it? Well, no matter. You'll have to learn if we're to get on. Now take the lines. . . ."

Five minutes later the two were on the road to London. Gordon gave instructions from time to time, and Lyna soon was able to handle the mare.

Leslie was pleased with himself, glad that he'd been able to help the lad, and that he now had a servant. "How old are you, Lee, fifteen?"

"At least." Lyna turned to smile at him, then said, "I thank you for taking me with you. I . . . I was in poor shape, sir."

"Well, we'll both have new careers, Lee," Leslie smiled. "I'll learn to be a soldier, and you'll learn to take care of me."

"Yes, sir!" Lyna stole a glance at the strong figure and the masculine profile. "I'll take care of you the best I can!"

9

"HE'S AS GOOD AS A WIFE, THIS LAD?"

AS SOON AS GORDON ARRIVED in London, Colonel White greeted the new officer with a cheerful air.

"First, you'll have to find a house, Lieutenant," he advised. "The regiment will be stationed here for at least a month, probably longer. The king wants his subjects to see His Majesty's military strength, so we'll be having regular parades and exhibitions to provide that. It'll be a good time for you to learn the ropes."

"I thought we'd all be living in tents, Colonel."

"We'll see plenty of that, Gordon—but for now, either rent a room in an inn or find a small house. Perhaps you could share one with one of the other officers. I'll ask around."

That very day Leslie met Captain George Mullens, a tall, rather plain man with a shock of straw-colored hair. When he mentioned that he had been advised to find a house, Mullens said at once, "I've got a small place—two bedrooms. If you'd care to come and share it, I'd be happy to accommodate you."

Leslie protested that he didn't want to be a bother, but Mullens shook his head and insisted. "Be company for me. I'm not too much of a social person, Leslie. And I could use some help with the rent. Come along, but it might not be fine enough for the son of an earl!"

Leslie found Lee, who was waiting outside headquarters, and said, "I think we may have a place to stay. Come along and we'll take a look."

As the two swung into the saddle, Captain Mullens joined them, mounted on a fine brown mare. "This is my servant, Lee Smith—Captain Mullens, Lee."

"Ah, yes. Been with you long, Gordon?"

Leslie winked at Lyna and said, "Long enough, I suppose."

Lyna felt nervous as the tall soldier examined her, but she met his eyes evenly. "Glad to know you, sir," she said, nodding at him.

"Can you cook, Smith?" Mullens asked.

"Why—yes, sir—a little."

"By George, you've got to come with me on the house, Gordon! I'm sick of my own cooking—if you could call it that! Come along, now."

Lyna took in the sights as the three of them passed through the busy streets of London. The streets were packed with people so determined to get to their destinations that they jostled one another furiously. One vendor driving a wheelbarrow of nuts yelled in a stentorian tone, "Make way there!" but he was drowned out by a tinker who stood at the door of his shop, bellowing, "Have you a brass pot, iron pot, kettle, skillet, or frying pan to mend?"

As they made their way down the twisting streets, sooty chimney sweeps with grave and black faces shoved past some fat, greasy porters. Some of the porters were laden with trunks and hatboxes, while others struggled along bearing aloft a wealthy woman in a chair. The noise was deafening and the rank odor of the garbage and ordure that had been thrown into the gutters burned Lyna's nose as they rode along.

They passed scores of inns bearing colorful images of their various names: Blue Boar, Black Swan, Red Lion, not to mention Flying Pig and Hog in Armor. The streets were lined with all kinds of vendors who hawked their wares. Lyna could have purchased a glass eye, ivory teeth, spectacles, and even cures for corns. She saw chemists' shops, where drops, elixirs, cordials, and balsams were advertised as cures for all ailments.

When they were out of the main section of London and riding through a neighborhood of houses, Mullens pointed with his riding crop. "There's the place. Not bad looking, eh?"

The small house was made of red brick with white windows and a slate roof. It sat right on the street, as did the others that joined it. Mullens led them through a gate into a spacious backyard that included a small stable, where they dismounted and tied the horses.

"Nice little garden," Leslie said, noting the profusion of colorful flowers that had been arranged in beds.

"Yes, I like to fool with them," Mullens shrugged. "So many things in this world are ugly and smell bad. It makes a difference to have a rose now and then. Come along."

He led the way through a door into a hall, then directed them to a drawing room lined with bookshelves filled with books. "They came with the house," he informed them. "The former owner must have been quite a reader." Next he led them into a small dining room. The room had a kitchen that occupied a small shed off the side of the house, which had been added to keep the heat out. Mullens waved at the shelves, which contained a random supply of food. "If you decide to stay, Gordon, perhaps your servant can try his hand at making us a decent meal."

Lyna was tense, waiting for the matter of sleeping arrangements to come up. She was relieved when Mullens led them to a large bedroom, which he said Gordon might like. "And there's a small room in the attic, used for a servant, I expect. It'll do well for you, Smith. Go take a look—right up those stairs."

"Yes, sir!" Lyna climbed the stairs and was delighted to find a tiny bedroom, complete with small bed, table, chest, and a washstand. Though the room was small, it was clean and had a large window that allowed in plenty of light and fresh air. *Oh, I hope he takes it!* she thought. When she descended the stairs, the two men were smiling.

"We'll be staying here, Lee. You like the room?"

"Oh yes, sir—it's lovely!" As soon as she said the word "lovely," she caught herself and made a quick mental note to be more careful about her speech. She knew certain words weren't right for a young *man*. Quickly she said, "Do right well, sir." Then she asked, "Could I fix a meal for you, Captain Mullens?"

"Yes, by Harry!" Mullens' long face brightened and he said, "You'll need to go to the green grocers and the butcher, I expect— right down the street."

Leslie drew out some coins and passed them to Lyna. "Get what you need—let's have a feast to celebrate our new home and our new friend. Captain Mullens wants to show me around, but we'll be back for supper."

Lyna left the house at once. As she walked along, she was very grateful that she'd been trained to do some of the cooking at Milford. She had a natural talent for it and enjoyed fixing meals. Determined to make the meal a success, she bought the ingredients necessary for her most successful dishes. It took almost all of the money Gordon had given her, but she wanted to make a good first impression.

When Lyna returned she set about getting a fire going. Then she cut the best meat from the leg of mutton and put it on to parboil. Afterward, she added three pounds of shredded mutton suet and seasoned it with pepper, salt, cloves, and mace. She also put in currants, raisins, prunes, and a few sliced dates. Mixing all this well, she put it all into a pan and placed it in the oven to bake.

While the mince pie was baking, Lyna decided to try her hand at baking a cake. She had made only two—and those were while she was at Milford—but both had turned out quite successful. So she began mixing flour, currants, butter, and sugar in a bowl she found. As she worked, Lyna thought of how things had favorably turned around for her in just one day. She smiled, remembering some of her mother's last words of encouragement, of how God promised to be the Father of the fatherless and take care of them. "I'd have been sleeping under a hedge if Mr. Gordon hadn't come along," she mused out loud.

Next she added cinnamon and nutmeg. When the spices had been mixed in well, she put in the yolks of four eggs, a pint of cream, and a full pound of butter. As she beat the mixture, the sun flooded into the kitchen, and the heat of the stove made her face glow. She worked quickly, finally pouring the mixture into another pan. Setting it aside, Lyna let it lie for an hour until it began to rise. Then she put the pan into the oven along with the mince pie.

Glancing at the position of the sun, Lyna decided that she had time to do more. So she put on a chicken to boil while she made two loaves of fresh oat bread. While the loaves were baking, she went into the dining room and found the settings for the table. Spreading a white cloth over the oak table, she set out silver plates, knives, forks, and goblets. She found a silver candlestick that held six candles and the tapers to go with it and inserted them firmly into their bases.

By then the sun was almost down as she lit the candles. *They ought to be back soon,* she thought. As she walked back into the kitchen, she smelled the pleasant aroma of the bread. Checking it and finding it done, she quickly removed the loaves and set them on the sideboard. As she lifted the lid on the mince pie, she heard the door open and the sound of voices. Quickly she stepped out of the kitchen and met the two men, saying, "Supper is ready, sir."

"Is it?" Leslie exclaimed. He sniffed the fragrance of fresh-baked bread and grinned at his friend. "Think you could eat a bite, George?"

"I could eat whatever that is that smells so good!"

"If you'll sit down, it's all ready." Lyna returned to the kitchen, picked up the mince pie, and took it into the dining room. When she lifted the lid and placed generous servings on the plates of the men, she was glad to see them both pleased.

"That's not mince pie?" Leslie exclaimed. "My favorite dish!"

"I hope you enjoy it, sir." Lyna made several trips to the kitchen to bring all the food she had prepared. While they helped themselves to the other dishes, Lyna brought a bottle of ale—part of Mullens' store—and poured their glasses to the brim. She hovered over the two men, pleased with their praise for the food.

Finally she brought in the cake and Mullens stared at it. "By Harry—I can't believe it!" he exclaimed. He took an enormous bite, and with his mouth full, nodded toward Lyna. "Smith—if you can't cook anything else—I can live on what I've had tonight!"

"Where'd you learn to cook like this, Lee?" Leslie inquired.

"Oh, I worked in a large house once as a cook's helper," Lyna answered quickly.

"Well, you certainly were a good pupil!"

"Thank you, sir. I'll bring your tea to the library if you like."

The two men moved to the library, where they smoked and drank tea for some time. Mullens spoke of the regiment, giving Leslie a quick analysis of the officers and the state of the troops. He was an astute man, knowing the army well, and was glad to help his new friend begin his military career.

"I'm glad we've met like this, George," Leslie said. He lay back in the Queen Anne chair, smoking a pipe and feeling pleased with his new surroundings. "I've been dreading it a bit. A fellow can put his foot wrong, and it's the devil's own trouble trying to get it right."

"You won't go wrong, old fellow," George replied. "Soldiering's a hard life—but a good one. If you're cut out for it."

"You've never married, George?"

"No. Not much of a ladies' man. I suspect you are, though." He laughed at the expression on Leslie's face. "No, dear fellow, I don't know your history. But it would be strange if you hadn't been subjected to the wiles of the fairer sex. Son of an earl, handsome and rich. I suspect you've had your share of love's delights."

"Oh, I suppose I've been a fool a few times."

Mullens smiled and looked over toward Lyna, who'd come in with a fresh pot of tea. "When your master's not present, Lee, you must give me the juicy details of his love life."

Lyna shot a startled glance at Leslie, then flushed. "I couldn't do that, Captain Mullens!"

"Don't tell him a thing, Lee," Leslie spoke up. "It's none of his business."

"No, sir, I won't."

Lyna kept the tea flowing, and while the men talked, she had her own meal in the kitchen. She enjoyed the sound of the two men speaking quietly at times, but sometimes they laughed rather loudly. While they were in the library, she went to Gordon's room, made the bed, and unpacked his uniforms. She had time to go downstairs and iron his shirts and trousers, taking pride in her ability to handle the iron.

She was hanging the garments neatly in the wardrobe when Leslie entered. He gave a startled look at the freshly made bed, then at the uniforms. "Why, Lee, you've done it all," he exclaimed. He grinned at her, his heavy eyebrows rising. "You're going to spoil me."

"I hope so, Mr. Gordon," Lyna smiled back. "It's the duty of a manservant to spoil his master."

"Well, if you ever want to leave me, you'd have a place. Captain Mullens is very pleased to have you."

"I . . . I won't be leaving you, sir."

Something in the tone of the youthful voice caught Leslie's attention. He studied the clear features, noting that the drawn cheeks made the gray-green eyes appear very large. There was, he noted, a vulnerability in the face, the expression of one not accustomed to kindness. He suspected that the lad had been mistreated by someone and determined to provide something better. "Well, I'm glad to hear that."

He stripped off his coat and began to remove his shirt. At once Lyna moved toward the door and said hastily, "I'll have your hot water when you're ready to shave in the morning, sir."

"Fine. And, Lee—"

"Yes, sir?"

Leslie smiled at the youthful face. He put his hand on the thin shoulder and said, "I'm glad to have you with me. I can see that life is going to be a lot easier with you around."

Lyna felt her eyes sting and blinked rapidly. Clearing her throat, she was very much aware of the pressure of his hand. "I'm very grateful for the chance to serve you, Lieutenant. Good-night, sir."

"Good-night, Lee."

Lyna went to her room and wanted to drop into bed at once. She undressed and washed in warm water, then put on the night shirt she'd purchased. She glanced at her reflection in the small mirror, noting that her hair needed cutting. It had a tendency to curl, and she knew that she had to make herself look as masculine as possible. Tired from her busy day, she slipped between the sheets and lay there exhausted. She was so tired she could not go to sleep at once.

She thought of Daniel for a time, then forced those thoughts away. Sleep began to come, and she smiled as the events of the past few hours came to her.

He's so kind—to take in a ragged beggar!

She had doubtful thoughts, knowing that to keep up the masquerade would take great skill—and some luck. She breathed a prayer of gratitude, then as she slipped into the warm darkness, a single image of the face of Leslie Gordon came to her—and she smiled faintly. . . .

🎺 　 🎺 　 🎺

Learning to transform herself from a young woman into a young man proved to be more difficult than Lyna had expected! Fortunately she had a rather low-pitched voice for a woman, which was a great help. The fact that she was taller than most young women was also a factor in her favor. Aside from those two elements, Lyna had to remain constantly alert, lest the many pitfalls cause her to slip up and reveal her identity.

As the weeks passed, however, she perfected her art. It was

like being on stage, and after the initial fright was over, she took a strange delight in the masquerade. The obvious danger was that someone would somehow take notice of something and recognize that she was not a young man but a young woman. At first she had feared that being in the presence of soldiers might be a dangerous thing—but it didn't prove so. As the days slipped by she went about her duties serving her master, and the times she was around the other officers, she was treated no differently than the other servants.

The regiment's assignment in London made her introduction to the world of the army much simpler than if it had been out in a field camp. Primarily she remained at the house, but at times she accompanied Leslie Gordon to the reviews and to meetings of the staff, along with other servants. The two officers found it very convenient to have their horses taken care of by the youthful servant—and even more enjoyable was the luxury of well-cooked meals and uniforms always clean and pressed.

"By Harry, Leslie," Mullens exclaimed one day when the two were eating a fine supper, "he's as good as a wife, this lad!"

Leslie glanced up at Lyna, who was bringing in a pudding. Her face reddened at the compliment, but he was accustomed to that. "Better than a wife, George," he said fondly. "From what I hear, that breed demands all a man has and makes life miserable for him if he doesn't provide it."

"That's the best definition of marriage I've ever heard," Mullens grinned. As Lyna passed by he gave her a slap on the backside. "Lee, don't ever leave us two old bachelors!"

Lyna flinched and quickly moved away from the captain's reach. "No, sir," she said shortly, turning and heading back to the kitchen.

Leslie laughed. "Don't embarrass the lad, George. We'd have a devil of a time without him."

"Well, he's so blasted *sensitive*, Leslie!"

"I know, but when we take the field we'll need a good servant. And I don't expect we could find a better one."

That night after finishing all her work, Lyna took an extra candle to her room when she retired. She had begun keeping a secret diary. She had no one to talk to during the day, since the men were gone attending to their army duties. So at night she would sit up and read until she was certain that the two men were asleep. Then she'd pull out a notebook from under her mattress, and by the light of the candle she would put her thoughts on paper.

The entry for the night of August 15, 1750, was typical:

> Captain Mullens is a kind man—but I could have crowned him when he slapped me on the backside! I know I blushed like a—well, like a *girl*—and Mr. Gordon saw it. He must think I am the most tender young man in the world. He was watching last week when Lieutenant Givins told that awful story at dinner. It was worse than anything I've heard yet, and I know my face lit up like a candle! Later he said, "Lee, the men are rough but don't mind them." I tried to laugh it off, but I'm sure he noticed it.
>
> Five weeks we've been here, and it's been wonderful! A place of my own to sleep, plenty to eat, all the books to read, and Leslie gives me a crown every week for spending money. If it weren't for thinking about Daniel in prison, I wouldn't have a worry—except for keeping my secret, that is. But I've managed so far, and God willing, I'll be able to keep it up!

Two days later, however, Lyna was almost unmasked.

It began when Leslie said at breakfast, "We'll have guests tonight, Lee. How much money will you need to fix a meal for six?"

Lyna thought for a moment, then named a sum. Leslie pulled out a pouch from inside his vest pocket and handed her a number of coins. "And here's an extra shilling to get something special," he said as he and Mullens left for their duties.

As soon as the men had gone, Lyna cleaned up from breakfast. Then she hurried to the market to buy the fixings for the meal that night. She spent the better part of two hours walking amongst the vendors trying to find all she needed. Besides, she wanted to make sure she didn't pay any more than she had to. Finally satisfied with her purchases, she started home. As she rounded the corner of the street where the small brick house was, a vendor stuck a bunch of flowers in her face.

"Flowers, sir, for yer sweetheart?" said the old lady.

Lyna almost laughed at the thought and, on impulse, handed the woman the last shilling she had and hurried on her way.

The first thing she did when she entered the kitchen was stir up the fire and add some wood. She quickly set about making meal preparations for the guests who were to come. In the last few weeks Lyna had experimented on some new dishes, which had turned out quite nicely. She planned to prepare some of them for the meal that night.

The rest of the day seemed to fly by, but everything went smoothly. Just as she finished setting the table and placing the flowers in the middle, she heard voices in the hall. On the way to the library, Gordon entered the dining room and said the guests should arrive in an hour or so. When Lyna heard a knock on the door half an hour later, she was surprised when she opened it. Standing there were not three officers, but Lieutenant Givins—and three women!

"Ah, Smith," Givins smiled. "We're a little early. Are your masters home?"

"Yes, sir. Won't you all come in?"

Gordon and Mullens came out of the library at that moment, and the air was filled with laughter as Givins introduced the three women. "This is Henrietta, this is Alice, and this is my own treasure, Mary."

As soon as they were seated at the table, Lyna was kept busy with the serving. But she was not deceived by the women. They were all of the same stamp, heavily made up and wearing cheap and rather revealing gowns. When some of the stories that Lieutenant Givins told grew ribald, they protested lightly but joined in with shrill laughter.

After the meal was over, the guests moved into the library. As Lyna was busy washing the dishes, Leslie came and said, "Bring some ale in, will you, Lee?"

"Yes, sir, right away." She wiped her hands, cut pieces of the cake she had baked that afternoon, then took them in on a platter. The three couples were playing a game, but Lyna paid little heed. However, the game involved some sort of penalty, it seemed, and Henrietta shrieked as she lost.

"And the penalty is a kiss for the handsomest man in the room," Givins laughed. "And I think we all agree on exactly who *that* gentleman is!"

But as Givins moved to collect the kiss, Henrietta winked at Gordon, saying, "No, I think not, Lieutenant." She turned and, without warning, embraced Lyna and planted a kiss on her cheek.

"Now *that'll* do you, Givins!" Captain Mullens laughed loudly. "Let that be a lesson to you!"

Givins flushed and gave Lyna an angry look. "I wasn't including babies, Henrietta," he said shortly. "Only *men!*"

Henrietta was thoroughly enjoying her joke. "Why, he's very handsome, Robert," she jibed. Lifting her hand she ran it through Lyna's shortly cropped blond hair. "He's young and innocent—just what I like!"

Leslie had been laughing at Henrietta's antics. But now he noticed Lee's embarrassment and said at once, "Well, let's get on with the game. My turn, I think."

Lyna fled to the kitchen and stayed there as long as she could. She went outside once. When she returned she found Leslie kissing Henrietta. "Oh—excuse me!" she gasped and hurried from the room.

Later that night after the guests were gone, Lyna moved about cleaning the house. Mullens had gone to bed, and when she went to the library to pick up the empty mugs, she found Leslie staring out the window. He turned and said, "It was a fine meal, Lee." He smiled and added, "Don't be embarrassed by Lieutenant Givins. It's just his way."

"No, sir."

"I think Henrietta took a shine to you." He grinned, but when she looked troubled, Leslie said, "She takes a shine to anything in pants, so never mind it." He crossed his arms and said seriously, "I've got news. The regiment is going into the field."

"Really, sir?"

"Yes, we'll be leaving London shortly." He shook his head thoughtfully. "There's trouble in India, I'm afraid. Colonel White has informed us that we'll be leaving in two weeks."

"India—that's a long way, sir!"

"Yes, and it will be very dangerous. You may not want to go along."

Lyna gave him a sudden look, which he could not fathom, but said, "Yes, sir, I'll go with you if I may."

"Of course both Mullens and I would like to have you." A smile crossed his lips. "In fact, he said he *wouldn't* go if you didn't. He's grown quite attached to your cooking. You've really spoiled us both, Lee."

Lyna felt strangely warmed by his words. "You've been very

kind to me, Lieutenant Gordon—you and Captain Mullens. I . . . wouldn't know what to do if I couldn't serve you."

Gordon came and stood before her. His eyes were gentle and his voice was low. "Why, Lee, you're a part of me—and a part of Mullens, of course." He put his hand on her shoulder and squeezed it gently. "We'll go together, then."

"I'm glad, sir!"

Gordon nodded, then dropped his hand and started for the door. He stopped and turned. "It'll be harder in India than in this little house." He looked around the room fondly, then back to Lyna. "I'll never forget this place."

He turned and left, and Lyna, still feeling the pressure of his hand on her shoulder, whispered, "Neither will I, Leslie Gordon!"

10

LYNA MAKES A DISCOVERY

THE SHIP THAT FERRIED THE ROYAL FUSILIERS from Liverpool to India was so crowded the men had to take turns sleeping in the narrow hammocks. Adding to the discomfort was the heavy weather the low-lying ship encountered almost as soon as the shores of England faded from sight.

For Lyna the misery of the voyage proved to be a mixed blessing. She felt queasy the first night out, but by dawn of the second day she had gained her sea legs. But Lieutenant Leslie Gordon did not fare as well. He was a poor sailor, worse than most. He turned pale even as the ship hit the first rolling swells of the open sea, and throughout the long voyage he never completely recovered.

Lyna had been nervously wondering how she could keep her secret on the crowded ship, but Leslie's seasickness made it possible. He had been assigned a small cabin with two bunks. Under normal conditions, any man would have discovered his roommate was a woman—but Leslie was so sick he would not have noticed if his partner had been the Queen of Sheba!

The two had made their way on board and found their tiny cabin. Excited about the voyage and what lay ahead, Leslie commented cheerfully as they stepped inside, "It's not a palatial suite, is it, now?" The room was only large enough for the narrow two-tiered bunk, a tiny table, a diminutive chest, and one chair. He smiled at Lyna. "You'd better take the top, Lee. If we hit rough weather, I'd crush you if I fell out of that top bunk."

"Yes, sir, that will be fine."

Leslie sat down on the lower bunk, speaking with excitement about the possibility of facing action in India. Lyna began to unpack his personal things, storing them carefully in the tiny chest. She found a place for his razor and shaving soap, wedged his pistols and loading equipment under his folded clothing, then began trying to do something with his wrinkled uniforms.

"Oh, we won't be able to do much about those," Leslie said as Lyna searched for a suitable spot to hang them. "Just stuff them anywhere. We won't be on a dress parade, Lee." He groaned and lifted his right boot, tugging at it. "These blasted boots! I *knew* they were too small! Give me a hand, will you, Lee?"

Lyna grabbed the heel of his boot. It was skin tight, and only when she gave a tremendous wrench did it budge. She fell backward, striking her head with a resounding *thud* against the oak bulkhead. Pain caused her to cry out involuntarily, and bright lights danced in front of her eyes.

"Lee! Are you all right?"

Strong hands touched Lyna, and she felt herself being lifted up. Leslie put his arm around her and sat her down beside him on the lower bunk. "That was a nasty bump! Let me see. . . ." He used his free hand to explore her head, moving it gently under the heavy blond hair. "That's going to be a pretty bad knot—but I don't think the skin is broken. Just be still for a moment."

Lyna was desperately aware that Leslie was holding her in a tight embrace. Afraid that he would notice he was not holding a tough young man but a softly rounded young woman, she pulled away from his grasp.

"I—I'm all right, sir!" she said, standing up. She made a joke out of the thing, saying, "Good thing I landed on my head, or I might have been hurt. My pa used to say it was the toughest thing about me!"

"Look, you just lie down, Lee," said Leslie, his voice still anxious. "I'll take a turn around the ship. Can't have you getting down, can we? Who'd take care of me?"

After he had pulled his boots back on and left the cabin, Lyna collapsed onto the bunk, trembling slightly. *If I'd been knocked unconscious,* she thought, *he'd have undone my clothes—and it would all have been up with me!* She lay there for a time, worrying about how she would share such a tiny place without being discovered. Finally she rose and made the cabin as neat as possible. "Maybe I can . . . can go out when he undresses for bed," she muttered. "But how will *I* ever undress with him in this little box of a room?"

But one factor came to her rescue—the weather. Just before the ship set sail, Leslie had eaten a large meal for supper at the captain's table. But as they pulled out into open waters less than an hour later, he felt the ship suddenly nose downward. Up until that time the deck had been as steady as his own floor at Longbriar— but as the ship slowly rose, his stomach turned over. Almost instantly he became deathly nauseous. He was walking with Mullens at the time, who gave him a sharp glance. "Are you all right, Leslie?" Then Mullens saw his friend make a lunge for the rail, and he shook his head. "No, I see you're not. Well, perhaps it'll be brief. It sometimes is, you know."

But two hours later Mullens found Gordon still hanging to the rail. "Look here, old fellow, you need to go below." He took Gordon's arm and steered him to the small cabin. When the two stepped inside, Mullens said, "I say, Smith—your master is a little under the weather. Put him to bed and see to him, won't you? That's a good fellow!"

Lyna had seen several officers suffering from the same malady as she had gone up top to get some fresh air herself. "I'll see to him, Captain," she said quickly. Mullens left, and she turned to Gordon and said, "Let's get that hot uniform off, sir."

Leslie's mouth was drawn up into a tight, puckered line, and his face was ashen. "Never knew—a man could be so *sick*—!" he gasped. He allowed her to pull his coat and shirt off, then she slipped a cotton nightshirt over his head.

"Lie down, Lieutenant—that's right—now, let's have these boots." She tugged the boots off, then the socks, and finally pulled his tight trousers free. "Now, cover up and let me bathe your face with cool water. . . ."

All night long Lyna stayed beside her employer. He lay still as though afraid to move—and when the ship began to roll more violently from side to side, he kept his eyes tightly closed. Whenever he quieted down, Lyna would go topside to empty the bucket over the rail. She could do little except bathe his face with tepid water and hold his head when he threw up. After a time he had nothing left in him, but the ugly retchings continued.

Sometime during the early hours of the morning, Leslie said

weakly, "Lee—go to bed! There's nothing more you can do for me."

"Yes, I will, sir—in a little while. Try to take a little water, Lieutenant Gordon." Lifting a cup to his lips, she gave him tiny sips of water, some of which he kept down. The only sleep she got consisted of short naps in the chair by the lower bunk. At dawn Lyna heard the door to the tiny cabin open. She looked up and saw Captain Mullens, who had come by for a report.

"He's so sick, Captain!" Lyna whispered. "He looks like death!"

"He may be sick all the way to India, Smith," Mullens said doubtfully. "Can you handle that?"

"Yes, sir."

Mullens gave Lyna an encouraging nod. "Good man! If it's a chronic case, you'll have to feed him like a baby. He'll spit it up, mind you, but he's got to have nourishment. I'll leave word with the cook to make some clear broth—and you just make him take it, no matter how much he curses!"

As soon as Mullens left, Lyna tried to sleep more. But an hour later she awoke when Leslie stirred. After fetching fresh water from the barrel in the galley, Lyna poured some into a basin and bathed his face. The day wore on and Lyna endured his bad temper as she alternately forced him to sip water and some broth the cook had prepared. Sometimes he was able to keep some of it down, but whenever the ship rolled, the poor man was overcome with nausea and the cruel retching plagued him once again.

For the rest of the voyage, Lyna had her hands full with caring for Leslie Gordon. He grew to hate the feeding sessions and did indeed curse on more than one occasion when she persisted in spooning food down his throat.

"What's the use of eating when it just comes right up again?" he cried once. "Leave me alone, can't you?"

"Some of it stays down, sir, and you *must* have some nourishment!"

Later Leslie looked up at her. His eyes were sunken and his skin had a gray pallor. "Didn't know you'd have a blasted puking baby to take care of, did you, Lee? Wish you'd stayed at home?"

Lyna took a cloth, dipped it in water, and then bathed his face. "No, sir, I don't wish that." She felt a strong maternal instinct, and for one moment Lyna had the impulse to put her arms around him and hold him—but she quickly put that thought aside! "You'll be fine when we get ashore, sir," she said softly.

"I might die before then," he muttered bitterly.

"No, you won't do that," Lyna said, trying to comfort him.

"Sure of that, are you? I wish *I* were!"

Most of her days and nights were spent sitting beside him for long hours. When she could, she took short naps in the bunk above. The other times were spent bathing his face or trying to feed him broth. She managed to change her clothes when he drifted off into fitful short sleeps, and once thought wryly, *He's not likely to be noticing he's got a woman for a roommate—and even if he did, he's so sick I don't think he'd care much. . . !*

One afternoon she left the cabin and stood beside the rail. Captain Mullens came to stand beside her. "How is he?"

"A little better." She looked out over the long line of waves that rolled endlessly, then asked, "When will we get there, sir? It's been a long trip."

"Not long now—maybe two days." Mullens leaned on the rail and gazed at the blue sky above. He seemed a lonely man, with no family except one sister in Yorkshire. More than once Lyna had wondered why he'd never married. Although he was not handsome, he had a kind spirit and flashes of humor that she found most appealing. Now he put his sharp blue eyes on Lyna and smiled. "Well, Leslie sure made the right choice for a manservant. You make a fine nurse, Lee—as well as being a great cook and valet."

Two days later, the ship dropped anchor in India. The months at sea had taken their toll on Gordon. He had lost a considerable amount of weight and was so weak he could hardly button his shirt. As Lyna helped Gordon dress, he complained, "I'm weak as a kitten! Don't know if I can walk down the gangplank, Lee." He slipped into his coat, then turned to face her. His face was gaunt and his eyes sunken, but he managed a smile. "Lee—thanks for everything."

Lyna dropped her eyes and stepped back. "Oh, I'm glad I was here to help you, sir. Once you get some land under your feet, you'll feel better."

"I sure hope so—I'd hate to think I was going to feel this bad the rest of my life." A trace of humor flickered in his eyes, and he nodded. "Now, sometime *you'll* have to get sick. Then I can take care of you—sort of even things up, eh? You've worn yourself out feeding me and giving me baths. Maybe I'll be able to do the same for you someday, right?"

Lyna smiled broadly at her employer and shook her head. "I hope not, sir—no, indeed!"

🛡   🛡   🛡

Lyna never understood properly the political issues that ignited the battle which brought Englishmen so far away from the shores of their homeland. For several weeks after the regiment marched down the gangplank, she had all she could do taking care of her employer. Gordon recovered quickly from the seasickness and now spent long hours day after day drilling his men—and learning the art of war from Captain Mullens and Colonel White. Finally, the troop marched to the outskirts of a small city called Trichinopoly, where they made their camp.

The heat of India was oppressive, and the sanitary conditions of the camp bred all kinds of sickness. Sometimes as many as a fourth of the men were down with some sort of illness. Lyna worried that sooner or later either she or Leslie would be added to the list.

Rumors began to fly through the ranks that they would soon be going into battle. Lyna's fears mounted as that day approached and the tension in the camp grew. Then one night Colonel White stopped by to caution the officers that the next day would bring on the battle. He was accompanied by a twenty-five-year-old officer named Robert Clive. As the officers sat around the fire drinking tea mixed with whiskey, Lyna hovered close, listening to the discussion.

Gordon said little at first as he sipped at his tea. He listened for a while, then finally said, "I hate to admit it, sir, but the issues of this thing still elude me. Exactly *what* are we fighting for out here?"

Colonel White smiled at the question. "Better men than you have asked that, Lieutenant. As a matter of fact, I suspect that few members of Parliament really know. Clive, why don't you enlighten our young friends?"

Clive was a man of no more than medium height, but he seemed taller because of his erect posture. He had a pair of steady gray eyes, and his voice was clear and confident.

"It all has to do with the East India Company," he said, looking around at the officers, who paid him close heed. "The nationals here have been fighting among themselves, so France sent a man named Joseph Dupleix to take over for France. And he succeeded—oh, my yes!" Anger swept over the face of the young officer. "I was at Madras when it fell to him. Only a few of us escaped to tell the tale. With that victory, France became master of southern India."

A wild dog not far from the camp lifted its voice in a long howl, and Clive waited, listening to the mournful sound. Then he waved his hand toward the east. "The French intend to drive us out—and we're here to make sure they don't succeed! They've besieged Trichinopoly, and in the morning we'll go out and hit them hard."

"It'll be a bit of a chore," Colonel White said evenly. "We'll be outnumbered considerably."

"But we are *Englishmen*!" Clive insisted. "We are soldiers of His Majesty—and we will overcome!"

The next morning Lyna was helping Leslie pack his gear for the battle when he said, "We'll be back to the base when we've whipped the Frenchies." His face was glowing with excitement, and he reached out and slapped Lyna on the shoulder. "We'll have a victory celebration, won't we?"

Lyna bit her lip, trying not to show the fear she felt. "Be careful, sir," she said, lifting her eyes to meet his. "I . . . don't like to think of . . . of anything happening to you."

"Bosh, nothing's going to happen!" A bugle blared and the roll of drums caught his ear, and he turned and left at a run.

As Lyna watched him go, Colonel White's servant, a burly man named Boswell, came to stand beside her. "Well, there they go, flags a-flyin' and drums a-poundin'! I've seen 'em go like that many a time—and some of 'em won't be a-comin' back."

Lyna shot him a startled look. "You think it'll be bad, Boswell?"

Boswell spat on the ground and shook his bullet head. "A battle's always bad, Smith," he grunted. "Ain't nothin' fine or noble about it, no sir! Oh, my eye! When they come a-draggin' the wounded back with their guts all hangin' out, you'll see!"

Lyna went about her duties nervously—and just before noon

135

she heard the distant boom of cannon. Running outside, she encountered Boswell.

"Startin' up, it is. I 'opes our lads give it to 'em!"

Lyna walked around the camp for hours worrying about Gordon. Late in the afternoon the wagons used for ambulances started arriving. She moved in close to watch as the wounded men were unloaded, praying she would not see Gordon. And she learned at once that Boswell had been right—there was no romance in war!

The wounded were moaning with pain, some of them covered with blood. As each wagon arrived, the downed soldiers were unloaded and placed on the hard floors to wait their turn with the field surgeons. Screams of agony rent the air, and more than once Lyna covered her ears to shut out the hideous sound.

Finally, moved by compassion for the suffering Lyna saw, she went over and offered to help. A doctor exclaimed fervently, "Lord, yes—we can use all the help we can get! See that those poor fellows waiting over there get water, will you—except those with belly wounds."

Lyna worked arduously all afternoon and even after darkness fell. She saw more than one man die, and her hands and clothes were stained with blood from helping raise men up for a drink of water.

When she finally fell onto her cot, she was relieved that Leslie had not been one of the wounded soldiers. But the thought that he might be dead gripped Lyna with a terrible fear. She slept in fits until dawn, then arose and began her vigil again as she helped tend the wounded. The distant sound of gunfire began and continued intermittently throughout the day. The wagons started arriving with the wounded, and once again she was relieved when Gordon was not among them.

Late in the afternoon, while Lyna was feeding a soldier who had lost his arm, Boswell came by. "They're a-comin' in—the regiment!" he said hurriedly.

Lyna carefully fed the soldier the few remaining bites and smiled at him. "Now, you try to sleep, Corporal." Then she moved with a hurried step outside the hospital. She saw at once the long line of men and horses coming back from the front line. Nervously, she searched for a glimpse of Gordon's company.

She heard a familiar voice behind her and turned to see Captain Mullens dismounting. When he faced her, she knew immediately the news was bad.

"I . . . I'm sorry, Smith," said Mullens.

"Is . . . is it bad, Captain?"

"I'm afraid it is." A bloody bandage was tied around the captain's left arm and he moved carefully, his face lined and hard. "He took a bullet in the stomach about noon."

A cold wave of fear ran through Lyna, for she knew how few who suffered that sort of wound lived. Most of them died of infection. "Where is he?"

"Come along. We'll see the surgeon gives it his best."

For Lyna the rest of the night was blurred. She could remember only bits and pieces of helping lift Leslie out of the wagon and into the hospital. He was barely conscious and didn't even recognize her. She was scarcely aware of Mullens beside her while they waited for the surgeon to do his work. Fear had a paralyzing effect on her, slowing down her thoughts. It was as if somehow she'd been numbed by the impact of the bullet Gordon had taken.

Finally the regimental surgeon came out, his apron stained with blood. "He's not going to make it, I fear," he said to Mullens, his face stiff and cold. "We got the bullet out, but it was a bad one. I think it may have done a great deal of damage to the organs."

"What can we do, Doctor?" Mullens asked. "He's a good man. I'd hate to lose him."

"Nothing much, I'm afraid." The surgeon looked at the young man beside the captain and asked, "You've been helping us—are you his servant?"

"Yes, sir," said Lyna, struggling not to show the emotion that was choking her.

"Well, he'll have fever. They always do. Try to keep it down. Keep him from moving too much. And pray. I wish I could be more hopeful."

"Can we go to him now?" Lyna asked.

"Yes. We'll have him put in one corner of the ward. You can stay with him all the time."

"A bad break," Mullens said soberly as they followed the doctor. "I'm very fond of him—as you are."

"Yes, sir, I am," said Lyna, her lip trembling.

When they stood looking down at the pale face of the wounded man, Mullens said, "I'll be on duty, but I'll come by when I can. Let me know what I can do, Smith." He started to leave but hesitated, saying, "Don't get your hopes up, my boy. I've seen this sort of thing often. He's in very poor shape. There ... really isn't much hope, I'm afraid."

"He won't die!"

Mullens blinked in surprise at Lyna's adamant response. He said no more but left at once.

Lyna sat down and picked up Gordon's limp hand, holding it with both of hers. All around her the cries of men in pain rose, but she was scarcely conscious of them. Her eyes were fixed on the still face of the man who lay on the cot. Sometime later the doctor came by, looked down at her, then shook his head and left.

Lyna fought down the fear that lodged in her throat and held her head up straight. Reaching forward, she smoothed the reddish hair from Gordon's forehead, her touch gentle.

"He won't die! I won't let him die!" she whispered.

Finally she leaned back and took a deep breath. The clock ceased to have meaning for her, for she had thrown her spirit into the task of saving this man. And as she sat there long after the ward had grown quiet, except for an occasional groan, a startling thought came to her. *Why am I hurting for him so much?*

She leaned forward and studied the pain-wracked face and whispered, "I think ... I love you, Lieutenant Gordon. . . !"

Her voice was low and there was no one to hear or see her. Picking up the still hand, she kissed it, then held it to her cheek. . . .

11

DISCOVERED?

It was like drifting in a sea of murky darkness . . . with muffled sounds that held no meaning.

Occasionally a voice broke through—unembodied, thin, far away. After a while, one of the voices became familiar, for it was different from the others—gentle and quiet. It somehow brought release from the fear that enveloped him as thoroughly as the darkness.

And searing pain—always pain that stabbed like the sudden thrust of a fiery sword, sending him back into the stygian blackness.

He could feel the difference between the hands that touched him. One touch was brisk and rough, probing, sending great waves of pain through his body. He would struggle faintly, attempting to get away, but there was no escape from the relentless torture.

But other hands were gentle, bringing relief from the scorching sense of burning. They would linger on his face and body, bringing coolness that washed away the heat of the fever. And he would relax at their sensitive touch.

Time had no meaning as he drifted in this realm of semiconsciousness. For all he knew, the Pyramids might have been built while he lay on the hard, narrow bed. Or it might have been a wild nightmare lasting only a few seconds. Darkness, heat, pain, coolness, the touch of hands—these were the boundaries of his shadowy world.

At times he dreamed of home—of Longbriar. Scenes from his

childhood drifted by, events he hadn't thought of for years—had long since forgotten. A trip to Portsmouth with his father, the delight of seeing the tall masts of the ships, and his father's hand holding his. A fragment of memory touched him briefly, of the first girl he'd kissed—her face turned up to his in the moonlight along the shore in Brighton. He twisted as he dreamed of the fight he'd had with Carleton Bennett when he was fifteen, almost feeling the hard knuckles on his face.

Gradually the dreams and the darkness faded, and he became aware of *real* voices.

One day he opened his eyes when he felt gentle hands touching him. A face swam into focus, and he whispered, "Lee—!"

The hands that were bathing his face stopped, and a familiar voice said, "Leslie, you're awake!" The tired-looking eyes brightened. "Well, it's about time you woke up! How do you feel?"

Leslie stared at his servant as if he were seeing a spirit. "I got shot," he murmured. He looked around the ward, noting the line of cots—most of them empty. "I'm in the hospital?"

"Yes, sir. You've been here since you were wounded—almost two weeks ago." Lyna felt the patient's forehead, then nodded. "You don't have a fever anymore. Let me take a look at your wound."

Leslie lay still while his servant carefully removed the bandages on his stomach. He lifted his head to look at the ugly, puckered scar, trying to pull his thoughts together. "You've been here all the time?"

"Yes, sir. But the infection's all gone. Doctor Simms will be by soon. Can you drink some water?"

Leslie's mouth felt as dry as the Sahara. He nodded and drank noisily from the cup of water held to his lips.

"Don't strangle yourself," Lee scolded. "You can have all you want after the doctor says so."

"What's happened?" Leslie asked. "Did we win?"

"Yes, you won," Lyna said, then described in detail how Clive had directed the troops and won a great victory.

Doctor Simms strode down the aisle between the rows of cots and stopped, his expression incredulous. "Well, Gordon, I see you're awake."

Simms examined the wound, giving Leslie a quizzical glance. "You're a very fortunate man, Lieutenant. Most men don't survive wounds like this." Turning toward Lyna, he said, "I'd say this young servant of yours made the difference. He hasn't slept a full night since you were brought in."

Leslie saw that his servant was indeed thinner. "I knew you'd do me good, Lee. . . ."

He dropped off to sleep in that alarming manner of badly wounded men, as if he'd been drugged. Simms was satisfied, however. "He's on the mend, Smith. Just needs lots of rest and good food. It's going to take some time for him to get his strength back." The doctor studied the tired face, then said gently, "I wish there were more nurses like you—but I'm prescribing more rest for you."

"Yes, sir. Have you heard when we'll be going home?"

"Yes, Colonel White said the wounded will be leaving at the end of the month. I think by then this young man will make the trip fine. See that he eats all he can."

"Yes, Doctor Simms, I'll do that." Lyna looked down at the drawn face of Leslie Gordon and murmured, "I'll take real good care of him."

♇   ♇   ♇

The voyage home was delayed for a few weeks, which was fortunate, according to Doctor Simms. It gave Leslie more time to regain his strength, so that when the *Dorchester* was ready to weigh anchor and set sail for England, he was able to walk on board. He needed a cane and Lyna's support, but he was out of danger and improving daily.

Every day at sea Leslie grew stronger; his color improved and he gained some weight.

"I can't believe it, Lee! I thought I'd be sick to death as soon as I got back on another ship!"

Leslie turned his gaze from the endless expanse of ocean stretching over the horizon to look at Lyna. The bow of the *Dorchester* dipped and rose, sending white foam over the deck. "Not like our trip over, is it? Thank God for that!"

Lyna held the rail to steady herself and gave Leslie a warm smile. "No, I was dreading it for you. But it's actually done you good, this voyage."

He took a deep breath of the salt air. "I don't know why I haven't been seasick. A miracle, I think." He studied Lyna carefully, then shook his head. "You've taken care of me, but now it's time for you to look after yourself. You've lost weight, Lee."

Lyna's brown trousers hung loosely; the short jacket and cotton shirt appeared too large. Although thinner, her face glowed from the invigorating sea air, tanned slightly by the southern sun. "You have some freckles—right across your nose," Leslie observed. "I had them when I was a boy, millions of them."

Lyna looked out at the rolling sea, thinking of the weeks that had gone by since the battle. She had been with Leslie Gordon almost constantly, nursing him day and night after he'd been wounded. As he got better, her role had changed to one of companionship. They had plenty of time together, so he'd taught her to play chess. To his chagrin, Lyna proved to be the better player.

They spent long hours playing chess, letting the days slip by. There was a strange peace about the time for Lyna. She could not remember when she'd been so free from pressures. She didn't think of England or their return, but let the days roll over her. They talked endlessly as Leslie grew stronger. And for hours she would read to him—usually a novel. She had always been a reader, though her selections had been limited. They disagreed on the worth of some of them and argued rather noisily defending their favorites.

One day as they stood at the rail, enjoying the serenity of the sea and sky, Leslie suddenly said, "You know, Lee, it's a strange thing, but I've gotten closer to you than I ever got to anyone."

"I suppose it's because you had no one else."

"No, I've been alone before. I think perhaps it's because I was so dependent on you." He stared out across the gray expanse, then turned and gazed at her, a smile on his broad lips. "First I was your patient on the voyage over—and after I was wounded, I was your patient again. You were always there." He placed his hand on Lyna's shoulder. "I suppose I've been the worst trouble you ever had—having to take care of me, I mean."

Lyna looked up at him and smiled. "No, sir. I'd not say that. We've had good times—since you got better." A mischievous light touched her gray-green eyes. "And I'd never have been able to teach you good taste in novels if I hadn't had you at my mercy— nor beat you at chess."

Leslie laughed at her impudence. "I just *let* you beat me at chess," he said airily. "And your taste in writers is *terrible. . . .*!"

The two of them walked around the deck for a time, arguing about the merits of Henry Fielding and Samuel Richardson. When Leslie grew tired, they returned to their small cabin. Lyna went to get his meal from the galley and, as had become their custom, ate her own meal with him.

When they were finished, she cleaned up, then set up the chessboard. This time Leslie won. With a hint of triumph in his voice, he said, "See, I told you so."

"I'm still ahead of you three games," she retorted. "Shall I read to you?"

"Yes—but not that interminable *Clarissa* by Samuel Richardson! I don't see how you can stand that sentimental book. All that silly woman Clarissa does is run away from the rascal who's after her—and squall! Lord, she runs on water power!"

"What do you mean sentimental? She's a respectable woman! It makes me so *angry* the way he treats her!" Lyna's eyes glinted and her back grew straight. "That man Lovelace—he should be hanged! He has no sense of decency or honor."

"Oh, come now, Lee!" They had had this argument before, and Leslie was mystified as to why his servant grew so incensed at the plot of a mere book. In the novel, a nobleman named Lovelace was determined to seduce an innocent young servant girl named Clarissa. "Lovelace isn't so bad. Most of our nobility have drunk from the chalice of love in their green years."

"I suppose *you* did?"

Leslie was taken aback by the anger in Lee's eyes. It was the only time he'd ever seen his young servant angry. "Why, I suppose I did. But she was willing enough," he added quickly. "I never forced myself on a woman."

"But many men do exactly that. They take advantage—it's wrong!"

Leslie studied Lee's face for a moment. Perplexed, he finally shook his head. "You ought to know this world's not a very fair place. You've had some hard knocks. Why does it shock you to see it set out in a mere novel that some men are evil?" A thought came to him, and he asked, "Has some woman given you a hard time, is that it?" He leaned back and said, "You've never shown any interest in the girls, Lee. You're too young to have had many serious problems along that line—or am I wrong? You're a handsome young fellow. Did some beauty do you in?"

"No!" Lyna shook her head, then realized she was getting into deep water. "It's not that, sir. It's just that—oh, I don't know, Lieutenant, things just aren't fair!"

"Well, go on and read the blasted book. Maybe someone will shoot the villain dead before he has his way with the innocent Clarissa." He sat on his bunk and rested his head against the wall. "Maybe by the time we get to Longbriar you'll finish the thing. . . ."

T　　T　　T

"Well, I must say, my boy, I'm proud of you!"

Leslie looked up startled, for his father had not made a remark like that for years. The two of them were riding across the meadows two days after Leslie had returned home. "Why, that's good of you, sir—but really, I didn't do much." He patted the mottled gray mare and shrugged. "I was just getting ready to start fighting, and the beggars cut me down like a cornstalk."

Sir Lionel shook his head, his voice firm. "Colonel White wrote me about you. I want you to read the letter. He speaks most highly of your gallantry under heavy fire. He's proud to have you in his command. Sees a great future ahead for you, Leslie."

The two men rode slowly, making allowances for Leslie's wound. Sir Lionel had welcomed his son home with delight, making much of him to his wife and Oliver. In fact, the two had been together almost constantly, so much so his wife had protested one day when they returned from hunting. "After all, Lionel, you can't neglect the rest of the world for Leslie!"

Oliver had been friendly enough, but he had little in common with his younger brother. His mind was occupied with business and music, and he spent little time with Leslie. "He'll be gone soon enough, Mother," he said when she had objected. "Father's always been fond of military things. Let them have their little visit."

Lyna had been nervous about coming to Longbriar. She knew a little about Leslie's family, for he had spoken of them at times on the voyage from India. When she arrived, Leslie had praised her to the skies. "This young fellow has been my good angel," he'd said warmly to his family in her presence. He told them of Lyna's faithful attention, and Sir Lionel had at once said, "Why, we're in your debt, young man! I thank you for your faithful service to my son!"

The living arrangement during the visit proved to be safe. Leslie had taken her upstairs and showed her where she was to sleep. "Look, this is my room, and it's joined to a smaller one—right through this door. You'll have a little privacy for a change—but it'll be convenient for you to serve me."

"It's very nice, sir," Lyna said, looking around the small room—which was much larger than any she'd ever had. It was a welcome relief from the cramped quarters on the ship, where it had been difficult on the return voyage to hide her identity. With Leslie feeling so much better she had had to come up with clever ways of concealing her secret. Somehow she had managed, but Leslie had teased her often, saying he had never before seen such modesty in a young man.

"Well, we'll be here until I'm fit enough to rejoin the regiment," Leslie went on. "I think you'll like it here at Longbriar."

Lyna did enjoy her stay. Her duties were light, and she had a great deal of time to herself. She took her meals with the rest of the servants, but made no friends among them. After three weeks she wrote in her diary:

June 12, 1752
I went for a long walk deep into the woods today. It's so lovely in the spring. Flowers blooming everywhere. I slept beside a bubbling brook, collected a bouquet of wild flowers. Leslie said he didn't know young *men* collected flowers—I must be more careful!

One of the maids has been flirting with me outrageously—her name is Rosaline, Lady Alice's personal maid. She thinks I'm a handsome young fellow, and yesterday she made an excuse to press herself against me—the hussy! She gives me all sorts of rather obvious invitations—and is quite peeved when I don't respond. It amuses me, but I keep away from such things. It could be dangerous.

I like Sir Lionel very much. He's kind to me and very grateful for what I did for Leslie. I wish all English lords were so considerate.

We will be leaving here soon. Leslie is almost completely recovered, thank God!

I will find a way to get to Dartmoor after we get back

with the regiment. I must see Daniel—I must!

⚑   ⚑   ⚑

A few days later, Lyna stayed up very late reading, enjoying the luxury of an evening off while Leslie had ridden to the home of an old friend to spend the night. It was a hot night, and being alone she decided to risk a complete sponge bath. Usually she bathed during the day when Leslie was out with his father.

She undressed and poured fresh water into the basin on the washstand. Taking fragrant soap and a clean cloth she washed her face, then began to sponge carefully. The water felt good, and she refilled the basin twice, savoring the coolness of it.

She was almost finished when she heard a slight sound behind her. She spun around and was horrified to see Rosaline standing in the doorway staring at her, her mouth open in amazement!

Lyna desperately made a grab for her robe, but it was too late. The girl whirled and disappeared, the sound of her footsteps fading as she ran down the hallway. Lyna stood motionless, then began to tremble. *She'll tell—I know she will!*

And she was correct in her assumption, for the maid went straight to her mistress the next morning. Lady Alice listened with disbelief, scoffing, "You've lost your mind, Rosaline! Or else you've had a dream."

But Rosaline said indignantly, "Do you think I don't know a man from a woman, ma'am?"

"What were you doing in that room anyway?" Lady Alice demanded—then nodded grimly. Rosaline was a pretty girl who could think of nothing but men. She'd had numerous affairs with the men on the estate and, no doubt, had had intentions that night of seducing Lee Smith while Leslie was away. "Oh, it's like that, is it!" Lady Alice raged. "No, don't bother to deny it. Don't say a word, you understand—or I'll have you whipped!"

Lady Alice was waiting when Sir Lionel and Leslie returned. As soon as they entered the house, she was there to meet them. "Come into the library, Lionel—and you too, Leslie." Her face was grim as she added, "This concerns you."

When the door was shut, she turned to lash out, "I thought I knew you, Leslie, but this deception exceeds even *your* misdeeds!"

Leslie blinked with surprise. "Deception? I don't understand—"

146

"Oh, don't bother to deny it!"

"What do you mean, Alice?" Lionel broke in. "What's wrong?"

"What's wrong? Leslie has brought his doxie into this house, that's what's wrong!" When she saw the perplexity on her husband's face, she snapped, "That servant of his—Lee Smith—is *not* a young man! She's a hussy dressed up as one!"

"Mother, don't be ridiculous!" Leslie broke out.

"Don't deny it!" Lady Alice cried. "I know you've been with women—but to bring that creature into your own home!"

Sir Lionel turned to stare at his son. "Is this true, Leslie?"

Leslie was stunned. "I . . . I don't know what to say. I had no idea!"

"You *must* have known!"

Leslie stared at his mother, then shook his head slowly. "I met him on the road—" He was thinking more quickly now, remembering how Lee had always been very private in personal things. He said suddenly, "Let me see about this."

He left the room and went at once to the second floor, entering his own room, then crossing to the adjoining door. For one moment he hesitated, then knocked. "Come in," a voice said quietly. He opened the door and saw Lee standing beside the window. One look and he knew it was all true!

Lyna said, "I almost left last night, but I wanted to see you one more time—to explain."

Somehow she had changed—or he himself had changed. She was still dressed in men's garb, but now that he knew the truth, Leslie saw as for the first time that the eyes were too large for a man, and the sweep of the jaw was smooth and feminine.

"Sit down, Lee," he said quietly. "Tell me everything."

"My name is Lyna Bradford. . . ."

Leslie listened patiently as Lyna related her story. She told him of her mother's death and the time at the workhouse with Daniel. Of how they had worked as indentured servants for a family. And of her brother who had been falsely accused and sent to prison. Twenty minutes later, Lyna ended her story. For a while, they both sat in silence. Finally, with a sad look in her eyes, Lyna said, "I'm sorry, sir, for bringing shame to you. I . . . I don't regret anything but that."

Leslie had not one doubt about the truth of her story. Everything suddenly made sense: comments she had made, her sensitivity Mullens always joked about, her modesty, her cooking, the flowers—so many things. He stood up and walked to the window, thinking of the unselfish care she'd lavished on him all this time. Turning back to her and seeing the anguish in her eyes, he said gently, "Lyna, you have nothing to be ashamed of. You did what you had to do to survive. And as long as I live—I'll never forget that you saved my life."

"Oh, I hardly did that!"

"Doctor Simms said so."

Lyna's heart was too full to speak. She knew he was not angry with her—and that was what she had feared most. But he was looking at her in a strange fashion, and she could only say, "I'll be going now, Lieutenant Gordon."

"Going? Going where?"

"Why, I can't stay here!"

"No, I don't think you can," Leslie said. His mind was working swiftly. He knew that his mother was angry to the bone. His father—well, he would be able to make him understand. But the situation would be intolerable for both Lyna and himself. Quickly he made a decision. "We'll be leaving together, Lee—I mean, Lyna."

Lyna stared at him, not understanding. "Sir, you can't leave your family—and I won't be able to serve you—"

"One problem at a time," Leslie interrupted. He sat back down beside her, looking into her tragic eyes. "Don't feel bad about this, Lyna," he said gently. "We'll manage—both of us. Now, you take your things and go saddle the horses. I've got some explaining to do."

Lyna quickly obeyed, and thirty minutes later Leslie entered the stables, carrying a small traveling bag. He looked tense but said only, "Let's be on our way."

The two of them mounted, and she noted that he didn't look back as they left the grounds. When they reached the top of the ridge, he did draw up and turn to look down on the estate. He was silent for a few moments, and finally Lyna could not bear what she suspected. "Sir, you can't leave your family on my account!"

Leslie faced her. "I've been estranged from my family for some time, Lyna. My mother and my brother are very angry with me—but my father believes me." He saw the tears of frustration in her eyes and said quickly, "Come now, things aren't so bad as that."

"I feel terrible!"

"No need." He marveled that he could have ever been so blind to the feminine qualities of the girl. Despite some doubts of his own, he said cheerfully, "Come along now, we'll be all right!"

The two rode away from Longbriar, and Leslie wondered when he would ever look on it again.

12

Sir Leo Rochester's Visit

THE CANDLE GUTTERED IN THE HOLDER, and Lyna glanced up, then snuffed the wick so that it burned more brightly. Her small room was still, as was the entire house. Outside her window the apple tree stirred in the rising breeze. It seemed to be clawing at the clapboards with bony fingers, but she was accustomed to this. Dipping the tip of her quill in the ink bottle, she poised it over the sheet of paper, a thoughtful expression on her face, then began to write:

> For two weeks we've been back in this house, and I still feel very—strange. I had expected Leslie would rent me a room and help me find work, but he wouldn't hear of it. The night we arrived, he said, "George kept up the house, and he told me to stay in it until he gets back with the regiment—and you're staying here, too."
>
> I remember how I argued, but he would not listen. He is a most *stubborn* man! When I said it wouldn't be right for a single man and a grown woman to live together under the same roof, he said we'd been living together under the same roof for months! I hinted that people would talk, and he just shook his head, saying, "Let them wag their tongues. We'll do nothing wrong, so it's none of their blasted business!"
>
> So, we did as he said. I kept to my same little room, and he moved back into his downstairs. I keep the house, and he is busy getting ready for the return of the regiment.

151

She heard a faint sound and looked up to see the mouse that came to take the crust of bread she always put out for him. He sat up and nibbled the bread, his silver eyes watching her. "Hello, Your Highness," Lyna whispered. He was a bold fellow, and she felt a companionship with him. He came regularly, and she enjoyed his antics. "Now, what have you been up to, sir?" she demanded.

He stopped eating, cocked his head, and studied her calmly. His nose twitched, then he began to nibble in an incredibly rapid fashion. When he was finished with his meal, he proceeded to calmly give himself a thorough bath. Lyna smiled as he suddenly scampered away; then she began writing again.

We were like two strangers for those first days—indeed we were. I'll never forget the look on Leslie's face when he came home and got his first glimpse of me in a dress. I'd gone to a shop and bought it, for we had agreed that would be best. It wasn't a fancy dress, just a simple blue gown, but with nice lace trim around the bodice and sleeves. I hadn't worn one in so long that it felt peculiar, to be sure! Anyway, when he came into the house I was dusting. He took one look at me—and I never saw a man look so shocked! His eyes flew open and his jaw actually dropped! I would have laughed—but I was too nervous! He swallowed and nodded, mumbling, "I see you got a new dress. You look—very nice."

I'd hoped for more of a compliment, but he seemed to be stunned. Two days later, however, he did say, "When I saw you for the first time in that dress, Lyna, I actually realized you were a woman." I did laugh at him then, for we'd gotten a little more relaxed about the whole thing. I said, "It takes a great deal to convince you, sir." After that I would notice him stealing glances at me—as though he had to constantly assure himself that I was a young woman and not Lee Smith.

The regiment will arrive soon, and I asked Leslie how he would explain me to his fellow officers. He looked doubtful and said only that he was sure they would understand. I wish I were sure of that!

Since he will never see this diary—nor will anyone else— I'll write here what I shall never be able to say aloud: I love Leslie Gordon! It's a hopeless love, for he is high above me— but I will never find a man as kind! He tells me he's been wild—but to me he has been nothing but gentle.

Lyna slowly read over the last lines, then wiped the quill and put it down. Lifting her mattress, she hid the diary, then went to bed, thinking of the strange fate that she'd fallen into.

"I'll talk to Leslie about Daniel tomorrow," she murmured. "I want to write him. Leslie will know if it's safe. . . ."

🜚   🜚   🜚

"Good to be back in England, isn't it, sir?"

Colonel White looked out at the ship that was disembarking the troops, then nodded. "Very good, Mullens! And I suppose you're ready for a little time off?"

"If it's convenient, sir."

"Of course! You've done a fine job! I'm mentioning your fine service in my report. I think it could be helpful to you."

"That's good of you, sir!"

The two men parted, and Captain Mullens caught a cab. As he moved through the city, he was thinking, *Glad I kept the lease on the house. It'll be good to have a place to rest in—and it's been good for Leslie.* He had told Leslie when he left India to be sure to use the house when he and Smith got back to England. Leslie had assured him he would keep the house fit until the rest of the regiment returned.

"Here we are, Captain," said the driver as he pulled his horses to a stop.

Mullens stepped out of the cab, paid the fare, then walked up to the front door. He had not known how much he missed the place until this moment. It was merely a rented house, but he'd been in and out of it for three years—the longest stay he'd had in any one spot. "By Harry—it's *good* to be back!" he exclaimed. He opened the door and stepped inside, calling out, "Leslie—are you here?"

Receiving no answer, he took two steps down the hall, then halted abruptly as a young woman stepped out of the door that led to the kitchen. Mullens yanked off his tricorn hat, somewhat confused. "Oh, I hope I didn't—ah, frighten you, ma'am."

"Not at all. Won't you come in, Captain?"

George Mullens' first thought was that his friend Gordon had married—or had taken a mistress. He stood there—his mind working rapidly—studying the young woman. She was very young, he saw, not over seventeen or perhaps a year older. She wore a simple blue dress that set off her trim figure well. Her hair was blond and she had a fine pair of gray-green eyes. Yet there was something about her that baffled him.

"We've met, have we not?"

"Yes, sir, many times."

The reply provoked Mullens, for he prided himself on his good memory. He cocked his head, thinking hard, but could not remember the woman. "I'm afraid you have me at a disadvantage, ma'am," he said. "My memory is failing me at the moment."

"Come in, Captain. Let me take your things."

As the young woman took his hat and coat, Mullens took a long look at her. Then when she turned, he said, "Why, you must be Smith's sister!"

Lyna's face became pale, but she faced him squarely. "I wish Lieutenant Gordon were here, Captain Mullens. It would be better if he could explain."

Suddenly a wild thought flashed into Mullens' mind— brought on by the sound of her voice. He exclaimed with astonishment, "Why—why, you're *Lee Smith!*"

Lyna nodded and stood quietly before the soldier. "Yes—I was. My real name is Lyna Bradford." She shook her head at the shocked expression on Mullens' face. "Come and sit down, sir. It's a long story. . . ."

Mullens accompanied the young woman into the library, where he sat and listened to her for the next quarter hour. When Lyna had finished, she said, "I feel you must despise me, Captain."

"Why, not at all!" Mullens was amazed, but he had no great social conscience. The girl's behavior might shock some, but he was a soldier—and had only admiration for the courage and ingenuity she had shown. "Why, Miss Lyna, you are a daring young lady!" He sat forward, staring at her, and shook his head in wonder. "You certainly fooled me—and Leslie as well!" He laughed with delight, exclaiming, "I'll have him for this! Imagine, living all this time with a lovely young girl—and not even *knowing* it!"

"Oh, please, Captain—don't tease him about it!" Lyna's eyes were filled with apprehension as she pleaded, "He's done so much for me! For my sake, don't torment him!"

Mullens sat staring at the lovely face of the young woman, wondering how he could have been deceived. But for her sake he agreed at once. "Well, it will be a sacrifice—but I promise. Now tell me more. How do you two get on? Are you staying here?"

The two talked for half an hour more, and as she explained, all of Lyna's fears vanished. She had always liked Mullens, and now knew that he was no threat to her. She heard the door close and rose at once, joined by Mullens. "Thank you for being so understanding, Captain," she whispered, then turned to face Gordon as he stepped inside.

"George!" he cried out, and the two men greeted each other warmly. Leslie glanced at Lyna, who nodded and gave him a warm smile. "Ah, Lyna has told you of our adventures? Well, now that the secret's out, will you throw us out?"

"Throw out the best cook in England? Not likely! You're welcome to stay as long as you like. Now sit down and let me fill you in on the regiment. I expect you'll be getting a medal, but I say you should hold out for a promotion. . . ."

While Lyna went to finish the meal she had been making, the two men sat and talked all about the regiment. Later, when they were alone after dinner, Mullens made his only comment about Lyna. "You did a noble thing for Lyna, Leslie. Most men would not have been so charitable."

After George had gone to bed, Leslie and Lyna sat down in the library to have a cup of tea. "I'm glad he's back," Leslie said. "He's a fine fellow."

"Yes." Lyna hesitated, then said, "I . . . wasn't sure he'd want me to stay. It's not a regular thing, is it?"

"You're a housekeeper for a pair of lonely bachelors. That's all there is to it."

They spoke quietly, and when she rose, Leslie stood and suddenly reached out and took her hand. Lyna was startled, for he had never done such a thing. He held it quietly, his fine eyes looking down on her. Finally he lifted her hand and kissed it gently.

Lyna's hand seemed to burn from the kiss, and when he released it, she whispered, "Why did you do that, sir?"

"I don't know. Perhaps because I admire you so much."

"Me, Lieutenant?"

"For heaven's sake, Lyna, *must* you call me that? After what we've been through, you might at least call me Leslie."

"It . . . wouldn't be right, sir!"

He put his hands on her shoulders and swayed her toward him. "I think all the time of how you cared for me—on the ship— and in India." Leslie could smell the faint fragrance of violets. He saw her eyes fixed on his. "You're a lovely young woman, Lyna." He hesitated, then said, "I know you've been misused. But do you trust me?"

"Yes! Yes, sir, I do!"

"Then . . . may I kiss you?"

If Leslie had tried to kiss her without asking, Lyna would have been frightened. But he was not demanding. She knew that if she said no, he would not be angry. She thought of all he'd done for her—when he'd thought she was a young man—and a sense of warmth and trust enveloped her.

She lifted her face, and when his lips fell on hers, she felt a gentleness she'd not known could come from a man. At the same time, there was a strength in his arm and a tender force in his lips that stirred her. She was aware of the muscles of his chest as he drew her close, and without thought, she lifted her hands and put them on his neck. Her lips had a pressure of their own, and a strange fluttering rose in her heart—reminding her that she was a woman. His hands were warm and firm, and he held her as if she were a very fragile and precious thing.

She felt herself pressing closer to him. Then to her surprise, he released her, but kept her in the circle of his arms. He looked into her eyes and whispered, "Lyna Bradford, you're woman enough for any man!"

Lyna was moved by his kiss, and she knew that most men would not have stopped as Leslie had just done. "I . . . I must go."

"Yes—but not until you call me by my proper name!"

Lyna reached up and laid her hand on his cheek. It was something she had longed to do but had not dared. She whispered, "Good-night . . . Leslie!" And then she was gone, slipping out of the room and leaving young Leslie Gordon to his thoughts.

🔔　　🔔　　🔔

A fresh layer of snow lay on the rooftops and streets of London, and though Christmas was still two weeks away, Lyna was looking forward to it. She had been working for weeks on two new shirts for Leslie, taking them out of hiding when he was gone with Captain Mullens to drill the men. Sometimes she would sit in bed sewing the fine seams, thinking of how happy she'd been in the past weeks.

Leslie had not kissed her again, but he was not unaware of her as a woman—she was certain of that. Often as they sat before the fire, reading or simply talking in the easy way that people who enjoy each other do, she would look up to find his eyes fixed on her. His expression she could not define, not completely. *Does he love me?* she would ask herself—then force the question from her mind.

She had written, on his advice, to the warden at Dartmoor prison, asking what procedures must be followed to visit a prisoner. Leslie had promised to take her as soon as they knew what the regulations were—and as soon as he was able to get a short leave.

The sun was glistening on the fresh snow as she made her way down the street to the market. Every post had become a rounded beacon, flashing with diamondlike gleams, and all the houses that had dirty, sooty roofs were now castles of smoothly rounded peaks. There were no sharp edges or angles—all the city had been smoothed and rounded as if by a magic hand.

Lyna bought her supplies, then walked home, delighting in the beauty of the city—white, sparkling, and fresh. A group of small boys emerged from behind a fence, waging war with snowballs, their shrill, yelping cries muted by the thick blanket of soft snow. One of the older boys called out, "Hey, now—watch out!" and sent a snowball winging toward Lyna.

She twisted quickly, causing it to miss, then put her package down and made a hard-packed snowball. "Watch out, yourself—" she cried, and hit the boy in the stomach with the missile. The rest of the pack began jeering at the wounded member, and one of them waved at her, hollering cheerfully, "Good on you, miss!"

Lyna retrieved her package and smiled. The incident brought back memories of how she and Daniel had learned to survive on the streets against rougher boys than those she'd just seen.

After arriving home, Lyna worked all morning cleaning. Later she began cooking for the evening meal. She prepared a thick roast in the large black pot, then stewed several vegetables. She also decided to make a plum pudding—a favorite dish of both men. She had learned from her mother how to make savory puddings by stuffing meat or blood, spices, and other ingredients into skins of an animal's intestine. Sometimes they'd smoked them, adding pepper, which improved the flavor and hid any foul taste if they started to spoil.

"I'm glad some smart person invented pudding *cloth*," she murmured. "I always hated those old intestines!" For the sweeter plum pudding, she carefully stuffed the cloth with fruit—mostly raisins and currants—and sugar, then added some rich cuts of beef. Forming the mass into a ball, she tied the top, then dropped it into a cooking pot.

At four o'clock she heard the front door open and close, followed by the boisterous sound of voices in the hallway. The kitchen door burst open and the two officers entered, their faces ruddy. Captain Mullens went at once and pulled the lid from a pot, then exclaimed, "Pot roast! Gordon, we're likely to end up with bellies as big as the general's if she keeps feeding us like this!"

Leslie winked at Lyna. "You ought to keep your trim appearance, George—as an example to the rest of us. Tell you what, I'll eat my share and most of yours. Can't say fairer than that, can you?"

"You two go wash your dirty hands," Lyna said. "You look like you've been playing in the mud." She shooed them out of the kitchen and began to set the table. By the time they returned with faces and hands clean, the food was on the table. They sat down and she served them; then she sat down and said, "It's your turn to say grace, Captain."

Mullens blinked. "Begging your pardon, Lyna, but what good does it do for a heathen like me to say a blessing? I mean to say— well, dash it all—God knows what a bounder I am!"

Lyna had insisted on one of them asking a blessing at every meal—a custom both of them found strange. But Lyna said, "You're not a bounder, Captain. And you *are* thankful for the food, aren't you?"

Mullens grimaced but nodded. "Can't deny *that*—since I intend to demolish a large portion of it. But I'm not a believer in God."

Lyna turned to him and said gently, "That may be, George— but He believes in *you*. That's why He sent His Son to die for you—and why He sent this food to you. Now—don't argue."

Mullens bowed his head and stumbled through a rather un-orthodox blessing, exploding with a loud, "*Amen!* Now, let's do our duty, Lieutenant."

The men ate with gusto, and when Lyna brought in the plum pudding, Leslie groaned. "Why didn't you *tell* me you had a plum pudding? I would have saved room!"

"Well *I* saved lots of room," Mullens asserted. "Just give me his share, Lyna—" Interrupted by the sound of knocking, he glanced toward the door. "Who could that be, I wonder?"

"I'll get it," Leslie said. "Don't let him have all that pudding, though." He made his way to the door and opened it. A tall, well-dressed man stood looking at him. He wore a heavy black over-coat, a tall silk hat, and carried a heavy cane with a gold head.

"I'm looking for a young woman named Lyna Bradford."

At first Gordon thought the man must be one of the officials of Dartmoor, come to give news of Lyna's brother. But there was something of the peerage about him; one could never mistake the air that such men had. "Yes, sir, Miss Bradford is here. Won't you come in?" Leslie said, stepping aside.

"Thank you."

As the man passed by, Leslie noted a rather wicked-looking scar on his left cheek. "If you'd like to wait in the library, I'll fetch her."

"Very well."

"And your name, sir?"

A smile touched the thin lips of the man. "Just say that an old friend has come to call. I'd like to surprise her."

Leslie was not entirely satisfied with that, but he nodded and returned to the dining room. "Lyna, there's a gentleman to see you."

"Oh, it must be about Daniel—about the letter I wrote."

"I don't think so," Leslie said slowly. "He said to tell you he's an old friend."

Lyna was surprised. "Oh, it must be Mr. Longstreet, then—the gentleman I told you about from Milford. He was very kind to Daniel and me." She rose and left the room. Leslie shot Mullens a troubled glance, then followed her. He was behind her when she stepped into the library and a startled cry burst from her lips. He moved into the room to find her standing before the tall man, her face twisted with fear.

159

"Ah, my dear Lyna, we meet again. It's been a long search, but I can tell you, it's worth all the trouble I've had."

Lyna was trembling, her face pale. Instantly Leslie stepped beside her, his eyes fixed on the face of the man, who was watching him carefully. "Who is this man, Lyna?"

"I am Sir Leo Rochester—and your name?"

"Lieutenant Leslie Gordon." Turning to Lyna he said, "Don't be afraid, Lyna."

"No indeed, I say the same as this officer." Rochester smiled with his lips, but it did not reach his eyes. "I don't suppose you've told this gentleman much of me? No, I thought not. Well, sir, I will inform you that this young lady is a runaway. She is indentured to me, with a year left to serve."

Leslie saw that Lyna was petrified. She was trembling violently, and he put his arm around her, as much to comfort her as to quell the red rage building in him. He had always known that someone had abused Lyna, and now he was positive that this arrogant man standing here was the man.

"Sir, the amount of the indenture will be paid. If you will name the sum—"

"Ah, but I do not choose to part with the girl. As a matter of fact, I intend to take her back with me this very night."

"Then I must inform you, sir, that you are bound to be disappointed."

Sir Leo Rochester stared at Gordon, anger twisting his face. "The girl is a thief, Lieutenant. She left my house with a large sum of money. She is liable to the law, and if you persist—"

"He's lying!" Lyna cried. "I ran away because he wouldn't leave me alone. I never stole anything!"

Leslie said, "Sir Leo, you have my permission to leave."

Rochester's face grew dusky with rage. "You realize that you are harboring a fugitive? And you must know that I will return tomorrow with representatives of the law to take the girl?"

"Get out!" Leslie snapped.

"I won't!"

Leslie Gordon stepped forward, his eyes blazing. "Do you need help to get out of this house, Rochester? I can provide it if necessary."

For a moment Rochester seemed ready to fight—but he forced himself to say, "I will not dirty my hands on you." He walked stiffly out the door, pausing to turn. "Tomorrow, we shall see who will give way!"

As the door slammed, Lyna turned blindly and fell trembling into Leslie's arms. She began to weep, and he held her tightly. She finally looked up, her face stained with tears. "I—I *can't* go back—not to him!"

"You're not going back!"

Lyna stared at his face. "I'll have to run away again."

Leslie shook his head. "No, you won't run away. But you won't be going back with him." When she started to protest, he suddenly bent his head and kissed her. Then he lifted his lips to whisper, "Will you trust me, Lyna?"

Lyna Bradford had known little kindness from men—but she knew that Leslie Gordon was different. She thought fleetingly of his kindnesses, then nodded. "Yes, Leslie—I'll always trust you!"

🎺   🎺   🎺

"This is the house. Are your men ready for trouble?"

Sir Leo Rochester had led the three large men to the door of the house early the next evening. He had informed them that there would be resistance, and he had paid them well, instructing them to batter anyone who defied them.

"Don't trouble yourself about *that*, Sir Leo," one of the men answered. He was slightly smaller than his two companions, but there was an air of authority about him. "We have the warrant, and it shall be served."

"Very well." Rochester knocked on the door, and it opened at once. A small man stood there, dressed in a rather dapper fashion.

"Yes, what is it?"

Leo nodded, and the sheriff said, "We have come to arrest a young woman named Lyna Bradford. We understand she's in this house."

"There is no woman by that name here, sir."

"He's lying!" Rochester said. "Make a search!"

The small man smiled. "Why, of course. Come in, all of you."

Leo walked in and moved down the hall, followed by the three officers. He turned into one door, saw the room was empty, then entered another. He stopped instantly. "There she is, Sheriff! Make your arrest!" He pointed at Lyna, but his eyes were on Leslie Gordon—who stood with his arm around Lyna—and on another officer next to the couple.

The sheriff stepped forward, but the small man who had opened the front door interrupted him. "My name is Jaspers, Sheriff. I think you know me?"

"Indeed, I do, sir." The sheriff had instantly recognized the foremost lawyer in London but had kept silent. He knew that the little man was feared by every opponent he'd faced, for he had a knack of winning cases that were supposed to be lost. The sheriff said carefully, "I have a warrant for Miss Lyna Bradford, sir."

"And there she is!" said Rochester.

Mr. Jaspers put his cool eyes on Rochester but then turned to the sheriff. "This is Mrs. Lyna Gordon, Sheriff. Here is a copy of her wedding license. And as you see, *I* am one of the witnesses, so there is no doubt of the legality of the marriage."

Rochester stared at the lawyer, then turned to face the man and woman who stood together. "You can't get by with that! I'll have you both arrested!" He saw the peaceful expression on Lyna's face—and how the tall soldier held her carefully, a smile in his eyes—and it infuriated him. "Sheriff—do your duty! Arrest her!"

But the sheriff was no fool. "Sir, the warrant is for a single bound girl. This lady has a husband."

"She broke her indenture by running away!"

"For which you may bring action for the refund of any money owed to you. I can recommend several good solicitors who will be glad to handle the matter—but Mr. Gordon has indicated that he will be happy to pay the sum. If you will submit it, it will be paid."

A silence fell over the room. Leo Rochester's face was pale as chalk, so that the scar stood out like a flag. He would have killed both Lyna and her husband if he could have done it without hanging. But he knew he was defeated. With a wild curse, he shouldered his way past the policemen and left the house. The sheriff and his burly assistants followed, after apologizing to Mr. Jaspers.

"Mr. Jaspers," Lyna said, coming to put her hands out to the diminutive lawyer, "how can I ever thank you?"

He took the hands of the young bride, leaned forward, and kissed her cheek. "I wish all my cases ended so happily. My congratulations to both of you!" He turned to Mullens, saying, "Now, sir, you come with me. This is the wedding night for these two."

Mullens was subjected to rather overwrought thanks—including kisses from Lyna and a massive bear hug from the groom. He grinned as he left, winking, and said rather loudly, "Our regiment has a reputation to maintain, Lieutenant. See you do your duty tonight!"

Then they were gone, and the house was quiet. The two stood in the middle of the library, stunned and subdued. Lyna came to him, burying her face against his chest. "I . . . I can't believe we're married!"

"You can't?"

"No . . . it all seems like a dream." She lifted her face to his. "I really can't believe it!"

"Well, then, Mrs. Leslie Gordon—I shall have to prove it to you."

A flush touched Lyna's cheeks, but she held his gaze. As he took her into his arms, she whispered, "Oh, Leslie—I love you with all my heart!"

She was soft and warm and sweet, and there was an innocence in her lips. He held her tightly, saying, "This isn't a dream, sweetheart. I'll love you until the day I die!"

PART THREE

—

THE VIRGINIA INCIDENT

1753–1760

13

A New Acquaintance

LEO ROCHESTER STEPPED OUTSIDE INTO the bright sunshine that sometimes comes in September in Virginia. He lifted his eyes to the rolling hills, feeling a sense of satisfaction with the fine yearlings that frolicked inside the white fences. He missed England, but he was quite pleased with the success of his plantation, which he had named Fairhope. Though it had been a risk leaving Milford Manor and starting over in the Colonies, it had proved to be a wise decision. Leo smiled at how profitable the venture had turned out to be.

The house was not equal to the ancestral home in England, of course, but, for the Colonies, it was splendid. He glanced at the two-storied structure with satisfaction. It was a square house, painted white with blue shutters. Smoke curled out of the six chimneys, scoring the blue sky, and a long white portico spanned the entire front of the house, whose roof was supported by white columns. Large and spacious stables lay to the back of the main house, and to the left of them were the slave quarters.

As Leo approached the stables, he found Daniel Bradford showing a chestnut stallion. He was intent on the job, and Rochester halted and studied his servant. Leo noted that the years at the forge had given Bradford a deep chest and broad shoulders. He had seen him once take a steel horseshoe and twist it as if it were made of putty. *Strong as a bear*, Rochester thought. *He'd be hard to put down in a fight.*

He knew the prosperity of Fairhope was to a great degree the result of Bradford's keen ability with horses. The young man seemed to have been born with an uncanny knowledge of which foals would be champions, and the planters in the area had flocked to Fairhope to buy the horses Daniel bred. He trained them as well, which had put a great deal of money into Leo Rochester's pocket.

He's done better than I expected, Leo thought grudgingly. *A good thing I brought him along.* Then he touched the scar on the left side of his cheek, and a flash of anger ran through him. The memory of how Lyna Bradford had escaped him had not faded. Even now he took a vicious pleasure in the memory of how he'd gotten at least a taste of revenge on the girl. He'd bribed the warden to alter the records concerning his agreement with Daniel, so they read that Daniel Bradford had died in prison. Then he'd made it a point to write a scathing letter to Lyna, telling her he was glad her worthless brother had died in Dartmoor—and wishing her the worst of fortunes.

It was a cruel sort of revenge, and looking at the swelling muscles in the back and arms of Bradford, Rochester had an uneasy thought of what might happen if Daniel ever found out his master had lied to both brother and sister. *He's capable of crushing a man's throat; and he'd do it, too!* However, Leo knew that Lyna's husband was in the regulars and that his military duties would take him and his wife to the distant assignments of the Royal Fusiliers. *I hope the wench gets fever and dies in one of those Godforsaken places,* Rochester thought.

Stepping forward, he said briskly, "Hurry it up. I've got a job for you."

Daniel didn't even look up but carefully continued to pare the hoof he was working on with a file. He was seldom hurried and over the years had learned to keep his dislike for his employer under control. His time at Fairhope had not been unhappy. After the horrors of Dartmoor, his freedom and responsibilities here were a paradise. From the very beginning, Daniel had thrown himself into the work with an intensity that surprised Rochester. As a result, he was now recognized as one of the best men with horses in the state. His time of indenture would be up in two years, and he didn't think beyond that.

He carefully set the hoof down, slapped the horse on the

shoulder, then turned to face Rochester. "What sort of job?" Daniel asked calmly. He pulled a clay pipe out of his pocket and filled it methodically as he spoke. "Whatever it is, you'd better get Ralph to do it. I'm busy training the new foals."

"Do what I tell you and keep your insolent remarks to yourself!" snapped Leo. He hated to admit that it was Bradford's efforts that drew the income to the estate, and he took every opportunity to display his spite.

"Suit yourself," said Daniel, knowing that nothing angered his employer so much as having to admit that he needed the help of his servant. "What is it?"

Leo had hoped to anger Daniel, but he seldom could. He suddenly grinned. "You won't like it," he said. "It's a matter of trading one female for another." He laughed at the surprise that came to Bradford's face. "We're selling Lady and getting a new maid."

"I don't mind a new maid, but it's not wise to sell Lady. She'll make you a lot of money if you hang on to her. She's the finest mare on the place."

"I know that—but I've got to have some ready money."

"If you'd learn that you can't play cards with the sharpers you run with, you'd not have to sell your finest stock."

Leo flushed and cursed Daniel. "Mind your own affairs! Do what I tell you or I'll have you flogged!" Leo looked into Daniel's steady eyes and knew it was a foolish threat. "I've sold the mare to young Washington."

"I thought Lawrence Washington bought the stock."

"He died last year. His younger brother George is handling the estate now. Do you know how to get there?"

"Mount Vernon? Yes, I know it."

"He'll give you cash. Give him a receipt."

"What's this about a maid?"

Rochester shrugged. "My mother thinks she needs a new maid to help with the house. She ran Ella off."

"That was foolish. Ella's a good girl."

"Bradford, you're insolent! What my mother does about a maid is none of your business! Now, the new girl will be at Pine Bluff—that's close to Mount Vernon. She's a raw girl, never worked out, but comes recommended by Squire Thomson. Her name's Holly Blanchard. Stop at his place and he'll give you the directions how to find her."

"All right. I'll leave right away."

Rochester said as he turned to leave, "If the girl's ugly, don't bring her."

Daniel stared at the retreating back of Rochester and thought, *If she's pretty, I'd like to leave her where she is.* Daniel shook his head as he thought about it. He knew well enough that though Rochester had come to a new country, he had brought along all his old ways where women were concerned. Daniel knew that several of the maids had left because of Leo's advances, and rumor had it that he was known to frequent the brothels along with his profligate friends. *I'll warn the girl—that's about all I can do.*

T   T   T

"Well, Daniel, I've never seen a finer mare!"

Daniel flushed with pleasure, for the praise from the tall young man, he suspected, wasn't given often. "Lady's the finest horse I've ever trained," he said proudly. "She can carry your weight I think, Mr. Washington."

It would take a strong steed to bear the weight of the master of Mount Vernon. At the age of twenty-one, Washington stood six feet three with broad shoulders, wide hips, and heavy legs. He gave the impression of great strength, and as Daniel had watched him ride the mare, he knew that Washington was the finest horseman he'd ever seen. Washington had bold features, including a broad nose and a determined chin. His eyes were deep-set, a gray-blue that seemed to look right into the heart of a man.

"I've heard fine things about your horses, Bradford," Washington nodded. He had met Daniel earlier on a trip to Fairhope, and the two had gone over the fine points of Lady then. "Your reputation has spread, Daniel. Mr. Rochester is fortunate to have a man of your skills. How did you learn so much about horses?"

Daniel warmed to the man, saying, "I had a good mentor back in England, sir. And I served a time in the cavalry."

"Did you indeed?" Washington's eyes lit up with interest. "I'd like to hear about that. Come along. We'll have something to eat." He led Daniel to the kitchen of the large house, where the two sat down and ate the meal set out by a female slave. Daniel was not a great talker, but Washington's genuine interest in his service with the cavalry was so intense he found himself speaking more than usual.

He halted once, laughing ruefully. "I'm talking like a magpie, Mr. Washington!"

"Why, I'm fascinated, Bradford!" He took a long pull at the mug of cider, then asked, "What did you think of the English as a fighting force?"

"The cavalry? There's none finer, sir!"

"So I'm told. What about the infantry?"

Daniel thought of the battles he'd seen and shook his head. "Well, Mr. Washington, to tell the truth, I wouldn't care to be a foot soldier in the king's service."

"Why not?"

"Well, the men are poorly paid, and they have to furnish some of their own equipment. It's a hard life, sir. But what I couldn't understand was how they could march into the face of enemy fire."

Washington pulled his chair closer. "I've never seen a battle fought that way," he admitted. "But someday I may. What's it like?"

"Well, the troops are trained to advance in close ranks. If a man in the front rank goes down, the man behind him in the second rank steps forward and takes his place."

"That must be fairly disconcerting to the enemy," Washington observed. "To see the lines keep filling up with new men."

"I suppose so—but it's chilling, at least it was to me." Daniel lifted his mug, sipped the cider thoughtfully, then set it down. "It's the way all armies fight in Europe, sir. The French do the same. What that kind of fighting means is that the army with the most men wins the battle. They just keep feeding troops forward until they overcome the enemy."

"Well, that's the object, isn't it?"

"Of course, sir, but in England and France there is more open farmland on which to fight." He glanced out over the fields toward the woods that lay in the distance. "That sort of tactic wouldn't work in this country. Here, there are too many forests and hills—no place to form large groups of soldiers."

Washington's eyes narrowed. "I've wondered about that myself. And I've heard that some of the king's troops haven't fared so well using those tactics in Canada against the French." His craggy face broke into a rueful smile. "I've heard that the French used the Indians to attack massed troops. *They* don't line up in nice neat formations, not the Indians! They hide behind trees and shoot from ambush."

Daniel grinned suddenly. "I expect the officers in His Majesty's army look on that with disfavor?"

"Indeed! They call them cowardly—but they don't seem to have found any new tactics to meet them." He frowned and shook his head. "We've fought two wars over territorial claims to the Ohio Valley and are about to wage a third, I fear."

"Against the French again?"

"Yes." Washington hesitated, then said, "As a matter of fact, that's the reason I bought the mare from Mr. Rochester. I'm leaving right away on a long, difficult trip. Governor Dinwiddie has commissioned me to take a warning to the French commander at Fort Le Boeuf against further encroachment on territory claimed by the king."

Daniel asked instantly, "Will they heed the warning, sir?"

"No, I think not," Washington answered. "It's gone too far for that. England's got her armies spread all over the world. The French are determined to keep their share of this new world. They'll never give it up without a fight."

"My indenture is up in two years, Mr. Washington," Daniel said. "I'd thought to settle in the Ohio Valley. With the way things stand, would you advise against it?"

Washington shook his head. "I'm afraid it would be unsafe. The French already are inciting the Indians to attack English settlers in that area." He paused for a moment, then smiled and added, "Come to Mount Vernon, Bradford. I can use a man who handles horses as well as you do."

Daniel was flattered by the offer and promised to think about it. Finally he rose, saying, "Good luck on your mission, sir. I wish I could go with you."

"When your indenture is up, come and see me. Governor Dinwiddie has made me an adjutant over a military district in this state. I could use a good man like you in the militia."

Daniel left Mount Vernon, highly impressed with Washington. The man possessed a steadiness that pleased him. Daniel would have liked the adventure of accompanying the big man on his trip to warn the French, but he knew that Rochester would not hear of it. His time of indenture stipulated seven years of service, and Leo would demand he fulfill the terms to the very day.

Two more years—and I'll be free to do as I please, he thought as he headed the team down the winding road.

He arrived at Pine Bluff at dusk and put up at an inn for the night. After a good meal, he retired early and slept soundly the whole night. Daniel woke up at the sound of the animals stirring in the stable. He went out to wash at the pump, combed his hair with his fingers, then entered the small dining room for breakfast. "I need to find a gentleman named Thomson," he said to the man who came and set a plate in front of him.

The innkeeper, whose name was Shockly, was a burly man with black curly hair. "That'll be Squire Thomson. He lives six miles down the road—but he ain't there. He's gone to Boston."

Daniel said, "I'm supposed to find a young woman named Holly Blanchard. She's going to work for my employer, Mr. Rochester. Do you know the girl?"

"Why, it happens I do." Shockly shrugged his heavy shoulders. "I heard her ma died. Didn't know she was leavin' the homeplace."

"How do I get there?"

Shockly gave careful directions as he filled Daniel's cup, adding, "The Blanchards are backwoods people. Don't come to town more'n three—four times a year. I knowed her pa and her brother. The old man died a few years ago, and I heard that young Blanchard married and moved on down to Georgia." He shrugged, adding, "That's all the family the gal had—guess she's got to work out."

Daniel finished his breakfast, thanked the man, then started out to find the Blanchard place. He had difficulty finding the old homestead, for it was far back in the woods. He finally drove up a narrow, twisting road and stopped in front of a dilapidated cabin. A man stepped out, and Daniel said, "I'm looking for a young woman named Holly Blanchard."

A voice came from inside the cabin, and a young woman stepped outside, carrying a small bundle. She was no more than sixteen or seventeen, he judged. "I'm Holly Blanchard," she said, stepping off the porch.

"My name's Daniel Bradford. Mr. Rochester sent me to fetch you to Fairhope."

The girl nodded, rather nervously, Daniel thought, then

climbed into the buggy as the man on the porch went back inside without saying a word.

"I'm ready," she said evenly.

Not much of a goodbye, he thought. Aloud he said, "Just put your things in the back."

"Yes, sir."

"You don't have to call me sir, Holly. I'm a servant for Mr. Rochester, just like you."

The girl nodded but said nothing. Daniel spoke to the team and guided them as they wound around the narrow road. "You lived here long, Holly?" he asked idly.

"All my life."

"Guess you'll feel bad leaving it." When she didn't reply, he said quietly, "I heard you lost your ma. I'm sorry about that."

The girl nodded slightly, and when Daniel glanced at her, he saw a tear running down her cheek. It disturbed him, and he remembered his vow to warn the girl about Leo Rochester. But she was filled with her private tragedy, and he refrained from adding to her burden. She would need some time to adjust to a new place and to settle in to a different way of life. He would keep an eye on her and talk to her at another time.

As they rode along, Daniel thought about his time at Fairhope. He had not formed close friends since he arrived in Virginia. He was fatalistic in his own way, preferring to keep those who would have been friendly at arm's length. It was not so much hardness, but rather caution that made Daniel build a wall around himself. Those difficult years after his mother died, along with the hard times in prison, had proven to him that life was fickle, so he had chosen not to make new friends. Better not to have them than to have them and lose them.

Daniel kept silent as they rode along, and the girl sat staring straight ahead at the road, saying nothing. At noon he stopped and brought out the lunch he'd had the innkeeper pack. "Well, let's eat," he said.

"I'm not hungry."

Daniel ignored her, saying, "I'm getting stiff. Here, we'll take a rest under those pines." He helped Holly down and handed her the satchel with the food in it. "You fix the lunch, and I'll take the team down to that creek for a drink." Without waiting for an answer, he unhitched the team and led them away. He took his time, giving the girl a few moments to herself. After the team had had a long drink from the winding creek, he led them back.

"That looks good," he commented, coming to where she'd spread the sandwiches and onions on a flat rock. He brought a jug out of the wagon and smiled at her. "No cups, but we can take turns with this ale." He sat down and began to eat. "Go on, Holly," he urged gently. "We've got a long ride ahead of us before we reach Fairhope. You need to eat something."

Slowly the girl reached out and took one of the sandwiches. As she ate, Daniel studied her covertly. She was not tall, and even though she was wearing a plain gray dress, Daniel saw that she was fairly pretty. She had thick brown hair and a beautiful complexion. Finally she looked at him with dark brown eyes and a heart-shaped face. "What's it like—where we're going?" she asked.

"Why, it's a nice plantation, Holly," Daniel replied. He told her a little about Fairhope, then asked, "You had no place else to go?"

"No. I got no kin—except my brother. He's gone to Georgia, with his wife's people."

Daniel bit into one of the onions, enjoying the strong flavor. "You didn't think to go with them?"

The girl hesitated. "We . . . didn't get on."

Daniel glanced at her and saw the troubled light in her eyes. *Well, she's got no other choice. She'll have to go to Fairhope, I reckon. And Leo will just have to keep his distance from her.*

The air was chilly, and when they got back into the buggy, he said, "Getting cold. You got a coat, Holly?"

"No, just a sweater." She rummaged through her sack, pulled out a worn brown sweater, and put it on. She had kept her right hand out of sight, but his eyes fell on it. She was missing the small finger and the one next to it.

Holly saw him looking at her hand and instantly thrust it under her sweater. Her fair cheeks flushed as if she'd done something shameful.

"How'd you hurt your hand, Holly?" Daniel asked, making his voice easy and natural.

"I . . . was holding a stick of wood . . . and my brother, he missed with his ax and cut my fingers off."

"That's too bad—but I'll bet you've learned to make do."

Holly turned and stared at him, her eyes betraying her fear at having to leave home. "I can do most anything," she said eagerly. "Even sew and spin and milk a cow. It don't hurt my work none a'tall, Daniel!"

She was so pathetically eager to convince him that Daniel was touched. "Why, I'm sure of it, Holly. You'll make out real fine."

The buggy moved along, and Holly whispered, "I ain't never worked out, Daniel. I'm scared I won't please them."

"Sure you will," Daniel assured her. "You'll be working for a housekeeper named Mrs. Bryant. She's real nice. I'll put in a word for you with her—you know, tell her you're new at this sort of thing and ask her to be patient."

Holly turned to him, her eyes warm. "Would you really?"

"You have my word on it." Daniel didn't tell her about Leo— or about how fussy Lady Edna was. He knew she'd just have to learn to put up with them as everybody else did.

By the time they reached Fairhope, the sun was almost down. "Come along and I'll take you to Mrs. Bryant," Daniel said. He leaped to the ground and came around to her side of the buggy. She picked up her bundle, holding it in her good hand—and looked to see Daniel extending his hand to help her. She had kept her maimed hand hidden. Now, however, she slowly withdrew it—and placed it in his hand.

Daniel was certain this was the first time she'd ever done such a thing. He saw the trust in her dark brown eyes as he gently closed his fingers on the injured hand and helped her to the ground.

"I . . . I thank you," Holly whispered.

I'll have to be a friend to her, he thought as he led her to the back door. *She's a pitiful little thing. . . .*

🕮   🕮   🕮

For the first two weeks of Holly's service, Daniel made it a point to stop at the house and visit with her whenever he could. He had spoken to Mrs. Bryant, who was a kindly woman, asking her to help the girl. The housekeeper had agreed, and just one week after Holly's being there, she reported, "Why, Daniel, she's as hard a worker as I've ever seen. Real awkward, but that's be- cause she's never been in a fine house like this. But tell her once, and she never has to be told again. She's a fast learner."

One morning Holly came out to the barn to milk the cows.

176

Daniel had been busy working on one of the carriages when he saw her cross the yard. Leaving his work, he walked over to the barn and entered. Holly was sitting on a three-legged stool, busily filling the pail. Seeing him come in, a smile brightened her face. "Oh, hello, Daniel."

"I hear good reports about your work from Mrs. Bryant," he said as he leaned against the wall.

"That's nice—I like Mrs. Bryant." She suddenly bit her lip, started to say something, then fell silent.

Daniel asked quietly, "What's wrong, Holly?" When she only shook her head, he asked, "Is it Mr. Rochester?"

Instantly her cheeks flushed, and she looked up at him, surprised at his question. "I'm . . . I'm afraid of him, Daniel!"

"I'll speak to him, Holly. Don't you fret anymore about it, you hear?"

"Thank you, Daniel," she said, a troubled look still in her eyes.

"Well, I need to get back to my chores," said Daniel. He went back to fixing the carriage and waited for a chance to talk with his master. Later that morning, Leo came to the stable to get a horse.

"Saddle Highboy for me," he said, his mind on his errand.

"Mr. Rochester, I want you to leave Holly Blanchard alone."

Rochester blinked with the shock of the blunt statement. His handsome face reddened, and he slapped his riding whip against his thigh. "Keep your mouth shut! I'll do as I please!" he blurted out.

Daniel came to stand before him. He was wearing a thin shirt and his chest swelled against it, the corded muscles clearly outlined. His hazel eyes were half-shut and his voice was controlled as he said coldly, "If you bother her again, Leo, I'll break your back."

Rochester lifted the whip, preparing to strike Bradford's face. However, something he saw in the eyes of the young man caused him to withhold the blow.

"Second thoughts are usually best," Daniel said.

Rochester flared out, "If you ever lay a hand on me, Bradford, I'll see that you rot in prison."

"Then who would make money for you to throw away at cards?" Daniel taunted. He had hoped Leo would strike him, for he was ready to retaliate.

Rochester hated to admit the truth. "You must be enjoying her favors, Daniel." He saw this as a way to extricate himself with some sort of dignity. "I want none of your leavings—go on and have the wench!"

Daniel said no more. He turned and went to saddle Highboy while Rochester glared at him. When he returned with the mount, Leo quickly mounted, struck the horse hard with his crop, and took off at a fast gait. Daniel stared after him as he disappeared down the lane. Later in the week Daniel questioned Holly. "Has Mr. Rochester been behaving himself?"

"Oh yes—thank you, Daniel!" She reached out and touched his arm with her left hand. Her eyes were bright and she whispered, "I don't know what I'd have done—without you!"

Daniel laughed and without thinking reached out and gave her a hug. "Really, it was nothing, Holly," he said, then walked back to the stables.

At the end of the day, Daniel stopped by the house. When he entered the kitchen, Mrs. Bryant looked up from her work. She walked over and slyly nudged him. "You've got a way with the girls, Daniel!"

"What's that?" said Daniel.

"I saw how Holly was staring after you today."

A little embarrassed, Daniel said, "What do you mean, I just gave her a little hug. That's all."

"You never looked at any of the girls—but you could have had some of them." Mrs. Bryant was a born matchmaker, and she leaned close and whispered, "She's a pretty little thing—and downright foolish about you! Why, she never takes her eyes off you!"

Daniel laughed. "She's from the backside of the woods, Mrs. Bryant. I don't think she's been around many men. You just wait and see. She'll take up with Henry or Jake!"

But as the weeks passed, Mrs. Bryant watched Holly and could tell that the girl was hopelessly enamored with Daniel. *She's moonstruck over him—that's what she is!* she said to herself. *And a good girl she is, too—not like some I could name!*

14

DANIEL AND THE LADY

"I've never been to a dance—I wouldn't know how to act," Holly said as she leaned on the fence rail and stroked the nose of the frisky new foal Daniel was training.

Daniel shrugged his shoulders and smiled at her. "Why, I'm not much of a dancer myself—but I could teach you enough to get by."

A few days earlier, George Washington had invited Daniel to a dance to be given by the local militia the following week. Daniel had mentioned it to Holly in an offhanded fashion, not knowing if she'd even consider his invitation. Now as she watched him work with the young chestnut stallion, he hoped she would say yes.

The colt lifted his head, snorted, then wheeled and galloped out across the pasture. Holly laughed. "He's a rowdy one, he is!" She had fit into her role as maid for Mrs. Bryant very well and, after almost a year's service, had become the lady's strong right arm. Holly had gained weight, and as Daniel glanced at her, he thought she looked very pretty in her blue dress covered with a white apron. Her glossy brown hair escaped from the white starched cap, and he noted that she still used her left hand to tuck it in. "I expect Micah will be jealous if you go with me," Daniel teased her. "He's moon-eyed over you!"

Holly made a face at him. "I'd as soon go with a *moose* as with

179

Micah." She looked up at him and asked abruptly, "When will your time be up, Daniel?"

"First of 1756." He walked over beside her and leaned on the rail. "It'll be a glad day for me," he said, staring out over the fields.

Holly's gentle eyes grew troubled. "I'll . . . I'll not know what to do without you here, Daniel. If you hadn't taken care of me . . . speaking to Mrs. Bryant . . . and to Mr. Leo . . ." She hesitated, then shook her head. "Maybe you'll settle close, do you think?"

Daniel shrugged his shoulders, saying, "Haven't decided." He reached over and picked up the bridle he'd stripped from the chestnut, then stopped and said thoughtfully, "I've thought of going into the army. Washington has asked me to join him. I could be an officer, in time."

The previous year, George Washington had been commissioned by Governor Dinwiddie to raise a force and proceed to the Forks of the Ohio and take command. He had asked Daniel to accompany him, but Daniel had to fulfill his time of indenture. Daniel was deeply disappointed at not being able to join the colonel's troops when they moved out. Washington's force met the French in battle but were completely outnumbered. Forced to retreat, he led his men to Fort Necessity, a small log stockade he'd constructed for just such an emergency. The French followed and Washington's small army was forced to surrender the fort. The French allowed Washington and his men to retreat to Virginia.

After Washington returned to Virginia, he spoke of the battle to his brother Jack. "I fortunately escaped without any wound, for the right wing, where I stood, was exposed and received all the enemy's fire. I heard the bullets whistle, and believe me, there is something charming in the sound."

Later Daniel had a meeting with Washington, who laughed at himself as he recounted his own words. "I spoke like a callow youth—which Horace Walpole insists that I am. He says that if I knew more of bullets, I would not find them 'charming.' "

But the excitement of the battle had bolstered Washington's confidence, Daniel could see, and he said, "Sir, if you take the field again, I hope to ride with you. My indenture is up in January of '56, so please keep me in mind."

"Of course I will! When we were having trouble with the horses, I told my second in command that if Daniel Bradford were here, we'd not be having such a hard time."

All this ran through Daniel's mind as he moved with Holly toward the barn. He was startled to hear Leo Rochester's voice to his left, calling out, "Bradford!"

At once he went to stand in front of the owner, noting that Holly quickly walked back toward the house. "Yes, sir?" he asked.

Rochester stared after the girl, then turned and glared at Daniel. It was obvious the proud man was still galled by being warned away from Holly. Despite Leo's threats, Daniel knew he'd never have any more trouble over it. He did, after all, bring in much income for the estate.

Leo struck his leg with his riding crop, then said, "We're having a visitor soon—a young lady. Her name's Marian Frazier."

"Yes, sir?"

"Well, she's crazy for horses, Bradford. I want you to see that she has a nice mare to ride while she's here—or whatever will please her." Daniel eyed him strangely, and Rochester laughed. "She has a very rich father in Boston. I may marry her someday, so I want her to see the best side of Fairhope."

"Is she a good rider?"

"Have no idea—but you see to it that she doesn't get hurt, hear me?" said Leo, an edge to his voice.

"I'll take care of it personally, Sir Leo."

The request was not unusual, for Daniel was normally asked to see to proper mounts for all the visitors that came to Fairhope. A week later, as the two of them rode to the small village where the dance was to be held, Daniel related Rochester's orders. "He's never mentioned marrying, that I know of. Her father must be pretty rich."

"Why would a rich man want to marry for money?" Holly asked in a puzzled tone. "He's got everything he wants."

"He that loveth silver shall not be satisfied with silver," Daniel responded. "That's in the Bible somewhere—can't remember where." He slowed the horses down to a walk and gestured at the cluster of houses that lay ahead. "There's Duttonville—the dance will be in the town hall, I hear." He sat loosely in the seat, his tall, strong form relaxed. He wore his best suit—a pair of brown knee breeches, white stockings exposing his muscular calves, and a maroon coat over his white shirt. Over his wheat-colored hair he wore a brown tricorn, which he now pulled down over his brow. "I'll bet she's homely—Miss Marian Frazier."

"But you've never seen her, have you?"

"No . . . but somehow I got it in my mind that she's a skinny old maid with a pointy nose and a shape like a rake handle!"

Holly laughed outright. "You're just silly! Why should she be plain?"

"Dunno. Just think she is." They were entering the village, and he admired the bright colors of the houses. They were mostly clapboard, with a few sober red brick homes. "Look like rows of dollhouses, don't they?" Daniel commented.

"I think they're pretty. Look, that one with the gingerbread trim—it's so nice!" A touch of longing came into Holly's voice, and she added, "I'd love to live in a little house like that. It wouldn't have to be big, though."

"You might have ten children," Daniel remarked, then laughed at her sudden surprised expression. "Why not? The girls would all be pretty—like you." He saw her flush as she always did when he paid her a compliment, then added innocently, ". . . and the boys would all be big and ugly—like Micah."

Holly sputtered and struck him hard on the arm with her fist. "You—you *blacksmith*!" she cried.

"*Blacksmith?* What kind of cussing is that? Maybe I'd better teach you something a bit stronger," Daniel said. He smiled at the reaction he saw in her face. He knew that Holly was a devoted Christian. From the day she'd arrived, she had faithfully attended the little Congregational church. "I tease you too much, don't I, Holly?"

Holly smiled slightly and blushed, then quickly changed the subject. "I don't think I want to try to dance. I'm too awkward."

But Daniel merely shook his head. "You don't go to a dance *not* to dance," he replied. "Besides, nobody will be looking at us."

He drove the wagon to the line of buggies and tied up the team. Reaching up, he helped Holly down—thinking of how she'd been ashamed to give him her maimed hand the first time he'd helped her down. *She's gotten over being uneasy about her hand—at least with me*, he thought. He liked the girl very much and took pride in the way she'd taken hold with her work. Even Lady Edna had made mention to the housekeeper how pleased she was with Holly's work. She reminded him of Lyna—whose memory was never far from his thoughts. Holly looked nothing like his lost sister, but she was kind, and Daniel felt like a brother to her.

When they were inside, Holly's eyes opened wide when she

saw all the decorations and the lights that glittered from a myriad of candles. "Oh, it's beautiful, Daniel!" she exclaimed.

He helped her off with her coat and, when he saw the dress she was wearing, shook his head in admiration. "Why, Holly...! You look very nice indeed."

Holly had been anxious for him to admire her dress. It was actually a dress that Edna Rochester had worn a few times, then tired of. Lady Edna had given it to Mrs. Bryant, telling her she could do with it as she pleased. And as soon as the housekeeper had heard that Daniel had invited Holly to the dance, she promptly offered it to Holly. It wasn't really stylish, but she'd worked on it, and now was happy at the admiration reflected in Daniel's hazel eyes. The dress itself was made of pink satin, and the Empire style with the bodice gathered lightly above and below her bosom looked very good on her. The skirt was full and clinging, with a row of satin swags near the hem line. The only jewelry she wore was a pair of small pearl earrings—borrowed from Helen, one of the other maids.

"Come along, Holly," Daniel said. "We'll see what sort of dancers we make." Taking her hand, he led her to the floor, noting that her heart-shaped face was tense with fear. *She's petrified*, he thought, and so he determined to make this an evening she'd never forget. "Now, isn't the music fine?" Daniel asked. To calm her he kept encouraging her as he led her through the sets. His tactic was successful—Holly moved over the floor with more ease than he'd hoped for.

The room was crowded with many Virginians who belonged to the militia. The uniforms were wildly different, for each unit chose its own, and yet there were many men, such as Daniel, who had no uniforms at all. The dresses of the women added touches of scarlet, green, pink, blue, and even such exotic colors as orchid and turquoise to the whirling kaleidoscope made by the dancing pairs.

It was a democratic sort of dance, for some of the wealthy planters such as the Lees and the Washingtons had come—mostly to encourage the men who served under them. Holly felt very much out of place among all the people, and when a tall man wearing a buff uniform came to speak to Daniel, she instinctively moved her right hand behind her back.

"Good evening, Daniel," Washington smiled, shaking hands

with Bradford. "Glad you could attend the Militia Ball. And this young lady is. . . ?"

"Miss Holly Blanchard, sir. And this is Colonel Washington, Miss Blanchard."

Holly curtsied and managed to return the greeting the tall man gave her. She had heard so much about Washington from Daniel and others that she was very glad to have a close view of him. He was not handsome, she saw, but there was a strength in his rugged features, mixed with a courteous demeanor. After the colonel left, she said, "He looks very kind, Daniel."

"He has a temper," Daniel replied. "But somehow he has a way with people. He can make men follow him."

The evening went by all too quickly for Holly, and when Daniel helped her down from the buggy back at Fairhope, he asked, "Did you have a good time, Holly?"

"Oh yes! I never thought I'd get to go to such a party."

It was late and a huge silver moon poured waves of light over the yard. "I'm glad," Daniel said, smiling at her. The light from the moon reflected in her eyes, and he said, "You looked nicer than anyone, Holly. I was proud to be with you."

She didn't speak for a moment, then she whispered, "Daniel . . . I want to tell you—"

She halted and Daniel saw that she was choked up. He leaned forward, put his hands on her shoulders, and gave her a kiss on the cheek—much as he might have done with Lyna. But then she leaned against him and looked up—and he kissed her lips. It was, he thought, a brotherly caress, but when her body brushed against his, he tightened his grip for a moment. Her lips were sweet and innocent, and he savored the youthful touch of them. Then he was aware that the kiss was not as brotherly as he had thought—so he drew back.

Holly had been roughly kissed twice and had disliked it each time. But there was a strength and comfort in Daniel's embrace that touched her. She was breathless as she looked at him, whispering, "Good-night, Daniel." She went to her room at once, which she shared with Sally, another maid, and went to bed. As she lay there, she knew she would never forget the evening, and she touched her lips with her fingers, thinking of his kiss—wondering if he would ever kiss her again.

T　　T　　T

"Are you Daniel Bradford? Mr. Rochester informs me you're to see that I get a suitable mount."

Daniel was examining the hoof of a tall jumper named Dunmore. When he dropped the hoof and turned to the young woman who'd entered the stable, he was speechless for a moment. He'd heard that Miss Marian Frazier had arrived—but he hadn't heard that she was a beautiful woman. He remembered telling Holly that she was probably very homely—but there was *nothing* homely about the attractive young woman who stood waiting for him to speak.

"Why, yes, miss," he said finally. "I'm Daniel. Welcome to Fairhope."

Marian Frazier was very tall, and her height was accented by the long green skirt she wore. She had a wealth of dark auburn hair, light green eyes, and a glowing complexion. In a day when many people had blackened or missing teeth, she had very even, white teeth.

"I've got a nice gentle mare that you'll like, Miss Frazier," Daniel said. He led her to the stalls and nodded. "Very good-tempered, Molly is."

"I'd prefer a more spirited horse. That stallion over there, I think might suit."

Daniel at once shook his head. "Oh, that's King, Miss Frazier—and he's a handful. Wouldn't be at all suitable."

"Put a sidesaddle on him, Bradford," the young woman commanded. When Daniel hesitated, she laughed at him, a musical sound. "Don't worry, I won't fall off."

Daniel protested, "I'm to give you whatever you require, Miss Frazier, but King has thrown some very good men."

"Well, he won't throw me!"

Daniel objected again, but in vain. He could tell from the determined look in her eyes that Marian Frazier was a strong-willed young woman, accustomed to having her own way. Finally she hinted that she would have to resort to speaking to Mr. Rochester. She was nice enough but totally determined to ride King, and in the end Daniel reluctantly gave in to her request.

He saddled the big horse and then his favorite in the stable, a black gelding named Midnight. When the horses were saddled, he came to hand her up. She mounted so gracefully he hardly felt the weight of her hand on his. He was holding the lines and handed them to her with a warning, "He'll try to get the bit in his teeth—so be careful!"

Even as he turned and mounted Midnight, he saw that King was up to his old tricks. The big stallion lunged forward in a move that would have unseated most riders—but the young woman merely swayed and laughed. She struck King lightly on the flank with the crop and turned to say, "Come along—see if you can catch me, Bradford!"

Daniel was a fine rider and had ridden and won many of Rochester's races. He leaned low over the gelding, whispering into his ear. Midnight was a fine horse, but not the speedster that King was. Still, the skill of the rider meant something, so he fully expected to catch the big horse soon enough.

The dust rose, swirling from the hooves of the two horses, as they galloped off. The young woman was riding perfectly, Daniel saw. He was a little shocked, for he was not accustomed to seeing such skill in a woman. And when Miss Frazier abruptly turned King's head and left the road for the rolling pasture, he was alarmed.

"Miss Frazier—there are holes in this field!" he called out. But she merely looked back and laughed at him. Gritting his teeth, he drove Midnight at top speed, intending to catch the fool woman and stop her!

But he had no chance at all, for King was running at top speed. Daniel looked ahead and called, "Don't try that fence—he's not a good jumper!" But there was no sign of obedience, and he held his breath as King took the fence, knocking down the top rail with his rear hoof.

Crazy woman—she'll kill herself!

Daniel guided Midnight over the fence, angry yet at the same time impressed with Marian Frazier's skill. Finally she pulled the stallion up short, and when Daniel caught up, he drew his own mount up alongside. He wanted to shout at her, but he knew that would never do—not after what Leo had told him.

The light green eyes of the young woman were gleaming, and her wide mouth turned upward in a delighted smile. Her cheeks were bright with color, and there was an air of freedom about her as she said, "Now—let's not argue about which horse I can ride, all right?"

Daniel felt his anger fade and was forced to smile at her. "Your father would probably take a stick to you, Miss Frazier," he said. "But my guess is that he didn't do too much of that when you were small."

"Not nearly enough!" Marian leaned forward and patted King's neck. "There have been plenty of people to tell me so. Now, show me the best trails."

Daniel spent the rest of the morning showing Miss Frazier around the plantation. She was intensely interested in everything—the crops, the advantages of slaves over free laborers, the problems of running a large business—and by the time they returned to the stable, he laughed, "You must be one planning to write a book!"

"Meaning I'm a nosy young woman? Well, I'm never bored, Daniel. Life is too short for that."

Daniel dismounted, and as she slid out of the saddle, King bucked unexpectedly. Daniel yanked his bridle down with a tremendous pull, at the same time catching the young woman with his free arm. He felt the pressure of her body for a moment, then set her on her feet.

Marian was embarrassed. "After all my boasting—to get thrown like a beginner."

"King's very clever. I think he stays awake nights thinking of ways to humiliate people." He held the big horse effortlessly with his iron grasp.

At first, Marian had not thought Daniel a very large man, but now she noticed with admiration the heavy muscles of his shoulders and arms and the swelling chest molded by the thin shirt. "You're very strong, Bradford," she remarked.

"A blacksmith has to be," he shrugged. "Can't shoe a horse with your brain."

Marian smiled. "Thank you for the tour. I expect we'll be seeing a great deal of each other. I love to ride—but your employer doesn't care much for it, does he?"

"Well, Sir Leo thinks of a horse as a means of getting from one place to another."

"And you don't?"

"No, I like the process." Daniel stood holding the lines of the big horse, the sun glinting on his light-colored hair. He was tanned and his hazel eyes grew warm as he added, "A horse is— well, more than just transportation. When you're on a fine horse and feel his muscles working as he flies over the ground, why, that's about the most exciting thing I know."

Marian stared at him, her eyes wide. "Why, that's the way *I* feel!" she exclaimed. "I get too emotionally involved with my horses—I cry when they hurt, and when my mare Lily died, I thought I'd like to die, too!"

The two stood there, sensing the excitement that comes when two people discover they have an interest in common. It actually matters little what it is, for it is the unity of the thing that joins them. When these people meet and discover that the other shares the same burning interest, the one wants to exclaim, "What! You *too*?"

Marian came to herself, conscious that she was showing too much of her inner heart to a servant she'd just met. Brusquely she nodded, "Well, we'll be seeing each other," and turned and walked back to the house.

And they did see each other—every day. Sir Leo had guests over, and riding around the grounds on the trails was a regular part of the activities. At night there were elaborate suppers and even a concert of chamber music one evening. But during the days, Marian spent a great deal of time in the saddle. Leo was tolerant, telling Daniel, "See she doesn't break her neck. She's worth too much money for that!"

Marian tried to keep a wall between herself and Daniel Bradford, but it proved impossible. She was a very rare creature—a wealthy woman with a genuinely democratic spirit. Most young women of beauty and wealth were snobs, but not so Marian. Her independent nature had no trace of arrogance, but rather an insatiable thirst to learn and experience everything she could. She enjoyed Daniel for his quick wit—and for his mastery of everything about horses. She would watch as he shoed a horse, asking question after question, and finally would sigh. "I wish *I* could do all the things you do—but I'm not strong enough."

"I don't think you'd like to have a blacksmith's muscles, Miss Frazier," Daniel grinned. "You'd look a bit odd."

A week flew by, and Leo sent for Daniel. When the young man entered his office, he saw Marian Frazier sitting in the window seat. He greeted her, then turned to Leo, who said, "Bradford, I've got a letter here from Colonel Washington. He wants to hire you for a time."

"Hire me for what, sir?"

Rochester frowned and snapped his fingers with some irritation. "You've heard about General Braddock's arrival from England?"

"Yes, sir. He's supposed to whip the Frenchies in the Ohio Valley."

"Yes. Well, Washington is going along as his aide. He wants you to accompany him. He's willing to pay for your time, so I'm sending you to join him." He scowled and flung himself into a chair. "I suppose you like the idea of playing soldier?"

"I'm sure he just wants me to help with the horses, sir—but I'll be glad to go."

"All right, be off with you—but don't dally after General Braddock whips the French, you hear me?"

"I'll come straight back to Fairhope, Sir Leo."

Marian looked up to smile at Daniel. "Good luck. Don't get yourself shot. You still haven't shown me how to train a horse to take a fence."

"I'll do that, Miss Frazier—and you watch out for King."

After he left, Leo stared at the young woman. "You like Bradford, don't you?"

"He knows more about horses than any man I've ever known. And he's handsome," she added slyly. "Does that make you jealous?"

Leo went to her, pulled her to her feet, and tried to kiss her. She avoided it, then laughed and left the room. "Come on, I'll let *you* ride King today!"

Daniel went and gathered his gear together, then headed for the barn. As he saddled Midnight, he was surprised that Sir Leo had granted his request to take the fine horse. When he turned to lead his mount out, he saw Holly standing at the entrance of the barn.

"Daniel, you're going to the army!"

"Just to shoe the horses for Colonel Washington, Holly. I won't be doing any fighting." There had been a reserve between them since he'd kissed her after the dance, and now he smiled and put out his hand. "Come now, say goodbye. I'll be back soon. We'll go to another dance."

She took his hand, felt its pressure, then he mounted and was away at a gallop. Turning slowly, she made her way back into the house, feeling lonely and a little afraid.

15

BLOOD AT
MONONGAHELA

"We must wipe out the shame of Fort Necessity!"

This one statement by King George set in motion the wheels of war. Determined to prove English soldiers were the finest in the world, he sent General Edward Braddock to America with two regiments of five hundred men each to fight the French. The general arrived in Virginia in February of 1755 with his troops. The Virginia Burgesses added their support by voting £40,000 to pay and equip four hundred fifty Virginians in nine companies to accompany the newly arrived general.

Braddock had had an exemplary army career for forty-five of his sixty years. However, his military expertise was about to be challenged. He was soon to learn that the wilderness of America was not suited for the tactics used on the expansive battlefields of Europe. As he organized his troops along with the colonial militia, he made one good decision. He had learned of George Washington and his military prowess and persuaded the tall man to accompany him as his aide.

Daniel Bradford joined Washington at Mount Vernon. Washington was accompanied by a deep-chested young man whom he introduced as Adam Winslow. "You two will be a great help to me," he smiled. "Adam is the best gunsmith in Virginia, Daniel, and you are the best with horses." The three men left at once, leading a string of fine horses for Washington's service. As they traveled, Washington explained his position to the two young men. "I will not be a part of the army itself—but an advisor on General Braddock's staff."

Later when the two young men were alone, sitting in front of a fire, Daniel said, "I don't think it's right, Winslow. Colonel Washington knows more about the enemy than the whole of Braddock's staff."

"I expect that's right, Daniel," Winslow nodded. He spoke slowly and thoughtfully. Adam was a husky man, with a ponderous strength in his movements. "It'll be more of a fight than these English officers think."

By the time Daniel and Adam arrived at Fort Cumberland, the two young men had become fast friends. The fort was bustling with activity as an army of 2,400 men was assembling. Daniel's first assignment from Washington was terse. "I'll meet with the general, and I want you to examine the horses. I want a thorough report on their condition. They will be vital to this campaign."

"Yes, sir," said Daniel.

Daniel moved among the troops, observing the various groups that had gathered. Some of the units included volunteers from Pennsylvania, Maryland, and the Carolinas. At one point Daniel stopped to talk with a steady-eyed man dressed in buckskin breeches named Daniel Boone and discovered that quite a number of the men were not soldiers at all. Many of them were simple backwoodsmen who had come along to help.

"Some of us are axmen," Boone informed him. "Our job is to clear a road to Fort Duquesne for the troops and all the equipment."

Daniel spent the rest of the day studying the horses carefully and was disappointed, to say the least. Many of them were spavined, broken hocked, and wind galled. He was staring at a sorry-looking specimen when a burly woodsman noticed him.

"Ain't much, are they?" grunted the large man. He studied Daniel carefully, asking, "Which unit you with?"

"I'm not with any unit. My name's Daniel Bradford. I came with Colonel Washington. . . ."

The man listened carefully while Daniel spoke, then spat an amber stream of tobacco juice at his feet. "Well, I was hired to drive this here wagon, but the shape these horses are in, I might have to pull it myself. I'm Daniel Morgan. You had anything to eat?" asked the man.

"No, and I have a friend who could use some grub, too."

"Well, go and fetch 'im whilst I fix somethin', and come have a bite."

Daniel went and found Adam Winslow and returned to Morgan's wagon a few minutes later. As the two sat down in front of the fire, Morgan poured cups of steaming coffee and handed them to the hungry men. Then he filled some plates with the stew he had made.

While Bradford and Winslow ate with the husky wagoner, Washington was speaking with General Braddock. The two men liked each other, and after introducing his new aide to his staff, Braddock outlined the tactics he was planning. The man was so thorough he had mapped out the expedition down to the last pound of bacon in the supply wagons.

Standing next to Washington, Braddock was a foot shorter, with more fat than muscle in his bulk. He wore a powdered wig under his winged hat, and his uniform blazed with bright decorations. "Tell us, George, what kind of fighting conditions can we expect?" asked the general.

"Well, it's not going to be like some of the fighting you're used to. The terrain around our objective," Washington said, noting the officers' reactions, "is one of thick forests and broken gullies. It will be difficult to maneuver troops, General," he explained. "And you will discover that the enemy will not meet you with a massed force. Indians know nothing about that sort of warfare."

"Ah, yes, they fight from behind trees, I am told." Braddock's bulldog face had a stubborn cast. "We will see them flee when they meet trained troops of England. They will be no match for us."

𝕀   𝕀   𝕀

Later, when Washington received Daniel's report on the condition of the horses, the colonel looked doubtful. "The train will break down, I fear," Washington said. "The general is taking two dozen six-pound cannons—not to mention four big howitzers and fourteen small mortars."

"Sir, the man has no idea of what he is getting into."

"I believe you're right, Daniel. I got the same impression when he asked me to explain to his staff about wilderness fighting. Some of those cannons he plans to take weigh over a ton." The tall man bit his lower lip, adding, "And then there's all the food for two thousand men and all the equipment."

"I met some of the men who'll be clearing the road," Daniel nodded. "But what bothers me is the lack of food for the horses. The general seems to have planned for his men but not for the animals. There's not enough in the train, and no horse can keep going on leaves!"

"Daniel, I want you to go buy a wagon and carry enough grain for our own animals," Washington decided.

Daniel waited until the man finished with some other instructions; then he went and found Winslow. They spent the next two days gathering sufficient supplies to take along. Daniel knew from his army days in England the rigors and demands that fighting put on the horses. He had learned in the battle at Culloden Moor against the Jacobites that if the animals weren't properly cared for, the army would suffer. It proved to be a wise decision, for later in the campaign, it was this food that kept their horses strong and active while others were starving.

The trek itself turned into a nightmare. The army moved out with all its equipment and slowly began its march north. Braddock sent a guard of highly trained British riflemen ahead of them with six blue-clad Virginians selected for their knowledge of the woods. On the flanks he kept outriders, and behind all these the three hundred axmen labored long and hard to clear the road. Every day was marked with endless hours of arduous toil. And the long train of men, horses, and supply wagons could only advance as fast as the axmen cleared the road ahead of them. The terrain proved to be an obstacle, as Washington had tried to inform the general. And the cannons Braddock had insisted on bringing were so large and cumbersome they slowed the advancing army down even more.

Washington wrote to his brother Jack about the difficulties they were having. He had tried to give advice to Braddock many times, but the general's arrogant responses had finally silenced him. As the days wore on, Washington learned to never give advice to Braddock unless asked for it.

In late June, the troops were plagued with dysentery, the old enemy of the soldier. Washington was among those who were afflicted. He became so weak he was forced to ride in the wagon, which Daniel drove. Unfortunately, the sickness came at a time when Braddock sorely needed the man's wise advice.

As time passed, Braddock grew more frustrated with the situation. He refused to listen to Washington's advice on fighting the enemy. And it was this inability to adapt to a new way of fighting and his harsh treatment of the troops that resulted in many bad choices along the way.

Braddock had been trained differently. For decades he prided himself as the general of highly trained soldiers who followed orders concerning military protocol down to the very details of a soldier's attire. The battles he had fought in Europe were often staged on large fields, where each day flanks of fresh troops in crisp red uniforms would advance across the battlefield like a colorful parade with guidons, drums, and trumpets. Here, each day was a lesson in survival as they cut through the thick forests. Some days the progress was slowed down by gullies, inclement weather, or broken wheels on the wagons. And as the troops trudged along through the wilderness, the stark contrast between the ideal soldier and the rag-tag appearance and behavior of the Americans grew daily in Braddock's mind.

The general made a grievous error one afternoon when a group of men from Pennsylvania came slouching in, offering to serve as scouts without pay. Their rugged appearance was so abhorrent to Braddock that he refused to use them. He was short with the Indians who accompanied the army, commanding them to wash off the grease on their faces—which they applied to repel mosquitoes. By alienating these men who knew the wilderness better than anybody, Braddock, in effect, lost the "eyes" of his army.

The British officers demanded the same sort of respect from the Americans as received from their own troops—which was impossible. One afternoon Daniel and Adam Winslow witnessed a scene neither of them would ever forget. Daniel was in line behind his friend Daniel Morgan, who was rebuked by an officer for moving along slowly. Morgan answered the man with a rough retort. At once the officer drew his sword and rushed toward the driver. Morgan snapped the sword from the hand of the officer and easily gave him a sound thrashing.

The cries of the officer drew instant help, and when Morgan was grasped by soldiers, the officer shouted, "Tie him to that wagon—give him twenty-five lashes!"

Morgan's shirt was stripped off, and a burly soldier stepped forward with a whip. Drawing it back, he brought it down across Morgan's naked back, raising a red welt. The beating went on forever, so it seemed to Bradford. Washington had heard the commotion and had lifted himself from his bed in the wagon to mutter, "Bad business!" When the last stroke was given, he said, "Take care of him, Daniel!"

Daniel and Adam joined Daniel Boone in cutting the unconscious man down. They bathed Morgan's back, applied ointment, then offered to drive his wagon.

"No! I'll drive it myself!" Morgan said, cursing the officer under his breath as he painfully climbed into the wagon. From that hour he nourished a bitter hatred for everything English.

🔔   🔔   🔔

Braddock's army arrived at the banks of the Monongahela River on July 9. The enemy lay directly ahead, and Washington had Daniel bring one of his horses with a pillow placed in the saddle. He had no fever, but he was extremely weak from suffering twenty days of the illness.

Getting into the saddle, he said, "Look—that's a beautiful sight, isn't it, Daniel?"

Bradford looked to see the red-coated regulars parade with unfurled guidons and drums beating and trumpets blaring. "I suppose the general's doing it to frighten the enemy," he said.

Adam Winslow said in his slow voice, "Somehow I don't think the enemy's going to run when they see a parade."

"Let's hope they do," Washington said, tight-lipped. "I don't like this ground. There's not much space to maneuver the troops and equipment. We need to get out of this thick wood."

The French commander, Captain Daniel Lienard de Baujeu, was well aware of the terrain and used it to his advantage. He was leading a heterogeneous army of Indians, and his scouts had kept him well informed on the progress of the advancing army. Now as Braddock crossed the Monongahela, Baujeu detected a weakness he could exploit. The British had moved into a *cul de sac*, with thickets on all three sides, and were flanked by deep gullies. At once he cried out, "Fire—kill the English!"

Lieutenant Colonel Thomas Gage was in the group that received the first fire from the enemy. He ordered his men into the battlefront and commanded them to return fire. The soldiers could see nothing, but they pointed their muskets at the bush and fired. The volley tore off leaves and twigs, leaving heavy smoke lingering around the trees.

Gage ordered his men to reload, then ordered again, "Fire!" Baujeu fell with a bullet in his forehead, and cannon came up to reinforce the foot soldiers.

The French fell back, and Captain Jean Dumas took command. "Do not fear them, my children!" he rallied. "See, when their officers order them to fire, there will be a time when they must reload. Take cover, then, after the volley, we will move in and have them!"

At this point, Braddock could have moved back to clear ground, but to retreat in the face of the enemy was a sign of weakness. His inflexibility in changing his style of fighting prevented him from ordering his men to take cover behind the trees. Instead, he rode to the forefront of the battle to urge the troops on. He was shocked to see the Virginians and the Pennsylvania axmen taking cover behind the trees. With the flat of his sword he beat his own men out of the cover and sent his aides to order the Virginians to fight in the open.

Boone was fighting beside Daniel Bradford and Adam Winslow. "It's like sending a cow to catch a rabbit!" he exclaimed. "Them Indians will cut them redcoats to ribbons—look at 'em, Dan! Going into them woods like they was on parade!"

Daniel Bradford was appalled at what he witnessed. To him it was plain suicide.

Adam shook his head, muttering, "They'll get slaughtered!"

Washington was also horrified at the sight. He rode up to Braddock to tell him to pull back.

Braddock saw him draw up at his side mounted on a powerful steed and said, "Now, sir, you will see how the English soldier handles an enemy!" He lifted his voice, shouting, "Charge!" and the troops slowly moved forward.

"Sir—this is the enemy's main body. We're outnumbered!" Washington protested.

"Nonsense! It's just a few skirmishers!" Braddock scoffed. But suddenly the general's horse was struck with a ball, and as he fell, Braddock screamed, "Charge the enemy!"

The massive force moved forward, marching in ranks, officers on horseback, drums beating the cadence. A wall of red filled the entire road as the men walked shoulder to shoulder.

Suddenly the woods erupted with a blaze of musket shots. Bullets hailed from the unsecured heights, and every bullet seemed to find a target! Within minutes the column was decimated. Yet the officers continued to order volleys into the woods at an enemy they could not see. Washington pleaded with Braddock to allow the Virginians to seek shelter, but Braddock insisted, "Let the French play the coward, but not we English!"

And so the senseless slaughter continued. The only remarkable thing about this battle was that the English lasted as long as they did. The first volley was fired early afternoon, and they remained on the field for more than three hours.

As the British officers fell, confusion and panic began to grip the remaining soldiers. Washington knew what would happen if they lost all sense of leadership. Seeing that most of Braddock's staff was killed, he took command and rode tall in the saddle, amid the screaming bullets, carrying out Braddock's orders. The soldiers sensed the man's courage and threw themselves back into the battle. Four bullets left burns where they cut through his coat. Two horses were shot from under him, but he never faltered. He secured a new mount and plunged back into the fray giving orders.

When a Mingo chief saw that no shot took the big man, he ordered his warriors, "Aim at somebody you can kill. The Big Man is under the protection of the Great Spirit!"

The fighting was so fierce that men were falling like flies all around. Daniel Morgan, his back a mass of scabs and scars, was struck in the back of the neck by a bullet that lodged in his mouth. He spat it out and kept firing!

Shortly after five-thirty, Braddock finally gave up hope. In two hours he had had four horses shot dead under him. Finally a bullet found its mark, passing through an arm and penetrating his lung. The fall of their leader sent the English army retreating in wild disorder. It was Washington who was the marvel of the day. He saved them by quickly organizing the Virginians and the Pennsylvania axmen into a rear guard, which held off the enemy.

Daniel Bradford was in the thick of the battle the whole time, fighting alongside Adam Winslow and Daniel Boone. The battle had been bad, but the retreat was even worse. All night they rode under the failing light of a dim moon. The casualties had been heavy, and at times their horses stepped on wounded men. Daniel was numbed by the agonizing cries of the dying. Some of the screams in the distance, he knew, came as Indians stopped to collect scalps. He shuddered at the thought and plodded on.

Fortunately the French were not able to follow up their victory. The fourth night after the battle Braddock died of his wound. Just before he died, he muttered faintly, "Who would have thought it? His Majesty's troops defeated by the French and Indians. We will know better how to deal with them another time."

The next morning Washington chose a burial place in the middle of the road and directed a brief funeral service. After the shrouded body was lowered into the grave, he ordered every wagon, every horse, and every soldier to march over it. The mound was flattened and no epitaph was written, so that the fallen general's body would not be dug up for a victory scalp and a resplendent uniform.

And so the battle was over—and the vaunted general and his trained troops were defeated.

As Washington and his two young aides made their way back home, they spoke little of the humiliating defeat they had just suffered. Only once did Washington give any indication of the tremendous grief he felt. The three were sitting before a campfire one evening, eating beef roasted on sticks. "All those brave men," he said suddenly, shaking his massive head. "And all for nothing!" Neither Adam nor Daniel replied, and finally George Washington added thoughtfully, "Perhaps one thing came of it—we know that the English method of war will not work in this country. Though it was a costly lesson that could have been avoided."

Washington and Adam Winslow left Daniel when they came to the crossroad that led to Mount Vernon. Daniel made his way back to Fairhope, depressed. His time of indenture was almost up, however, and he consoled himself with the thought that he would soon be a free man. Boone had invited him to join a group going over the mountains to settle in Kentucky, and Washington had offered him a job at Mount Vernon.

Finally he said aloud, "I'll be my own man—and that's more than I've been lately!" He thought of Lyna with sadness, wishing she were still alive so that the two of them might find a life together in this new world. Then he spurred his horse toward Fair-hope, anxious to see Holly—and thinking about Marian Frazier.

"I wonder if Marian has missed me." But then he shook his head, knowing that even if she had, such things were not to be.

16

Two Women

AFTER THE EXCITEMENT OF MILITARY LIFE, Daniel discovered that getting back into the flow of life at Fairhope was difficult. He had hated the blood and the suffering he'd seen at the Monongahela. But after years of indentured servitude, the freedom the adventure had offered was very appealing. It had opened up new vistas to Daniel and made him anxious for his time to come to an end at Fairhope.

Leo Rochester noted Daniel's restlessness as soon as he returned. One day Leo came to the stables and said sarcastically, "I suppose farming is too tame for a military hero?" Daniel said nothing but continued to fix the strap on the saddle he was working on. Rochester impatiently slapped his hands against his sides. "I'll not get much work out of you before you leave, I suppose."

"You've gotten your money's worth out of me," Daniel shrugged. His time of indenture would be up on the first day of 1756, and he was aware that the scent of freedom from Rochester was another factor that added to his restlessness.

Rochester hesitated, then nodded. "I can't deny that. Your knowledge of horses has helped line my pockets quite well. As a matter of fact, I'd like you to stay on." He laughed at Daniel's look of astonishment, adding, "I know—we've not been friends, but I need you around here. I'm no farmer—never will be. You've got the experience it takes to run this place properly." Leo had been mulling it over for weeks. Things had not run as smoothly during Daniel's absence. "You'll be manager of the whole estate. I'll give you a percentage of all the profits. Contract for five more years, and at the end of that time, you'll have enough money to buy your own farm if that's what you'd like."

"A generous offer, Mr. Rochester—but I'll be moving on."

Rochester felt a tinge of regret, but he was not surprised by Bradford's response. He had expected no other. "Very well, I'll have to get what I can out of you before you leave. I have an important errand for you. I want you to take six horses to Boston and deliver them to John Frazier."

"Miss Marian's father?" said Daniel in surprise.

"Of course." Leo noted the interest in Daniel's eyes and laughed. "You two were pretty thick when she visited here— spent almost every minute together riding. Well, one of the horses is a gift for her. I think it'll make her give in—stubborn wench!" His courtship of Marian had not prospered, but Rochester was a patient man when he wanted something—and he wanted the fortune that would come along with the only child of John Frazier, who owned a profitable foundry.

"When do you want them delivered?"

"Leave in the morning," said Leo.

Surprised at the suddenness of it, Daniel listened as Leo discussed the details. He had misgivings about Leo's interest in Marian, but said nothing as Leo went on.

Finally Leo cocked his head and smiled sardonically. "I don't suppose I can expect you to put in a good word for me, Daniel— just don't pour any of your hatred for me into my intended's shell-like ear." He laughed, then turned and walked back to the house.

Daniel was glad for the chance to get away from Fairhope. He even found himself anxious to see Marian Frazier again. He had never met a woman who intrigued him so, and he felt rather foolish for thinking of her. *She's in another world, Dan Bradford! Besides, Leo Rochester has his eyes on her,* he scolded himself.

He spent the rest of the afternoon preparing Lonnie Bates, his helper, on what to do during his absence, then went to say good-bye to Holly. Since his return he had spent little time with her. As he walked toward the kitchen, he wondered again what was troubling her. When he'd left, she'd been happy, but on his return he'd found her pale and subdued. She kept to herself and didn't talk as much to him as she used to. He was worried about her, for he could tell that something was wrong, yet he could not find a way to help.

"Well, Holly, I'm off again," he said when he entered the kitchen. She was sitting at the table shelling peas, and at his words, she looked up at him with an expression he couldn't define. Her eyes, which were usually bright, were dull, and her lips were drawn into a thin line. He hesitated, then sat down across from her. The kitchen was deserted for the moment, and he hated to leave her in such a despondent condition. "What's the matter, Holly? Are you sick?"

"No. I'm all right," she said as she worked.

Daniel noted that her voice, which was usually cheerful, had no joy in it. She looked—*different*, somehow, though he couldn't put his finger on what made her appear so.

She asked diffidently, "Where are you going, Daniel?" She listened as he explained his errand, then said quietly, "I hope you have a good time."

Daniel sat beside her for twenty minutes, but she was withdrawn, responding to his questions in a lackluster manner. Finally he said in a perplexed voice, "Something's wrong with you, Holly. I wish you'd tell me what it is. Maybe I can help."

For a moment, he thought she meant to speak out about whatever troubled her. She lifted her eyes to him, and for one brief instant he saw a ray of hope, and her lips opened slightly—then she closed them and shook her head. "There's nothing, really," she said, but he thought he saw tears beginning to form.

"I've got to leave, but as soon as I get back, we'll have a long talk," Daniel said. He rose and put his hand under her chin, entreating her to look up at him. Seeing the pure misery in her eyes, he said gently, "I don't like to see you like this, Holly. Whatever's bothering you, when I get home, I want you to tell me about it."

He gave her a quick farewell, then spent a troubled night worrying about her. Awake before dawn, he saddled up Midnight, and, with Mr. Frazier's horses in tow, started out on his journey to Boston. All along the way he thought about the troubled look in Holly's face. *She was so happy when I left to go with Washington—and now she's downright miserable. Guess I know a little of what that's like.* He realized how fond of her he'd grown, so he determined to get to the bottom of it as soon as he returned from delivering the horses.

🜊   🜊   🜊

The city of Boston was a busy place, and Daniel had some trouble guiding his small herd of horses through the crowded streets. He threaded his way through multitudes of horse-drawn wagons filled with heavy loads of produce. As he led his animals past Back Bay and through the town gates, geese and chickens exploded in noisy flocks in front of him. He had some difficulty finding the Frazier residence, but finally, after getting two sets of wrong directions, he pulled up in front of a very large white house set thirty yards back off the street. Most of the houses opened up right on the sidewalks, but this one, he saw, was built more like a country house, with large pillars holding up a portico and mullioned windows on the front and the sides.

He led the horses down the circular drive, stopping to ask the black man who was carefully clipping the green grass, "Is this Mr. Frazier's house?"

"Yes, indeed, sir." The man was tall and thin, with chocolate-colored skin and large intelligent eyes. "These must be the horses Mr. Rochester is selling. I'm Cato. Come with me, sir, and I'll help you stable them." He led the small procession around to the back of the house, where a brick stable offered ten stalls. As Cato helped Daniel put the horses into individual stalls, he said, "I'll feed them, Mr. Bradford. You'd best go see Miss Frazier." His white teeth gleamed as he smiled. "She ain't talked 'bout nothin' but these here horses for a week. Just go to the side door, and Emmy will fetch Miss Marian."

Daniel followed his instructions, and shortly Marian Frazier came running into the foyer, her green eyes alive with pleasure. She came to him, offering her hand, exclaiming, "I thought you'd *never* get here, Daniel! Did you bring the horses?"

Very conscious of her smooth hand in his, Daniel nodded. "I don't think I'd be very welcome if I'd come without them, would I?" He released her hand, intensely aware of her vibrant beauty. She was wearing a rose-colored dress that clung to her body, and her full lips were smiling with the same excitement he remembered.

"We'll go riding right away—but first I want to see them." She practically towed him out of the house and into the stables. Going from one horse to another, she demanded to know the names, the virtues, and the shortcomings of each one. When she came to the fine chestnut mare, the prize of the lot, she whispered, "What a beauty!"

"This one's for you, Miss Frazier—a present from Mr. Rochester."

Instantly Marian turned to face him, a strange expression on her face. "A present? What sort of present?"

Daniel couldn't repeat what Rochester had said, so he merely shook his head. "Just a present, I guess. She's the finest mare I've seen since I've been at Fairhope. Her name is Queenie."

Somehow the gift disturbed Marian. She stood there, absently stroking the nose of the mare, her eyes thoughtful. Finally she turned and asked, "Did he give you a message to go with the present?"

Daniel felt very awkward and wished she hadn't asked about Leo Rochester. He felt that she would be making a terrible mistake to marry the man—but how could he tell her that? Looking at the clean lines of her face, he hated the idea of her being the wife of a man who had no scruples or sense of decency. But he could only say, "No, Miss Frazier—no message."

The first wave of excitement that had brightened her eyes now faded away. Her voice was more restrained as she said, "Come along. I'll take you to my father and you two can get acquainted. Later, perhaps you'll come for a ride with me."

"Like we used to do at Fairhope?" Daniel suggested. "I've thought of our rides many times."

Marian looked at him and her good humor returned. "Have you? So have I." Mischief caused her eyes to gleam, and she suddenly laughed. "I can still beat you in a race—you'll see!"

Daniel spent a pleasant half hour with John Frazier and took an instant liking to the man. Frazier was a rather short man with piercing blue eyes and a set of fine whiskers, which he stroked fondly. He was an astute businessman, having worked his way up from a hired hand to becoming the owner of one of the largest foundries in the Colonies.

"My daughter tells me you're a fine blacksmith, Bradford," he said after they had settled the details of the sale. "Perhaps you'd like to see my foundry before you leave Boston. Be glad to show you around."

"I'd like that very much, sir," Daniel said eagerly.

"Well, *if* you can get away from Marian in the morning, you can go with me. She thinks you know more about horses than any man alive, and I think she has plans to keep you pretty busy."

The gentleman's words proved true, for Daniel spent the rest of the afternoon with Marian, trying out the new mare. They rode outside the city, and he discovered that she knew every inch where a horse could be ridden. When they were on a level green bordered by fences, she gave him an arch look. "Are you prepared to let me beat you in another race?"

Daniel was mounted on a tall, rawboned gelding named Fred and knew he had little chance to beat the speedy mare. "No bets— but we'll see."

Marian spurred her horse and took off across the field. Daniel followed her in pursuit, but as he had expected, Queenie beat the big horse easily, but he didn't care. He pulled up beside Marian, whose light green eyes were gleaming with pleasure. "You like to win, don't you?" he asked.

"Of course! Don't you?" she breathed, her face aglow from the ride.

"Haven't had much experience along those lines." Not wanting to sound pitiful, Daniel quickly added, "Next time I'll ride Big Red—he'll show you his heels."

"Tomorrow morning," Marian nodded. "We'll come early."

"Your father offered to show me around the foundry in the morning."

"Oh, Daniel, it's just a sooty, black, noisy old place!"

"It makes the money that buys you fine horses and pretty outfits like that one." She flushed slightly at his compliment, which surprised him greatly. *I'd think she'd be up to her pretty neck in pretty speeches.*

They moved along through the countryside, and he enjoyed the ride more than anything he could remember. When they returned and pulled up in front of the stables at the back of the house, Daniel helped her down.

"So you'd rather go with Father to the foundry than go riding with me?" she pouted. "I think I resent that, Daniel." But she was smiling and added, "All right—but tomorrow afternoon is *mine*!"

Daniel agreed, and the next morning he went with Mr. Frazier to see the foundry. He enjoyed his visit and watched everything carefully. Once he offered a suggestion that brought an approving glance from Mr. Frazier. Afterward, when he was leaving, pleading his promise to ride with Marian, Mr. Frazier said, "I'm always looking for good men, Bradford. Would you ever think of leaving your present position? I think I could find a place for you."

Daniel thanked him, and later when he was riding beside Marian down a shady lane, he told her of her father's offer.

"But would you like to leave Fairhope?" she asked at once. "Leo told me he planned to offer you a good position there when your indenture is up."

Daniel hesitated, then shook his head. "I'll be leaving the first of the year."

A few minutes later they came to a stream and dismounted. Daniel held the lines and let the horses drink, then tied them to a sapling. Coming to stand beside her, he looked around, "Pretty here—like Virginia."

The clear water murmured in a sibilant fashion over the smooth stones, reflecting the sunbeams with tiny flakes of light. The trees formed a natural canopy, giving the spot the air of a cathedral, and the green turf was soft under their feet.

"Daniel . . ." Marian said hesitantly, her eyes coming to rest on him. "What sort of man is Leo?"

"Why, you know him, Miss Frazier!"

"No, I don't. He's handsome and witty—and rich, of course." She bit her lower lip, which was a most attractive gesture to Daniel. She seemed uncertain for the first time since he'd met her. "I . . . I suppose all young women about to be married get nervous. It's . . . such a big thing, isn't it? I'll have to live with the man I marry until one of us dies. What if I make the wrong choice?" She suddenly took his arm, her grip tight, and there was something close to fear in her eyes. "You've been with him for a long time—and nobody knows a person as well as a servant does. You've seen him when he's off guard. So tell me, Daniel, what's he really like?"

Daniel had never been at such a loss for speech. All the years he had known Leo Rochester only confirmed the first opinion he'd formed that day so long ago in England. Leo was a self-serving man spoiled by his aristocratic upbringing, a man of unbridled desires who did not care what happened to others who got in his way. Marriage to such a man would be disastrous for this young woman. He knew that Leo Rochester was selfish to the bone, that he would never be faithful to any one woman. *How can I say that to her? But she needs to know what he is like,* he thought as they stood by the stream.

Turning to her, he said quietly, "I can't tell you what to do. But I can say, be very careful, Marian. He's a strange man."

Marian listened to his words, and for one moment she seemed completely vulnerable. She was an impulsive young woman, filled with the joy of living, but as she looked up into his eyes, she seemed to be begging for assurance.

She closed her eyes and whispered, "Oh, Daniel—I just don't know anymore!"

Daniel felt a great desire to protect her, knowing what lay ahead for her if she married Leo. He didn't deserve a woman who could give herself so totally to life. Moved by his thoughts and the moment, Daniel put his arms around her. She looked up, a startled expression in her eyes. He expected her to draw back, to protest, but she did not. Instead she leaned against him and whispered, "Daniel!"

Somehow a dream formed that he knew he'd had for years—yet he could not bring it out of the misty background, nor cause it to take shape. When she looked up at him with those light green eyes, he bent down and kissed her. He felt her wishes come up to him and suddenly knew that she was thinking of him as a woman thought of a man.

Marian welcomed his kiss. She had never given herself to a man's tender touch, but now as she felt the power of his arms, she made that surrender that she'd never been able to make. She had been struggling with her decision, but as she leaned against Daniel's chest, all that seemed far away.

Somehow a barrier had fallen, and she knew it would never be completely restored. In one brief moment, they had crossed the line between friends who care for each other to a man and a woman who feel the powerful surge of a new love. The effect of this kiss, she knew, would be with her for a long time. They were on the edge of the mystery which made love so desperate and so desirable a thing—and she wished she could always have this feeling of security—and of being loved.

"Marian . . ." he whispered as he looked at her. In that brief instant, he had hoped that what he felt could last forever. But he knew there could be no future for them. "I . . . didn't mean to do that."

Marian straightened at once and saw the desire in his face—and the hopelessness. She suddenly understood what he was thinking—*We're separated by everything. No one would understand—and life would be impossible.*

Marian felt a sharp stab of regret but knew what she had to do. "We're entitled to one mistake, Daniel," she said in a weary tone. She turned to the horses, and he helped to hand her up. They rode in silence for a few moments, then finally began to speak of unimportant things.

The next day Daniel left Boston at dawn. He had bid farewell to Mr. Frazier the night before, but he had not seen Marian. Daniel knew he would not see her again.

All the way back to Virginia, he was morose and withdrawn. Somehow he knew he'd lost something precious—*But it was never mine—never could be mine!* he told himself.

When he finally pulled up in front of Fairhope, he stared at it and said aloud, "I can't have her—but I'll not stay here and watch her be married to him!"

☤   ☤   ☤

If Daniel had not been so depressed by what happened on his trip to Boston, he might have noted that Holly was even more withdrawn than ever. But he was kept busy by new orders from Rochester, and on his free time, he kept mostly to himself.

About a week after he'd been back, Mrs. Bryant approached him while he was working with a new horse. She came right up to him, put her hands on her hips, and said, "Daniel, can't you talk to Holly?"

Later that day Daniel came to the house to get some scraps of linens, and her words caught at him. "Holly? What's wrong with her?"

Mrs. Bryant clucked her tongue and shook her head. "Men! You're all as blind as bats! I could drown the lot of you!" Her face was red with anger, and she faced him squarely. She was an angular woman, as tall as Daniel, and there was something formidable about her. She studied the face of the young man, then lowered her voice. "She's in trouble—bad trouble!"

Daniel stared at her blankly. "What kind of trouble?" he asked.

"What kind of trouble would a pretty young girl be in?" Mrs. Bryant was a plain woman and had been exposed to a bad marriage. She had a low opinion of most men, and now she shook her head almost fiercely. "Poor thing! She's green as grass, and some man's gone and taken advantage of her, Daniel."

Shock rolled along Daniel's nerves. "She told you this?"

"No, she didn't tell me—but I have eyes, don't I?" The angry eyes of the woman fastened on Daniel. "I thought it might be you—she's been in love with you ever since she came."

"Why—that's foolish!" Then Daniel added abruptly, "No, I've done nothing to her. And you may be wrong."

"She's leaving, did you know that? Why would she leave here if she didn't have to—and where's the poor thing going to go?"

Daniel felt a heaviness settle on him. Then anger rose at the thought of some man deceiving the innocent girl, but he fought it down. "I'll talk to her, Mrs. Bryant."

The woman studied him, then nodded, pain etched in her eyes. "Be kind to her, Daniel. She's the sort who knows all too well what rough treatment is." She turned, saying, "I'll send her out to you—go down to the grape arbor. It's quiet there."

Daniel left the house and walked down toward the arbor, his mind struggling with the tragedy. He felt a mixture of sympathy and concern; but at the same time, a burning anger at whoever had done it gripped him. He knew that Holly was a devoted Christian—and if this was true, it would make it even worse for her. He knew she had no place on earth to go, and the weight of that lay heavily on him.

Ten minutes later, she came down the path slowly. Daniel rose at once. "Holly, sit down," he said. Her face was pale and drawn, and her eyes were pools of despair. She sat down dumbly, and Daniel said, "Mrs. Bryant's told me about . . . about your trouble." He waited for her to speak, but she seemed to be paralyzed. Finally he asked quietly, "Are you going to have a baby, Holly?"

She dropped her head and tears rolled down her cheeks. Daniel put his arm around her, murmuring, "I'm so sorry, Holly. Is there anything I can do to help you?"

Holly turned to face him, her soft lips forming the words, "Oh, Daniel—I wish I were dead!"

"Don't talk like that!" Daniel was deeply moved by the terrible grief and shame he saw in the girl's eyes. His heart went out to her, and for a long time he sat beside her, gently assuring her that things would work out. Finally he said, "You can't leave here, Holly—"

Instantly she said, "Oh, but I must! I can't stay here!"

Abruptly Daniel thought of why she was so determined. "Who's the father of the child, Holly? He may want to marry you."

"No!" Holly cried. Leaping to her feet, she ran back up the path, leaving Daniel to stare after her. A mockingbird hopped up on the limb of the cherry tree to his left and began to chirp. Daniel stared at the bird, then whirled and ran after the girl, calling her name. . . .

17

A Free Man

AS THE LAST DAYS OF HIS INDENTURED time passed, Daniel became strangely moody, going about his work in a half-hearted fashion. His fellow servants couldn't understand his lack of excitement.

"Lord, if I was about to get myself out of this place and be my own man," Micah Roundtree exclaimed, "I wouldn't be mopin' around like you've been, Daniel! What's wrong with you?"

But Daniel had merely shrugged and gone about his duties. When the last week of his time rolled around, Leo called him to his office in the house. It was not as large as the one at Milford Manor, but Leo had furnished it quite well with the profits from selling the fine horses Daniel raised. When Daniel walked in, Leo was standing behind a large oak desk, a glass of brandy in his hand. Coming around the side, he shoved a small sheaf of bills at Daniel, saying, "There's the cash your papers called for." He hesitated, then said, "Now that you're a free man, what will you be doing?"

Daniel had kept his plans secret until now, but he saw no reason not to tell Rochester. "I'll be opening a blacksmith shop in Dentonville," he said evenly. It was a small town far enough away from Fairhope to escape his memories but close enough to Mount Vernon to serve as Washington's blacksmith. He did not add that it was George Washington himself who had suggested the matter and had, in fact, underwritten Daniel's initial expenses.

Leo Rochester stared at Daniel and said only, "You've earned your freedom, Bradford. We're not the same sort, are we? The first time we met, it was a fight. We're just not the same cut of cloth. But good luck to you."

Daniel took the bills, then turned and walked out of the office, hoping he never would have dealings with Leo Rochester again. He strongly disliked the man's vile character, and that would never change. He had suffered at the hands of the man more than once during his indenture. Many times the anger almost consumed him, causing him to strike out. But over the years Daniel had learned to control it, knowing that Rochester would have no qualms at throwing him back into prison.

He spent the rest of the day in the forge, his mind on the future—but when dusk came, he laid his tools down for the last time at Fairhope and went to gather up his belongings. As he tidied up the cabin he'd built and put on clean clothes, he thought of Holly—as he had done almost unceasingly since he'd found out she was in trouble. Every day he'd sought her out, trying to cheer her, but nothing seemed to lift her spirits. She had insisted that she was leaving, and when he tried to discover her plans, she seemed to have none—except to escape from Fairhope as soon as possible.

The wind was sharp when he stepped outside, and he sniffed the cold air. Tiny flakes of snow burned on his face, and he knew that by morning the ground would be covered. He went to the back door of the house, entered and found Mrs. Bryant cooking supper. "Where's Holly?" he asked at once.

Mrs. Bryant gave him a sharp look. "She's not been down this afternoon. I think she's getting ready to leave, Daniel. There's no talking to her."

"Go and get her, will you, Mrs. Bryant?"

Wiping her hands on her apron, she left the kitchen to get Holly. Daniel waited, and shortly Mrs. Bryant came hurrying back, her eyes wide with disbelief. "She's gone, Daniel—look, she left a note."

Daniel took the note and read it quickly. He could tell it had been written in a hurry. It simply said, "I can't stay here any longer. Thank you for your many kindnesses, Mrs. Bryant. Tell Daniel I couldn't bear to say goodbye to him."

Daniel scanned the note again quickly, then his mind began working. "You didn't see her leave?"

"I haven't seen her since two o'clock. She was in her room

then. Oh, what will the poor child do in her condition?" Mrs.
Bryant said, her voice breaking.

"She's headed for town," Daniel said instantly. "It's the only
place she could get a coach to leave here. I'll find her, don't
worry." He left the house, hitched a horse to the buggy, and drove
out at a fast gait. Doxbury was the closest stage stop, and it was
fully ten miles away. He turned west and kept the horse at a trot
as the snow began to leave a soft white blanket on the ground.

As he drove he thought of Holly's plight, and the image of her
tragic face came to him. His affection for her had grown over the
months, and now he realized he was going to have to do something. *She can't take care of herself*, he thought, his eyes probing the
road ahead. *She's as helpless as a kitten!*

He had not gone three miles when he saw her—a pathetic figure trudging along the whitened roadway struggling with a bundle. He felt a gust of relief and hurried the horses on. When he
drew close, he pulled the buggy to the side of the road.

"Holly!" he called, leaping down and running to her. She
turned to him and met his eyes with a hopeless expression. He
took her arm and held it tightly. "Come on, get in the buggy."

"I can't go back, Daniel."

Seeing that she was adamant, Daniel nodded. "All right, we
won't go back. Give me that!" He took her small bundle and led
her to the buggy. When he'd helped her in, he put the bundle in
the back and wrapped a blanket around her. "We'll go to Doxbury," he said. "I'll get you a room in the inn."

She didn't answer. All the way to town, Daniel tried to get her
to speak, but she could only answer in monosyllables. Finally they
reached the small town, and he pulled up in front of the White
Hart Inn. "Come along," he said. When they entered, they were
greeted by the innkeeper, a rotund, elderly woman named Mrs.
Bixby. "I need a room for this lady, ma'am," he said quickly.

"For how long?"

"Well, overnight at least."

Mrs. Bixby gave a curious glance at the pair, then nodded.
"Come along, I'll show it to you." She led them to a room upstairs.
It was small, but at least it was clean. Besides the bed, it had a
stand with a washbasin, a single chair, and a fireplace. "That'll be
two dollars—in advance," she said. Taking the coins from Daniel,
she asked, "Will the young lady be wanting supper?"

"Could you bring something to the room—for both of us?" Daniel asked.

Mrs. Bixby's eyes narrowed, but she nodded at Daniel. "Certainly, sir."

When she left, Daniel said, "I'll get a fire started, Holly. It's going to be cold tonight."

Soon a cheerful fire was blazing in the fireplace and Mrs. Bixby brought them some roast beef, bread, and a pitcher of ale.

"Here, this looks good," Daniel said, offering one of the wooden trenchers to Holly.

"I'm not hungry."

Daniel hesitated, then said, "You've not got only yourself to think of. There's the baby to consider now."

Holly started and gave Daniel a shocked look. It was as if she had not been aware that the child she bore was a person who had to be considered. She had been so overwhelmed by the shame of her tragedy that she had forgotten the baby growing within her. In her mind this little one was not yet a living, breathing human who would be a part of her life. Now she was brought face-to-face with the hard fact that she could never again think only of herself—the baby would be part of her in everything.

She took the wooden plate, ate a bite, then took a swallow of the ale. "It's . . . it's good, Daniel," she said, trying to smile.

"Did you eat anything this morning?" asked Daniel, a tender look in his eyes.

"No. I was too sick."

"Well, you'll have to have good food. Even I know that much about having babies."

He was encouraged as Holly ate a little more, and as the fire crackled, he began to speak gently of unimportant things. Finally she finished her meal, and he stirred up the fire. The flames flared up, sending myriads of sparks swirling up the chimney. "Fire's nice—nothing like a good warm fire when snow's falling."

"I've always loved the snow." Holly curled up in the chair, drawing her feet under her. The food had made her sleepy, and she sat quietly as Daniel spoke of his boyhood, and of the heavy snows he'd seen back in England.

Seeing that Holly was exhausted, Daniel said, "You need to rest. I'll be leaving you now." When fear leaped into her eyes he added reassuringly, "I'll be back tomorrow. You sleep late, and

we'll have dinner together. Maybe take a walk in the snow—
might even build a snowman." He saw her relax and smiled at
her. "Good-night, Holly. You get some rest, now."

Daniel left the White Hart and started back to Fairhope, but
he was troubled with Holly's situation. All the way back his mind
was filled with disturbing thoughts. She was so young and vulnerable. He shuddered at the thought of what could have become
of her if she had run away. As soon as he arrived back at Fairhope,
he unhitched the horse and rubbed it down, then went to the
kitchen and told Mrs. Bryant where Holly was staying. "She's all
right, but something's got to be done," he said, shaking his head.

"She's too young, Daniel, to be facing this alone. She only has
her brother, but she don't get along with that wife of his. What's
she going to do?" she said, wringing her hands.

"I don't right know, Mrs. Bryant, but we have to figure out
something." Excusing himself, Daniel went to his cabin and sat at
his handmade desk, racking his brain. An hour later he heard a
knock at the door and got up to open it.

"Hello, Mistuh Daniel." Horace, the slave in charge of the
grounds, smiled at him. "I come to ask you how Miss Holly is."

"Come in, Horace." Daniel stepped back, and when the small
man stepped inside, he said, "She's all right for now. I got her a
room in Doxbury."

"Poor little chile!" Horace was the pastor of the small black
congregation that gathered every Sunday. He and his wife, Molly,
had become very fond of Holly since the first day she had shown
up for the Sunday service. She had come to his services faithfully,
and now Horace asked, "Whut she gonna do, Mistuh Daniel? I is
worried about her."

"So am I, Horace. . . ." Daniel bade the man sit down, and for
some time the two of them talked over the problem. Finally Daniel
said, "I can't think of a thing, Horace. Don't know *what* to do!
She's got to go somewhere to have the baby."

Horace shook his head. "If we could, me and my Molly would
take her in—but Mistuh Rochester ain't gonna allow dat." His
kindly face was twisted as he sat there thinking. Finally he looked
at Daniel and said, "Is you a praying man, Mistuh Daniel?"

"I . . . I don't think I am," said Daniel, a bit surprised by the
man's gentle question.

"Well, mebby you ain't been up to now—but it 'pears to me

dat you is gonna *have* to start lookin' to de Lawd." Horace spoke for some time, giving Daniel several scriptures, including one that Daniel had never heard. "De Book, it say, 'And thine ears shall hear a word behind thee, sayin', This is the way, walk ye in it, when ye turn to the right hand, and when ye turn to the left.' Now *dat* is the promise of God, Mistuh Daniel!"

"Where is that, Horace?" Daniel demanded. "I never heard it."

"Right smack dab in Isaiah thirty, the twenty-first verse."

Daniel was not a great reader of the Scriptures, and his religion had been of a perfunctory nature. He had never forgotten his promise to his dying mother, however, and now he said doubtfully, "I don't think I'm in much favor with God, Horace. I haven't served Him like I should have."

"Why, dere's no better time to start than now. De good Lawd, He ain't particular 'bout dat! If He *wuz*, why, ain't none of us sinners could get nothin' from Him! But He say He loves you—and when you find a promise, why, jest hang on to it!"

Daniel suddenly nodded. "Well, I sure *need* to hear from God, Horace. You better pray that He gives me an answer—and pretty fast."

After the slave left, Daniel went to his trunk, pulled out his Bible, and found the verse Horace had just quoted to him. He read it several times, then found pen and ink and marked it carefully. He sat for a long time, doing what he'd never done—seeking God. . . .

🔔   🔔   🔔

On the fourth day of the year 1756, Holly was in her room waiting for Daniel. He'd promised her that he'd come early, and she had risen and was already dressed when his knock came.

"Come in," she said, opening the door. The days she had spent at the inn had restored some of her good nature, and she smiled as he entered. "Well, you're a free man now, aren't you, Daniel Bradford?"

"Yes, I am, Holly." Daniel was somber, she saw, and looked tired. But there was a peace in his eyes that was different. He suddenly took her hands, saying, "I'm not a servant of Leo Rochester, anyway." He hesitated, then said, "Holly, something's happened to me. . . ."

Holly listened as he told her of Horace's visit, and how he'd spent the last three days seeking God. She was very much aware that he was still holding her hands.

" ... and I've been praying for God to tell me what to do—and He has, Holly!" Daniel's eyes suddenly grew misty—something that was rare indeed—and he was struggling for words. Finally he said, "Last night ... God spoke to me!"

"Daniel...!"

"Oh, not in a literal voice, Holly, but it was God, I know it!"

"What did He tell you?" said Holly, looking at him intently now.

"He told me what to do with my life—and it was about you, Holly." Daniel dropped her hands and gripped her shoulders. With a tenderness in his hazel eyes, Daniel rushed on, "Holly, I know this is sudden, but I truly believe God has shown me that He wants me to be your husband and a father to your child. Holly, you and I will be together! You'll never be alone again!"

Holly was so shocked she couldn't speak. Daniel's words fell on her ears, but she couldn't believe she'd heard him rightly. And then he took her in his arms and kissed her. She surrendered to his strength, clinging to him fiercely. Leaning against him, she whispered with her face pressed against his chest, "Daniel ... are you *sure* it's of God?"

Daniel Bradford held her possessively, whispering, "Yes, I'm sure, Holly. We'll have our troubles to face, like anybody else ... but whatever happens, I'll always know that God is with us ... because He's the one who's telling me to take you for my wife!"

T   T   T

April sunshine splashed on the big man as he galloped into Dentonville. He pulled his gray stallion up with a flourish under the sign that read, DANIEL BRADFORD, BLACKSMITH. He came off his mount with the smooth motion of a natural-born horseman and greeted the man who came out to him. "Good morning, Daniel—what a day, eh?"

Daniel wiped his hands on his apron, then took the hand offered him. "Yes, it is, Colonel Washington. Reminds me of the time we were on our way to the Monongahela."

Washington smiled briefly, saying, "That seems long ago now, but it was just last year. I'll never forget it." Since that time, Washington had thrown his energy into restoring Mount Vernon. In the last year, he had already erected new buildings, refurnished the house, and even experimented with some new crops.

"How is the farm, sir?"

"Oh, business is excellent. And your good wife? Anything new? I'm ready to fulfill my duties as godfather anytime."

"Any hour, the doctor says, Colonel." He glanced toward the house where Holly was in bed on Doctor Fox's orders. "I'm more nervous than I was in that battle with the French."

Washington laughed. "Natural enough for a first-time father. Now, two things—first, you'll have to come to Mount Vernon sometime next week. That will be easier than bringing all the horses here. Second, I've got to press you to join the militia. I know it's taken all your time getting established in a new business—and it's commendable that you'd want to be with Mrs. Bradford for the birth of your firstborn. However, as soon as possible after the child is born, I would very much like for you to join. I need good men like you in places of leadership, Daniel. You'd be a tremendous asset."

Washington was a man to whom Daniel could refuse nothing. "Yes, of course, sir. I'll do my best for you."

Washington smiled with pleasure, then swung into the saddle and left at a fast gallop. Daniel thought of how fortunate he'd been to have had Washington's support. His business had been highly successful, for the patronage of the colonel had been enough to bring him more work than he could handle. He had been forced to hire an assistant, and now he was working on plans to build a larger shop and hire on another man to keep up with all the work.

He returned to his work, but half an hour later, Mrs. Stevens, who had been sitting with Holly, came hurrying into the smithy. "Mr. Bradford—it's time!"

Daniel dropped his tongs and ripped off his apron. "Take over, Tim!" he called over his shoulder as he ran toward the house. When he reached the bedroom, he took one look at Holly, then said, "I'll go and get Doctor Fox!"

He made a wild ride to the doctor's office, practically carried the physician to his buggy, and harried him all the way back to his wife's bed. Fox, irritated by the jostling, said shortly, "Go back to your shop, Bradford. I'll tend to this. You'll just get in the way!"

Daniel, however, remained in the house, pestering the doctor and Mrs. Stevens with nervous questions. It was a hard birth, but finally at midnight, Doctor Fox came out of the bedroom. He was tired as he wiped his brow, but he had a smile on his face. "You have a fine son, Daniel—go give him greetings."

Daniel rushed into the room, fell down beside Holly, and took her hands. "Are you . . . all right?" he whispered.

Holly was pale and worn, but she turned a tender smile at him. "Yes, I'm fine."

"And here's this fine boy!" said Daniel proudly.

Daniel rose to take the bundle Mrs. Stevens handed to him. He stared down at the little red face, unaware that Holly was watching him intently. Although Daniel had assured her repeatedly that he would love the child regardless of who his father was, she was still apprehensive. She had never spoken of the father, and Daniel respected her silence about the matter.

Looking down at the child, Daniel said nothing for so long that Holly grew fearful. But then he turned to her, a smile on his broad lips. He reached down and took her hand.

"I have a fine son," he said quietly. "What would you think of Matthew for a name?"

"Yes!" Holly's eyes filled with tears, but she squeezed his hand and whispered, "His name is Matthew—and may God make him the finest son a man ever had!"

18

MARIAN'S MISTAKE

THE GREATEST ARGUMENT AGAINST MONARCHY as a form of government might well be the century-long reign of the Hanoverian kings over England. Foreign bloodlines, political incompetence, and even insanity began to weaken the monarchy in the eyes of nobles and paupers alike.

George I ruled for thirteen years and never learned to speak English. His ineptitude was known throughout the empire. Rumors flew out of the palace and all through the kingdom that George I loved pleasure and would gladly add to his mistresses any woman who was very willing and very fat. The German-born ruler had little interest in the internal affairs of the country. As a result, he left politics in the hands of his incapable ministers, ushering in the role of Prime Minister—and letting the real power of the empire slip from the hands of the monarchy. The stage was set for others to wield tremendous power over the people of England.

Unfortunately, the royal bloodlines produced no competent successor to the throne, for George II was no improvement. Short and stout with the puffy, gargoylelike features of a true Hanoverian, he possessed all the petty vices, including raw avarice. He had an undying hatred for his son, Frederick, the Prince of Wales, whom he banished from the court. Once he stated flatly, "My dear firstborn is the greatest beast in the whole world, and I most heartily wish he were out of it." The true power behind the throne came by subtle influence from a very capable source, his wife, Queen Caroline, along with Horace Walpole, the Prime Minister.

But on June 4, 1738, a son was born to the Prince of Wales, a boy named George who was destined to rule England after the death of his father. He was so frail at birth that his parents had him baptized at midnight, fearing that he would not live through the night. He survived, however, and was so carefully sheltered in his nursery that by the time he was eleven he was still unable to read English. His education was flawed, lacking in the preparation required of one who was to ascend to the throne. When his father was killed in 1751 in the most undignified manner—struck in the head by a tennis ball—his mother turned his upbringing over to Bubb Dodington, whose evil influences greatly effected the ruining of the mind and character of young George. His mother then took a lover, Lord Bute, who completed the task.

At the age of seventeen, the young prince read a book that changed his life. Unfortunately it was not the Bible, but a political tract titled *Idea of a Patriot King* by Viscount Bolingbroke. It set forth the notion that monarchs should be above all influences, including party or profit. His only concern should be the welfare of the people. Corruption should be stamped out wherever it existed.

The American patriotism that cried for independence was just such corruption. Young George took the motto of this book as his creed and determined to crush any resistance to the monarchy. When George III was crowned King on October 15, 1760, the angels in charge of England wept!

T   T   T

The crowning of a new monarch may have been all important to some, but Daniel Bradford took no notice of the event. He had more pressing matters to consider. His wife, Holly, was pregnant with her fifth child and was not doing well.

He was trying to keep the children entertained while Doctor Fox examined Holly. Rachel was the only one who was quiet, but at the age of one she had not yet developed the lungs her three brothers had. She sat propped up against the wall, her thumb in her mouth, large green eyes watching owlishly, her bright red hair glinting in the amber beam of the whale-oil lamp that glowed on the table.

Dake and Micah, identical as two beans, swarmed over Daniel, who was sitting on the floor. At two the twins were large for their age, and their wheat-colored hair and hazel eyes made them miniatures of their father. They had his high cheekbones and broad forehead, and the same cleft in their rather pugnacious chins. The resemblance to their father was almost comical, but Daniel delighted in it. "Now you'll never have to ask what I looked like when I was a boy," he was fond of telling Holly.

The twins loved to wrestle, and when Daniel allowed himself to be pinned to the floor, Dake yelled, "See, Pa! We win!"

"You sure did, Dake." He had named the boy Drake—after the great English seaman—but Matthew could not quite manage that, so he had become "Dake" to all of them.

"Come on, Pa," Matt pleaded. "You promised to take us for a ride." At the age of four, Matt was not as large as the twins, though he was quicker in mind and body. He had light brown hair and blue eyes, and gave promise of becoming a handsome man someday. His features were more sharply chiseled than those of the twins, and he was far more restrained. Dake and Micah were loud, boisterous, and outgoing, while Matt was given to quiet periods and was somewhat withdrawn when it came to meeting new people.

"A little later, Matt. You can ride to Mr. Lassiter's with me." Looking at the boy, he thought of the years that had passed since he'd first held him. Daniel was proud of Matt, and he had been careful to play no favorites between him and the twins. It had not been difficult, for somehow he had never been troubled by the fact that Matt was not his real son. He'd asked God to give him a love for the boy—and his prayer had been more than answered. Time had softened the memories of the circumstances surrounding the birth of his firstborn, and he was tremendously grateful for Holly and for the wonderful children God had given them.

When Doctor Fox walked out of the room, Daniel rose quickly. "You fellows wait here. Take care of Rachel, Matt." He led the physician into the parlor and asked at once, "How is she, Doctor Fox?"

Fox had aged somewhat since Matt's birth. His hair and beard had turned silver, and his face was more lined. He stroked his beard slowly, hesitating as he formed an answer. "She's having a hard time, Daniel." He shrugged, adding, "I'm sorry she's having this child, to be truthful. She nearly died when Rachel was born."

Daniel remembered the doctor's warning that Holly should not have other children, but she had longed for another baby. Now he felt a stab of regret that he had allowed her to override his own wishes. He talked to Doctor Fox quietly, attempting to elicit an optimistic outlook, but the physician was gloomy. "Don't let her out of bed and send for me as soon as the labor starts. Will Mrs. Taylor be with her?"

"Yes, and her daughter will help take care of the children." Mrs. Taylor was a widow who lived close-by, and Fox had great confidence in her. After giving a few instructions, the doctor picked up his black bag and left the house, shaking his head.

As soon as Doctor Fox left, Daniel went at once into the bedroom. Going to the bed, he leaned over and forced a hearty note into his voice as he kissed Holly. "Well, now, Doctor Fox says it won't be long."

Holly looked very ill. The pregnancy had been worse than her others, and her skin had a pale color. Her cheeks were drawn in, and her eyes sunken. "He's not happy with me," she said quietly. Reaching up, she took his hand and held it, her grip weak.

"Oh, you know Fox." Daniel forced a grin. "He's never satisfied with any of his patients. You're going to do just fine, Holly." He sat down and held her hand for some time, speaking of the arrangements he'd made with Mrs. Taylor and her daughter, then of the children.

Holly lay very still, her eyes on his face as he spoke. She had been different during this pregnancy, Daniel had noticed—quieter and somehow lacking in the joy that had been with her before. Once Daniel had found her weeping—something that had very rarely happened in their marriage. She had shrugged it off, saying that she was just weepy and that there was nothing to worry about.

Now as she lay quietly, Daniel saw some sort of expression in her face that he could not read. He finally asked tentatively, "Holly, what's the matter? Are you frightened?"

"No, Daniel . . ." Holly hesitated, then a struggle seemed to take place in her. Her drawn face moved, and her lips seemed to draw into a tight line. She stirred restlessly, then finally whispered, "Daniel, I've been thinking so much of Matthew these last few days."

"Matthew? Why, he's fine, Holly!"

But she shook her head, and her grip on his hand tightened. "I don't mean that he's sick or anything like that." The sunlight streaming through the window fell across her face, a pale yellow

light that accented the lines in her face, making her look older. "It's
. . . about his father."

Daniel blinked with surprise, for they had not spoken of this
since their marriage. He had told her that the past was dead, and
that Matthew was his son. Holly had been happy with that, and
now he was somewhat shocked at her words. But he saw she was
troubled—more than he'd seen her in years. "What is it, sweetheart?" he asked gently.

"If anything happened to me, no one on this earth would ever
know who Matthew's father is." She reached up with her maimed
hand and stroked his face in a tender fashion. "Oh, Daniel, you've
been a *real* father to Matthew—and I've loved you for it! No man
ever loved his son more than you love him!" Allowing her hand
to drop, she fell silent. Daniel waited, troubled by this, and wondered why she was so burdened.

"Does it matter, Holly?" he finally asked.

"I hope not . . . but somehow I keep feeling that I should tell
you. I've been praying about it, and I think I must." She looked
up at him, her eyes filled with pain. "I think you should know,
Daniel . . . though I don't know why I feel this way. Somehow I
think God is putting this on my heart."

Daniel could see the hesitation in her eyes, yet he could tell it
was very important to her. "All right, Holly, if you feel that way,
maybe you should tell me." He was suddenly aware that she had
carried this burden alone for all these years. The important thing,
he realized, was not that he knew Matthew's father, but that Holly
must not carry the weight of it alone any longer.

"It . . . was Leo," she whispered, her lips twisted. "He forced
me, Daniel. He caught me alone and had his way with me. I
fought him . . . but he was too strong." Tears overflowed and ran
down her pale cheeks. "When I found out I was with child, I was
afraid I'd hate the baby—because of that. But then you came and
I loved you so much! And you've been so good to Matthew!"

Daniel was not too shocked at her words. He hadn't allowed
himself to think much about whom the father had been, but he
remembered now that back at the time, he'd been suspicious of
Leo Rochester. It had been wise of Holly not to tell him the father's
name. *I'd probably have killed him,* he thought—but the passage of
time had dulled the rage that would have come when the wound
was fresh. Now he felt a dull anger and bitterness. But he knew

as well that he would never say a word to Leo Rochester about Matthew.

He leaned over and stroked Holly's hair, then kissed her cheek. "Now I know," he said softly, "and you've done what God asked you to do. I don't want you to have one more troubled thought about this. It means nothing, Holly—nothing! Matthew Bradford is my firstborn son—and nothing under God's heaven is going to change that!"

"Oh, Daniel—" Holly cried, a light touching her eyes. "I love you so much!"

Daniel sat beside her, speaking of other things. He could tell she was relieved, and soon she grew sleepy. He kissed her, saying, "You sleep now. I'm going to make a quick trip to Mount Vernon. Mrs. Taylor is here if you need anything."

When he emerged from the room, Matthew and the twins swarmed him, reminding him that he'd promised to take them for a ride. "All right, but just a short one," he agreed. While they were scrambling to get ready, he went to Mrs. Taylor in the kitchen. "I'm going to take the boys for a ride," he said. "I won't be long, but I'll have to make a quick trip to Mount Vernon. You'll see to Mrs. Bradford?"

Mrs. Taylor was a motherly woman of fifty. "Of course, sir. You go right on." After he left the kitchen, she resumed mixing dough, but her thoughts were on Holly Bradford. Mrs. Taylor was knowledgeable in all matters relating to childbirth, and her brow wrinkled as she thought, *I don't like the way she looks—she's going to have a bad time, I fear. . . .*

🔔　　　🔔　　　🔔

Martha Washington smiled as she said, "Mr. Bradford, have you met Mrs. Rochester?"

Daniel kept his expression free of the quick stab of emotion that ran along his nerves. He bowed to Marian, saying, "Oh yes, Mrs. Washington. Mrs. Rochester and I met several years ago."

Marian had seen Daniel coming across the room talking to Colonel Washington, so she had been able to compose herself. She had seen Daniel Bradford only once since he had left Fairhope, and that had been a brief encounter at which they had murmured but a few words. Daniel had never returned to Fairhope, and their paths had not crossed anywhere else. As the wife of Leo Rochester she normally moved in higher social circles and was taken aback to see him now.

"Yes, Mr. Bradford is responsible for the fine stock we have at Fairhope." She managed a smile, adding, "Queenie is still my favorite, Mr. Bradford."

Daniel had gained control of himself enough to make a comment about the horses, and then Colonel Washington and his wife were called by a servant. When they had moved away, Marian said, "Colonel Washington has told me how you've prospered. I'm glad to hear of your success." She took in the plain dark broadcloth he wore, noting that he still looked roughly handsome.

Daniel asked, "Mr. Rochester isn't with you?"

"No. He's in London on business," she replied, her answer very clipped. Afraid that Daniel might suspect how unhappy she was in her marriage, she at once asked, "You have a family, I understand?"

"Yes, three boys and one daughter. Mrs. Bradford and I have been greatly blessed." He hesitated, then added, "We're expecting our fifth very soon. As a matter of fact, I must hurry back home right away."

Marian nodded. "I have no children," she said, the statement stark and unadorned. "I hope to see you again—but give my best wishes to your good wife."

"I will, and thank you," Daniel said politely, yet noticed how distant she seemed.

She turned to go, but then suddenly said, "I still remember our rides, Daniel. They were very good."

"Yes, I think of them often. You were very kind to me."

Her lips parted and her eyes brightened—and then she abruptly said, "I must go now. Goodbye."

The brief encounter unsettled Daniel somehow. All the way home he thought of how troubled she seemed. *More beautiful than ever—but her eyes have so little joy! She was always so full of life, and now it's as if she's been drained dry.* He thought of the kiss they'd shared, and how he'd never forgotten it. For years he'd felt guilty and disloyal, had tried to bury the memory, but it would lie dormant for months—only to rise again.

His marriage to Holly had been good. She had been a loving wife, and he loved her dearly. But it had not been a grand passion—in all their married life he had never felt for Holly what he had felt for Marian Frazier that one day by the creek. As he approached his home, he thought, *What sort of a man are you, Daniel Bradford? You've got a wife who's been faithful and true in every way—and you think of a boyish love!* He shook his head angrily, determined to put out of his mind forever that feeling he'd had for Marian Frazier—no, for Marian *Rochester*.

Dismounting in front of his house, he was met at the door by Mrs. Taylor. One look at her face and his heart seemed to contract. "What is it?" he demanded. "Is her time come?"

"No—not yet. But she's having other problems." Mrs. Taylor's plain, round face was drawn with worry. "I think Doctor Fox had better come and look at her, Mr. Bradford." She shook her head, adding, "She's not strong—and I'm concerned."

Daniel left at once and went to find Doctor Fox. Fortunately, he was not out making rounds. He was sitting behind his desk in his office when Daniel burst through the door.

"Doc, you've gotta come. Mrs. Taylor thinks something's wrong with Holly," said Daniel, his face drawn with worry.

Fox grabbed his coat and bag and quickly followed Daniel outside to where his horse was hitched in front. He told Daniel to ride on ahead and he'd be there shortly. Daniel took off at a fast gallop as the doctor followed behind at a fast gait. When Fox arrived and entered the kitchen, he saw Mrs. Taylor coming out of the bedroom, concern etched on her face. Daniel was in the kitchen trying to keep the children quiet, but Fox could tell from the drawn lines on his face, he was scared.

Doctor Fox examined Holly, then came out into the kitchen. "Stay with her as much as you can. I don't know exactly what the problem is—but she's having difficulties, Daniel."

For the next three days Daniel scarcely left the house. He tried to help out with the children the best he could, but he spent most of the time just sitting beside Holly. A gnawing sense of dread was growing inside him, and he was frightened. The other births had not been easy, but this one was—different. Holly was suffering terribly, and when she did sleep, it was a fitful rest, waking up in pain and drenched in sweat. Daniel tried to comfort her, soothing her brow with a cool cloth. Often, she would lift her hand to his cheek and tell him how grateful she was for his presence.

Finally she went into labor, and Alice Taylor came and took the children away. Daniel walked the floor, enduring the strain badly. He slept in short naps and ate only when Mrs. Taylor forced him to.

After hours of hard labor, a baby boy was born. Doctor Fox came out, wiping his brow, and said in a hard tone, "Get the children here!" He chewed his lip, then shook his head. "She's going, Daniel—there's nothing I can do. I'm sorry."

Daniel's mind went numb. Mrs. Taylor left instantly at the doctor's word and returned a few minutes later. When they came through the door, they all looked at once toward their father. Daniel took Rachel in his arms, saying, "Boys—your mother—she wants to see you."

Matthew gave him a look that Daniel never forgot. His eyes were filled with fear and he whispered, "Is she dying?"

Daniel could not answer the boy nor bear to look into his face. He said hoarsely, "Hurry, son—!"

They all gathered around the dying woman, and when she held up her arms and called them by name, Matthew, then Dake and Micah were embraced. "Let me have her—" Holly said and took Rachel in her arms. She kissed the silken hair, whispered endearments, and then asked for the baby. Cradling the small form in her arms, she tenderly looked into the tiny face. She said softly, "Tell him his mother loved him dearly—and call him Samuel." Then she held up her hand to Daniel, whispering, "Husband—" When Daniel bent and held her, she whispered faintly in his ear, "All my love—to you, my dear husband—as it's ever been!"

Daniel's eyes were burning with scalding tears, and he held her with trembling arms. He felt the strength going out of her, and wanted to call her, to keep her from slipping away.

But he heard her whisper, "I love you—but—I must go—to Him who loves me—!" She said clearly in a stronger voice, "Lord Jesus—!" and then she was gone.

Daniel held her for a long moment, then straightened up. He kissed her cheek, and the boys came, all of them weeping. Daniel picked up the baby, held him tightly and, looking down at his face, thought, *I'll do the best I can with the children, Holly, I promise!*

🎺　　🎺　　🎺

The funeral was difficult, and afterward the children were a problem—especially Matthew. The sudden loss of his mother affected him terribly. He would sit for hours staring at nothing. He became irritable easily, and at times would cry inconsolably. The twins were not affected as deeply, but it took all the patience that Daniel had to keep his promise to Holly.

He let his assistants run his business, and for two weeks he threw himself into caring for the children. The women of the neighborhood came and helped, often bringing some sort of dish or baked goods to help out. But Daniel was growing weary and cast down by the tremendous grief and responsibility that he bore. Finally Mrs. Taylor took him in hand one day and said, "Go hunting—go to town, Mr. Bradford!" she exclaimed. "You can't stay with the children all the time. Now go!"

Daniel stared at her, but realized that she was right. He left the house and walked all day in the woods. He was spiritually and emotionally exhausted, and for three days he roamed the hills. Slowly the silence of the forest seeped into him. At night he built a small fire and cooked a rabbit he'd shot earlier. Finishing his meal, Daniel lay on his blanket looking up into the starry heavens. The gentle breezes rustling through the leaves soothed his jangled nerves, and finally he began to pray. On the third day, God gave him a great peace that settled down into the depths of his troubled heart.

When he returned home, he entered the house, calling out, "Matt, where are you? Micah—Dake?"

The three boys came running to greet him. He picked them up, hugged them, and was relieved to see that they were well.

And then he turned to see a woman holding Rachel. At first he thought it was Mrs. Taylor—but it was not. He swallowed hard, then exclaimed, "Marian—!"

Marian was holding Rachel tightly in her arms, and her eyes were fixed on Daniel. "I—came to offer my respects." She seemed embarrassed, and said quickly, "Mrs. Taylor's daughter is ill, so I volunteered to help with the children until she recovered."

Micah cried out, "She can make the *best* taffy, Pa!" And at once Dake and Matthew joined in with Micah and began singing the praises of their new keeper.

Daniel went at once and held out his arms to Rachel, who was squirming in Marian's arms. "How are you, sweetheart?" he asked, kissing her silken cheek. She patted his cheeks and began pulling at his hair.

Finally Daniel and Marian were able to get the children settled.

She had made taffy and put Matthew in charge of letting them throw it at a nail on a board. While they were noisily engaged in pulling the sticky confection, Marian found herself alone in a corner of the big kitchen with Daniel. She was flushed, but her eyes were bright as she related how she'd kept the children entertained. When Daniel tried to thank her, she shook her head. "It's been such a joy, just being around them," she said softly. "I love children, and they're so sweet!"

The two of them spent some time with the children, and then Marian said, "I must go, now that you're here to take over."

Daniel asked before he thought, "Will you come back, Marian?"

Marian gave him an odd look, then shook her head. "I don't think that would be wise."

At once Daniel knew what was in her reply, what Leo Rochester might do if he knew his wife was seeing a former servant. He said quietly, "I understand."

Marian left at once, and on her way back to Fairhope, she thought in bleak despair, *I've made the worst mistake a woman can make. I never loved Leo—not as I love Daniel Bradford!* It was the first time she'd allowed that thought to surface in her mind. And now as she rode along under a gray cloudy sky, she knew that the future would be as bleak as the sky above.

As for Daniel Bradford—he went about pulling his life together, refusing to entertain thoughts of anything except his promise to Holly. *I'll do the best I can for the children.* He knew that he had missed something that could not be replaced, but doggedly he set his heart to give his children—including young Samuel who would never know his mother's caress—the best he could.

PART FOUR

—

THE SHOT
HEARD ROUND
THE WORLD

1770–1775

19

MASSACRE IN BOSTON

THE BRAZEN CLANGING OF HAMMERS on iron filled the enormous high-ceilinged room. Men blackened by smoke from the furnaces pounded white-hot steel into curves, angles, and concentric shapes, sending showers of sparks swirling upward, flickering brightly, then fading like diminished miniature stars. The air was thick with scorching leather, sweat, and acrid smoke that burned Daniel's eyes as he passed along between the two lines of workers. His quick glance took in the apprentices who pumped the leather bellows, and he stopped long enough to ask one of them, "How's your mother, Timmy?"

The young man, no more than sixteen, nodded quickly. "Oh, she's better, Mr. Bradford—and she says to thank you for lettin' me off to help until she got better." A rash grin flashed from the boy's sooty face as he added, "And she said to tell you she's prayin' for you every day!"

Daniel slapped the young man's shoulder, saying as he moved on, "Well, I need all the prayers I can get, Timmy. Tell your mother I'm glad she's better."

Moving on, Daniel was not aware of the glances of approval his simple act of pausing to speak to the boy drew from the other workers. When he had bought a half interest in John Frazier's foundry, the workers had been aloof, but soon they'd discovered that not only was Daniel Bradford as good at the forge as they, but he was a good boss as well.

When John Frazier had written and offered him a partnership, Daniel had almost refused. *It will put me too close to Marian,* he had thought instantly. However, after thinking it over and deciding that his feelings for Marian were not a factor, he accepted Frazier's fine offer. As soon as he'd found a buyer for the smithy, he had packed up his family and moved to Boston in 1765. Now five years later he was in charge of the day-to-day operations of the foundry—and not a man was unhappy with Bradford.

Leaving the shop by a side door, Daniel walked up a flight of stairs, moved down a narrow hall, then stepped through a door into an outer office. He nodded at Blevins, the bookkeeper, asking, "Is Mr. Frazier still here, Albert?"

"Yes, sir, he is. Said he wanted to see you before he went home." Blevins was a tall, cadaverous individual with sharp features and a thin-lipped mouth. He had been with John Frazier from the beginning, and the astute man knew every aspect of the company better than either partner. He had been stiff with Daniel at first but had warmed to him when he'd discovered that Bradford was willing to learn. Despite his craggy, rather sour look, Blevins was a kindhearted man who was thoroughly devoted to John Frazier. "I don't like the way Mr. Frazier's looking," he said. "He's never gotten over his bout with pneumonia he had last year. Why don't you try to get him to go south for a time?"

"I'll do that." He winked conspiratorially at the bookkeeper, adding, "You're the real boss around here, but don't let anybody find out about it." He moved through the door to the inner office and found his partner sitting at the desk, staring at some designs. "Hello, John," he said, taking off his apron and hanging it on the wall. He peered down at the drawings and nodded, "What do you think? Can we do it?"

John Frazier had sold half interest in his business to Daniel five years earlier because he was beginning to have health problems. He needed a young, energetic partner, and he had found him in Daniel Bradford. It had proved to be a wise decision, for his health had not gotten better. Frazier was only fifty-nine, but he had the frail look of an invalid. His color was pale and ashen, and he had lost considerable weight since Daniel had come.

Looking up, he nodded, "Yes, these are good, Daniel. But can we make money on casting cannon?"

"Don't know," Daniel shrugged. "Not much market in the Col-

238

onies, and we can't sell them in England. But we ought to find a market, John. Men are going to fight, and they need cannon."

Frazier's mouth drew into a straight line. "If those fools in Parliament keep digging at us, we might need cannon to teach them a lesson." Seeing the surprise on Daniel's face, he laughed shortly. "I sound like one of Sam Adams' Sons of Liberty, don't I? Well, I don't go that far—but it's getting worse, Daniel."

"Yes, it is. I had hoped that the Stamp Act fiasco would have brought the Crown to its senses."

As the two men talked about the growing tensions between the Colonies and the Crown, Daniel expressed his incredulity at the king's stubbornness in the face of American resistance. England's attempt to tax all legal papers in the Colonies had exploded when Sam Adams and his Sons of Liberty had gone into action. These patriotic rowdies had rampaged through the Colonies, spreading their zeal for liberty from Maine to South Carolina, encouraging people to refuse to buy the stamps, and stirring up a storm of violence. King George was stunned by it all and quickly backed down.

But no sooner had the king repealed the Stamp Act than he suffered the first of his terrible fits of madness. He hid from the public behind his palace walls, existing on potatoes and water, and avoiding any direct contact with the people. He blundered into handing over control of the empire to Charles Townshend—the new Chancellor of the Exchequer—who used his power to cripple the Colonies further by slapping heavy duties on all imports from England, which only fueled the colonists' growing hatred.

The death of Townshend in 1767 did nothing to alleviate the situation, for the mad King George replaced Townshend with the *one* man in England who could stir the anger and bitterness of the colonists even more than Charles Townshend—Lord North. North pursued a headstrong course of forcing the colonists to obey his predecessor's tax laws.

Daniel recalled that tense day in May of 1768 when two British warships had sailed into Boston Harbor and began "impressing" men into service—a British euphemism for kidnapping unsuspecting colonists and enslaving them into service in the Royal Navy, with no chance to alert their families of their whereabouts. Incensed, the Sons of Liberty mobbed the Crown's Inspector of

Customs, and England retaliated in typical fashion by sending troops into Boston.

"If only Britain hadn't sent those troops here," Daniel said. "It was like pouring gunpowder on a fire! No good can possibly come of it."

John nodded solemnly. "No, I expect not, Daniel. I'm afraid we are facing difficult times indeed." Rising painfully to his feet, Frazier took his coat and allowed Daniel to help him into it. He settled his tricorn hat on his head, then said, "A letter came from Marian this morning."

At the mention of Marian, Daniel felt a peculiar jolt. He had felt odd about becoming a partner of John Frazier's—for he had known for years that his love for Frazier's daughter was hopeless. He had kept his relationship with her under careful control. He had seen her and Leo only a few times, but neither he nor Marian ever referred to their brief moments of intimacy they'd shared during her first visit to Fairhope years earlier.

"How is she?"

"Very well. She doesn't like it in England. Says she's coming home soon." Frazier hesitated, then said briefly, "Leo won't be coming—he's not finished with his business, Marian says."

Daniel knew that Frazier was very much aware of what kind of "business" his daughter was referring to. Through the years he had sadly discovered that Leo Rochester centered his life around wenching, gambling, and heavy drinking. Leo's reputation was bad, and it was the grief of Frazier's life that his daughter had not gotten a different husband. However, Daniel carefully avoided any mention of Leo's name, saying only, "You've missed her, John. It'll be good for you two to have some time together."

"Yes, it will. Well, good afternoon, Daniel. Let me know what we're going to do about casting these cannon," said Frazier as he turned and left the office.

Daniel moved to the window and watched the frail figure climb painfully into his carriage. He thought for one instant of Marian but quickly put away the small but insistent feeling that rose at the thought of seeing her again. *Can't be thinking like that!* he rebuked himself, then turned and sat down to work on the drawings of the cannon.

After working for an hour, he rose and put on his coat. He left the office, bidding Blevins a good day. He saddled his gelding at the stable and rode out, his mind filled with cannon designs. It was a project he'd been interested in for years, and now he was determined to be one of the few men in the Colonies who could produce such powerful guns.

As he passed along the streets of Boston, Daniel saw several red-coated soldiers and thought of how tense the situation was getting. Confrontations between soldiers and citizens were growing uglier each week. The animosity had grown so deep that there had been a few incidents of rocks being thrown at the soldiers, and the soldiers had retaliated by leveling their bayonets and threatening to draw blood. They had not made good on those threats—not yet.

He pulled his coat closer about him and shivered in the early March chill. The gray skies and raw wind seemed a portent of troubled times ahead. Daniel jumped as a man on the street shouted, "Filthy lobsterbacks!" He swung around in the saddle to see two British soldiers riding by, their faces stoic, staring straight ahead, ignoring the taunts and jeers of a small group of men who had joined their comrade.

Daniel had never had a hatred for the Redcoats. He knew too well that they were a miserable lot themselves—so poorly paid that most of them were forced to seek part-time work to furnish the bare necessities. And for this the working class in Boston resented them highly, since jobs were hard to come by.

Lobsterbacks! He really couldn't blame the colonists for using the epithet, a reference to the bloody floggings with which the British army enforced its brutal discipline. He remembered such a flogging years before on his trip to the Monongahela. *Daniel Morgan—he's become quite a leader in resisting the Redcoats. Little did that British officer know what he was doing when he laid a whip to Morgan's back,* thought Daniel as he rode along. He continued on toward home, anxious now to get out of the cold and rest by a warm fire.

As Daniel drew close to his house, he saw a small crowd gathered in the street, surrounding a tall British soldier. It was easy to identify the man by his red woolen overcoat and the pointed hat of an infantryman.

A poorly dressed workman was standing in front of the soldier, and Daniel heard the man cry out, "Lobsterback—go back where you come from. We're tired of the looks of you here!"

"Out of my way, Yankee Doodle!" replied the soldier. He lifted his Brown Bess rifle and the bayonet gleamed faintly. "Let me pass—I have work at the docks."

The colonist shouted, "Work at the docks?! You already have a job!"

"I need the money—now back up!" he threatened, nervous at the gathering crowd.

Daniel caught a flicker of movement, and even as he dismounted, he saw a stone flying through the air. It struck the soldier's hat and a cry went up from the crowd. Daniel caught a glimpse of the boy who'd thrown the stone and saw others reaching down for more.

"Stop that!" he cried loudly and, stepping forward, put himself between the soldier and the crowd. He made a formidable shape in the fading light, his broad shoulders and solid neck tense. "Be off with you now!" He watched the crowd reluctantly move away, then said to the soldier, "Sorry about this."

"Thank you." The soldier nodded, turned on his heel, and marched stiffly down the street.

Daniel went back to his horse and led him to the small stable behind his house. After he unsaddled and fed the animal, he descended the narrow stone steps leading to the back door of his house. When he stuck his head into the kitchen, Mrs. White said, "Dinner's ready, Mr. Bradford."

"All right. I'll wash up and be right there." Mrs. Letty White was his housekeeper, a strong woman of sixty who served as cook—and kept the children under her strong hand. Daniel asked, "Children give you any trouble today?"

"No, sir—none that I couldn't handle," she said as she stirred a thick soup in the cast-iron pot suspended over the open fire.

Daniel went to his bedroom, washed, changed clothes, then came back to take his seat at the head of the table. After greeting each of his children, he bowed his head and said grace, then helped himself to a generous serving of the rich soup. "How was school today?" he asked. He listened as the five of them related the events of their day, examining each one—thinking of how different they all were.

Matt, only thirteen—so different from the others! So quiet that I wonder what's going on in that head of his—and sometimes something seems to break out in him and I see a temper that could be frightening. He studied the straight back, the light brown hair and blue eyes, wondering if he had done his best for the boy. *Holly could have drawn him out, but I haven't been able to touch whatever's in him. Maybe it's the artistic streak in him—not at all like me in that way.*

He shifted his eyes to the twins, who were two years younger than Matt, but broader and stronger. He took in their straw-colored hair and hazel eyes—so much like his own—and noted the small scar on Dake's left eyebrow, almost hidden by his hair. He remembered how Sam had administered that scar. Dake had been teasing his younger brother and Sam had hit him in the head with a stick. Ever since then, it had been an identifying mark—the only way most people outside of the family could tell the two apart, but the twins' personalities and behavior were distinctive to their own father.

Dake will always be that, not Drake which I named him. Matt couldn't say it—so Dake it is. Always involved in some kind of mischief—too quick to speak and just as quick to jump into things. A temper like a firecracker— but never holding a grudge. I wish he had more of Holly and less of me in the matter of temper.

He looked over at Micah, who was sitting across from him, noting how precisely he used his knife. Whereas Dake shoveled his food into his mouth, Micah cut his meat into small, neat portions and ate almost as daintily as a woman. *That's Holly, that gentleness,* he thought almost sadly. *Never loses his temper and always has a smile for everyone. Loves books just like she did, but the best worker of the three—steady as a rock!*

Now Daniel had to smile as he looked on his youngest son, age nine. *Sam—you're a different breed!* He admired the strong, short figure, the rich auburn hair and abundant crop of freckles and the electric blue eyes. *You'd take the house—or anything else— apart if I didn't watch you! Got the most mechanical touch I ever saw in a boy—and not afraid to tackle anything.*

Finally, there was Rachel—with her red hair and green eyes. Daniel hardly ever looked at her without thinking of Holly, for she had her mother's heart-shaped face and widow's peak. *More beautiful than your mother—but not as sweet, perhaps.* At the tender age of ten, she was the tyrant of the household—able to get her own way, in most cases, from her brothers or her father. She looked at him now and smiled—and a poignant memory touched Daniel, for he'd seen her mother look just so a thousand times.

Finally the meal was over, but they stayed at the table talking, a custom Daniel both enjoyed and insisted on. It was a time he used to instruct the children in something, and now he said, "There was a soldier in front of the house as I came in. Someone hit him with a rock." He saw Sam cast an involuntary look at Dake but ignored it. "I'm asking you not to join in harassing the soldiers. Those men you see had no choice about coming here. They're only following orders, and most of them hate it."

Dake stuck his chin out pugnaciously. "But, Pa—it ain't *right*! They make hardworking colonists quarter them!"

Daniel saw in Dake's set features a reflection of himself at that age and said easily, "I know, son, but we can't do anything about that. What we can do is act like gentlemen."

"The Sons of Liberty say we ought to fight them," Dake argued.

"That's treason, Dake," Matthew spoke up, his lips drawn tight. "They're the servants of the king—and we are, too."

"Aw, who cares about Old Mad George?" Sam quipped. His hair was standing up wildly, and he waved his square hand in a wild gesture.

Daniel allowed the argument to go on for some time. He believed his children had the right to think and speak their minds. He often joined in heartily, taking sides with one of the boys. This time it was Dake and Sam against Matt and himself. Rachel merely sat and listened. The argument came to an end when Sam lifted his head and said, "Listen—it's the bells, Pa! There must be a fire!"

Daniel heard them, too, and said, "You all stay here!"

"Pa, let me go with you," Dake begged, and the others joined in. But Daniel rapped out his order to stay in the house, then rose and grabbed his coat.

Outside he found men running toward the center of town. "Is it a fire?" he asked Thomas Sealy, his neighbor.

"No, it's the Redcoats—they're shooting some of our people!"

The words cut along Daniel's nerves, and he ran with the rest toward the commotion. When he reached the Customs House, he saw Henry Knox and went up to him at once. Knox was a fat young man who owned a prosperous bookstore, but who was highly interested in military matters. He and Daniel had gotten to know each other well, and they had spent much time talking about guns and cannons.

"Ed Garrick's been hurt by that lobsterback," Knox said, his fat face glowing with anger. He looked around and muttered, "This is an ugly crowd, Daniel—and it could get worse."

As more people gathered in the street, the scene started to get out of hand. Soon they began throwing snowballs and chunks of ice at the soldier. Dodging the missiles, he tried frantically to get inside the Customs House, but the door was locked. In the dim flickering light of the moon, Daniel could read the hatred on the faces of the mob. "Henry, these are toughs from the waterfront," Daniel said. "We've got to do something."

Knox nodded and the two men shoved their way to the front, trying to speak, but loud voices kept screaming, "Kill him! Knock him down!" The situation was getting worse by the minute. Then Daniel saw a British officer and a few soldiers at the edge of the crowd. He knew the officer, Captain Thomas Preston, and respected him. Daniel pushed his way through the mob and said, "Captain, take care of your men!"

Knox was alongside him, his face pale. "If they fire on these people, they're dead men!"

"I'm aware of that," Preston replied. He looked over the crowd, which seemed to contain much of the male population of the town. "Fall in, Private White," Preston ordered the beleaguered soldier.

At the officer's command, a roar went up from the crowd, and when they charged forward, Preston ordered his men to form an arc. By then snowballs and ice and curses began to fly from all directions toward the soldiers, and the mob began chanting, "Fire! Why don't you fire!"

The situation had turned into a powder keg ready to explode. Just as Preston was moving his men slowly away, a club came flying out of the crowd, striking one of the soldiers and knocking him down. The soldier struggled to his feet, fury spreading over his face. He fired but the shot flew high, hitting no one. The crowd yelled and surged forward, and a private lifted his musket, aimed, and squeezed the trigger. A man fell dead with a hole in his head, and another musket roared, downing a huge black man named Crispus Attuck.

Daniel knew Crispus well, and he dived into the crowd to try to reach the dying man. His attempts were futile, though, as he was carried helplessly along by the surge of the angry mob. Pandemonium broke out and other shots were fired, wounding more men. One man broke free from the crowd and ran, only to be struck in the back and killed instantly.

At the sight of dead and wounded men lying in the street, the crowd suddenly grew silent. In the dim light of the pale moon Daniel saw the shock on wild faces. Rumor had it that the muskets of the Redcoats were loaded with only powder, but now in the face of death, a pall fell over the mob.

Henry Knox said in a strained voice, "Daniel, this means war! American blood has been shed—and our people will never forget!"

Sickened by the sight, Daniel turned and stumbled down the street—the crowd dispersing now in all directions. He knew that what had taken place this day would never be forgotten. Blood would bring forth blood, and he felt the crushing weight of it as he slowly made his way home.

20

A Spot of Tea

DAKE SMELLED THE RICH AROMA OF COOKING even
before he entered the house. He'd been outside chopping wood,
and when he entered and dropped a huge armload of split oak
into the box, he turned at once toward the fireplace. "Donkers!"
he exclaimed and moved to where Rachel was cooking.

"Stay away from here, Dake!" Rachel said sharply. At the age
of fourteen she was on the verge of young womanhood. "You can
wait to eat with the rest of us."

Dake suddenly swooped down and picked Rachel up, swinging her lightly as a feather around the kitchen. At fifteen he was
as tall and strong as most men, and he delighted in tossing Rachel
around as though she were a child. "Aw, sis, you wouldn't deprive
a starving man of food, would you?"

"Put me down, you—bear!" she squealed.

Dake set her down but managed to sample the donkers. This
was his favorite food, made out of leftover meat from the past
week's meals. Rachel had chopped it all up along with bread and
apples and raisins and some savory spices. Fried and served up
with boiled pudding, it made a delicious dish. "Nobody makes
donkers like you, Rachel," he said and gave her a hard hug. "No
girl in Boston's as pretty, either!"

Rachel sniffed, but she allowed Dake to sample the donkers.
She knew very well that he was getting around her, but she was
very fond of Dake. The two of them were close—much closer than
Dake and his twin, Micah. Rachel had said once, "I think God got
mixed up and put the wrong twin with you. Twins are supposed

to be alike—but you and Micah are as different as night and day. You and me are the same inside."

"Go call everyone to breakfast," Rachel ordered.

Dake smiled and simply stuck his head outside the kitchen door and yelled in a stentorian voice: "Breakfast! Come and get it!"

"Well, *I* could have done that!" Rachel said tartly.

"It isn't polite for young ladies to yell."

"And it is for young men?" she asked in a teasing tone.

"Sure. That's because men are crude and rough, and you ladies are sweet and nice." Dake grinned at her, then helped her set the table in the dining room. As he did, Sam came stumbling in, his eyes puffy with sleep. Dake rubbed the head of the thirteen-year-old, saying, "Don't you *ever* get enough sleep? Wake up!"

"Let me alone or I'll bust you, Dake!" Sam was a good-tempered lad—after he'd had breakfast. Until then he was as sullen as a young boy could be.

Micah entered, and he and Dake sat down beside each other. Except for the clothing, few could have told the two apart. Looking at her identical brothers, Rachel smiled to herself and thought, *If it weren't for that tiny scar on Dake's face, our friends would never know who is who.*

Daniel came in, dressed in a dark green suit, and Rachel smiled at him. "You look nice, Papa." She came over and straightened out his cravat, then patted his cheek. "Try not to get so dirty, will you?" She took her seat, adding, "You're the *owner* of the foundry, not one of the hired workers. You can just tell people what to do."

Daniel grinned at Rachel, for they'd had this argument often enough. Even though he was a partner in the foundry, he often worked side by side with the workers, showing them what to do. "It's just not in me to sit in an office and shuffle papers all day," Daniel joked. "A man's got to get his hands dirty or he doesn't feel like he's done a day's work!"

Sam said rebelliously, "Well, when *I* get to be boss, you won't see *me* working myself to death!"

Dake laughed outright. "I don't remember seeing you ever hurt yourself working. That wood I split this morning was supposed to be your job. Now you get out there and split the rest of it after breakfast."

"You're not my boss, Dake!" snapped Sam.

"Well, I'm your father, Sam," Daniel spoke up. "And Dake's right. You get all that wood split today." He eyed Sam, waiting for an argument, but Sam saw something in his father's eye that caused him to keep silent. Daniel bowed his head and asked the blessing, and as he said "Amen," he saw Sam's hand close on a piece of bread.

Micah noted Sam's grabbing hand and asked with amusement, "How do you time it so well, Sam? You always have your hands on the food just as Father says the amen."

Sam stuffed a mouthful of donkers between his lips, mumbling, "Because he always says the same thing. I know when he's almost finished."

Despite himself, Daniel laughed aloud. "I'll have to cross you up, Sam. Next time I'll ask a blessing that lasts for ten minutes."

The family enjoyed their mealtimes together. They had managed to keep house with the aid of Mrs. White. And now that Rachel was older, she had taken over much of the responsibility for the meals. Looking around the table, Daniel had a quick thought: *Holly would be very proud of them!*

"When's Matthew coming home, Papa?" Rachel asked.

"Not for a while, Rachel. He's enjoying his time in England studying painting." Daniel had reluctantly given his permission when Matthew had asked him to go. Yet Daniel knew the lad was intent on following his art, so in the end he had given in to Matthew's wishes. He had only been gone a few months, but Daniel already missed him considerably.

Rachel sipped from her cup, then made a face, exclaiming, "This is *awful!*"

"Might as well drink dishwater," Dake agreed. "But it's better than nothing."

The tea was raspberry tea, or "liberty tea," as it was sometimes called. Most Americans—except for Tories—had substituted this for tea shipped from England. None of the Bradfords liked it, and Sam shoved his cup away. "Don't see why we have to drink this slop!" he grunted.

"I've explained that to you fifty times, Sam," Dake snapped. "The English are trying to make us pay for the French and Indian War. And that's not right!"

"I can't see how drinking this swill is going to make things any better!" Sam shot back.

Dake stared at his stubborn younger brother and began to speak loudly. "Look, Sam, the East India Tea Company lent the Crown money to fight the war. Now to pay them back, King George has slapped a stiff tax on tea."

"And that's like taxing the Company's customers to pay off the Company," Rachel nodded. "It's stupid!"

Daniel said mildly, "The East India Company has seventeen million pounds of tea in London warehouses. If they don't sell it, the Company could go bankrupt."

"That's *their* problem, Father," Dake said heatedly. "They don't have the *right* to tax us for their stupid wars!"

"If the English hadn't stood against the French," Daniel remarked, "we might be living under the French flag—and then you'd be going to mass instead of to a Protestant church."

The discussion became heated, with Dake and Rachel hotly disputing the right of England to tax the tea without the consent of the colonists—while Daniel and Micah took a more moderate view. Sam didn't care about anything but his own tastes and said, "I don't see why we don't drink what we want!"

Daniel rose and slipped his coat on. "You just split the wood, Sam," he said. Then he turned to the twins, saying, "I'll be getting a report from your tutor later in the week. It had better be good."

After their father left, Dake said, "Don't see what good it does to study Latin. Everybody's dead who spoke it."

Micah grinned at Dake. "It's an exercise for your mind, Dake."

"If that old man hollers at me one more time over some stupid verb, I'll throw him in the bay!" The "old man" was Dr. Silas Jennings, a retired minister and scholar who had taken the twins as students in his school.

"If you do, Father will do worse to you," Micah replied calmly. "Come on, we're going to be late. . . ."

🔔   🔔   🔔

"Dake—you can't get mixed up in this crazy business!"

Paul Revere stared at the two young men, his dark eyes gleaming with excitement. "You must be Micah," he nodded, then turned to say, "Dake, Mr. Adams has sent us word that we must do something about this tea tax." He hesitated, glancing at Micah.

He had grown rather close to Dake Bradford, but he was uncertain about his twin brother. Dake had simply pushed himself into the Sons of Liberty, coming with an older friend. Revere had found the young man just the sort of recruit he needed and overlooked his youth. He had talked with Dake about his family and discovered that neither his father nor his twin was sympathetic with the Sons of Liberty.

Dake saw Revere hesitate. "You can speak in front of Micah, sir. He won't say anything."

Micah said at once, "I'm going to Dr. Jennings' house, Dake— I wish you'd come with me." He stood there feeling uncertain, disturbed as he always was over Dake's rabid enthusiasm for the revolutionary activities of the Sons of Liberty. He was a calm young man, not given to bursts of excitement as was his twin.

"You go on, Micah," Dake said. "I've got to do this."

Micah started to say something, then shook his head sadly, turned, and walked away. Revere waited until Micah had gone, then said, "It's not just another meeting, Dake." His eyes glowed with excitement as he added, "This time we're actually going to *do* something!"

"What's going on, sir?" asked Dake, curious at the man's obvious excitement.

"We're going to raid three of the Crown's ships," Revere said, speaking quickly. "It could be dangerous, Dake. You may not want to go on the actual raid, but I want you to help me get word to all the Sons of Liberty. Will you do that?"

"Of course! But I'm going on the raid, too!" Dake was twitching with anticipation and soon was off at a dead run. In his pocket he carried a list of men to be alerted. As he ran, Dake thought of his father, knowing he wouldn't approve of what he was doing. *I hate to go against him,* he thought grimly, *but I have to do this!*

T   T   T

Thomas Hutchinson, the Governor of Massachusetts, was a flexible man—but his fine home had been wrecked earlier by a "patriot" mob. He responded to the crisis with a bitter spirit and set in action the events that had long-reaching effects. Patriots at New York and Philadelphia had prevented ships carrying tea to their ports from docking and unloading their cargo. The resistance was so strong that the ships' captains had been forced to return to London. In Charlestown, shiploads of tea had been landed, but it had been locked up in a warehouse near the docks. With the unrest growing throughout the Colonies, people were asking, "What will Boston do?"

Hutchinson made a fatal decision. He allowed three ships—the *Eleanor*, the *Beaver*, and the *Dartmouth*—to enter Boston Harbor, all loaded with tea. He then ordered Admiral Montagu to close the harbor mouth so that no ship could return to England.

Sam Adams seized the opportunity and called for a quick assembly of the Sons of Liberty at the Old South Church. Adams had sent a warning to Hutchinson, but he knew what the governor's answer would be. Standing in front of the gathered men, Adams could sense the excitement coursing through them. He looked out over the group and asked, "Who knows how tea will mingle with salt water?" At once a great shout of laughter erupted around the room.

Dake was one of the crowd that milled around the church, and at six o'clock when Governor Hutchinson's refusal to heed the warning came, he was waiting outside with the rest for Adams to respond.

Sam Adams read the paper and looked out over the faces that looked at him eagerly. "This meeting can do nothing more to save our country," he cried in a shrill voice. Instantly yells rose from the throats of the men.

"Are you sure you want to do this, Dake?" Paul Revere demanded.

"Yes, I'm sure!"

"Well—so be it! Here's the paint—and get into this outfit!"

Dake scrambled into the Indian garb Revere handed him and then smeared his face with paint. When he was ready he joined the others and went screaming like a true Mohawk toward the harbor where the ships were anchored. Adams had planned for fifty men in each of three parties to attack the three ships. Dake fought for a place in one of the small boats and soon was standing on the deck of the *Dartmouth*. Captain Hewes, who was in charge of the raiders, demanded of the ship's captain, "Give me the keys to the hatches!"

The captain put up no struggle, and soon Dake and the others were wrestling the heavy chests to the deck. Dake took great delight in splitting them open with his tomahawk, laughing with the other men as the tea fluttered down to coat the surface of the water.

Everything was done in an orderly fashion, with no interference from the captain or crew. Finally the "Mohawks" returned to their bobbing boats and rowed back to shore.

Dake made his way home, his heart stirred with the event. He knew his father would have stern words for him—but he could bear that.

"At last—we've actually *done* something!" he cried aloud, throwing his tomahawk high into the air. He'd kept it for a reminder of the tea party, and as it spun in the air, he shouted, unable to keep back what rose to his throat, "Now, George the Third—how did you like *that* little tea party?"

21

Out of the Past

BOSTON HARBOR LOOKED LIKE A FOREST of masts, but Daniel only had eyes for one of the ships. He stood straining his eyes, and when he saw Matthew making his way along the rail of the *Bristol Queen*, he shouted, "There he is, Dake!"

The two waited until the passengers came ashore; then they made their way through the bustling crowd to the trim young man. "Matt—by George—it's good to see you!"

Matthew dropped his luggage and rushed forward to take the hug his father gave him. He was slender but only an inch shorter now than his father's six feet. At the age of nineteen he had grown into a handsome man with thick brown hair and fine blue eyes. "Pa, it's good to be back," he said, then took his brother's hand, saying, "Dake—how are you? You look strong enough to pick up the ship!"

Dake nodded, his blond hair ruffled by the sea breeze. "Good to have you back, Matt. Let me take that suitcase. . . ."

Dake made it his business to get Matt's trunk, then the three men made their way to the carriage. "I'll drive, Pa," Dake announced. He was six feet tall and weighed one hundred eighty-five pounds, all solid muscle. When the three were on their way, Dake asked, "Well, are you ready to start painting portraits? I'll be your first model!" He grinned at his brother, adding, "You don't find good-looking fellows like me to pose very often, I bet!"

Matt gave Dake a smile, saying, "My rates are pretty high, but I'll put you on my list." His interest in art had taken him to England and France to study painting. He turned now and looked at

255

his father, asking, "Have you ever forgiven me for becoming a painter instead of a blacksmith, Pa?"

"Why, Matt, I never put up that much of a struggle," Daniel protested. At first he had been apprehensive over Matthew's choice, but he had been supportive, which included paying his son's expenses for the past two years. "I'm proud that a Bradford has that kind of talent."

Matthew touched his father's arm, saying at once, "I was just joking, Pa. You'll never know how much I appreciate your help." He looked at the crowded streets, noting the many red-coated soldiers. "Looks like half the British army's here," he remarked.

Dake gave the lines a sharp jerk, which caused the horses to quicken their pace. "I wish they were all back where they came from," he growled. "They've got no business here in Boston!"

Matthew gave his brother a sharp glance. "You don't think so, Dake?"

" 'Course I don't! And if I had my way we'd send them packing."

"Be a little difficult to do that, I'd think," replied Matthew.

Matthew spoke more crisply, Daniel noted, and he looked different—the effect of the English style of clothing. He was wearing a maroon velvet jacket and a pair of ash gray wool trousers tucked into a fine pair of leather Hessian boots. He also wore a square-cut vest of colorful striped satin, and a watch fob of striped red and green silk. His hat was made of beaver, high crowned and narrow brimmed.

"After all, Dake, this is an English colony."

"We're not slaves, Matt!" Dake shot back. "I guess you've been listening to the wrong people over there. I hope you've not come home a Tory."

"I'm a subject of His Majesty King George the Third, Dake—and so are you. There's such a thing as loyalty to one's country."

Dake was framing a hot reply, but Daniel said quickly, "Now, let's not get into political arguments. I want to hear about your painting, Matt. What are your plans? I don't have the vaguest idea of how an artist goes about getting started."

The tense moment passed as Matt began to speak of the future, but Daniel knew that the peace was only momentary. In the year of 1775, Boston was a powder keg, waiting for only one spark to set off a war. Dake had become such an enthusiastic member of the Sons of Liberty that he was one of Sam Adams' favorite fire-brands. As much as he had tried, Dake had failed to entice Micah into the group. And Samuel, at the age of fifteen, had to be forcibly restrained by Daniel from getting involved.

Finally they arrived at the house, and Rachel ran out to greet Matthew. "Why—I can't believe it, Rachel," he exclaimed, stunned by the change in his sister. "You were a scrawny pest when I left—and look at you now!"

Rachel was now sixteen and had blossomed into a beautiful young woman. She had her mother's heart-shaped face, but little else from her. Her hair was flaming red and her eyes were green as eyes can be. This along with a flawless complexion combined to make her very attractive. She kissed Matt, saying, "Now, when will you paint my picture?"

But Sam had come to stand before his older brother, claiming his attention. "Tell me about the machines in England," he demanded. He was not tall, but strong and filled with an endless supply of energy. He was fascinated by any sort of machinery, and Daniel boasted that he would become another Benjamin Franklin someday.

Micah stood back, letting the others greet Matthew, which was typical of him. He was a carbon copy of Dake, tall and strongly built, with yellow hair and blue eyes, but he was very quiet, almost withdrawn. He loved books, Dake often said, more than people, and there was some truth to this charge.

When they all had settled down, Rachel said, "Now, we're going to the Fraziers' for dinner, Matt, and I want to show you off. You wear your best clothes and we'll show them what a real artist looks like!"

Matthew Bradford looked around at his family. "I've missed you all," he said. "It's good to be home."

Daniel was warmed by his words. "We've been looking forward to your return for months. The family's not the same without you, Matt." He was happy and thought, *I wish Holly could see him—she'd be so proud!*

🎺   🎺   🎺

Marian looked over the dining room, pleased with the arrangement. The room was illuminated by a suspended gleaming ceiling lamp which threw amber gleams that reflected on the large sideboard and long table. She noted the Wilton carpet that was protected by a baize floor cloth. The portraits on the wall caught the light from two small patent lamps set on tripods resting on the mantel. It was a rich, lovely room, which held many special memories for Marian.

Hattie came in, saying, "Everything's ready, Miss Marian. Is Mr. Frazier going to come down?"

"Yes, Hattie. He's feeling better this evening—" A knock on the door sounded, and she said, "I'll let the guests in, Hattie." She moved down the hall to open the door. Her eyes went at once to the central figure. "Good evening, Daniel," she said softly. She smiled to cover the stirrings of old memories, then said, "Come in—all of you, please."

Daniel had not seen Marian but a few times in all these years, yet he felt awkward as he stood there in the doorway facing her. Old memories stirred unbidden in his mind, and he felt drawn by her beauty, which had not changed since their first meeting. Finally he said, "I think you've met all my family, Marian, but they've all grown up, so let me introduce them."

Marian warmly greeted each of them. To Rachel she gave a compliment on her lovely dress; to the twins she avoided making the usual trite remark about telling them apart, which pleased them greatly. "Sam, you weighed only about ten pounds the last time I saw you," she smiled. When Daniel informed her about Matthew's recent study in Europe, she extended her hand. Matthew took it and kissed it with a grace that startled Daniel and made him rather envious. "Did you meet Mr. Joshua Reynolds in London?" asked Marian.

Matthew's eyes widened. "Why, he was one of my teachers, Mrs. Rochester."

"He's my favorite painter," Marian smiled. "We dined with him several times the last time I was in England. You had a fine teacher, Matthew."

Matthew at once attached himself to Marian, monopolizing her. This attention continued all through the dinner, and finally Dake leaned over and whispered to Micah, "You'd think he'd never seen a woman before! He's a pretty slick talker, isn't he?"

Micah smiled and nodded. "She's a beautiful woman. Pa never told us that. He's known her forever, hasn't he? You'd think he might have mentioned it."

Dake shrugged his broad shoulders. "You know Pa, Micah. He's not looked at another woman since Mother died."

Rachel, who was seated beside Dake, had been listening to their conversation. "Sometimes I wish he would marry. He gets lonely," she added. She looked across the table where her father was sitting between Major John Pitcairn of the Royal Marines and John Frazier. He was wearing a new dark brown suit that she'd bullied him into buying and looked very handsome. At the age of forty-five, Daniel Bradford looked ten years younger. Rachel had been surprised by the beauty of Marian Rochester and noted that her father hardly ever looked directly at her. *He acts as though he's afraid of her—I wonder why?* she thought as she observed them.

Daniel was not aware of Rachel's eyes. He was listening as Matthew and Major Pitcairn were speaking. Pitcairn was a fine-looking man of forty who had gotten acquainted with John Frazier when he'd first arrived in America. Frazier had been drawn to the officer, and he'd become a frequent guest. The major had traveled all over the world and was a fascinating spinner of tales.

Matthew asked, "What sort of a commander is General Gage, Major?"

"A little cautious for my taste, but a sound man."

Dake started to speak, but his father caught his eye and he clamped his lips shut and listened to the men discuss the political matters of the day. He knew that Adams felt that General Thomas Gage had been sent by George the Third to clamp a lid on the rebellious activities of the Colonies. Since it was Gage's troops that had precipitated the Boston Massacre in 1770, Adams had warned the Sons of Liberty that Gage had come back to destroy their liberties. The Tories joyfully welcomed him, rejoicing that the king had finally sent them a man to make the Yankee Doodles dance.

"The man has pressed the colonists so hard with his strict regulations that Massachusetts, I hear, has called for the First Continental Congress," said John Frazier casually.

Pitcairn only smiled and shrugged. "Nothing to worry about. They will blow off steam and do no harm, John."

After dinner Pitcairn excused himself, pleading another engagement. Before he left, he turned to Daniel and said, "I mentioned to General White that we'd be dining together, Mr. Bradford. He sends you his invitation to attend a reception for the new officers who've arrived. It's tomorrow at six."

"My compliments to the general—and tell him I'll be there."

Pitcairn gave Daniel a curious glance. "He tells me you served under him once. Says you had the makings of a fine soldier."

Daniel was embarrassed, saying, "I think he makes too much of that."

"A man's likely to make much of a thing like that." Pitcairn studied the large man in front of him, then asked abruptly, "What would you do if these Sons of Liberty led Boston into a treasonous rebellion?"

Daniel shook his head. "I pray it won't come to that, Major Pitcairn. It would be tragic!"

After the major left, Daniel went to sit with John Frazier. He was worried about the older man, thinking, *He looks worse every time I see him.* The two of them listened as Rachel played the harpsichord and sang. When she was finished with the piece, they all joined in the applause. Afterward, Marian came to sit beside Daniel. "She's got a marvelous talent, Daniel," she said warmly. "You must be very proud of her."

"I am—and of all of them," he said.

They sat there talking about the rest of his family, and Daniel enjoyed her company. When it grew late, he said, "Marian, this has been most pleasant."

"We must do it again," she said quietly. She was very much aware that Leo's name had not been mentioned except by her father, who'd explained his absence. When she arose, he rose with her, and she turned to him suddenly, saying, "I'm surprised you never married again, Daniel."

Daniel hesitated, then said slowly, "I never found a woman I could share life with. I've often thought that was a selfish view. For the children's sake I should have married. They were so young when their mother died."

He stood there, the past rising unbidden like a faint echo from a far distance. Daniel was thinking of the time so many years ago when he'd kissed her—and she'd responded so passionately. He felt stirred by the memory, then wondered, when he saw her smooth cheeks color slightly, if she too remembered. She was, to him, more beautiful at thirty-two than she had been when she was eighteen. He wanted to put his arms around her, to take her from this place where they could be alone—but he knew it was a foolish thought. Carefully he said, "Marian, you've been in my thoughts for years. I'll never forget—" And then he broke off, bitterly knowing he was making a fool of himself. He said abruptly, "It's late. We must be going home."

The moment passed, and when the guests were all gone, John Frazier said, "A fine family, eh, daughter? I wonder why Daniel never remarried after the death of his wife. He'd be a fine catch for a woman—still would be. He's a young man."

"I don't know, Father," Marian said quietly, her face paler than usual. "I suppose he didn't fall in love with anyone." Even as Marian spoke, she knew it was false, for in her heart she was saying, *He loved me when he was young—and he still loves me! He couldn't even look at me tonight.* And then she suddenly admitted to herself what she had long denied: *If he asked me—I'd leave Leo and go with him!* Her lips trembled, and she blinked back the tears as she said good-night to her father and quickly went to her room.

♜   ♜   ♜

When Daniel arrived at the reception the next night, he was warmly greeted at once by Major General Adam White. White was over sixty and was retiring from the army. When he'd come to Boston, Daniel had looked him up and the two had shared some good memories. The general was beaming and shook his hand firmly. "Now then, this *is* fine! Come in and let me introduce you to the staff, Bradford."

Daniel allowed himself to be pulled into the large room and introduced to General Gage himself. Gage had come to welcome his new officers, and he impressed Daniel as a man of sense. White spoke highly of Daniel, insisting, "If you want a man to see to your horses, General, here he stands. I've always said he was the best in the army!"

Gage smiled at White but then added, "I may need some help with the horses, Mr. Bradford. Would you be able to serve in that capacity?"

Daniel was somewhat taken aback by the suddenness of the question and said only, "I have a business that takes most of my time, General Gage. About all I can offer is advice—which is cheap enough, I believe."

General White took Daniel to meet the other officers and finally said, "Well, that's the lot, except for a colonel I'd like you to meet. Where *is* the colonel, Simms?"

"Oh, he said he'd be a little late, Major." The man who spoke was a small lieutenant with a bristling mustache and a pair of sharp gray eyes. "I think his wife lost a shoe or something."

"It's a chronic disease with wives," White grinned. "Never knew one of the fairer sex to be on time for anything!" He led Daniel to the reception table loaded with food and drink, saying, "You'll like this man, Daniel. He's a fine officer!"

Daniel and General White moved to a small room where they could talk more easily. They sat at the single table drinking some of the cider and reminiscing about old times. Daniel had a thought and spoke it to White. "You know, General White, if things had gone differently, I might have been one of you. I always liked the army."

White grinned, saying, "No, Daniel, you're a rich colonist—no ducking lead for you—" He broke off abruptly on seeing a couple pass by the door. "I say—Colonel!—come in, will you? There's someone here I want you to meet."

Daniel set his tankard down on the table and rose to meet the tall officer and the woman who heeded General White's invitation. "This is Colonel Leslie Gordon—and this is Mr. Daniel Bradford, Leslie. Present your wife to him."

Gordon stepped forward and took Daniel's hand. "Happy to make your acquaintance, Mr. Bradford."

Daniel was impressed with the officer, and then he turned to meet the woman who was standing slightly behind her husband. "This is my wife, Mrs. Gordon."

Daniel turned to the woman with a smile—and then he saw her face and halted. He felt as though he'd been struck in the pit of the stomach, for he could neither speak nor move, so great was the shock that paralyzed him.

Lyna Lee Gordon's face turned chalky white, and her husband at once came to take her arm, exclaiming, "Lyna—what's wrong? Are you ill?"

Lyna's eyes were staring with wild disbelief at the man in front of her. She was trembling and was aware that her husband and General White were staring at her, asking her what was wrong.

Then she took a deep breath and moved forward.

Colonel Leslie Gordon could not have been more shocked if the sun had fallen—for his wife walked right into the arms of the tall man and clung to him fiercely! Gordon saw Bradford's arms go around his wife—saw him hold her tightly. He felt as if the world had gone suddenly insane and whispered hoarsely, "Lyna—who *is* this man?"

Lyna was clinging to Daniel with all her strength, but at the sound of Leslie's voice, she drew back and stared up into a face she'd never expected to see again until she reached heaven.

She turned and held to the arm of her brother, tears unashamedly streaming down her face.

"Leslie—this is—my brother, Daniel!" She swayed and suddenly the room seemed to spin around her. She was aware that she was losing consciousness—and the last words she heard were, "Lyna—I thought you were dead. . . !" She felt his hands reach out to support her and then she fainted.

22

A MOMENT OF PASSION

"DANIEL—COME IN!"

Lyna took Daniel's arm and practically hauled him into her small house. She turned, saying proudly, "This is your uncle Daniel!"

Lyna had come out of her faint at the reception the night before to discover that she was not dreaming—that Daniel was *alive*! She had clung to him, and he to her. They had seemed unwilling to lose physical contact and sat holding hands, taking turns relating what they had each been through over the years. General White and Leslie Gordon had sat back, shocked by the revelation—not understanding how the two could have been separated, each thinking the other dead.

Lyna and Daniel understood instantly, however. They didn't mention Leo Rochester's name—but it was clear that he had lied to both of them. Daniel felt a streak of fury roar through his brain as he thought of the deceit the vile man had used for revenge. *What kind of a devil would take pleasure in separating us?* thought Daniel, but he forced the tormenting thought away.

Finally Lyna had said, "Come visit us tomorrow, Daniel. I want you to meet our children."

"Of course—and then you and Colonel Gordon must visit us."

Daniel had left the reception in a daze. Finding his sister alive after all these years was a miracle to him. He had said nothing to any of his family when he arrived at the house but kept it to himself. That night he had lain awake thinking of Lyna. The next morning he'd gone at once to the house where Lyna and her family were living.

Now as he stepped forward and saw the face of Grace Gordon, he smiled, saying, "Well, I've never had a niece to spoil—but I intend to begin at once."

Grace was a small girl of seventeen with dark honey-colored hair and gray eyes. She had an oval face and was clearly flustered by the appearance of an uncle she'd never dreamed of having. "Mother's told us all about you, Uncle Daniel," she said at once. "She's never forgotten a thing the two of you did together, I don't think. She still laughs when she remembers how you carried that turkey off right out from under the noses of all those nobles."

"And this is Clive, our older son," continued Lyna. "He's twenty-two and wants to be a rich businessman, don't you, Clive?"

"Oh, don't be foolish, Mother!" Clive Gordon was very tall, at least six feet three, and roughly handsome. He had reddish hair, cornflower blue eyes, and a strong tapered face. He took his uncle's outstretched hand with a firm grip and said, "Happy to meet you, sir. But I warn you, Grace is right. Mother's made you out to be quite a fellow! No man could live up to her tales of that older brother of hers!"

"I'll not try, Clive." Daniel turned to shake the hand of David, who was fifteen and too forward, or so Lyna informed him. David was a lean boy, with dark brown crisply curly hair and merry brown eyes.

"It's customary for uncles to give their nephews a shilling or two from time to time," he announced brashly. "If you'd care to catch up for lost opportunities, Uncle Daniel, please feel free to do so."

"Why, you young rascal!" Lyna exclaimed. "You're incorrigible."

Daniel laughed and winked at David. "See me when we're alone, David. I think some sort of arrangement for back payment might be made."

"Don't spoil him, Daniel! He's the world's worst at getting exactly what he wants!" warned Lyna, enjoying the moment.

She was, Daniel saw, very fond of her children, and as they sat down to tea, he demanded to know more about them. He sat there looking from face to face, and finally when Lyna shooed the children away, said, "Lyna, what a wonderful family! God's been good to you!"

"Yes, He has," Lyna nodded. She was wearing a simple dress, but somehow she lent grace to it. She was as attractive as a young girl, and her hair was crisp and still glowed like honey in the sunlight streaming through the window. Sitting down beside Daniel, she took his hand and squeezed it. "I can't believe it's true, Daniel—that you're alive and we're together!"

Daniel put his hand on her cheek, whispering, "I thank God for bringing you back to me, Lyna. Part of me died when Leo told me you had died in that cholera epidemic. Now I feel alive again."

They sat in front of the fire, and Daniel listened as Lyna related how she'd nearly died—and how she had the best husband in the whole world! Her eyes glowed as she proudly spoke of how kind Leslie Gordon had been to her from the first time she had met him at the Red Horse Tavern when she had run away from Milford Manor. He listened quietly as she told him how Leslie was all that a woman could desire in a man. "His brother Oliver is Lord of Longbriar now—rich and secure. But I wouldn't give the love I've found with Leslie for all of it!"

When she was done, Lyna insisted that Daniel tell her his story, leaving out none of the details. It took a long time, for she wanted to hear everything. And he was unaware of how much of himself he gave away as he spoke, for he didn't know that this sister of his had a quick mind and was very observant. When he finally ended his story, Lyna asked one question, "What about Marian Rochester, Daniel?"

Daniel stared at her, confused. "What about her, Lyna?"

"It sounds as if you were in love with her when you were younger," Lyna said. "Are you still in love with her?"

"Lyna—she's Leo Rochester's wife!" said Daniel, shocked at the bluntness of her question.

Lyna leaned forward, her eyes fixed on him. "Of course—but you're not answering my question. Do you love her?"

Daniel felt awkward, for he had tried to keep his love for Marian Rochester buried deep down in his most secret thoughts. Now he could only stammer, "Why . . . do you ask such a thing?"

Lyna's face was filled with compassion. "Why, Daniel, you can't even say her name without showing how you feel! And you're not the first man to love another man's wife."

"Don't . . . don't say such things!" Daniel looked down to see that his hands were trembling. He clenched them but saw that Lyna had noticed his weakness. "I've got a family and she has a husband—and that's all there is to it." He looked at Lyna but could not hide the misery in his eyes. "Please, Lyna—let's not mention this again!"

Lyna nodded slowly. "Very well, Daniel. I'll not speak of it— but if you ever need to talk, I'll be here for you." She began to speak of other things, and soon afterward Leslie arrived. Kissing Leslie as he entered, she left the two of them to talk while she began to fix the noon meal.

T   T   T

Daniel had been badly shaken by Lyna's intuitive assertions, and as he made his way back through the city, he thought about his behavior, wondering how many other observant people had seen his feelings for Marian that he'd tried so desperately to mask. The gusty March wind pulled at his hat and snatched his coat open, but he paid no heed. *Got to learn to keep my feelings for Marian hidden—no, I've got to forget—God knows I've tried to do just that!*

He made his way to the foundry and spent the rest of the day burying himself in the work. When he finally arrived at home, he was exhausted not only physically but emotionally. As soon as he came through the door, Sam clamored for his help on a clock he was attempting to make. The two of them worked on it until Mrs. White came to announce that dinner was ready. "Come along and let's wash up, Sam," he said, and the two of them made a quick job of it.

When everyone was seated, and after Daniel said a brief prayer, he smiled, saying, "It's good to have you here, Matt. Tell me what you've been doing today."

Matt was wearing a fine wool coat and an elegant white silk shirt from Paris. "Oh, I walked along the harbor and studied the light."

Dake had lifted a knife loaded with peas to his mouth. He dexterously ladled them in, chewed hastily, then demanded, "Studied *what*, Matt?"

"The light—the sun and the way it changes the color of the sea." Matt's eyes grew distant and he seemed to be *seeing* the ocean through the wall of the house. "Sometimes in the morning when the sun is red, the sea is sort of a pale green—about the color of Rachel's eyes—but an hour later it turns to a whispering blue."

"*Whispering* blue?" Dake said with a puzzled look on his face. "What in thunder is *that*?"

Micah rarely interrupted his twin, but now he leaned forward and said, "I know what you mean, Matt—it's sort of pale, like the first violet, just *tinged* with blue. And it sort of—well, *quivers* when you try to stare at it."

Matt stared at his younger brother with interest. "You may be a painter yourself, Micah. That's as good a description of that color of the sea as I've ever heard."

Micah, not accustomed to compliments, flushed, and Rachel reached over and ruffled his hair. "You could do it if you wanted to, Micah." She was partial to Micah, for the two of them had been close all their lives. "*You should have been Micah's twin, Rachel*," Daniel had told her once. "*You're closer to him than Dake is*."

Dake scoffed loudly. "Well, just plain old *blue* is good enough for me. I reckon it's all right for you, Matt, but I like to have things black or white."

"Most things aren't that simple, Dake."

Dake stared at Matt and shook his head. "Don't see why not. If a thing's right, it's right."

"The Bible says, 'Thou shalt not kill,'" Matt responded, "but good Christians kill all the same. In a war soldiers have to obey their orders, even Christian soldiers. So 'Thou shalt not kill' becomes a little more complicated, doesn't it?"

Dake was an argumentative young fellow and at once plunged into the fray. "Why, that makes no sense, Matt! The Bible means not to kill anyone—like to *murder* somebody. But it's different in a war. . . ."

Daniel listened as the two young men went on, noting that Sam agreed with whatever Dake said, but that Micah seemed to be less willing to go along with his twin's opinions. And as he knew would happen, Dake grew angry when he discovered that he could not answer Matt logically.

He said angrily, "Look, we've got a king over in England, but he's not an American. He sends soldiers over here to enforce all his taxes. And *you* may have forgotten that they butchered some of our people right here in Boston a few years ago, but some of us haven't!" Dake was a handsome young man, and now his hazel eyes were glowing with feeling. "And I don't think God will hold it against me if I shoot a lobsterback who's killing my people with his bayonet!"

"I don't think it's that simple, Dake," Matt said evenly. He had determined not to argue with Dake, and he could see that his father was distressed. He picked up his knife and began slicing his meat into bite-sized portions. "But I'm not going to argue with you about it."

The evening went fairly well after that, but later Daniel took Dake aside and said, "Don't pester Matt with politics, Dake."

"But, Pa—"

"No, don't argue with me. I know you think he's wrong—but he's your brother. I won't have this political mess causing rifts in my family."

"But he doesn't—"

"I'm not going to argue about this, son," Daniel said firmly. "I don't usually demand something from you, and I don't like to order you to stop your wrangling. I'm *asking* you to do it. Will you heed my wishes?"

Dake was a good-hearted young man and at once nodded. "Well, I'll *try*, Pa—that's the best I can say."

Daniel slapped Dake's shoulder, smiling with relief. "I've never known you to try something you couldn't do, son. And I appreciate it."

The next day at the foundry Daniel worked hard on getting the final designs ready for the cannon he hoped to cast. He spent the whole day working with Isaac Cartwright, the most experienced man in the shop. Finally, at four o'clock, Daniel smiled at him, saying, "This thing will probably blow up and kill both of us, Isaac."

"No, sir!" Cartwright denied vehemently. He was a short barrel of a man who knew iron and other metals like most men know their own bodies. "It'll be a *fine* piece, Mr. Bradford! Good enough to blow a few of King George's red puppets to bits!" Cartwright was a fiery patriot and had already been jailed twice for insulting Gage's officers.

Knowing that talking to Cartwright was like talking to a lamppost, Daniel shrugged and went back to his office. As he entered, Albert Blevins met him. "A note from Mr. Frazier. He wants you to stop by on the way home with all the information on the Miller project. I have it all ready."

"I'd better leave now, Albert." Daniel took off his working apron, donned his coat, and left the office. It was growing dark, but he reached the Frazier house shortly. The black woman Hattie opened the door, saying, "Mistuh Frazier, he say for you to come right to his room, suh. Lemme have your hat and coat, Mistuh Bradford."

"Thank you, Hattie."

Daniel found Frazier feeling poorly, so he stayed only a few minutes, going over the papers on the project he'd been working on. "I'll stop by tomorrow, John, and we'll go over these more thoroughly."

"Thank you, Daniel. I appreciate how hard you've been working on this," said Frazier.

Daniel bid the man good-night and left the room. When he reached the foot of the stairs, ready to leave, he was startled to see Marian.

"Do you have a moment, Daniel?"

"Of course," he said as she motioned for him to follow her into the parlor.

"I'm worried about Father. He's not doing well at all."

"What does the doctor say?"

"Oh, just that he's never recovered from the fever he had last month. But he had a strange spell of some sort yesterday. It frightened me, Daniel."

Daniel saw that her eyes were cloudy with doubt and said, "What kind of a spell?"

"He . . . couldn't describe it very well. Just said he felt peculiar and had trouble breathing. And he said the fingers on his left hand were numb . . . as if they were asleep."

Daniel listened as she spoke of her father. He noted that she was no less attractive when she was dressed in a plain dress than when she wore a rich gown and glittering jewels. He knew he should leave, but he hated to leave her when she was so distraught. Just then Hattie entered the parlor and said, "You want me to take Mr. Frazier's dinner up to him, Miss Marian?"

"Yes, please." Marian looked at Daniel and asked, "Would you stay for dinner?"

Daniel could tell that she was lonely and worried about her

father and made a quick decision, "Well, I haven't had anything since noon—"

"Come along—I hate to eat alone."

Daniel followed her into the small dining room, and soon the two were eating a simple meal of lamb and vegetables. Hattie returned and served them from time to time, then said, "I got to tend to Enoch, Miss Marian—you just leave them dishes when you gits through. I'll tend to them when I gits back."

"All right, Hattie. Be sure and tell Enoch I said for him to get well."

When Hattie left, Marian said, "Enoch is her youngest boy. He's got some sort of ague." She sipped the wine from a crystal goblet, then added, "She's a wonderful cook—and a fine nurse. I don't know what we'd do without her."

"She's a fine woman from what John's told me. He said he's setting her free," said Daniel.

"I'm glad!" Marian nodded and her light green eyes glowed. "It must be awful to be *owned*—like you were an animal!"

Daniel listened as she spoke for some time about her hatred for slavery. He was pleased to discover she felt exactly the same as he did. They talked for a time, then Daniel said reluctantly, "I've got to go, Marian."

"Oh, just one cup of tea before you leave! I've got a new service and a fresh shipment in the library."

Daniel was starting to feel awkward but agreed. He waited while she went and fixed a kettle of boiling water. When she came back they moved to the library where she brewed a pot of tea.

"I feel guilty drinking tea," she said, pouring the boiling water into a cup. "Most of my friends have fasted from drinking it. They've made it a symbol of independence ever since the Boston Tea Party. In fact, some of them have sworn not to drink the brew until England stops taxing the Colonies."

"I don't see how my refusing to drink tea helps the situation much," Daniel said dryly. He spoke for a time of the volatile politics of the country, then somehow found himself telling Marian of his sister, Lyna—how he'd found her after believing she was dead all these years.

Marian was fascinated by the tale and kept asking questions about the matter. She was half aware that she was drawing Daniel out to prevent him from leaving. Somehow she felt no shame over this and wondered at herself.

As for Daniel, a sense of comfort had come to him. He had not had anyone to share his inner thoughts with for years. Since Holly had died, he had kept to himself. All of his time was spent working hard at the foundry and giving himself to the task of being a good father as he'd promised. There had been little time for any social life. He'd been attracted to two women, but not seriously. Now as he sat in the light of the fire drinking the delicious tea—and speaking with a woman who listened so carefully—he longed to stay.

Finally he got up and she rose with him. "This has been very pleasant, Marian," he said. "I can't think of an evening I've enjoyed more."

Marian came to stand in front of him. The amber light of the fire gave her face a coral glow, and her dark auburn hair had been loosed so that it cascaded down her back. Her green eyes glowed and she seemed infinitely desirable as she said softly, "It's been good for me, Daniel—very good!"

He could smell her scent, a faint sweetness that came to him with a strange potency. She looked exquisite in the simple dress she was wearing, and there was an innocence in her face that reached out to Daniel. "You . . . you're very lovely, Marian," he said unsteadily.

Marian felt powerful feelings stir at his words, and yet she knew she should not listen. She was a lonely woman, married to a brute who had never given her tenderness. For years she had hoped that this kind of love would come between her and Leo, but he grew more thoughtless and even cruel. She had learned in a short time that she had made a tragic mistake in marrying Leo, but there was no retreat in her world. She had thought often of Daniel Bradford, with a bittersweet memory of things that she had allowed to slip past her.

And now as she faced him, tracing the strength in the solid planes of his jaw and the steadiness of his hazel eyes, she longed for him. And being a woman, she knew that he longed for her in the same way. She leaned forward, spoke his name in a broken whisper, and he came to her—as she knew he would.

His kiss was firm and inviting, and she responded equally so. She clung to him, knowing only that he loved her and that there was something good in him. His arms were enfolding her closer, determined and strong, and there was a protectiveness in his embrace that made her weak.

For how long they stood there, holding each other, swayed with passion that threatened to break out in a flood, she never knew—nor did Daniel. They were both like two enraptured people, their minds blinded by their love, on the edge of a deep chasm, teetering on the brink—

And then a voice broke through the moment—loud and jeering.

"Well, my dear wife—I see that you're entertaining your lover! Quite a welcome home from England!"

Marian and Daniel broke apart, and Marian uttered a cry of distress. "Leo—I didn't know—!"

"Obviously you didn't," Leo said. He had been drinking, and his mouth was tight with anger. He was wearing an overcoat and carrying a gold-headed cane, which he gripped until his knuckles were white. He stared at Daniel, finally saying, "I think I will kill you, Bradford!"

Daniel had never felt so helpless. Guilt raced through him, and he knew that nothing he could say would have the slightest influence on Rochester. He said evenly, "I wouldn't blame you too much, Leo. And I make no defense. But it's all my doing. Marian has never—"

But Rochester laughed harshly and glared at Daniel with red-rimmed eyes. "Oh, *spare* me that, Bradford! Don't play me for a fool. Do you think I don't know a guilty woman when I see one? Just look at her—she's guilty as Jezebel!"

Daniel glanced at Marian. She looked so vulnerable and pale standing there, her lips trembling. "Leo, I've never lied to you," Daniel said. "You know that, don't you? Never!" When Rochester hesitated, he said, "I swear to you that this one moment of indiscretion is the first—and you must blame me, not Marian."

Rochester seemed for a moment to sway, as though he were half convinced of Daniel's impassioned plea. Drunk as he was, he did know that Daniel Bradford was a man of honor. Perhaps it was, for some complex reason, the cause of his hatred for the man. But it lasted for only a moment, then he sneered, saying, "A man will lie for a woman when he'll lie for nothing else. Get out of my house, Bradford."

Daniel moved stiffly past Rochester and picked up his hat and coat. When he reached the door, Rochester cried out, "This isn't over, Bradford! You'll regret touching something of mine!"

Daniel did not respond but left the house. He moved woodenly and was so shaken by the scene he had difficulty mounting his horse. He never remembered riding home, for the ugly scene played itself again and again in his mind.

What a fool I was—and it's Marian who'll have to pay for it!

As soon as Bradford left the house, Rochester crossed the room where Marian stood and struck her with his fist. She fell to the floor, blood salty in her mouth, but as he cursed her, punctuating his curses with more blows, she did not utter a word. Her silence infuriated Rochester worse than anything else she might have done. After he finally stopped hitting her, he snarled with a terrible intensity, "We'll see how much you love him after he's a corpse—which is what I intend to make of Mr. Daniel Bradford!"

23

LEO SEES HIMSELF

THE EVENTS LEADING TO THE SHOTS heard round the world at Lexington and Concord were only a preamble of what was to come. Much later those in Massachusetts would look back upon them as a series of dress rehearsals for the inevitable war that broke out between the American Colonies and Britain.

General Gage had been steadily accumulating troops, but when he called for workmen to build barracks, none came forward to help. He sent to New York and Halifax for workmen, but the Sons of Liberty began a campaign of sabotage. Brick barges were sunk, straw for soldiers' beds was burned, and supply wagons were overturned.

Enraged by this show of resistance, Gage sent soldiers to Charlestown and Cambridge to seize colonial powder and cannon. When the Continental Congress heard the report of Gage's action, it exploded in outrage. Many of the patriots viewed it as a violation of the very fundamental liberties that had been set down in the original charters. Almost overnight four thousand armed and angry men thundered into Cambridge, while all over New England others organized units and were on the march. This unbelievably swift response would have alerted most that the colonists were on a trigger edge, teetering on the brink of a revolution. But Gage was a general and did not read the signs of the times. Instead, he kept his head well hidden in the sand of military protocol. The fact that the men of America could gather almost instantly into a host seemed not to trouble him.

Another incident occurred when Gage sent a military expe-

277

dition to Salem on February 16, 1775. The British met the colonial militia under Colonel Timothy Pickering's command at an open bridge. The staunch Pickering faced the British troops down! As they turned to march sullenly back to Boston, a nurse named Sarah Tarrant taunted them from an open window, "Go home and tell your master he has sent you on a fool's errand and broken the peace of our Sabbath. What, do you think we were born in the woods to be frightened by owls?"

Angered by the woman's jeering, one of the soldiers lifted his musket and aimed it at her. Sarah Tarrant scoffed at him, "Fire if you have the courage—but I doubt it!"

And so the British empire was challenged by Americans willing to sacrifice all to defend their rights. All through the Colonies fiery voices demanding freedom from the English Crown began to blaze. The fire was fanned in Virginia by Patrick Henry, who was well known as a revolutionary and great orator. He rose before the newly formed Virginia Provincial Convention and declared:

"There is no retreat but in submission and slavery! Our chains are forged. Their clanking may be heard on the plains of Boston! The war is inevitable—and let it come! I repeat it, sir, let it come!

"It is in vain, sir, to extenuate the matter. Gentlemen may cry, 'Peace! Peace!'—but there is no peace. The war is actually begun. The next gale that sweeps down from the north will bring to our ears the clash of resounding arms! Our brethren are already in the field! Why stand we here idle? What is it that the gentlemen wish? What would they have? Is life so dear, or peace so sweet, as to be purchased at the price of chains and slavery? Forbid it, Almighty God! I know not what course others may take, but as for me, give me liberty or give me death!"

The thundering rhetoric of Patrick Henry was soon carried well beyond the walls of the Virginia Convention. It was carried on the lips of all true patriots throughout the Colonies. Unrest was mounting and troubles were stirring again in Boston.

General Gage was facing a dilemma that threatened to weaken his military strength. It was not with American militia, but with his own troops. Sick of the poor pay, rotten food, and the unforgiving lash, the disparaged soldiers were deserting by the hundreds. The offer of a new start in a new land appealed to many of them, causing them to flee from Boston. Gage, with the typical mentality of many British officers, gave orders to severely punish anyone who was caught trying to escape. Ordinarily under military law they would have been hanged, but with the growing resistance among the colonists Gage could not spare them, so the sentence was "milder"—a mere 1,000 lashes to be administered at the rate of 250 per week! The only effect this inhumane discipline had was to encourage more men to flee!

The tension between the militia and Gage's soldiers continued to build as April approached. The British soldiers tried to ignore the dismal conditions by staying comfortably drunk, for liquor was cheap in Boston. Their officers found feminine companionship of the lower sort and even went so far as to put on amateur theatricals at which the more effeminate of the officers sometimes quarreled over who should play the feminine parts, complete with dresses.

Colonial Leslie Gordon was appalled by the deteriorating morale of the men. As an officer in His Majesty's service, he was repulsed at how the troops were behaving. "We're looking like buffoons, Lyna," he said one morning at breakfast. "I can't imagine what General Gage must be thinking!"

Lyna poured him a fresh cup of tea, concerned about the situation. "But it won't come to a war, will it, Leslie?"

"It might if Lord North doesn't stop issuing those idiotic regulations. His taxations have already pushed people to the edge."

Later in the day, Gordon was walking through the camp on an inspection with Major John Pitcairn. They paused to watch a squad of soldiers taking target practice—and were disgusted when every single soldier missed the mark.

An elderly farmer had come along with his son to bring a load of lumber to the camp. He stopped unloading long enough to watch the shooting, then laughed aloud. The sergeant in charge of the squad cursed him, asking what was so funny.

"They ain't much for shootin', are they?" the farmer grinned. He was one of the few who had agreed to sell supplies to the British, so he was not afraid of the sergeant's scowl.

"I suppose you could do better?" the officer scoffed.

"Why, I got six boys—and this here"—he waved at the dark-haired fifteen-year-old boy who stood watching—"he's the worst shot of 'em all, but I reckon he can do better than them soldiers."

"Let's see if he can!" challenged the Redcoat.

Leslie said at once, "That's a mistake, John! We'd better stop it."

"Oh, let him try," Pitcairn said carelessly.

The sergeant set five loaded muskets in front of the lad, and the boy proceeded to hit the target five times in a row, two of them bull's-eyes.

Leslie Gordon turned away in disgust, stating flatly, "Just what we needed! Our men beaten at their own game by a farmer boy! And the old man is probably telling the truth, John. These Americans have grown up with a musket in their hands, and a man is a lot easier to hit than a squirrel!"

"Aye, but squirrels don't shoot back, sir," Pitcairn shrugged. "They're a rabble in arms, this militia of theirs. They'll never stand against the trained troops of the Crown."

🔔　　🔔　　🔔

Dake Bradford stood before the three men, his heart beating fast. Sam Adams, Paul Revere, and Dr. Joseph Warren had asked for him to remain after the meeting was over! He had seen them at many of the secret meetings the Sons of Liberty had convened, where he'd listened to them speak many times. But now face-to-face with his heroes, Dake could barely keep still.

Sam Adams had pretty much failed at everything he'd tried. He was a man fueled by a passion for freedom and soon turned his zeal into writing. He was born for this moment in time. He had become a gadfly, able to powerfully stir up the people of America against the British rule with his polemical writings. Every time he gave an impassioned speech, his eyes burned with the light of a true believer. His clothes were shabby, and he was an average man in height, weight, and appearance. He had a great head, which he held at an angle, always in motion.

"Mister Bradford, I have had good reports of you," Adams said abruptly.

"Why, I want to do my best, sir!" said Dake, drinking in the man's praise.

"You're a fine horseman, I understand? And you have a fast mare?"

"Fastest in Massachusetts!"

Dr. Warren laughed at the quick response. "I like a man who believes in himself—and his horse, Mr. Bradford." Warren was the most popular physician in Boston, a hero to many for his work in the smallpox epidemic of 1763. His chief interest, however, was not medicine, but liberty. He had opposed the Stamp Act with all his power and had risen steadily in the hierarchy of the patriots' cause, serving as the chairman of the Committee of Safety and president of the provincial Congress. And this tall, handsome man would be the first to be clapped into prison—and perhaps hanged—if a real war broke out. "Would you be willing to use this fabulous mare of yours for the cause?"

"Yes, sir!" said Dake eagerly.

All three men smiled at the instant and enthusiastic reply. Adams nodded, saying, "Fine! Fine! Mr. Revere will give you your instructions." He hesitated, then asked, "Your father—is he a patriot?"

Dake hesitated, then answered carefully, "Well, Mr. Adams, he doesn't really understand what we're trying to do. But when the fighting starts, I assure you, he'll be with us!"

"He's a good man by all reports," Revere said. He was a short stocky man, dark complected and square faced. "He's working on a new project—learning to cast cannon. That would make him an invaluable man for our cause."

Dake blinked with surprise. He knew nothing of his father's work in casting cannon and realized that the Sons of Liberty had spies in practically every house in Boston. "I wish you'd talk to him, Mr. Adams," he said. "You could make him see how important this is."

"I will try to see that we have a talk, your father and I."

As soon as Adams and Warren left, Revere waved Dake to a table, his dark eyes glowing as he said, "Now, when the revolution begins, we must have men who can get the word out to our people all over New England. I will be one of those, and you will do the same, Dake."

"Will it be soon, Mr. Revere?" Dake asked as the short man rose finally.

"Sooner than you think, young man!"

T   T   T

Resentment had burned with a vitriolic rage in Leo Rochester ever since he'd seen his wife in the arms of Daniel Bradford. He had not been completely sober since that night, and abusing

Marian had not been enough. He had not struck her again after that first outbreak of anger, but verbally he lashed her with cruel words that cut deeper than any whip.

If it had been any other man, he thought as he sat in the Eagle Tavern three days after his return, *I wouldn't have been greatly disturbed. She's never been the kind of woman I've wanted! I've had to find warmer women than her!* He was just drunk enough for his thinking processes to be slowed down considerably, and he defiantly drained the glass of whiskey and shouted, "Innkeeper—blast you! Bring me a bottle!"

He snatched the bottle from the resentful innkeeper, poured a glass, and drained it off. As the liquor hit his belly and sent a fine mist of fiery fumes into his head, he thought of Marian. Their marriage had been a disaster from the start, and he had a brief moment of regret, knowing that he had been a poor husband. He thought of their wedding night—how she'd looked so beautiful in her white gown—and how fear had overwhelmed her that night. He'd been drunk and had thought of nothing but himself. He was rough, without a thought to tenderness. He remembered he'd felt bad the next day, but the damage was done. When he approached her, she shrank back, her eyes filled with fear and disgust.

The memory angered him, and he took another swig. "Let her have her men," he muttered. "But not *him*—not Bradford!" For years he had bred resentment for Daniel Bradford, knowing that he'd wronged him. Now he reveled in the savage pleasure of knowing that Bradford was not the perfect man some thought him to be.

"Hypocrite—blasted hypocrite! No better than me! Puts on a front, but he's as rotten to the core as the rest of us!"

Rochester drank steadily, and finally a purpose grew in him. *Got to show him—he can't treat Leo Rochester this way!*

Rising to his feet, he had the innkeeper fill the silver flask he always carried with brandy. Tossing several coins to the host, he staggered out of the tavern. "You—over here!" he shouted. When a carriage pulled up, he had to grasp the side of the vehicle to keep from falling. "You know where Daniel Bradford lives?"

"No, sir, don't know the gentleman."

"Well, do you know the Frazier foundry?"

"Oh yes, indeed, sir!"

"Go there, find out where Bradford lives—then take me there—but first go by Anderson's shop over by Faneuil Hall."

Half an hour later, Rochester walked out of Anderson's Gun Shoppe with a pistol, primed and loaded, under his coat. He climbed into the carriage and ordered the driver, "Take me to Bradford's house!" He then drew the flask and drank half the contents, swallowing convulsively. As the carriage rattled along, he muttered, "Nobody will blame me—injured husband! Got a right to—defend my honor!" He soon grew dizzy and lay down on the seat, falling at once into a drunken stupor. He was aware once that the carriage stopped, but he could not rouse himself. He felt sick and fought down the nausea that came as the vehicle started up again. He fell asleep and did not move until he heard a voice that seemed to come from far away.

"Sir? This is where Mr. Daniel Bradford lives."

Rochester muttered, "Go—away—" but the voice became more insistent. He struggled to a sitting position and blinked uncomprehendingly for a moment at the round face of the coachman.

"Shall I get help, sir? You ain't feeling too well, are you?" the coachman asked diplomatically, noting the drunken stare on Rochester's face.

"No, blast you!" Rochester heaved himself out of the carriage, cursing when he staggered, but shoving the stocky driver aside when he tried to help him. "Keep your hands off me—!" Fumbling in his pocket, he tossed a crown at the cabman, but then realized he had no way to get back to his home. He shook his shoulders together, blinked his eyes and said, "Wait here—there'll be another fare and an extra crown for you."

"Yes, sir—I'll wait right here!"

The street was nearly empty and darkness was falling over Boston. Leo felt sick and his legs trembled as he walked toward the white clapboard house set back from the street, but the bitterness that had burned in his belly seemed to ignite again. He reached the door, touched the pistol in his belt, then lifted his hand and knocked resoundingly on the door. As he waited, he thought of what he was about to do, and fear ran through him. He had never killed a man, nor even been involved in a brawl. But he was too drunk to realize much, and when the door swung open to reveal a tall woman with white hair, he muttered, "Mr.

Bradford—have to see Mr. Bradford!"

Mrs. White gave him a cautious examination, then nodded. "Come in, sir. I'll tell Mr. Bradford you're here." She stepped back, and as Rochester stepped into the entryway, she smelled the raw liquor and saw that he was very drunk. "The family is at dinner, sir. If you'll wait in the library, I'll tell Mr. Bradford you're here."

"All right." He followed the woman into a small room lined with books and illuminated by a whale-oil lamp. The woman turned and left, and he stood there, sobering considerably as the significance of what he planned to do began to sink into his mind. He was not at all concerned with the wrong of killing a man, nor was he at all troubled by what might follow. Men who took the wives of others were fair game, and no jury or judge would convict him for killing a man who had violated his home and his wife. He was thinking only of the possibility that his hand might not be steady enough, that he might miss with his one shot. He knew the prodigious strength of the man. If Bradford didn't fall dead, he might well get his hands on his assailant. Rochester had seen Bradford twist a heavy horseshoe with his bare hands, and he shuddered at the thought of what those hands would be like on his neck.

He positioned himself with his back to the bookshelves, directly opposite the door, and waited. A large clock on the mantel over the fireplace filled his ears with an ominous, steady cadence. As it ticked off the seconds, the thought leaped into Leo's mind: *In a few minutes—if I miss—I may be dead, and that clock would go on with its infernal ticking!* He had given little thought to death, for despite his indulgences, the man had never been ill. Now, however, as the *ticktock, ticktock* of the clock repeated in a remorseless rhythm, he felt fear crawling along his nerves. *To be dead—to die at the hands of Bradford!*

And then the door opened and Daniel Bradford entered. Instantly Rochester's hatred revived, and he watched as the big man closed the door carefully, then turned to face him squarely. "Well, Leo," he said evenly, "what brings you here?"

Bradford's coolness served to anger Rochester, for it made his own weakness seem suddenly contemptible. He wished he were sober, for he hated the thought that his drunken condition must seem a flaw to Bradford. But the sight of Bradford's face gave him a sudden determination to finish what he'd come to do.

"You're a hypocrite, Bradford!" he cried. "I've known it for years. You've deceived some, but all that religious talk of yours—that pious churchgoing you've shown to the world—it's all an act!"

"I've given you cause to think so, Leo," Daniel said quietly. He had known as soon as Mrs. White had come to whisper in his ear that a gentleman somewhat under the influence was in the library asking to see him that his visitor was Leo. He had been expecting such a thing but had rather thought that the encounter might occur elsewhere. Now as he looked at Rochester, he saw the hatred that burned in the man's bloodshot eyes. "Sit down, and I'll try to tell you how—"

"I know how it was! You're a liar and a cheat, Bradford!"

"As I say, I've wronged you, but not as you think."

"Go on, Daniel," Leo taunted. "Tell me how it was all just an innocent little embrace. You felt *sorry* for the neglected wife, I suppose? And I know she's told you what a beast of a husband I've been!"

"Marian's never said one word against you, Leo."

"Oh, that's likely, isn't it, Bradford?" Leo's anger rose higher, for he had convinced himself that Marian had indeed revealed the truth about her failed marriage. The thought enraged him and he shouted, "Don't bother to lie—I know what you've done! You're both alike, you and her! Why, she hasn't even given me a son! She's barren as a brick—!"

Rochester broke off, for he had not intended to say this. It was a shame—the only one—that lay in him. He had wanted a son for years, had expected one from his marriage. But none had come, and he was angered and hated Marian for failing to provide him one. Deep down he was not at all certain that the lack of a child was her fault—as he often told her it was. For all his affairs, he had never heard that he had fathered a child. This would have been something to boast of, but it had not happened—and deep inside, a scalding sense of inadequacy had burned in his heart. He had hated Daniel for his sons as much as for anything else, and now staring at him, he realized he'd blurted out something about himself that he never wanted anyone to know.

Daniel had not missed the desperation in Rochester's voice. He thought at once of Matthew. Knowing that the son for which Leo Rochester so obviously longed was no more than a few feet away troubled him. However, he masked his alarm, saying, "You're not able to talk about this in your condition, Leo. Go home and sober up. Tomorrow we'll—"

But he had no opportunity to complete what he planned to say, for Leo had drawn the pistol from beneath his coat. Had Leo been sober, Daniel would have died, for he was only five feet away. But Leo fumbled as he drew back the hammer of the pistol. In that one small instant, Daniel leaped forward and knocked the weapon aside.

The pistol exploded. The powder burned Daniel's coat, but the ball passed through the fabric, tearing the shirt underneath, and plowing into the heavy oak door instead of into his heart.

Daniel easily wrenched the pistol away from Leo, and one look at the man's face revealed fear. "I'm sorry you did that, Leo," said Daniel. The echoes of the shot reverberated in the small room, and the sound of running feet came down the hall outside. Then the door burst open and Dake ran in first, followed by the family and Mrs. White.

"Pa—are you all right?" Dake cried, rushing to his father's side, his eyes fixed on Rochester. He noted the pistol in his father's hand and the powder burns on the coat. "Are you shot?" he demanded.

"No, I'm all right." Daniel swept the faces of his family, wishing heartily that the incident had not happened. He did not think of the fact that except for the short interval of time Leo took to draw the pistol's hammer, he would be on the floor with a bullet in his heart. He saw all of them staring at Rochester and said quickly, "We've had a little accident—nothing to worry about. This is Mr. Leo Rochester. You met him once, but you were all very young."

Rachel came and looked at the bullet hole, her face pale. "Let me see, Pa," she said. "You're hurt!"

But Daniel took her hands, saying quickly, "No, there's no harm done." He shot a quick glance at Rochester and saw that the man's complexion had turned pasty white. "Why don't all of you go back? I'll have a few more words with Mr. Rochester—"

At that moment Matthew came into the room. He had left the table early, going to his room, and now he came rushing in, demanding, "What's the matter? I thought I heard a shot!"

Instantly Daniel shot a glance at Rochester and saw that the man's gaze riveted on Matthew. Quickly, he stepped in front of Matthew, saying, "Just an accident—all of you, please leave us alone."

They all reluctantly moved to the door, but Dake turned to put his eyes on Rochester. "I'll be right outside, Pa, if you need me."

"Thank you, Dake," Daniel nodded, then shut the door and turned to face the ashen-faced man opposite him. "That was a fool thing to do, Leo," he said tightly. "You'd have swung from the gallows if you'd killed me."

But Leo Rochester was staring at the door, his lips drawn in a thin pale line. His voice, when he spoke, was a hollow whisper. "Who was that?"

Daniel knew it was hopeless to try to turn Rochester's mind from what he had seen. Both he and Holly had seen from the time Matt was an infant that he bore an astonishing resemblance to Rochester. To both of them it was a tragedy, and especially for Holly. Every time she looked at him, she saw the features of the man who had so brutally taken advantage of her. She had never mentioned the resemblance, nor did Daniel while she was alive— but they had both watched silently, dreading the day when somehow the two might meet. However, there had been little chance of that—at least so it seemed.

And now it had happened—in his own home—but Daniel resolved to give no ground to Matt's real father. "It's time for you to go," he said, ignoring Leo's words.

But Rochester turned to face him, his eyes wild. "Who is that?" he repeated. He forgot himself enough to come closer and grasp Daniel's arm. "Tell me—who is he?"

"He's my oldest son, Matthew Bradford."

Rochester blinked and stared at Daniel. "No—he's not!" A shiver seemed to run through him, his body shaken by the young man he'd seen. "He's as like me as a mirror image! He's me— when I was his age!" He grabbed wildly at Daniel, catching the lapels of his coat, whispering hoarsely, "He's my son, isn't he, Bradford?"

Daniel removed Leo's hands with his iron grasp. "Don't be a fool! He's my son—"

"He's Holly's son—but not yours!" Leo was thinking quickly and gave a startled look at the door. He was suddenly aware of a tremendous surge of joy. He was not childless—he had a son! "She was with child by me when she left Fairhope," he said slowly, tracing the history in his mind. "You married her and gave the child a name, didn't you?"

A grim despair seized Daniel Bradford. *All for nothing—all the years we kept the secret—gone in one second.* He had often wondered about the right of keeping Holly's secret from the boy, but never once had he seen any profit for the boy in telling him the sordid story. Now he knew that all that was changed. He knew instinctively that Leo wanted a son desperately, and he knew as well that there would be a fight to save the boy.

"Forget what you've seen, Leo," he said finally. "The boy is my son. He was born to me and Holly, and any court in the world will certify that I'm his father. Holly is gone, and she's the only one who knew the truth. Go away and leave the boy alone. You can bring him nothing but misery."

"I can give him the truth—and I can give him his heritage!" The sight of his son had sobered Rochester completely. He stared at Daniel for a long time, then nodded. "He'll know the truth, Bradford. He has a right to that—and I have a right to my son!"

At that moment Daniel Bradford felt overpowered by a blinding rage. "You have a *right*? You who disgraced an innocent girl and never gave it a thought? If justice were served, you'd die for that!" Daniel stepped forward and lifted his powerful hands, unconscious that he was doing so. Fighting off the rage, he slowly lowered his hands and said, "Get out, Leo. And don't ever come near me—or my family!"

Rochester stared at Daniel. "I'll go, Bradford—but this isn't over." He walked stiffly to the door, then turned abruptly, his face changed. A light came to his eyes, and he said, "There may be a way out of this."

"There's nothing for you, Leo. Get out!"

"You love my wife, I take it? And I want a son. Does that suggest anything to you?"

The hideous offer, veiled as it was, revolted Daniel Bradford's sense of honor. He stepped forward, uttering through clenched teeth, "Rochester, you're a *monster*!"

Rochester didn't flinch. "You want Marian—and I want Matthew. Sooner or later, you'll come to your senses and see that it would be best for all of us. I assume she loves you, and she detests me. We have no marriage—never have! As for Matthew, I can give him the world! And I will!" He turned and purposefully strode out of the house, his footsteps firm and determined.

Daniel stood in the center of the room, not believing what he had heard. "He'd trade Marian to get what he wants!" he gasped—and then with incredible power, the whisper came to him—something deep inside, from a place he'd kept locked and bolted.

Why not? Matthew would be rich—and you and Marian would be happy!

Daniel was paralyzed by the enormity of the evil thought. Whirling he picked up the pistol that lay on the desk and threw it at the wall with all his strength. It clattered to the floor, and he stared at it, then cried, "Oh, God forgive me!" Then, gaining control of his emotions, he picked up the pistol, placed it on the desk—and walked out of the room. He forced himself to smile, but when he entered the dining room and saw Matt looking at him, a sword seemed to pierce his side. He looked like Holly— something in his eyes—but his face was an unspoiled version of Leo Rochester's visage.

"Come now, let's finish our dinner," he said calmly.

Matt looked at him carefully. "Is . . . everything all right, Pa?"

"Yes, Matt. Everything is all right."

24

A Town Called Lexington

GENERAL THOMAS GAGE HAD LITTLE USE personally for spies or traitors. "If they will betray their own," he once remarked to General John Burgoyne, "what's to prevent their betraying us?"

Now as he listened to his visitor, an urbane, handsome gentleman by the name of Dr. Benjamin Church, he felt stirrings of disgust. He kept an impassive look on his face, however, for he knew that Church was a longtime member of the Committee of Safety—the heart and core of the resistance against the king. Gage was also aware that Church had fallen in love with a wealthy woman and was in need of funds to carry on his courtship.

Church looked over his shoulder nervously, as if afraid of being seen. He had come late under cover of darkness, and even so, he spoke in a whisper. "Ah, General, I trust things go well with you?"

"They do not, sir." Gage's voice was almost harsh, and he had to force himself to modify it. *The fool may have something for us—have to smile and charm him.* "Sorry to be so short, Dr. Church, but I've just received orders from London. The Crown is unhappy with me. They demand that action be taken at once." He rose and went to stare out the window into the inky darkness. He was caught in a trap and well knew it. Gage knew the Americans better than Lord North, better than the king—better than any man thousands of miles away insulated from this boiling spirit of revolution. But he was a soldier and bound by duty to obey orders.

Turning to Church he said, "I need your help, sir. I must make a showing of some sort. I intend to arrest some of the leaders—Sam Adams and John Hancock to begin with. Where are they, can you tell me?"

"In Concord," Church rapped out. "You must move quickly, however, for they won't stay there long." He coughed and said, "I find myself a little strapped for funds, General, but I might give you a very good bit of information if—"

Gage knew the rules of the game and pulled out a bag of coins from a small desk. "There—" he said, counting out a quantity of them into Church's hand. "What do you have for me?"

"When you send a force to arrest Adams and Hancock, you can seize the arsenal of the Committee. It's in Concord, well hidden, but I can give you the location."

General Gage's eyes widened at the news. He did not expect such valuable information from Church. This was more than he had hoped for. "Give me their guns and powder, and I'll have them! Give me the details. . . !"

🔔   🔔   🔔

"What is it, dear?" asked Leslie Gordon as he hurriedly donned his uniform. Drawing on his boots he turned to Lyna, who had entered the bedroom.

"Who was that at the door?"

"Orders, Lyna. I've got to be gone for a time."

"Can you tell me what it is?" Lyna knew Leslie didn't like her to pry for information, but she was worried about the growing tension between the colonists and the soldiers.

"General Gage has decided to arrest some of the rebel leaders and to seize their store of muskets and powder."

"Will there be trouble?"

"Gage doesn't think the rebels will fight—but he's wrong." He stood and pulled on his coat, then turned to her. "Don't worry about me—but that's foolish for me to say. You always do when I may be in action, don't you?"

Lyna went into his arms and lifted her face. She took his kiss, returned it, then drew back with a frown on her face. "Yes, I do worry about you. And now I worry about my nephew. Dake is caught right in the middle of this trouble. Daniel's worried sick about him."

Leslie hesitated, weighing something in his mind. Finally he said carefully, "Lyna, I can't give away military information, but if you could tell your brother to keep his son at home for a few days, it might be wise. This thing will blow over, hopefully, but I like that young man—hate to see him get hurt."

As soon as Leslie had ridden away, Lyna dressed quickly and left the house. She drove to the foundry and was shown into Daniel's office by Blevins.

Daniel smiled as he rose from his desk and greeted her, but he saw that she was troubled. "What is it?" he asked. He listened as she spoke, then the two of them talked for a long time. Finally he said heavily, "This is hard. I wish you and Leslie were stationed anywhere but here."

Lyna nodded but said, "God will have to take care of Leslie and Dake. There's no way to stop this thing, is there?"

"No, I'm afraid not. It's certain to break out—just a matter of time." He shook his head doubtfully, adding, "Dake's seventeen years old. He's a young man now, not a boy. If I tell him not to fight, he'll leave the house, and I don't want that to happen."

"What will you do, Daniel?"

"I don't rightly know. But we're all in God's hands. My family comes first, of course."

"Will you fight if it comes to a war?" Lyna knew that her question was a painful one and said quickly, "I shouldn't have asked that." She rose, and when he thanked her for the warning, she said, "I'll be praying for you, Daniel, and you must pray for Leslie and my own boys."

"I already have, Lyna, and I will continue," said Daniel.

☉   ☉   ☉

Paul Revere spoke hurriedly, his dark eyes glowing with excitement. He and Dake were standing under the shelter of a large elm tree, watching the British officers as they harried their men into formations. Revere had sent for Dake and now pointed toward the soldiers. "Those are the grenadier and light infantry companies—the best troops Gage has," he murmured.

"I've been watching the harbor, sir," Dake spoke up. "They've been pulling the whaleboats up for repairs."

"Have they now? Good work, Bradford!" Revere thought rapidly, then said, "I think these troops will be sent from here to Cambridge—then they can take the road to Concord—that's about twenty miles." He gave the younger man a steady look. "I must see Dr. Warren—I suspect we'll have some riding to do!"

The next morning Warren sent Revere to Lexington to warn Sam Adams and Hancock to be ready to make their escape. He returned that night, having agreed that if the British went by water he would have two lanterns placed in the North Church steeple, and only one if Gage sent them by the overland route.

On April 18, Gage sent patrols along the Concord road on the alert for rebel couriers. That night eight hundred of his elite troops were awakened, startled out of a sound sleep. They fumbled into their uniforms, then formed ranks under the eyes of their commander—a fat, slow-thinking man—Lieutenant Colonel Francis Smith. Smith had under his command Major John Pitcairn. Also accompanying the troops was Lieutenant Colonel Leslie Gordon. At half past ten the British ranks began to move out. As soon as word reached Dr. Warren, he sent William Dawes and Paul Revere flying from Boston to warn the countryside.

Revere rowed over to Charlestown, sprang onto a waiting horse, and rode off at top speed. Behind him two lanterns began to glow in the steeple of Old North Church. When Revere reached the home of Parson Jonas Clark, he shouted the names of Adams and Hancock. When they emerged Revere excitedly relayed the news to them. Sam Adams turned to Hancock and exclaimed, "What a glorious morning this is for America, Hancock!"

On his way back to Boston Revere was captured by the British. The senior officer put a pistol to Revere's head and threatened to blow his brains out if he didn't cooperate. Revere admitted that the whole countryside was aware of the march of the British on Concord and would be ready for it. Later Revere was released and returned to the Clark house. With fresh mounts, the three patriots began their journey to Philadelphia where the Continental Congress was in session.

And on the clear, cold morning of April 19, 1775, the pale sunlight fell on the long British columns that were marching into Lexington.

🔔   🔔   🔔

"The men are in poor shape, John." Leslie Gordon rode alongside Major Pitcairn, and both men were dismayed as they watched the troops move out. The Sons of Liberty were constantly making it difficult to secure adequate supplies. And the continuing desertions had greatly affected the morale of the remaining soldiers. The march itself lacked the professional manner Pitcairn expected of his men.

Pitcairn was a strange choice for second-in-command, for there were no Royal Marines in the column. Nevertheless he was a fine officer and agreed with Gordon's statement. "Poor business!" he nodded. "We'd be better off to pull back and try on another day."

The soldiers were angry, wet from the waist down because of the moist white paste that was used to keep their breeches white. Now the breeches were stained with mud, and their slow-thinking commander had kept them waiting two hours for rations before forcing them to wade up to their chests in cold water to get into the whaleboats. They had been on their feet now for five hours. Each man was dragged down by sixty pounds of equipment in a pack and a ten-pound musket, the unreliable Brown Bess, which was carried at their side.

At the sound of bells and a musket being fired, a private lifted his head and said, "Well, they knows we're 'ere, Simon," he announced disgustedly to the man beside him. "We ain't about to sneak up on 'em, is wot I says. Wisht I was back at the tavern with Molly!"

Even as he spoke the brightly polished barrels and glittering bayonets of His Majesty's troops were visible to a handful of patriots drawn up on Lexington Green.

🔔 🔔 🔔

"Pa—? Wake up!"

Daniel came out of a fitful sleep with a start at the whisper that penetrated his bedroom door. Throwing back the thin sheet he used for a cover, he came to his feet and stumbled through the darkness to open the door. He was blinded at first by the yellow light of the lamp that flared in the darkness of the hallway, then made out Micah's face. "What's wrong?" he demanded quickly.

"I have to talk to you," Micah said. The amber light threw his face into sharp planes, making dark shadows of his eyes. When his father stepped back, Micah entered and stood waiting until Daniel took the taper and lit the lamp. Micah could see the troubled expression on his father's face.

"What is it?" Daniel asked. Of his four sons Micah was the most steady, the least likely to be alarmed—and yet Daniel could tell he was disturbed.

"Pa, I hate a sneak," Micah said, looking down at the floor for a moment. "But I got to tell you—Dake's gone to fight with the militia."

Daniel felt a coldness seize him, but he said only, "I knew it would come to this. You're right to tell me, Micah—don't worry about it."

"But that's not all, Pa—he took Sam with him!" he blurted out.

"Sam!" Daniel knew Dake felt he had to be a part of this, but he was disappointed that Dake had influenced Sam.

"Yes, Pa. I tried to stop him, but Sam said he'd bellow and wake you up, and Dake didn't want that. He said he'd look out for Sam—but I don't like it."

"Nor do I, Micah." Daniel stood there, thinking quickly, then asked, "Did Dake say where he was headed?"

"He said Mr. Parker was calling the Lexington militia out. The whole countryside's up in arms, Pa. The British are going that way—a lot of them," Dake said.

"I'll have to go bring Sam back," Daniel said at once. "Dake's old enough to do as he wants, but I'll not have Sam mixed up in this thing."

"What's wrong?" asked Matthew, who had stepped into the room. "It's something about the Sons of Liberty, isn't it?"

"The British are on their way to Concord to arrest Sam Adams," Micah explained. "Dake took Sam with him to join the militia."

"Why, that's foolish! The militia can't stand against regulars!"

"I don't know about that, but I'm going to get Sam," said Daniel.

"I'm going with you, Pa," Micah insisted. "I'll saddle the horses." He glanced at his older brother. "Want me to saddle your mare, Matt?"

"No. I won't get involved. And if you're wise, Pa, you'll grab Sam and get out of it. Everyone who's in this thing could be arrested and even hanged."

"That might be—but I'll have my son or know the reason why! Go get dressed, Micah. We'll take the road to Roxbury, then cut north to Cambridge. The British will be taking the northern road directly into Lexington, but we can beat them if we ride hard!"

Fifteen minutes later the two men were riding at a full run, muskets tied to their horses. They kept up a steady pace, and Daniel was thankful for the fine horses they had. They passed through Roxbury and found the town up in arms. Men were scurrying around, gathered into a line of march by their officers. Later when they passed through Cambridge, they found the same activity. They rested the horses and got what news they could from the excited officers of the militia.

They rode at a steady pace through the night, and as dawn began to turn the east into a reddish glow, they saw the town outlined ahead of them. Drawing the tired horses to a walk, Daniel nodded. "I think we're in time, Micah. Don't hear any kind of firing."

As they rode into the town, a sentry stepped forward and challenged them. But when he identified them, he said, "Captain Parker's got the men out on the Green—go join 'em!"

The two men moved forward toward the masses of men ahead and dismounted and tied their horses. "Come on," Daniel said tersely. "We'll find Sam and pull out of this."

"Yes, sir."

They walked over to two young men who were standing tensely observing the Green. Daniel asked the older one, "What's going on?" When the tall young man hesitated, Daniel said, "I'm Daniel Bradford."

Instantly the young man turned to stare at him. "I think you might know my father—Adam Winslow."

"Why, I certainly do! We served with Colonel Washington together back in fifty-five."

"I'm Nathan Winslow, and this is my younger brother, Caleb." He indicated a very young man standing beside him, "This is Laddie Smith." His face was grim and he said, "My father always speaks highly of you, sir."

"I'm glad to hear it. He's a fine man," Daniel said. "I'm trying to find my two sons. I want to get them out of this affair."

Nathan Winslow grimaced. "And I, sir, am trying to get my brother out of it. This is going to get bad!"

Daniel stared at Nathan, then at the stubborn face of his brother. Shaking his head, he said, "Both of you should leave. As soon as I find my sons, we're all getting away."

Daniel turned away, feeling a sense of hopelessness. Finding Sam was less difficult than he feared. They had not gone more then twenty paces before Micah said, "Pa—there's Dake and Sam!"

Daniel at once spotted the two and walked up to where they stood waiting. He led Micah toward the pair, noting that they had seen them. Dake's face was stubborn, and Sam's no less so. "Dake, I'm disappointed in you," Daniel said, stopping to face him.

"It wasn't his fault, Pa!" Sam protested. "I threatened to wake you up—"

"Be quiet, Sam," Daniel said firmly. "Dake, you're old enough to decide for yourself about this—but why did you bring your brother along? I thought you had more sense."

Dake was unable to meet his father's eyes. He had known from the moment he'd agreed to take Sam that it was the wrong thing to do. Several times along the way he told Sam to go home, but Sam had stubbornly refused. Now he lifted his head to meet his father's eyes. "You're right, Pa. I'm sorry."

"Well, that's something. I want to—"

"Here they come!"

Daniel was interrupted by a shrill, yelping cry. He whirled, hearing at the same instant the clipped cadence of drums. He saw the flash of bayonets and red uniforms approaching. Captain Parker called out an order, and the seventy or so men of the militia fell into line inside a triangle formed by the three roads. The road to Concord was at its base. Parker's men stood about a hundred yards above it, and Daniel and his sons could see the approach of the advance guard.

"There ain't many of us, Captain," one of the militia called out. "And they's a heap of them lobsterbacks!"

"The first man to run will be shot down," Parker responded.

Across the way, John Pitcairn ordered his men into a line of battle. At once the trained troops formed a line three men deep. They made an awesome sight to the untrained Americans—a solid mass of soldiers, all carrying glittering bayonets.

"Stand your ground," Parker ordered. "Don't fire unless fired upon. But if they want to have a war, let it begin here!"

Daniel watched helplessly, knowing that one false move would ignite the battle fury. He watched as Pitcairn rode forward, shouting, "Lay down your arms! Disperse!"

The militia seemed to hesitate, and it seemed that the crisis would pass. Parker realized that the situation was impossible and commanded his men to disband, taking their weapons with them. But a shot rang out.

Afterward, the arguments raged about who fired it—both sides claiming that the other had done so. Pitcairn and Gordon both moved out, ordering the men to hold their fire, but the regulars were angry. A volley rang out from some militia behind a wall. One British soldier was wounded and two balls grazed Pitcairn's coat.

One of the officers yelled out, "Fire!" and the regulars fired a volley. One of the shots must have been high, for an older man standing not ten feet from Daniel fell back, clawing at his side. Daniel saw that the militia had no chance to stand and said, "Come on, we've got to get out of here!" The four of them turned, and as they moved back from the Green, Dake turned to see Jonas Parker standing alone. He was reloading his musket, and Dake cried out as four British soldiers reached him, thrusting their gleaming bayonets into his body.

Dake lost his reason and turned to run toward the oncoming soldiers. Daniel raced after him, followed by Sam and Micah. He caught Dake, swung him around, saying, "Don't be a fool, Dake!"

At that moment Sam cried out, and Daniel and the other two whirled to see the boy falling. He grabbed his upper leg, and Daniel saw that he'd taken a ball. Without a word, he leaped at Sam and picked him up. The balls were whistling around the four of them, and he yelled, "Come on, boys!"

He glanced over and saw that Caleb Winslow had been shot and that his brother Nathan had picked him up and was running with him. He felt a stab of grief, thinking how terrible it would be for Adam Winslow if he lost a son in this useless slaughter.

The militia were all scattering in the confusion. And if Daniel ever was grateful to God for his prodigious strength, it was during those minutes when he raced along bearing the sturdy form of his son. He kept up with Dake and Micah, and finally they drew up in the shelter of a clump of large trees.

"Let's have a look at that leg," Daniel said. He pulled Sam's trousers down and with glad relief said, "Missed the bone!" Pulling off his scarf he made a quick bandage and bound up the wound. Sam pulled his pants up, his face pale. "It don't hurt much, Pa," he said grimly. Then he looked around and said, "Look, there's some of the men forming over there."

Daniel looked in the direction and saw that Sam was right. One of the men, evidently an officer, had managed to stop the rout. They could hear him saying, "All right, men, they got the best of us—but we'll have our revenge. They're bound for Concord—but they've got to come right down that road to get back to Boston!" He was a tall, thin individual with a hatchet face. "By the time they get back, we'll have reinforcements. We'll lay for 'em, and by the Great Jehovah and the Continental Congress we'll show 'em they can't kill our people! Are you with me?"

A cry went up, and Dake said abruptly, "Pa, I'm staying. You and Micah take Sam back home."

"No, I'm not going!" Sam Bradford got to his feet, his face pale. "They murdered Captain Parker and the others. If they can do it to them—they'll do it to anybody who stands against them!"

Daniel saw the determination of his son. Despite his objection, Daniel felt a thrill of pride at the spirit of this youngest son of his.

"Pa, I'm only fifteen, but I'm old enough to fire a musket— don't make me go home, Pa!"

At that moment a strange thing happened to Daniel Bradford. He was an Englishman—had never had a desire to be anything else. He'd stayed clear of the rabid politics of the day, hoping to walk a middle road. But now he thought of the dead who lay on the Green at Lexington, and he looked down at the bloody bandage on Sam's right leg. *It could have been him—or Dake or Micah— lying dead*, he thought. Suddenly he knew that the shots that had been fired had changed the world for him. Sam had put the matter into its simplest form. *If they can do it to them—they can do it to anybody who stands against them!*

Dake and Micah were watching their father closely—as was Sam. He was the best man they knew. Now they saw that his face was tremendously sober, his eyes half closed. Dake held his breath, and then he heard his father say, "I guess you've been right about this thing all along, Dake. No man's going to be able to straddle a fence anymore." There was a deep sorrow in Daniel Bradford's voice, but he straightened himself, and anger glowed in his eyes as he added, "We'll do whatever honest men can do."

Micah knew what this cost his father to say, and he remained silent for a moment. Then he said, "Pa, I don't think I can do this."

Daniel said instantly, "Go home, Micah. Stay out of it if you can."

"No, I'll stay, but I won't fire on British soldiers—not yet."

Dake looked at his twin, not understanding. But he said only, "You'll have to come to it someday, Micah." Then he said to his father, "Sir, I honor you!" Then he turned and walked away toward the officer and began speaking to him.

"Sam, can you make it on that leg?"

Sam's broad face was pale, but he smiled. "Yes, sir—if you'll give me a hand from time to time."

"We'll have to do that from now on, son!"

T   T   T

"We're being cut to pieces, sir!" John Pitcairn was hot and thirsty as he came to protest to Colonel Smith. The column had proceeded to Concord, found a few stores, had a brief engagement with some local militia, then turned and headed for Boston.

But four thousand men had gathered around that sixteen-mile gauntlet running back to Charlestown. They had not formed into ranks but had fired from behind stone walls or trees. Redcoats slumped to the dust, dozens of them, and there seemed to be no defense. The wagons were piled high with wounded, and still the carnage went on.

Gordon had come with Pitcairn to reason with the commander. "Sir, we've got to get in their flanks!" he exclaimed. "If we can double back on them, we can drive them from those fences."

"All right, Colonel Gordon, take some men and do so!"

Gordon quickly formed a force, and for a time his tactics worked—but the militia faded into the woods, only to re-form farther down the road. They would allow the column to get even with them, then rise up and fire a solid sheet of volleys, mowing down the exhausted soldiers like ripe wheat.

The strain of the long march and the heat of the battle caused the discipline of the British to fade. They had been on their feet for more than twenty hours, carrying heavy packs of equipment. As the men continued to fall, some of them tried to escape in a stumbling run, only to be shot down by the sharpshooters positioned along the road.

Finally at three o'clock a relief column led by Lord Percy appeared, and Gordon whispered, "That's good, John. They'd have killed us to a man if Percy hadn't come."

The fight continued all the way to Charlestown, and the casualties continued to mount. The British had 73 men killed, 27 missing—probably dead—and 174 wounded. The Americans had 49 killed, 5 missing, and 41 wounded.

Sam had fought for a time, but Micah had taken him home when he grew faint. Dake and Daniel had followed the fight, moving along the road all the way. When they were less than a mile from Charlestown, Dake finally ran out of ammunition and ran back to get more. Daniel was behind a fallen tree as the column passed. The soldiers were firing at his group, and he heard the whistle of musket balls like tiny bees around his head.

He lifted his musket and carefully trained it on the tall officer who was helping a wounded soldier into the creaking wagon. His finger started to pull on the trigger. Suddenly the man's face came into focus, and Daniel saw that he was aiming at Colonel Leslie Gordon, his sister's husband.

Time stood still for Daniel in that instant. He had killed men that day, hating every moment of the battle. He had taken a stand from which he could not retreat. Now he was committed, and the man in the red coat was his enemy.

In that frozen fraction of a second, a picture of Lyna's sweet face rose in Daniel's mind. He thought of their terrible times as children, and he thought of how much she loved this man—and he her.

Slowly he loosed the trigger and let the muzzle drop. He watched as Gordon straightened up, his face twisted with pain. *He hates this as much as I do,* Daniel thought.

As the column moved out Daniel stood up, his shoulders slumped with fatigue from riding all night and then fighting. He turned and walked wearily along the road looking for Dake. Deep inside he had the premonition that the last few hours had brought the Colonies to a pivotal place in history. The yearning for freedom had now broken out into a fight for the pursuit of inalienable rights that every patriot longed for. And he knew that the world that had existed for him the day before when he set out to come after Dake and Sam was gone forever. Whatever lay ahead, it would not be the peaceful life he so valued. He studied the faces of the tired men around him and realized that his own face had the same determination as theirs. Sides had been taken, and there would be no turning back!

It'll be a long time before I can find what I had before this day—maybe never. . . . The sun slowly dipped down behind the hills, casting a purple haze over the world, and a nightingale murmured a few notes in a plaintive voice.

25

FAITHFUL TO GOD

"LESLIE!" LYNA RAN ACROSS THE ROOM and threw herself into her husband's arms. His face was smeared with black powder stains and his uniform was filthy. Lyna clung to him fiercely, feeling a tremendous gust of relief that he had come home safely from the battle. She kissed him and placed her hand on his cheek. "Sit down—I've got tea."

Leslie slumped into a chair beside the trestle table and began to pull off his boots. He had not slept since the battle and was trembling with fatigue. His feet were aching, and he groaned with relief when the high-topped boots were off. "Lord, that feels good!" He picked up the mug of black, sweetened tea and drained it.

Lyna refilled the cup, saying, "Are you hungry, dear?"

"No, but I'm so tired I could sleep on the floor."

"You'll have to eat a little—then you need a bath." As she moved quickly around the room throwing a hot meal together, she asked, "Was it very bad, Leslie?"

"Bad? It was terrible, from beginning to end, it was awful!" Gordon sipped the tea, then as he ate the hot stew, he told Lyna of the carnage that had taken place on the road back from Concord. "As ill-planned and awkwardly executed as ever a battle I've seen!"

"Did we lose many officers?" Lyna listened closely as he gave her the details of the British losses, then, when he finished, asked,

"Were . . . were many of the Americans killed?"

Instantly Leslie understood what was troubling her. "I'm afraid so, Lyna. Not as many as we lost, but some of the men went wild—started killing civilians who'd done nothing."

Lyna felt a cold fear grip her heart but said no more. After Leslie had eaten and she'd seen to it that he had a hot bath, she bullied him into bed. She kissed him, whispering, "Thank God you came back unhurt!" Then she moved to get her cloak, saying, "I'm going to find out about Daniel. I'll be back as soon as I can. Sleep well, my dearest!" When she reached the bedroom door she turned and looked back. Leslie was already asleep. Slipping out the front door, she hurried her step, trying to control the cold fear that rose inside her.

🔔   🔔   🔔

Leo stepped into the bedroom to find Marian sitting in front of her dressing table. Coming to stand behind her, he studied her face in the mirror for a moment before speaking. He had never ceased to admire her beauty, even though their relationship had deteriorated years earlier. The afternoon sun slanted through the window, bringing out the rich auburn tints in her hair. Over the years she had kept her trim figure. Many of his friends had wives who had turned fat, and a faint regret threaded its way through him for what he had lost. However, Leo Rochester was a realist, with a strong cynical strain in his makeup, so he put away the thoughts of what might have been.

"Have you heard about the battle?" Leo noted with interest that his question caught her attention instantly. "I expect your lover is right in the middle of it," he said, then took out a cigar and lit it, waiting for her to answer. When she said nothing, he grunted, "Don't play games with me, Marian!"

"I've told you the truth, Leo," she said quietly as she continued to pin her hair.

Irritated at her simple answer, Leo snapped, "I come home to find you in the arms of another man, and you tell me it's all innocent? I'm not a simpleton, Marian!"

Marian had fastened the last pin and stood to face him. She was wearing a pearl gray dress with green trim at the bodice and sleeves. Except for her wedding ring, her only jewelry consisted of two small pearl earrings. The strain of the whole thing had left its traces on her face, small lines at the outside corners of her eyes and a tenseness in her mouth. But she answered evenly, "I'm sorry for what happened. I was wrong. I can only say again that what you saw was all there was."

Somehow Leo knew she was telling the truth—and that was somehow painful. He had been with dozens of women, and when he'd found Marian in Bradford's arms, he'd been incensed—but somehow almost pleased. He wished to see her brought down to his level—both her and Bradford—but deep inside he knew that Marian was telling the simple truth.

He asked suddenly, "Are you in love with him?"

"I'm your wife, Leo."

"That's not what I asked—but I think we both know the answer to my question." A faint, humorless smile crossed his lips, and he said, "I know you pretty well, I think. You're cold to me—but you'd never let another man kiss you unless you loved him." He gave her a sudden angry gesture of his hand, his voice hard. "I didn't come here to talk about you and Bradford—or maybe I did." He puffed on the cigar, studying her thoughtfully. "He loves you—I think he has for a long time."

"Leo—!"

"Did you know that he's not the father of that oldest boy?"

Marian stared at him blankly. "What do you mean?"

Leo's eyes grew suddenly bright and he straightened his back. "He married Holly Blanchard when she was carrying a child—and the child was mine!"

"I don't believe it!"

"Don't you? All you have to do is *look* at him."

An image of Matthew leaped into Marian's mind. She had been vaguely aware that he looked nothing at all like Daniel physically. And she had noted that he was very different from his three brothers. She had assumed that he resembled his mother, but at Leo's words she now was forcibly reminded that every feature of the young man was like that of her husband.

"Comes as a shock to you, doesn't it?" Leo walked to the window and looked out, not seeing the tall trees that spread their large branches over the house. He had thought of little else but the fact that he had a son since he had seen Matthew Bradford. He had not admitted to a single soul how the failure of his marriage to produce children had been a sign of personal failure in his own mind. If Holly Blanchard's child had been a girl, he would not have been so affected, but he was very English in the deep-seated desire to see his name carried on through a son.

Turning to face her, he said, "I want Matthew to become my son. He's the only hope of the Rochester line. I don't want my name to die with me."

"It's too late, Leo. He's not a child anymore—and even if he were, Daniel would never give him up."

"It's not up to Daniel," Leo snapped. "As you say, Matthew's not a child. He's nineteen years old and able to make up his own mind."

Marian stared at him, the shock of the thing etched on her features. "You can't do this thing, Leo," she said, a pleading light in her eyes. "It would shake his whole world. Daniel Bradford's the only father he's ever known. Think what it would mean to him!"

"Mean to him? It would mean that he'd be the son of nobility instead of a blasted tinker! The boy's not a fool, I can tell you that, Marian. Why, I only saw him for a moment, but I could read his face like a book! He's sensitive and there's nothing of Bradford in him. When I offer him everything—including Fairhope and a proud name—he won't hesitate!"

Marian could see that Leo was set on the thing and, for a moment, felt a twinge of pity for the man. She had been humiliated by him for her failure to produce children. And in truth she did feel the sting of that failure more keenly than she ever allowed him to know. But somehow she knew that the desire of Leo to have a son would not be met in Matthew Bradford. But she had never had the slightest influence on Leo and saw that it was hopeless to try to dissuade him now.

Leo gave her an odd look, his lips twisting into a travesty of a smile. "I've already made Bradford an offer. He wants you, and I want a son. Not a bad trade, I'd say."

"Leo!" gasped Marian.

"Why looked so shocked, my dear? It happens all the time. You must know that." Leo shrugged lightly. "Men get rid of their wives as they get rid of horses or houses. Most of the time they do it to get a younger woman. I think my motive is a little more noble than that."

"You—can't be serious!"

"I am serious—deadly serious." He suddenly fixed his eyes on her in an intense stare. "You're so conventional, Marian—you and Bradford. He was as shocked as you are. The two of you are alike, and I think you've found that out. But after all, I'm not trying to trade you off for another woman. You love the man, and he's so in love with you I can read it in his eyes. And for what it's worth to you," he added, "I believe you're telling the truth about your *affair*. Both of you are so self-righteous you wouldn't consider doing anything sinful. But if you were free, you'd go to him in a heartbeat."

Marian tried to protest—but she knew instantly that this much of Leo's speech was true.

He saw her hesitate and nodded. "I see you agree with me. Well, let's be honest with each other. Divorce is an ugly business and pretty difficult to come by—but there are ways. Money will buy anything."

"That's not so!"

"Isn't it? But think what it could be like, Marian—you could have Bradford—which is obviously what you want. He could have you, which is what *he* wants. I could have a son, which is what *I* want. And despite what you or Bradford think, it would be a good thing for Matthew. So all four of us get what we want. Can't you forget your little moral quirk and see that I'm right?"

"Leo, marriage isn't like other agreements," Marian protested. "It's forever in God's eyes."

"I know that's the way the storybooks speak of it. 'And they got married and lived happily ever afterward.' But life isn't a fairy tale, my dear. I sometimes wish it were." Strangely enough the cynical side of Leo Rochester gave way to what seemed to be a wistful air, and for that brief moment, he appeared more vulnerable than Marian had ever seen him. He dropped his eyes and seemed to study the pattern of the carpet for a long moment, and when he lifted them, he had none of the hard edge that a life of self-indulgence and dissipation had brought him. He said almost gently, "I know I'm not a good man—never have been. But in this one thing at least, I think I'm not asking for myself—at least not *only* for myself."

"Leo, you can't just step into a thing like this. You can buy a house or a carriage, and it's yours as soon as you pay for it. But you must see that being a father isn't like that—not at all!"

"It's too late for me to go back and change nappies and walk the floor with the boy," Leo said sharply. "I know that—and I'm not fool enough to think I'd have been any good with an infant. But I can be good with Matthew as a man. He's just ready to begin his life, and I can give him everything a young man needs— money, a fine name, an estate. . . ."

Leo spoke for a few moments of the advantages Matthew would enjoy and finally said, "I see you don't agree. Well, I don't care whether you do or not, Marian. It would be easier if you and Bradford would see this thing in the proper prospective. You'll do all you can to turn him against me—but in the end, he'll come to me!"

Leo spun around and left the room. Marian stood staring after him, her mind seeking some sort of answer—but none came. She well knew the stubbornness of her husband, and a heaviness settled over her as she moved out of the bedroom and made her way to see to her ailing father.

She found him sitting in his chair, fretful and nervous. "I'm worried about this battle, Marian," he said at once. "I want to know what's going on." She tried to soothe him, but he shook his head. "I'm stuck in this house like a mouse in a trap. I don't get any news about anything. Go see what you can find out, won't you, daughter?"

"All right. I'll be back as soon as I can. Try not to be upset."

"Why shouldn't a man be upset with the world falling down around him?" John Frazier halted abruptly, then smiled and reached out his hand. "I'm sorry, Marian. Don't pay any mind to my ways."

"It's all right, Father," Marian said quickly. Leaning down, she kissed him, saying, "I want to know as badly as you do. I won't be too long."

"Go by and see Blevins at the shop. He seems to know everything."

Marian left the house and went at once to the foundry. As she expected, Daniel was not there, and she learned that Blevins had gone to the town hall, where there was a meeting of the leadership.

"He'll be back soon, Mrs. Rochester," Edward Jenns, the foreman, assured her. "Why don't you just wait in 'is office?"

"Thank you, Edward, I think I will." She went to Blevins' office and tried to be patient but found she was more nervous than she'd been in years. Finally the door opened, and she turned from the window expecting to see Blevins. Instead Jenns said, "Lady 'ere to see Mr. Bradford—but I expect she can wait in 'ere."

"Quite right, Edward." As Jenns left the room, Marian nodded to the woman who entered. "I'm Mrs. Rochester," she said. Marian was curious, wondering who this tall, attractive woman could be. There was a genteel air about her, and she looked familiar somehow.

"I'm Lyna Lee Gordon, Mrs. Rochester—Daniel's sister."

"Oh—yes!" At once Marian saw the strong resemblance between sister and brother—the same light hair and features. In the sister, these were smoothly refined, of course, but she had the same steady eyes and strong chin. "I've heard about your marvelous reunion with your brother. You must be very happy."

Lyna answered, "Yes, it's been like nothing else in my life. . . ." She was very conscious of the woman who stood before her and was favorably impressed with Marian's bearing. *This is the woman Daniel loves,* she thought and determined to probe deeper than a casual conversation. "I'm very concerned about Daniel," she said, seeing a flicker of fear flash in the large green eyes of Marian Rochester. "He's gone to fight with the Americans, you know."

"I . . . didn't know for certain." Marian felt that Lyna Gordon was one of the most perceptive women she'd ever met. There was a steadiness in her gaze that revealed a more than casual interest. *I wonder how much Daniel has told her about . . . how we feel?* Aloud she said, "It must be very difficult for you, Mrs. Gordon—with your husband in the king's forces."

Lyna could sense that Marian was a woman of compassion. She moved closer and nodded. "It is difficult—and will become worse, I fear. My husband is a soldier and is very loyal to the Crown. I know Daniel will be drawn to the patriot cause. Two of his sons are already involved. . . ."

For half an hour the two women talked, and each discovered the other to be kind and gentle. Finally Lyna decided that honesty was what Marian needed. "I'm very fond of Daniel," she said quietly, then added, "And I believe you are, too, Mrs. Rochester." When Marian started and turned pale, Lyna came to put her hand on the arm of the other woman. "Oh, he's not said how he feels about you—not directly, that is. But he's such a dear, honest man! He can't speak your name without revealing how he feels."

Marian was trembling and said, "I . . . I can't speak of him, Mrs. Gordon!" She hesitated, but the kindness in Lyna's face gave her the courage to say, "Once—a long time ago—we were very close. But that's all over!"

"Is it?" Lyna murmured, then started to say more when the door burst open. The two women turned to see the tall form of Albert Blevins. Seeing them he halted and exclaimed, "Mrs. Rochester—Mrs. Gordon—!"

"Albert—what is it?" Marian asked.

Blevins was flushed and for once his stolid features were contorted with worry. "It's Mister Bradford!" he exclaimed. "I was on my way back from the city hall when some of the militia got back from the battle—some of 'em wounded. I knew the sergeant, and he'd heard that Mr. Bradford was hurt bad!"

"Where is he, Blevins?" Marian demanded.

"The sergeant didn't know for sure—but it's likely they took him to Doctor Rush's house—that's where they're setting up a hospital for the wounded."

"Where is it, sir?" Lyna cried out. "I must go to him!"

"Yes, Mrs. Gordon," Blevins nodded. "I'll take you myself."

But Marian spoke up, "My carriage is downstairs, Albert. You wait here. Someone may bring word. I'll take Mrs. Gordon to her brother." Turning to Lyna she said, "Come with me. We'll find him, Mrs. Gordon . . . !"

"Why, it's nothing but a scratch!" Sam protested vehemently. "I could have stayed at the fight if—"

Doctor Claude Bates was a short, rotund man with a shock of gray hair and a pair of sharp black eyes. "You hush, Sam Bradford!" he said loudly. He had the loudest voice in Boston, though he was not aware of it. His great booming baritone voice numbed the ears of all his patients, and he seemed incapable of whispering. "Your father ought to give you a caning!" He looked down at the bandaged leg and turned to the men who stood around Sam's bed. "Keep him off that leg," he thundered as though they were half a mile away.

"What's that you say, Doctor?" Dake asked, cupping his hand behind his ear. "I didn't quite get that."

"Stop your foolishness, Dake!" Micah had taken over Sam's

care, ignoring his protests. He'd rousted Doctor Bates out and now asked, "Any chance of infection, Doctor?"

"Certainly! Always a good chance of that." The doctor collected his gear and said irritably, "Well, I'll go see to some of the other fools who didn't have sense enough to stay out of a fight!"

"The doctor's not a patriot," Daniel said as the door slammed. He looked down at Sam's leg with concern. "But he's a good doctor. You'll mind what he says, Sam."

"But I want to be in on the fighting!"

Dake shook his head. "Won't be any fighting for a spell, Sam. The lobsterbacks have holed up here. They can't get out, either," he added grimly. "Our men have thrown a ring around Boston. We've got 'em!"

"There's a little more to it than that, Dake." Matthew had been sickened by the whole thing. Now he looked at the pale face of his brother Sam and shook his head. "King George will send twenty thousand trained soldiers here if he has to. He's vowed to stamp out patriot rebellion!"

"So—we'll train ourselves," Dake countered. "We did all right in the battle, Matt. Whipped them completely!"

"And what would have happened if the battle had been fought in the open?" Matthew shook his head. "Sooner or later the British will catch you in a battle where you can't hide—and that'll be the end of it. But I won't be here to see it."

Daniel lifted his head sharply. "What does that mean, son?"

Matthew turned to face Daniel. "I'm going back to England— maybe to France. All I want to do is become a painter—the best artist I can be. And you know that until this revolution is over, there's no place for that in this country." He saw the disappointment on his father's face and said, "We'll talk later."

Dake stared at the disappearing form of his brother and shook his head. "I don't understand him, Pa. I guess I'm just too dumb to see why a man won't fight for his family and his country."

Micah saw that Sam was looking sleepy. "Come on, Dake," he said at once. "Let's go see if we can find out what's going on."

"That be all right, Pa?" Dake asked, obviously anxious to go.

"Yes, both of you go on. I'll stay with Sam."

The twins left and Daniel sat down and talked with Sam for the next fifteen minutes. He saw that the boy's face was tense and said quickly, "That leg's hurting. Let's see if some of this medicine Doctor Bates left will help."

Pouring a large spoonful of the dark liquid down Sam's throat, he said, "That smells bad enough to be good medicine."

"Yahh—!" Sam grimaced. "Tastes awful!" He squirmed in the bed, then asked, "Pa, what's going to happen? Is Matthew right?"

Daniel pulled his chair closer to the bed and began to talk with Sam. Soon he saw the boy's eyelids droop, and finally his breathing became slow and measured. Rising to his feet, he tiptoed out of the room and went to the library. He sat down and began to think of all that had happened and wondered about the future.

Sometime later, he was startled by a knock at the door. Quickly he came to his feet, and when he reached the door and opened it, Daniel was surprised to see Lyna.

"Thank God, you're all right, Daniel," said Lyna, throwing her arms around him and embracing him. "I was so worried!"

"Lyna, what's wrong? Is it Leslie?"

"No—I'd heard that you were wounded. . . ." She explained what she had heard from Blevins, then asked, "Are the boys—?"

"Sam got a ball in his leg—but he's all right."

After Lyna had listened to the details of the battle, she said quickly, "I'll sit with Sam. There's someone in the carriage who's very worried about you." When he stared at her, Lyna said, "It's Marian Rochester. She was at the foundry when we got word that you'd been hurt, so she offered to bring me in her carriage to help find you." Lyna hesitated, then put her hand on his arm. "Go to her, Daniel. She's very concerned."

Daniel blinked with surprise, then gave his sister a straight look. "All right—I will." He stepped outside and walked to the carriage. Marian gasped when she saw him approach. "I'm all right, Marian," he said quickly. She was staring at him, her face pale. "Come into the house," he offered. "It was Sam who was wounded, not me. But he's going to be all right."

Marian shook her head, saying, "No, Daniel, I can't come in. Please get in and tell me about Sam."

Daniel stepped into the carriage and sat down beside her. When he turned to face her, explaining Sam's wound, he saw that she was shaken. Finally he said, "Marian—!" and reached over and took her hands. They were cold and he held them tightly. "I . . . I don't want to make things worse for you."

"I know, Daniel!" Marian was struggling to hold back the tears that formed in her eyes—but in vain. She had been terrified that he was dying, and now that he sat beside her, she knew that never would she love any man as she loved this one. His hands held hers tightly, and she longed to know the strength of his arms around her, holding her close.

Daniel saw the tears gather in her eyes and run down her face. "Marian. . . !" he whispered. "I hate to see you like this!" His voice was husky, and he wanted to kiss the tears away—but knew that would be wrong, and such a thing would only make matters worse. He sat there, aware that they were trapped in a hopeless situation. He wanted her more than he'd ever wanted anything in his life, but deep down he knew that he must let her go.

"Marian," he said softly, "I'm not a wise man—but one thing I know—" He paused, thinking how to frame words to express what he felt, then said more strongly, "I want you more than I want anything except heaven. But I've watched people all my life take things that they wanted—and leave God out. And every single time, I've seen the thing they wanted most turn to bitter ashes in their mouths."

Marian nodded, very conscious of the warmth of his hazel eyes. She noted the scar on the bridge of his nose, the high cheekbones, and the strong forehead. She wanted to reach up and touch the cleft in his chin, to smooth his thick hair back—but knew that she must not. "Yes, you're right," she nodded. "I've seen the same thing."

They sat there quietly, and finally Daniel said, "If you and I took each other, Marian, we might have some joy for a time—but it would be wrong. Sooner or later we'd lose what we have now—respect and trust—and love." He hesitated, and then spoke again, saying, "But I feel something inside me—something I can't really understand. It's like God is saying, 'Be faithful to me—and I will give you the desires of your heart.' My desire is to wholeheartedly follow God. I love you, but I *must* honor your commitment to Leo."

"Oh, Daniel—I feel that, too!" Marian exclaimed. She stared at him, her eyes filled with tears, but now there was joy in them instead of misery. She had been unhappy and alone for so long, and the future looked even more bleak—but somehow his words had touched a spring deep inside her heart. The weight seemed to lift, and she whispered, "If I remain faithful to God—He won't fail me, Daniel. And He won't fail you, either."

He lifted her hands and kissed them, then reached out and put his hand on her cheek. A quietness filled his spirit and he said softly, but with a strength that gathered in him like a rising wind, "No matter what the future holds, God will uphold you, my dear!"

Marian felt his strength in the touch of his hand, heard it in the firmness of his voice—and somehow she knew that what he said was true.

"Yes, Daniel," she nodded. "God will not leave me!"

He got out of the coach and entered the house, not looking back. Marian sat quietly in the carriage, her heart beating strongly, then picked up the lines and spoke to the horses. As she drove along the streets, she was aware that the city was humming with the excitement of the beginning of the war. Ahead the future looked bleak and terrifying. The sound of the trumpet had roused the specter of war, and soon there would be men dying on bloody fields. The wheels of destiny were turning, and the world would never be what it was since the first shots fired at Lexington. A great beast was slinking over the land and would demand the blood that war always seeks.

But despite all this, Marian was more conscious of the feel of Daniel's touch on her cheek, and of his words that seemed to linger in her heart.

Looking up into the sky where dark clouds marched along in ranks, she whispered, "Thank you, Lord God—for a man with strength to love You more than he loves his own way!"